GC
MR

MORTAL
SINS

MORTAL SINS

PENN WILLIAMSON

WARNER BOOKS

A Time Warner Company

This is a work of historical fiction. In order to give a sense of the times, some names of real people or places have been included in the book. However, the events depicted in this book are imaginary, and the names of non-historical persons or events are the product of the author's imagination or are used fictitiously. Any resemblance of such non-historical persons or events to actual ones is purely coincidental.

Warner Books, Inc.,
1271 Avenue of the Americas,
New York, NY 10020

Visit our Web site at www.twbookmark.com

 A Time Warner Company

Printed in the United States of America
First Warner Books Printing: June 2000
10 9 8 7 6 5 4 3 2 1

Library of Congress Cataloging-in-Publication Data

Williamson, Penn.
    Mortal sins / Penn Williamson
        p.   cm.
    ISBN 0-446-52154-X
        1. Serial murders—Louisiana—New Orleans—Fiction. 2. Police— Louisiana—New Orleans—Fiction. 3. New Orleans (La.)—Fiction. I. Title.
    PS3573.I456288 M67 2000
    813'.54—dc21

                                                                99-052357

For Tracy Grant, beloved friend

Acknowledgments

I owe an enormous debt of gratitude to my agent, Aaron Priest, for seeing me through this. I am sure there were times when he despaired, but he never gave up on me or the book. And my gratitude goes as well to Maureen Egen and Frances Jalet-Miller for their superb editorial guidance.

Once again, I would like to thank Lindsay Casablanca for her assistance with the research, although any mistakes found herein are all mine.

As it is, I have taken literary license by inserting the Flying Horses of Audubon Park into the story even though they wouldn't come into existence for another two years, and I created an outing to the Fair Grounds Race Track in the summer, quite arbitrarily choosing to ignore that the season only ran from January 1 through Mardi Gras. These are two of my favorite childhood memories of New Orleans, though, so I selfishly decided to include them in this fictional tale.

Finally, I would like to thank the city of New Orleans herself for giving me so many wonderful moments and memories over the years.

MORTAL SINS

Prologue

He stood naked on the sagging porch of the old slave shack, with moonlight burnishing his skin to the smooth ivory of a marble gravestone. He might have been waiting for his lover to come.

The night smelled of death, heavy and smothering. It was summer in New Orleans, when the streets steamed in the morning and the rain teemed in the evening, when the brown river flowed thick and muddy, and the bayous spread in a primal ooze of putrefying lily pads and crawfish. In the old St. Louis Cemeteries, where the raised crypts had cracked and sunk into the earth, water lapped at the rotting bones so that the sweet smell of decay rose into the air and took on the breath of resurrected life. A summer's night in New Orleans, rancid life and ripe death, and always—the heat.

The porch he stood on faced the Bayou St. John, although he could barely see it through the huge live oaks. Streamers of moss hung from the gnarled branches, limp in the still, heavy air. The water curved like a slow, silver snake around the low moon.

If he turned his head and looked across the yard he could have seen the big house. An heirloom of slender white colonnettes and broad galleries, and as much a part of him as his bones and breath.

If he turned his head he could have seen the window of his

wife's bedroom, but he didn't need to look to see her as he was remembering her. Linen sheets twisted around her naked legs, lamplight pooling on her belly. Her eyelashes spiking shadows on the bones of her face.

He breathed, and the sultry air panted with him. He imagined her looking out her window now, seeing him standing naked in the night.

He turned and went inside, leaving the door open. His shadow leaped out ahead of him in the wash of the brass gasoliers. Years ago they had brought electricity out to the shack, but he loved the gaslight. Once, in his grandfather's time, slaves had lived in this place. Of course in those days the floor had been packed dirt, the furniture a rotting table and a stool or two, rough ticking stuffed with moss and swamp grass to sleep on. Certainly no green leather chairs, no ormolu-mounted bureau, no big brass bed. When he and his brother were boys, these two small rooms had served as a sort of *garçonnière.* Out here where their mama wouldn't have to let herself know better, he and Julius had indulged in a lot of expensive bourbon and cheap women. Sure enough, some sinning had gone on in those days, most of it his.

Most of the sins had been his, yes, but not all. Not all.

Pulled by memories, he looked through a curtain of blue glass beads and into the shadowed bedroom. He saw, in the silver shawl of moonlight floating through the gauzy bed netting, the sweet curve of a woman's breast.

His breath quickened, and a hot flush prickled his bare skin. "That you, darlin'?" he said.

He took a step and the netting stilled, the shadow disappeared. His excitement died, leaving behind a melancholy ache. He wanted suddenly to be done with it all. He wanted to live a life without old longings, free of the past and old sins. Free of new sins and all the chaos and pain in his mind.

He picked up his silk robe from where he'd left it lying on the floor and shrugged it on. He went to the bureau, and his hands shook as he opened the flat silver box that was filled with not cigarettes but shaved cocaine. With the blade of a penknife, he scraped up the fine white flakes, then spilled it onto the back of his wrist. He brought it up to his nose, snorting deep, blinking.

His lips pulled back from his teeth and his eyes opened wide as the rush hit him. Beyond the open door the knife-like leaves of the banana tree stirred, sounding to his ears like a hurricane. He could feel his heart beating hard now.

He took a silk handkerchief out of his robe pocket and wiped his nose. He poured a glass of absinthe and spiked it with more cocaine. He tossed back most of the cocktail in one long swallow. The rush hit him again, harder this time, making him shudder.

Time spun away from him, letting go. He stood, swaying, drifting, caught up in the unraveling threads of a dream. Something brought him back, a noise. The locusts in the canebrakes, singing for their mates. He sucked in a deep breath and felt his chest expand with the force of it, felt the oxygen feed his blood. His blood pulsed now with the locusts' scratching song.

And then they stopped.

A wicker rocking chair creaked out on the porch. He jerked, almost stumbling, to peer back through the open door. The chair was still. The beaded curtain clicked softly, and he spun back around. He held his breath now, listening, but he heard only the whirring of the ceiling fan and the dripping of rainwater off the fronds of the banana trees. The tripping thump of his own heart.

A chill moved down his spine, in spite of the oppressive heat. There was something dangerous about the night, a sense of ancient, predatory creatures stalking silently through the tall grass or flying among the trees on soundless wings.

He laughed.

The mosquito netting in the next room stirred again, flashing white across the corner of his eye. The netting floated open and a woman rose from the bed. A woman, naked, her body glowing silver as moonlit snow. A snow dream, he told himself. She's only a dream.

He took a step backward though, even if she was only a dream, and still she came toward him. The beaded curtain parted around her, clicking and clacking. Thick worms writhed in her hair and

3

her face was flat and dead, the color of the old bones rotting in the cemetery down the road.

She raised her arm, and at the end of it was a cane knife. The blade, long and flaring, bled red with a liquid fire.

"No," he said, although even then he didn't really believe in what he was denying.

She came closer, the snow woman with the horrible dead face, and then he realized what he was seeing and he laughed again.

"Remy," he said, smiling, laughing. "Hey, you comin' to get me, baby?" He backed another step, grinding his hips a little now, almost dancing, and she followed. She liked to play at dangerous games, did Remy, but in the end they were only games. "Come on, come on, come and get me."

The cane knife slashed across his belly.

He grunted and looked down, he saw his flesh gape open and the blood well thick and black, and he wondered why it didn't hurt, and then he screamed.

The knife cut him again, lower, and his scream broke into a wail. Run, he had to run; he ran but the knife came after him, came for his eyes this time, and he threw up his hands to stop it. The blade sliced across his palms, and he saw a finger go flying, but it wasn't real and so he laughed, and then he screamed, and then he whimpered. "Please," he said, as the knife slashed again. He opened his mouth and the screams filled it so he couldn't breathe, rising and swelling in his throat like big wet bubbles.

He could hear her harsh panting in a wet darkness now filled with pain. He wanted her to stop so that he could breathe again, so that he could scream. He wanted to tell her he was sorry. He wanted her to understand that he wasn't supposed to die.

He fell instead, and still she came. To cut out his heart with her knife.

He was slipping down, down deep into a hot black cocoon, his chest bursting, burning. His eyes filled with a black light, and then the light brightened into a whiteness and the world became new and sweet again. Night rain still dripped off the fronds of the banana trees, but the camellias outside the window smelled of tomorrow's sunshine, and she was kissing him, warm, lingering kisses, her lips begging him to stay, and he didn't want to go.

Slowly, he turned his head and looked up into her face. The screams were still trapped in his throat, beating like moths against glass. He opened his mouth to say her name one last time.

It came out in a gush of hot blood.

Chapter One

Blood was splattered and sprayed all over the walls and furniture. It lay in dark smears on the oiled wooden floor and pooled beneath the dead man's cut throat, glossy and syrupy, like blackberry wine.

Daman Rourke stood just within the shack's open door and tried not to breathe in the rank smell. He winced as the magnesium explosion of a flashlamp illuminated for an obscene moment the gashes in the dead man's white flesh and his bulging, glassy eyes.

"Sweet mercy," Rourke said.

The cop with the camera cast him a glance and then leaned over and pointed the lens at a cane knife that lay glued to the floor by a puddle of blood. "Day, my man. Welcome to the party," he said, as the flashlamp blew with another burst of white light. "Where you been at? I've had guys looking for you in every gin and hot pillow joint this side of the river."

Rourke resisted the urge to rub his hands over his face. It was past midnight at the end of a long day, beneath his linen suit coat his shirt was sticking to his back like wet paper, he had a scotch-and-rye headache throbbing behind his left eye, and he hated the smell of blood.

He shoved his hands in his pockets and smiled. "What can I say? I guess you didn't look in low enough places."

The other man's thick shoulders, which had been hunched up around his ears, relaxed. The smile worked, as always. Daman Rourke could charm anybody, and he knew it. Sometimes he did it for a reason, and sometimes just to get in the practice.

Rourke stayed where he was and let his partner come to him. The other cop's loose pongee suit was rumpled and sweat-stained, and his sparse light brown hair stuck up like tufts of salt grass on a sand dune. In this, the year of our Lord 1927, Fiorello Prankowski was the only homicide dick in the City That Care Forgot who wasn't Irish, but then he had been born and raised in Des Moines, and allowances were made for Yankees, who couldn't be expected to know better.

"The stiff's Charles St. Claire," he said. Fio had a sad, haggard face, as if all the cares New Orleans had forgotten he felt obliged to remember. "But then I guess I don't need to tell you that, since you both were probably altar boys together at St. Alphonsus, where you used to jerk off Saturday afternoons in the sacristy. Your mama likes to tell the story of how she got a little tipsy at his mama's wedding, and you, you bastard, once tried to screw his sister."

"Charles St. Claire never had a sister."

"Know him well, do you?"

"No," Rourke said, which was not the same thing as saying he wasn't acquainted with the man at all.

He knew it drove Fio crazy that in a city of half a million people, everybody was connected to everyone else—through blood or marriage, through shared secrets and shared desires. All those connections formed concentric and interlocking circles that no outsider could ever penetrate or understand.

Neither living nor dying in New Orleans was ever completely and truly what it seemed, but the trappings, the traditions, the rituals were all enshrined and made inviolate by a collective act of faith. You buried your family secrets deep and spun intricate, invisible webs to hide your sins from yourselves and from the world. And sometimes, thought Rourke, it was far better that the sins stayed hidden, the secrets safe.

"The Ghoul is here," Fio said, pointing his chin at the corpse, and at the man who was squatting over it.

Not that anyone could have missed him, for he had the thick, blubbery roundness of a walrus. The cops called him the Ghoul because he always smelled of rotting flesh. He spent his life in the bowels of the Criminal Courts Building, cutting open dead bodies and examining disgusting specimens under microscopes, drawing conclusions too wild ever to be admitted into court.

The feelings of aversion and distrust were mutual. Moses Mueller, coroner for New Orleans Parish for less than a year, already held to the firm belief that the collective intelligence of all the detectives on the force was only slightly above that of a mollusk.

"So what's he think?" Rourke asked as he made his reluctant way to the body. He hated looking at dead things.

"You asking me?" Fio said, following after and rolling his shoulders like a horse with an itch. "You know the Ghoul—he never gives us squat. He told me it was murder, like I was supposed to run out and stop the presses. Hell, I had to give up on my theory that the stiff went chasing himself around the room hacking at himself with a cane knife."

The Ghoul had leaned over to sniff at the corpse's gaping, blood-caked mouth. "Oh, man," Fio said. "Why does he *do* stuff like that?"

Rourke was trying to keep from stepping in the blood. It had dried in some places, in stacks like glossy black tiles scattered on the floor, but in other places it was still wet and sticky, and he had just bought his expensive-as-hell alligator wing tips with last week's winnings at the track. No matter how low he did go, he always went there in style.

Charles St. Claire had not died in style. His paisley silk robe gaped open, revealing naked flesh that had been literally bled white. His throat had been slit, his chest cavity ripped open, and his guts oozed out of a cut in his belly. A slash across his pelvis had left his penis hanging by a small string of what looked like gristle.

The Ghoul was smelling the corpse's hair now. Ash from the burning cigarette that drooped from a corner of his mouth sifted down into Charles St. Claire's open and glazed gray eyes.

Rourke almost flinched, half expecting those eyes to blink. With his gaping throat and his eyes wide open and filmed with a milky caul, the dead man almost seemed to be wearing a look of laughing surprise. *Death: life's one sure thing. So what's the matter, Charlie St. Claire? Weren't you ready?* The trouble is, Rourke thought, it was easy to forget what a playful trickster was good ol' Death. How, like a naked girl popping out of your birthday cake, he could still catch you bright-eyed and smiling foolishly.

The Ghoul had lifted the dead man's hand to peer at it closely. It had a deep gash across the palm and was missing a middle finger, but a gold watch and diamond pinkie ring glittered in the light from the flickering gasoliers.

"Any ideas as to when it happened?" Rourke asked as he hunkered down on his heels beside the body.

The coroner wiped the sweat off his upper lip. Cigarette smoke curled in steady streams out his nostrils. "Certainly not within the last hour or two or, perhaps, even three—regrettably one cannot be more precise." His words, as usual, were very precise, although with a flavor of the Old World about them. "Rigor mortis has started to set in in the eyelids and cheek muscles."

"He talks to you," Fio said. "How come he only talks to you?"

"He likes me." Rourke leaned over for a better look at the knife. It was heavy, wide-bladed, and hooked, and was supposed to be used for cutting sugarcane. "Well, diddy-wah-diddy," he said on a soft whistle. For a thumbprint, flashy as a neon sign, was etched in blood at the top of the blade.

"If that quaint colloquialism is meant to convey awe," the Ghoul said, "then I find I must agree with it." He pushed back up to his feet, his bulk shifting in lurches. "Such splendid arches and loops and whorls, and all distinct enough to be seen even with the naked eye. But before we do too much celebrating, I should point

10

out that they could belong to the victim, who might have tried to wrest the weapon away from his attacker. Although it is, of course, always dangerous to speculate."

"Yeah? So maybe I'll just go on ahead and speculate that they're the killer's anyway. Just for what the hell." Not, Rourke thought, that he could count on it mattering. Many juries in New Orleans still tended to view the evidence of fingerprints as just so much hoodoo.

"Hey, get a look at this," Fio said. He had knelt to peer under a green leather wing-backed chair and now he lumbered back up, laughing. "It's the poor bastard's finger. His diddling finger." He laughed again and tossed the severed digit between the dead man's sprawled legs. "Better wrap it on up with the rest of him. What with his dick only swinging by a thread, he's gonna be needing something bonier to use on the chippies in hell."

Moses Mueller stared at the big cop, blinking against the cigarette smoke that floated before his face. "You are speaking," he said, "of a man."

"Hunh?" Fio said, and Rourke had to look down to hide a smile.

The smile faded, though, as he slowly stood with his gaze still on the dead man's face, on the sightless eyes. It wasn't so long ago some cops believed that the retinas captured their final view of life, like a photograph. Daman Rourke wished he could believe that those dying eyes had come to grasp all the truths that the living man had failed to see, but he knew that for a vain hope. If anything lingered in the eyes of the dead, it was what they had last felt in their hearts. Surprise, fear, perhaps, and an immense regret that this time the dying was happening to them, and that it was all, finally, going to be too late.

He lifted his head to find the coroner's eyes, small and hard like buckshot, studying him. "You have not asked me how he died, Lieutenant."

Fio blew a snort out his bent nose. "Gee. Maybe the cane knife and the big red grin he's wearing across his throat are some kinda clues."

"He drowned," Rourke said.

Fio laughed, but the Ghoul's shaggy eyebrows had lifted a little. He even took the cigarette out of his mouth long enough to almost smile. "You surprise me," he said.

He went to the back of the green leather chair, where he'd taken off an old-fashioned frock coat that was so worn in places it shone. He slung the coat over his shoulder while his gaze took a slow gander around the room, returning at last to the two detectives.

"Someone, or something, either evil or desperate, took a long, sharp implement, most likely a cane knife, and slashed it in a backhanded blow across the victim's throat—severing the jugular vein, the carotid artery, and the windpipe, with the result that the air passage filled with blood." He lit a fresh cigarette from the butt of the old one, then anchored a battered black fedora on his head. "Charles St. Claire did quite literally drown in his own blood."

He stopped on his way out the door to take one last look at the corpse. "This was not a quick way of dying, you understand. Not even in the final moments, after his throat had been slit open. It would have taken him a very long three or four minutes to die, and he would have spent that time in an agony of terror and pain."

He took a step, then paused again, half turning. The rotting porch groaned beneath his weight. "And it was likely that he was right-handed. The murderer, I am speaking of."

"He?" Rourke said.

The Ghoul stared off down the drive, where his chauffeured green Packard awaited him. The tip of his cigarette seemed to pulse red in time with his thoughts, then he sighed, shrugged, and began to make his slow, ponderous way down the steep and narrow steps. His voice came back to them from out of the night. "It could have been a woman."

"Well, la-di-da and kiss my achin' ass," Fio said once they'd heard the Packard's engine start up and its tires crunch on the oyster-shell drive. He fished a cigar out of his shirt pocket and scratched a match on his thumbnail. He turned, grinning, and winked at his partner as he curled his lips around the end of the cigar and drew deep to light it. "Drowned, hunh?"

The tobacco caught and he took the cigar out of his mouth,

waving it through the air and trailing smoke. "Jesus, I don't know what stinks worse—the stiff or the Ghoul."

The smoke did help cut the rank smell, for Fio indulged in only the finest Havana Castle Morros. They were part of the juice he got for pretending not to know about the numbers running going on in the back room of a certain pipe and tobacco shop on the corner of Rampart and Bienville.

Rourke said nothing. He stuffed his hands in his pockets and walked around the small room, forcing himself to look at things, to think and not feel, and there was no way, really, to keep from stepping in the blood. He wondered if a place like this old slave shack could have a memory. If inanimate things like wood and stone could absorb pain and sorrow and fear like a sponge. If so, he thought, then these walls ought to be weeping, and long before now.

He found himself looking at the top of an ormolu-mounted bureau. At a tipped-over glass, a penknife, and a silver cigarette case—all coated with aluminum and carbon powders. Fio dusting for more fingerprints. Fio, his partner, who he would have to remember was much, much smarter than he looked.

Rourke dipped his finger in the dregs left in the glass and licked, and tasted absinthe and the cold, numbing bite of cocaine.

He closed his eyes for a moment, his hand curling into a fist.

He pushed abruptly away from the bureau and brushed through a glass-beaded curtain, into the second room. The beads clattered again as Fio followed in his wake. Fio, his partner, who had the air now of a man anticipating the moment when he would be able to spring the punch line of a joke he'd been dying to tell.

It was a small space and the brass bed filled it. The mosquito netting draped open, and the counterpane was a little wrinkled, as if someone had sat or lain there, but only for a moment. A small rag rug lay crooked on the floor and looked out of place, but then it hadn't always been there.

If he lifted it, Daman Rourke knew what he would find. Because some stains, some crimes, could never be washed away.

He went to the window instead.

"You know," Fio said from behind him, "how you figure it's a good bet that the person who found the corpse is the person who made the corpse . . ."

The window was open but the air outside was hot and still. You couldn't see much, with the way the bamboo and banana trees crowded against this back part of the shack. You could stand behind that curtain of green, though, shielded from sight, and watch what went on in this room, on this bed. He knew, because once he had done so.

"So who did find him?" Rourke finally asked, although he knew that as well. God help him, but he knew.

Fio plucked the cigar out of his mouth. He moved his jaw as though chewing his thoughts, then his battered face split into a wide grin.

"Cinderella."

They called her the most beautiful woman in the world.

Her image was everywhere, in rag sheets and magazines, on candy boxes and postcards. It flickered on the silver screens of movie palaces, and on the midnight stages of a million erotic dreams.

The newspapers called her the Cinderella Girl sometimes too. It came from the first movie she had made, *The Glass Slipper*—a dark and sultry interpretation of the classic fairy tale. It was the role that had shot a young woman by the improbable name of Remy Lelourie into the galaxy of celluloid stardom. The world had seen nothing like her, before or since.

For it wasn't only her beauty—which was a strange kind of beauty anyway, with her eyes set too far apart and her face too bony, her mouth too wide. She seduced you in a way you didn't dare confess, not even to your priest. You looked at her and you saw a raw hunger and desperation for life, not redemption and not salvation, but *life*. The down-and-dirty kind of life that happened on a hot, wet night, in a seedy room, with whiskey and desire burning in your blood.

You looked at her, thought Daman Rourke, and you saw sin. Dangerous, delectable, unaccountable sin.

He stood in the middle of the yard and looked at the old French colonial house. He hadn't come near her yet and already he felt the pull of her. "Remy," he said, seeing how it would feel to say her name again after all this time.

He stayed where he was, not moving, looking toward the bayou now. A wind had come up, rattling the banana trees and bringing with it the smell of sour mud and dead water. He saw a pair of lantern lights floating among the dead cypress, where Negro boys often gigged for frogs at night.

A hundred years ago this place had been a sugar plantation, before the city had grown up around it. Only a few acres and the house remained, but her beauty and charm were there still. In her tall and elegant windows, in the finely carved colonnettes and balustrades. In the wide galleries that spread all around her, like the dancing skirts of a southern belle. The man who built the house had called her Sans Souci. *Free of worry, without a care.*

The spell was broken by the chug and rattle of the coroner's hearse turning down the drive, come to take away the earthly remains of Charles St. Claire, who was free now of not only worry but everything else.

A gaggle of reporters with cameras slung over their shoulders was riding on the running boards, and the sight of them sent Rourke sprinting the rest of the way across the yard to the house and up onto the shadowed gallery. Light from the headlamps bounced off the brass uniform buttons of a beat cop, who stood at stiff attention in front of the door.

Rourke showed him his gold shield. "Sure is a hell of a hot night for it," he said, and smiled.

The patrolman, who looked barely out of school, read the name on the badge and stiffened up even straighter. "Lieutenant Rourke, sir?" he said, wariness and wonder both in his voice. His round, freckled face was red and sweating beneath his scuttle-shaped hard hat.

Rourke turned up the wattage on his smile. He had no illusions that the young man's awed reaction had anything to do with Lieu-tenant Daman Rourke's sterling reputation as an ace detective.

Even being Irish and the son of a cop wasn't going to take you from walking a beat to carrying a detective lieutenant's badge by the time you were thirty. Promotions can come fast and easy, though, when your father-in-law is the superintendent of the New Orleans Police Department.

"Are you feeling generous tonight?" Rourke said.

The patrolman swallowed so hard his Adam's apple disappeared into his collar. "Sir, I . . . Sir?"

The reporters were leaping off the running boards now as the meat wagon rolled to a stop. They would go first to the slave shack to pop photographs of the body. Pictures too gory to be printed, but not too gory to be passed around and cracked wise over in the newsroom.

Rourke brushed past the young cop, flashing another smile as he did so. "So be a pal, then," he said, "and promise them anything short of a night with your sister, but keep those press guys out of my face."

The boy finally relaxed, grinning. "Well, I don't got me a sister, but I know what you mean. Sir?"

Rourke paused, the cypress door swinging open beneath his hand. "She couldn't have done it. Not Remy Lelourie. Could she?"

Rourke crossed over the threshold, saying nothing. He entered a hall that was wide and cool beneath a high ceiling fan, and sweet with the smell of oiled wood. The sliding doors between the double parlors were thrown open, and he could see into rooms that were dressed for summer in flowered slipcovers and rush mats. The French windows were open to the night, and a breeze stirred their long saffron draperies.

A small, slender woman in a gray silk dress stood before a yellow marble fireplace with her back to the door, her head bent. Her dark hair was cut boyishly short, baring her long neck. Her legs were bare as well, her feet caked and splattered with dried blood.

Rourke had to stop a moment and lean against the jamb. It was a strange high, to be seeing her again and with the smell of blood filling his head. A high as powerful as any that came from a glass of absinthe and cocaine.

"Hey, Remy," he said. "How you doin', girl?"

Slowly she turned, lifting her head. The softly tragic expression on her face looked drawn there as if by a knife. For a moment the wrench of memory was so strong he nearly choked on it.

"Day," she said, and that was all, but hearing it tore something loose inside him.

He walked up to her, holding her fast with his gaze. She waited for him, allowing him to look, daring him to see behind her eyes. The front of her dress looked like someone had taken a bucket of blood and drenched her with it. She even had blood in her hair.

Her right hand was pressed to the hollow between her breasts, as though he had startled her. Her fingers were wrapped around a stained handkerchief that had been twisted into a ragged string. He took her hand and she let him, her eyes the whole time on his face. Her eyes were exactly how he remembered them, wide-spaced and tilted up at the corners. Dark brown with golden lights, like tiny bursting suns.

He unwrapped the makeshift bandage. A ragged cut gaped open across her palm from little finger to thumb.

"Why did you do it, Remy?" he said.

She wrenched free of him and turned away, gripping her elbows with bloodstained hands. She didn't appear to be wearing any-thing underneath that single sheath of blood-soaked silk.

Rourke leaned against the mantel and stuffed his fists deep into his pockets. He allowed the space between them to empty into a hard silence, but she didn't fill it with any words. To Fio she'd spun a tale that she had been in bed, asleep, when she'd been awakened by screams coming from the old slave shack and she had gone out there to find her husband expelling his last breath through a rip in his throat.

"Now this was supposed to've been around nine o'clock, you understand," Fio had said. "But it was a whole two hours later when Miss Beulah, the colored lady who does for the family, comes down to the kitchen for something or other and she looks out the window and thinks something 'ain't quite right' about the shack. So she goes on out to see what's what, and lo and behold 'what' turns out to be Cinderella covered in blood, sitting 'longside of Prince Charming here, rocking back and forth and telling him over and over how sorry she is about it all."

Rourke took a step closer to her. "You going to tell me what happened?"

She raised her head as though meeting the challenge, but her voice when she spoke was dry and scratchy, as if she'd spent the night weeping. Or screaming.

"Why? What good will it do, when you've already made up your mind not to believe me?"

"Just think of it as a dress rehearsal for the jury, then, because things sure don't look good, baby. You saying you sat there and stared at the gaping raw wound of your husband's slit throat for all that time and did nothing."

The banjo clock on the wall chose that moment to strike one o'clock, and she flinched as if the soft gong had been a blow. "He was . . . there was this awful gurgling sound, Day, and all this blood came spurting out his mouth. It was like he was trying to talk to me, to tell me something, but I couldn't, couldn't . . . And then the next thing I remember is hearing Beulah scream."

"Yeah, I guess a couple hours of time must've just sort of slipped away from you there. It does that sometimes after an absinthe and happy dust cocktail."

"That was Charlie's poison. And yours, or so I've heard tell." She had lifted her head again, met his eyes again.

Her mouth trembled and twisted into a smile, but it was a wry one, full of memories and pain. "We've always been willing to believe the worst about each other, haven't we, Day?"

All he could manage was a shake of his head.

She held his gaze a moment longer, then the smile faded from her face and she turned away. He watched her in silence while she picked up a mother-of-pearl smoking set from off the mantel. He waited until she fitted a cigarette into the holder and lit a match before he said, "Who was your husband sleeping with, besides you?"

The flame trembled slightly, but that was all. "Now, whatever would Charles want with anyone else, when he already possessed the most beautiful woman in the world?"

He watched as the wild self-derision burned sudden and bright in her eyes. That cruel and destructive pulse of wildness that had once, long ago, seduced them both over the edge.

Jesus save me, he thought.

He cleared his throat. "Uh-huh. And how often did he beat you?"

Her hand flew up quicker than she could stop it, although she tried. It got as far as her neck, and so she pressed her palm there as if feeling for a pulse. The color around the bruise on her cheek drained away, so that it stood out as stark as a smudge of soot.

"Oh, this little ol' thing . . . You remember how the rain came up so hard and fast this evenin'? Well, I went to close the windows and the wind caught one of the shutters and it up and smacked me right in the face." She breathed a soft, girlish laugh, and he almost laughed himself at this vision of Remy Lelourie suddenly turning into a southern belle with cotton bolls for brains.

"Cut the shuck, Remy," he said. "One thing you've never been is a magnolia blossom."

She put the cigarette down in an ashtray without having smoked it and wrapped her arms around herself again. "And you've always been one mean, tough bastard, haven't you?"

"Somebody has to be. And here's another interesting fact for you: The human body holds about ten pints of blood, and Charles St. Claire left most of his splattered all over the floor and ceiling and walls of an old slave shack on his way to being hacked to death with a cane knife. Now, Lord knows I was never all that fond of poor Charlie, but that sort of last moment I'd reserve only for my worst enemy, and I got this sick feeling in the pit of my gut that the big fat juicy thumbprint on that knife is going to turn out to be yours. Was he your worst enemy, *Mrs.* St. Claire?"

Her eyes had grown wide and stark. "I might have touched it— the knife. It was stuck in his chest. I tried to pull it out, but it was caught on . . . on something . . . and blood was spraying all around us, and then . . . then all at once it came gushing up out of his throat."

Her hands fell to her sides and she looked down at herself as if suddenly just realizing what a mess she was. "It got all over me."

She lifted her head and there was a wounded look on her face now, and he wondered, as he'd always wondered, which of all the Remys in the world was the real one. "They wouldn't let me take a bath," she said. "When can I take a bath?"

"You'll have to take off all you're wearing in front of your maid, so's she can pass it along to us. Then tomorrow mornin' you're going to have to come on down to the Criminal Courts Building and give us your fingerprints."

"Oh, God, Day. You're not just . . . You really do believe I . . ." He watched her eyes brighten and grow wet with tears. Even though he knew it for the act that it was, he also thought that maybe a few things were getting through to her at last. That while she might be Remy Lelourie and the most beautiful woman in the world, there were going to be some in the city of New Orleans at least who would believe she had done this terrible thing.

He pressed his shoulder hard into the mantel to keep from touching her. She was still the most dangerous moment of his life. She had lied to him and used him and left him, hurt him in ways uncountable and unmeasurable, but he'd always wanted her anyway. He had never stopped wanting her.

"You remember how I worked the docks that summer, unloading banana boats? How I always had welts all over my hands and arms from getting bit by the rats and spiders that lived in those banana bunches?"

"Day." She had said his name on a sigh.

" 'Cause I remember it. Just like I remember other stuff about that summer," he said. Welts on his hands and welts on his heart. "Like how you cried that last afternoon. Big fat crocodile tears, just like these." He was cupping her face, gathering up her tears as if he would keep them.

"I loved you," she said. "I loved you so bad it almost killed me."

"You were slumming. And—funny thing—but this is the part I remember best: You were the one who left."

She wrapped her fingers around his wrist and held his hand in place so that she could turn her head and brush her lips across his palm, and the wetness of her mouth mixed with her tears. "I was afraid. Of you, Day. I wonder if you've any idea how frightening you can be."

Him frightening. That was a laugh. He leaned closer, until only a breath-space separated their mouths. He was opening the throttle wide now, putting his money down.

"You were always good, darlin', the best I've ever seen, and worth every bit of the ten G's a week they were paying you out in Hollywood." Her fingers were pressing hard on the pulse in his wrist, so that it seemed his blood flowed into hers. "But just like any two-bit hooker who finds herself owned by a cheatin', heavy-handed pimp, one day you up and killed your man."

He took a step back, pulled loose from her, let go of her. His face felt as though it were made of lead, but his breathing was fast and hard.

"You killed him, Remy girl. And I'm going to nail you for it."

Chapter Two

A specter folk called the gowman was said to haunt the cypress swamp beyond the Faubourg St. John. Dressed all in white and prowling the night, the gowman lured his victims to a hideous death. He murdered the innocent, but what he did afterward was worse: He stole away the corpses he made, so there would be no body for friends and loved ones to view at the wake, no casket to put in the crypt. To those old Creole families like the St. Claires and the Lelouries, those families whose names, like their cypress houses, had been built to last forever, such a fate was beyond bearing.

The gowman was innocent of this murder at least, thought Daman Rourke as he watched the coroner's hearse roll back down the drive. For this funeral there would be a wake and a casket, and a widow.

He leaned on the balustrade of the upstairs gallery and watched the wind blow fresh rain clouds back across the moon. Before he'd allowed her to go upstairs and get out of her bloody dress, he had gone up and taken a look at her bedroom. At her big tester bed with its canopy of rose garlands and frolicking cupids. At the semen stains on the messed sheets.

At her cloche hat and pearls laid out on her dressing table, a pair of stockings draped over the back of a chair, her shoes lined up beside it. At her tapestry valise stuffed so full of clothes, and done in such a hurry, that one of the straps wouldn't fasten—as if she'd packed up and gotten ready to run before she'd killed him.

But then people never change, and she had run before.

The old cypress floorboards creaked beneath Fiorello Prankowski's heavy tread as he joined Rourke at the gallery railing. Fio hooked a hip on the worn wood, folded his arms across his chest, and stared at his partner.

"You gotta figure the wife for doing it," he said.

"Yes." The word tasted sour in Rourke's mouth. The way he'd behaved with her in there—like the jilted lover he once was, who had wanted to make her hurt as much as he was hurting, who had wanted to make her suffer, and never mind that whatever pain he might have owed her was eleven years too late.

Fio flipped his cigar butt out into the night. "Blood all over her, those missing two hours, and the maid finding her with the body, crying about bein' so sorry. Yeah, she did it, all right, as sure as I'm a poor Italian-Polack boy from Des Moines. And ain't it almost always the one who is supposed to love you best," he said, voicing an old cop truism. "Her story's pretty half-assed, but it might hold up. I mean it's gonna be tough to find a jury who'll send Remy Lelourie upriver to fry, even for killing her old man."

"Even tougher if enough folk figure he was asking for it."

"Was he?"

From where they were, up on the second-story gallery, you could look across the bayou water and see the lights of the gates to City Park, where seventy years ago, beneath a grove of live-oak trees, a St. Claire had shot a Lelourie to death in a duel over lost honor and a game of faro.

"I played a game of *bourré* with the gentleman once," Rourke said. "Charles St. Claire had no fear, and no limit."

"Hunh, you should talk. So who won?"

"I did."

Fio huffed a laugh. "There you go . . . Everybody's got something, though. If he didn't have fear, what did he have?"

"Money, pride, greed, lust. And secrets." Rourke smiled. "All of the usual southern deadly sins."

"Aw, man, don't tell me that. What secrets?"

"He had a sterling silver name, and juice in all the high and mighty places, but he's been a hophead for years, and one who really got his kicks out of walking on the wild side. He liked to use people—men, but especially women. And then he liked making them pay for the privilege of being used."

Fio had turned his head back around to look at him, and Rourke could feel the dissecting edge in the other man's gaze.

"He was also," Rourke went on, "the only white Creole lawyer around these parts with enough brass to defend a Negro in court, and on rare occasions he even won. That Charles St. Claire was able to save a few sorry black asses from a life of hoeing sweet potatoes and cutting cane on an Angola chain gang—well, certain folk will tell you that was his very worst sin."

"And what will they tell me is Remy Lelourie's very worst sin?"

"That she left us all those years ago. Or tried to."

Fio waited two slow beats before he said, "I know you want her to be innocent, but she probably isn't, so don't—" He cut himself off, blowing a big breath through his teeth.

"Don't what?" Rourke said.

"Don't let it break your heart this time."

"This time?" For a moment Rourke wondered how much his partner knew—if he'd heard something somewhere, a whisper, a rumor. It was impossible, though. The real secrets, the sins, were buried too deep. Only he and Remy knew what had really happened down in that slave shack eleven years ago, and Remy would never tell.

Fio shrugged. "I'm only saying, she's young and beautiful and it's an ugly thought that she's responsible for that mess down there." He waved his hand in the direction of the slave shack. "But you always end up letting yourself care about them too much, the murdered ones and their murderers—you care too much and they end up breaking your heart."

Rourke stared at the other cop, letting an edgy silence fall between them. "You done?"

"Yeah, I'm done."

Rourke stared at Fio some more, then he smiled and shook his head. He waited until Fio smiled back at him, and then he said, "Jesus, Prankowski. You are so full of shit."

He pushed off the balustrade, turning his back on the bayou. His headache was blinding now, and his legs and arms felt weightless, invisible, as if he were disappearing back into the past where once they had been, he and Remy.

"You know," Fio said as they left the house by the back gallery stairs, "that's the part about all of this that I don't get the most. She had it all—she was a friggin' movie star, for Christ's sake. So what did she come back here for, to up and marry a man like St. Claire?"

"Maybe it was true love."

"Yeah? Then true love sure doesn't last long. When did they tie the knot—back in February sometime? That makes it five months."

They crossed the yard to the oaks that lined the drive, where Rourke had parked his Indian Big Chief motorbike. It had started to rain again, in large, fat drops.

He had straddled the leather seat and kick-started the engine when Fio's big hands gripped the handlebars and he leaned over, bringing his face close to Rourke's. "You mind telling me where you're going? Partner."

Rourke stared back at him, but his answer when it came was mild enough. "To a speak."

"If you need a drink, I got a flask in my pocket."

"I'm looking for a woman. You got one of those in your pocket too?"

Fio blew his breath out. In the white light from the bike's headlamp, his face looked drained of blood the way Charles St. Claire's had been. "What do you know that you're not telling me?"

"Nothing," Rourke lied, smiling so it would go down easy.

He rolled down the drive and along the bayou road until he turned onto Esplanade Avenue, where he opened the Indian's throttle into a roar and tore down the rainslick pavement. The bike shuddered between his legs, and the hot, wet wind slapped him in the face, while a saxophone wailed "Runnin' Wild" in his head.

Three years before, a Prohibition agent—strictly in the name of research, of course—had decided to prove how easy it was for a thirsty man to buy himself a glass of hooch in various cities throughout the dry country. It took him a whole twenty-one minutes to find and make his illegal purchase in Chicago. It took him three minutes in Detroit.

In New Orleans it took him thirty-five seconds.

Daman Rourke wasted even less time that wet and bloody summer's night, but then he knew where he was going.

The speakeasy was on Dumaine Street, masquerading as a laundry, although a few shirts occasionally did get boiled in the big copper tubs out back. Enough so that you could detect a faint smell of soap and scorched starch beneath the reek of tobacco smoke and booze-soaked sawdust.

Rourke leaned his elbows on the water-marked bar and ordered a scotch and rye from a slope-shouldered, slack-lipped man in a greasy apron. When the man came with his drink, Rourke put his dollar down. The bartender figured him for a cop and so he didn't pick the money up, but Rourke would leave it lie anyway, for no matter how low he did go, he always went there in style and he always paid his own way.

The hooch was good, straight off the boat from Honduras, and still it burned when it hit his belly. Tonight, the speak seemed sad and quiet. From the back room drifted the clatter of billiard balls and the murmur of men playing cotch. A man in a red-striped vest slumped, passed out, at a piano, his black hands gently folded together on the silent ivory keys as if in prayer.

Yet under the tarnished light of a copper-shaded lamp, a couple danced anyway, lost in music only they could hear. Feet shuffling in a slow drag, bellies pressed close, hips grinding together in a parody of love. The woman's tawdry yellow dress was coming unraveled at the hem, her brassy hair was black at the roots, and her eyes were clenched tightly shut. As if not looking was as good as not knowing.

When the bartender came back to see if he wanted another, Rourke nodded, even though his headache was now pounding loud as a Mardi Gras band. "Last time I was in here," he said, "must've been, oh, 'bout a week back—you had a gal singin' the heartbreak blues so damn fine. Made a man want to crawl into bed with a full bottle and a willin' woman, and drown his sorrows deep in the both of them."

Rourke paused to trace a pattern through the water rings with his finger, and when he looked back up his smile was backwoods friendly, with just a hint of bashfulness in it, as if he hadn't tried this particular game before and was seeing how far he could go with it. "Since then, well, I just haven't been able to get that lil' gal's song out my mind."

The bartender took a vague swipe at the scarred wood with a corner of his apron, while he sucked on his fat bottom lip and tried to assess if the cop leaning on his bar was looking to get laid or be put on the pad. "You're pro'bly thinkin' of Lucille. Only thing is, she said she wasn't feelin' so hot this evenin', so I told her to take it off."

"What a cryin' shame," Rourke said, while inside he felt sick, and cold with fear at the trouble he could see coming his way. Lucille's way. Lucille, who should have been here in this speak, singing the blues, and yet wasn't, and so she probably had no alibi now for where she had been while Charlie St. Claire was out in that shack, drowning in his own blood.

The bartender chewed on his lip some more, while his gaze flitted everywhere but on Rourke's face. Finally he leaned forward and lowered his voice to a hoarse, whiskey-fed whisper.

"If it's a hankerin' for blackberries you got, there's a place 'round the corner on Burgundy. Look for a brown door faded to the color of a drunk's piss. They got 'em from ripe to green, and every which way in between."

Rourke knocked back the last of his drink and laid another dollar down on the bar. He smiled again, and there was nothing backwoods or bashful about it. It was the smile of a boy who had grown up with a drunk for a father in the Irish Channel, where they had corner saloons that made this one resemble a Sunday school room, and bartenders who kept the peace with brickbats and bolo knives.

"You have yourselves a good night now," he said. The slack-lipped man didn't answer or nod, he just turned and walked carefully down to the other end of the bar.

Outside the rain had come and gone, but it hadn't taken the heat with it. Rourke had already started down the street when he saw a woman leaning against a mist-haloed street lamp. She was naked except for a faded blue wrapper and an old-fashioned corset.

Even with her standing in the shadows he could see that the skin of her legs glowed smooth and coal black, but her face was a pasty pink. Sometimes a country girl, young to the business and before she'd learned what it was a man really wanted, would buy pink chalk, wet it with perfume, and smear it on to make herself look white.

This one had at least got her hustle down. She rolled her belly in a little dance and made a wet, smacking noise with her lips. "Hello, daddy. Wanna do a little business?"

Rourke shook his head, then said, "No, thank you," to ease the rejection, and then had to laugh at himself for thinking she would care. She was young, but not that young. Yet as he passed her by, he thought that underneath the pink chalk she'd been someone he knew.

He walked down Dumaine, along a brick banquette slick and silver with rain, toward the mouth of the alley where he had parked the Indian. Off in the night someone was playing a trumpet. Whoever it was, all the misery of his life and the sorrow in his soul was coming out of that horn. Daman Rourke stopped to stand beneath a dripping balcony and listen as the trumpet went crying up the last note, making music so sweet it hurt, like the slash of a cane knife to the heart.

It hadn't all been a lie, what he'd last said to Fio about needing to get laid.

Memory could be like a train whistle in the night, sucking you deep into the low-down blues. You could stop it, sometimes, with booze or drugs, but the best way he'd found was to lose yourself in the arms of a woman, if she was your woman, maybe. If she hadn't left you yet, or died on you, or just plain given up on you.

No trumpet sobbed out its heart in this uptown neighborhood of double shotgun and camelback houses. Rourke killed the bike's engine as he rolled it to a stop alongside Bridey O'Mara's front stoop.

Shadows stirred on a gallery smothered with purple wisteria. A porch swing creaked.

He stopped at the bottom of the steps and looked up at the woman on the swing. His woman, maybe. She sat with her knees drawn up beneath her chin and her arms wrapped around her legs. Her head was tucked low, as if she were trying to hide behind the long fall of her Irish red hair.

"Hey, baby," he said. "It's after two in the mornin'. What're you doing still up?"

She raised her head, and the curtain of her hair parted. Light from the street lamps bled through the thick vines and onto her face. Her cheeks glowed damp with sweat, or maybe tears.

He stayed where he was at the bottom of the steps, staring up at her. She stared back at him a moment, then jerked her head away. "A couple of cops were here looking for you. I had to tell them I hadn't seen you in over a week."

Her voice had come out broken and rough. She gripped her legs tighter and rocked a bit. The swing moaned. "I was sitting out here remembering the night Sean didn't come home. Lordy, how it did storm—do you remember? Thunder and lightning and pouring down like it wasn't ever going to quit."

Rourke climbed the steps and sat down next to her on the swing. Her eyes were bright and hot.

"I sat out here on this swing that night, too," she said, "waiting for him to come home, with the storm going on all around me, and it was like I was falling through a long, black silence. I think that must be what dying's like, Day, don't you? Falling through a long, black silence."

He started to touch her, then didn't. "I won't go disappearing on you, Bridey."

She let go of her legs and leaned against him, her shoulder pressing against his. She wore only a thin cotton wrapper, and he could feel the heat of her body.

Memory could be like a train whistle in the night, and sometimes you felt the pull of its call in spite of all your good intentions and best defenses. He thought of Charles St. Claire lying in puddles of blood, his eyes wide open to death. He was afraid he knew well what horror those eyes had seen in their last moments, because long ago his own eyes had watched Remy Lelourie kill.

This was the place where his thoughts kept getting stuck, like a scratch on a record: If she'd done it once, once, once, she could do it again. Yet he knew already that she had the power to make him believe otherwise. Or not to care.

"I know he's dead," said the woman sitting next to him on the swing, and Rourke's mind made a dizzying jerk as he thought that she, too, was seeing that slashed body in the bloody slave shack. Then he realized her thoughts were back in another rainy night, waiting for a man who never came.

"I know his boat went down in that storm," she said. "I know that's what happened, I do. But sometimes . . ."

Sometimes.

Rourke turned into her and pulled her close, so he could lay his head between her breasts, and it felt so good. He thought he might have felt her lips in his hair, and then she pulled away from him and stood up. She took him by the hand and led him into her bedroom.

Her eyes were the golden gray color of pewter caught in candlelight. She had dustings of freckles on her breasts that were wet now from his tongue. He lay upon her, and as she looked up at him, her face was full of feelings and memories that he didn't want to know. He wanted to stay wrapped up in her, lost in her, forever.

It had been them against the world, growing up poor and tough and running wild on Rousseau Street in the Irish Channel. Daman

Rourke, Casey Maguire, Sean O'Mara, and Bridey Kinsella. The summer they were twelve, they went to Mamma Rae, the voodooienne, and for a dollar apiece she tattooed blue eight-pointed stars on the inside of their left wrists. She made up a charm and walked backward three times counterclockwise around a virgin's fresh grave in the light of a waning moon, and then she pronounced them blood brothers for life. It hadn't mattered that Bridey was a girl; she was one of them. They were all three half in love with her, even then.

Sean had been the one to marry her in the end, though, and he'd kept her until one Sunday two months ago, when he had taken his small trawler out onto Lake Pontchartrain for some spring evening fishing and hadn't been seen or heard from again. If you didn't know Sean O'Mara, you would say how he was a cop who'd gone bad, a boozer and a loser who had racked up big debts with his bootlegger and his bookie. You would say there were riverboats and trains leaving New Orleans all the time, and that sometimes the only way out from under was to start over.

Only if you grew up together in the hard-luck, hard-scramble neighborhood of the Irish Channel with him watching your back while you watched his, you would know that Sean O'Mara could run wild at times, but he would never run away.

Or this was what you told yourself on those nights when you lay in Sean O'Mara's spool-turned bed, with Sean O'Mara's wife. When strands of her long hair were caught on your chest, and you could feel the heat of her breath against your face.

"Bridey," he said.

She sighed in answer and pressed her hip into his belly, and his throat closed up on some emotion he couldn't name.

He had sat up with Bridey all that night, and several nights after, while they dragged the lake and the city's underbelly of speakeasies and hot pillow joints, looking for Sean. He hadn't meant to touch her, not even when she'd cried and asked him to hold her, not even when she had covered his mouth with hers in a kiss full of despair. For her, he knew, their touching was only a way of taking comfort from an old friend. For him it was a different sort of comfort—sweetly lonesome, edged with pain, like the wail of a saxophone. His own wife had been dead going on seven years. He had photographs to remind himself of what she'd looked like, but he had long ago forgotten the music her voice could make when she spoke his name.

He touched the woman who was lying beside him now, on the inside of her left wrist, where the small faded blue star was but a shadow, like a birthmark. "Bridey," he said again.

A smile was beginning to grow at the edges of her mouth and eyes when the telephone rang.

He saw her face change, saw the hope flare like a struck match for just an instant in her eyes, and he looked away. She would always, he thought, be out on that swing, waiting.

"It's probably only Mama," she finally said when the bell had jangled a third time. "She has a hard time sleeping nights since Daddy died."

He watched her rise naked from the bed and walk into the parlor, where the telephone rested on a narrow mahogany stand. She answered it with one hand and gathered her hair up off her neck with the other, and the movement arched her back and lifted her breasts. In the light cast by the parlor's red-shaded lamp, her breasts glowed pink, like rare seashells.

He heard her say, "Yes, he's here. Just a moment, please."

He got up, glancing at the camelback clock as he passed by the dresser. It still lacked a couple of hours before dawn.

He went to her, their bodies brushing together, then parting. He took the handset from her and spoke into the receiver. "Yeah?"

Fiorello Prankowski's voice, thick with static, came at him out of the night. "Day? We've got us another one."

Chapter Three

The dead man lay wet and bloated, facedown on the bayou bank in a web of green algae and swamp trash. Rourke had to pick his way through sucking, sour yellow mud, cattails, saw grass, and the remnants of a rotted pirogue. He really, really hated looking at dead things, and the night was ruining the hell out of his new shoes.

He squatted down next to the body and motioned to the young patrolman who was holding a lantern to bring the light closer. "You done?" he said to Fio, who'd been photographing the scene. "I want to turn him."

The flash lamp on Fio's camera strobed one last time over the black water and clawed branches of the dead cypress trees. "Yeah, yeah, do it," he said. "Christ." He shuffled a couple of steps backward, rubbing his nose. The stench was bad: thick and gray and fetid.

Rourke grabbed the dead man by the left arm and shoulder and heaved. The guy was strangely light, but soggy, as if he'd soaked up the swamp like a soft sponge. He landed on his back with a sodden plop.

"Shit!"

A baby water moccasin, its black head flaring, darted out of the gaping hole of the dead man's open mouth. Rourke jerked backward, his heel slipping on the wet ooze, and he almost fell on his butt. The snake slithered out of the corpse's mouth and around his throat to disappear into the canebrakes.

"Jesus," Fio said.

"Get some light back over here," Rourke said to the rookie cop, who had dropped the lantern in the mud. Rourke leaned back over the body. He thought at first the man's throat had been cut, and then the light caught the glint of a piano wire buried deep in the white, poached flesh.

"A professional hit," Fio said. In the tangle of weeds and abandoned trotlines wrapped around the dead man's legs was a thick rope with a frayed end. The rope's other end was tied in a bowline knot around one thin, twisted ankle. "Looks like he's been in the swamp at least a couple of weeks, maybe more. You recognize him, what's left of him?"

The face had begun to undergo adipocere from so much time in the water, turning bloated, grotesque, the color of yellowed old wax. But a lurid birthmark the size and shape of a cauliflower flared up the man's neck and over his right cheek, and memory clicked in Rourke's mind: of a round, chinless face marked by that terrible purple stain and made even uglier by a flattened nose pitted with acne scars and small, cement-colored eyes. You couldn't tell if they'd seen any truths at their moment of the death, those eyes, because the crawfish had been at them.

Rourke searched the past for a name. "Could be a kid from the Irish Channel, name of McGinty. Vinny McGinty. If it's the guy I'm thinking of, he tried to make it as a prizefighter a couple of years back, but he had lead feet and a glass jaw—couldn't even last past the first bell. After he quit the ring, though, he still used to hang out around the Boxing Irish club, trying to talk the contenders into sparring a few rounds. He made his broad and booze money by collecting vigs for the Maguires."

Fio blew a thick breath out his nose. "Wonderful, just wonderful. Casey Maguire's got so much juice he can't take a leak without the mayor offering to come along and hold his dick for him . . . Jesus, what a friggin' night. First a high-society blue blood gets himself slashed to bloody ribbons by the Cinderella Girl, and then one of Maguire's goons comes floating up out of the bayou with his eye sockets sucked clean by the crawdaddies. We're fucked, partner. Fucked. We got ourselves one murder suspect who's a matinee idol and more famous than Babe Ruth, and another murder suspect who fancies himself the New Orleans Al Capone."

Casey Maguire was indeed a force to be reckoned with of hurricane proportions in the city of New Orleans. He was what the tabloids called a mobster and City Hall called a businessman. He owned a sugar refinery and a slaughterhouse, along with pieces of all the usual nefarious rackets, but the Volstead Act had truly made him a king. He had a monopoly on all the hooch sold in the city's many speakeasies; he owned the smugglers' boats that brought the brand-name liquor in from Mexico and South America; and he owned the cutting plants where it was watered down and put into bottles. He owned the courts and the federal revenue agents and the city police who were sworn to uphold the laws that made most of what he did illegal.

Very few people knew, though, that beneath the starched white cuff of his shirt, on the skin of his left wrist, was etched the tattoo of a small blue eight-pointed star. Even fewer people knew what it meant. The juju woman had told them, the summer they were twelve, that they'd all be cursed if even one of them ever broke faith with the blood oath.

"I guess there's no reason to figure he was actually dumped all the way out here," Fio was saying as he frowned down at the body. "He could've been floating along for a while, once that rope broke."

Rourke stood up, dusting off his hands. "Who found him?"

"A cootch dancer who works at that Negro smoke joint on down the road. She said she was taking a walk to get a breath of air. What she'd probably done was take a walk to turn a trick, but whoever the john was—if there was one—he's vamoosed."

The girl had straightened brown hair and coffee-brown skin.

She sat on the running board of the patrol car, her thin shoulders hunched around the jelly glass of *spotioti* she had cradled in her hands.

Her head tilted slowly back as Rourke walked up to her. She had a booze-glazed look in her dark brown eyes, but she wasn't so far gone that she didn't know she was looking at the white man's law. He saw the fear and wariness settle over her face, like closing the shutters up tight on a storm-battered house.

He nodded at her. "Thank you for waiting, Miss . . ."

She heaved a deep sigh that smelled of the muscatel and whiskey. "Sugar. Well, my given name is Dora, but everybody calls me Sugar. Sugar Baudier." She tried to put a smile on, but it didn't stick. "I'm a dancer. I work at Jack's Place, on down yonder."

She waved her hand at the road that was little more than parallel tracks cut through the saw grass. The road led to a row of weathered shacks with sagging stoops set up on stilts that backed up against the train tracks and faced the bayou. Anchoring the row of shacks was one more shack as dilapidated as the rest, knocked together from scrap boards and tin, which Rourke figured to be Jack's Place from the noise and light leaking out around its rotted shutters. Laughter, the bawl of a saxophone, and a woman crooning "The Mean Lovin' Man Blues."

The singer was letting the pain of heartbreak bleed into every aching note. Rourke hadn't even realized he'd paused to listen, until the girl, scared by his weighty silence, started giving him the answers to the questions he hadn't even asked yet.

"I come out here for a walk, 'cause it was hot inside, and the smoke got to botherin' my asthma, and there he was, out 'longside the bayou, lyin' there in the mud and lookin' like he been dead for a good long while, so I said to myself, Better you go tell Jackson that he better get on down to Mr. Morgan's grocery an' telephone the po-lice, which is what we done. He done."

"Was there anyone out here with you, or just hanging out down along the bayou, when you came for your walk?"

She shook her head so hard he was surprised her ears didn't start ringing. "No, suh. Uh-uh. No, suh."

"How about going back a couple of weeks ago? You see or hear anything out of the ordinary happening along the bayou or 'round Jack's Place?"

"I di'n't see nothin'. No, suh."

Her salt-faded dress hung on her scrawny frame and was stiff with dried sweat. In spite of the hard grip she was putting on that jelly glass of *spotioti*, her hands still trembled. If she was on the hustle she wasn't making much of a living at it, Rourke thought; she looked half-starved and wrung down to nothing on bad booze. But then the men who frequented Jack's Place wouldn't have much more than a quarter to pay for what she had to sell.

"Miss Baudier," Rourke said. "You probably don't know this, but the city of New Orleans gives a reward to any citizen who assists the police during the investigation of a suspicious death." He pulled out what bills he had in his pocket, which amounted to all of five dollars, and held them out to her.

She stared up at him and he could see she didn't believe him, but she took the money anyway.

"Giving out rewards again, I see," Fio said as Rourke joined him. He was waiting at the top of the bayou bank for the Ghoul to show up in his chauffeured green Packard. "You go and try to put that on the report under expenses and the captain's gonna have your ass."

Rourke stared out over the bayou. False dawn was bleeding the sky a bone white, and a mist was creeping up around the cypress roots. He thought he could hear the *Smoky Mary* coming at them, rumbling along the train tracks that ran in back of the shacks.

"This Jack's Place—we ain't exactly talking high class," Fio went on. After almost a year of working together, he was used to Rourke's silences, had learned to talk through them. "Didn't some poor saps get blinded by drinking a white lightning made of wood alcohol and Jamaica ginger out here one night?"

It could have happened, Rourke thought. Or maybe that was some other joint. The singer had come to the end of her song. He thought he should probably amble on down there and ask around if anyone had seen anything. Nobody would have; this wasn't a part of town where you let yourself pay much attention to what went on around you.

It wasn't even a part of New Orleans city proper—this large expanse of bays and channels and flooded cypress and willows that comprised the swampy wasteland northeast of the river. In the old days they'd called it the "wet grave," but that was because of the yellow fever and not because it was a dumping ground for murdered goons.

The gray light picked out the body of Vinny McGinty lying on the bank of the bayou, bloated, decaying, dead. As dead as Charles St. Claire. Charlie St. Claire had been the flamboyant, handsome son of a fine old New Orleans family—rich, dissolute, and married to the most beautiful woman in the world. Whereas Vinny had been nothing but an ugly immigrant scrub from out of the Irish Channel, who'd dreamed of glory in the ring and ended up busting kneecaps for a living instead. No two men could have been more different in life, and yet, in their final moments, in their surprise and fear and their agony, they had been the same.

Maybe Fio was right, Rourke thought, maybe he did care too much. But the murdered ones at least deserved the dignity of having the world know why they had died and who had killed them. The ones responsible ought to pay, even if only by being found out.

Fio stretched his arms up to the paling sky, popping his bones. "Man, I'm way past tired to almost dead myself. But you know soon as I roll on home, the wife is gonna jump on my case about being out all night."

"Remy Lelourie has kindly offered to give us her fingerprints," Rourke said. "She will be paying us a visit first thing this mornin'."

"Oh, joy," Fio said just as the *Smoky Mary* clattered over the rails behind them, her whistle wailing long and shrill and lonely.

The house where Daman Rourke lived on Conti Street had once belonged to his mother's lover. In the last few years he'd been able to look at it without remembering that, but not tonight—or rather, this morning.

The honey wagons were rattling over the cobblestones, carting away the refuse from those places that still had outhouses, by the time Rourke finally made it home. He let himself in through the carriageway of the beautiful old Creole cottage and into the courtyard. In the murky light of dawn, the wisteria vines and elephant ears sent blue shadows splashing across the paving stones. It smelled wet, of rain-soaked leaves and black earth.

The courtyard was an oasis of peace in a rather rough-and-tumble part of town. The Faubourg Tremé was now known for its speakeasies, jazz, and bawdy houses. A hundred years before, though, it had been the custom for white plantation owners and their sons to maintain homes for their quadroon mistresses here.

In those days the *gens de couleur libres* had also lived in the Faubourg Tremé. They had been free men of color, not slaves; although some of them owned slaves themselves. They were tailors and blacksmiths and cabinetmakers. Some became rich, and so they built houses in the Creole style, and then they filled them with mahogany furniture, hung their walls with silk, and lived within them lives that were genteel, but separate.

They spoke French and sent their sons to school in Paris. Those sons whose skin was light enough they sent north, to disappear into the white man's life. Some sent their daughters to parade in their satin gowns and bare brown shoulders across a quadroon ballroom, to attract the eye of a protector with money and property and a pale face. For when put on a scale, the word *color* outweighed the word *free*, and if one of them had dared even to raise his voice to a white man, he risked being lynched from the nearest green-iron lamppost.

That was long ago, though, in another time, and some things were different now. Now much of the neighborhood was little more than a slum, where you could buy any brand of sin you cared to name. The wrought-iron balconies on the old town houses drooped like tattered swags of lace; rats and dogs fought over the bones in the garbage-strewn courtyards. Yet somehow through it all the old houses and cobbled streets had kept their romance and charm, along with their secrets and hidden shame.

Daman Rourke, coming from the scenes of two brutal murders, stood within the smothered emptiness of the courtyard as if not quite knowing how he came to be there. For a moment he thought it was raining again, and then he realized it was only the water splashing in the iron fountain.

Light leaked out from around the shutters of the small rear *cabinet* where his mother's housekeeper slept. Augusta always got up with the dawn; she was certain the day couldn't begin without her and no one had ever been able to prove otherwise. Where he lived, in the *garçonnière* over the old kitchen, all was shadowed.

He thought of the brass bed in the old slave shack out at Sans Souci and how so like Charles St. Claire it would have been to meet his mistress there, close to hearth and home and wife. Snort a little snow, drink a little wormwood, and do a little jig on the edge of the moon.

So she walks out there, the wife, and she sees . . .

Maybe it was true love, he had said to Fio, and thought that he'd been lying. And maybe he'd only wanted it to be a lie.

If you love, desperately, passionately, and the one you love loves another, would you kill in the name of your love? Maybe. Probably.

Yes.

Seeing her again after all this time, in the same room, close enough to touch, to smell, had been like wrapping his fist around broken glass. Once, he might have killed her just to keep her his.

He made a sudden movement with his hand, as if he could fling the thought away. A flock of starlings rose off the roof in a black cloud of flapping wings. He turned to watch them fly away and saw his mother.

She sat on a bench, deep in the shadows near the fountain. He had walked right by her when he came in through the carriageway. Anyone else would have said something, but not Maeve Rourke. Some people used silence as a weapon; she used it as a shield. He had long ago given up waiting for her to explain herself to him.

In the dawn light, her face was white and ethereal as mist. She had on her wine-colored silk dressing gown, and her long dark hair was down and fell along the sides of her face like a nun's veil. He started toward her, and that was when he saw that she wasn't alone.

His daughter lay sleeping on the bench, her head in his mother's lap. She wore a nightgown of white cotton and eyelet lace, but she had a Pelicans baseball hat on her head, and she was hugging the mitt he'd given her for her sixth birthday to her chest as though it were a teddy bear.

"Hey, Mama," he said as he knelt and kissed his daughter's cheek, which was soft and sticky and smelled of watermelon. "What y'all doing out here this early in the mornin'?"

"She was walking in her sleep again last night, and then she went and had a bad dream on top of it. Woke herself up with her crying, the poor thing. I thought she'd do better if I brought her out for some air."

His mother waved a palmetto fan in a slow, drowsy motion in front of the child's face. Maeve Rourke had been born and raised in Ireland, in County Kerry, but she was southern all the way to the bone now. As if she'd absorbed her southernness from this house and the Faubourg Tremé, and from the man who had brought her here.

"She dreamt the gowman was coming to get her," his mother said, her voice soft. She laughed, then, and the sound of it too was soft in the dawn's half-light, yet it surprised him, for she so rarely laughed. "I suspect it was either the gowman, or too much watermelon on top of supper."

Ever so gently he followed with his finger the length of his daughter's fat brown braid, where it curved over her shoulder and down her back, and he relieved some of the ache in his chest with the whisper of her name.

"Katie . . ."

Something brushed his cheek, a touch so light he might only have imagined it. "You looked so sad there for a moment," Maeve said. "What's happened?"

"Nothing. Well, no more than the usual. Two murders."

"And now you've taken it all upon yourself to see the culprits are brought to justice. You shouldn't care so much, Day."

He had to smile. "What did you and Fio do—get together and write a script?"

"I'm sure I don't know what you are goin' on about." She was quiet a moment, then she breathed a soft sigh. "People will always be doing ugly things to each other, bringing each other pain."

He didn't say it, although he could have: that she had been the first to teach him about ugly doings and pain, and she had taught him young. They had their own family secrets, he and Maeve Rourke. Their own buried sins.

His mother waved the fan between them, while the sky lightened from cinder gray to ash. He thought he should tell her about Charles St. Claire's bad death and that Remy Lelourie had probably killed him.

"Give her over to me," he said instead. "I'll put her back to bed."

His daughter felt heavy in his arms as he lifted her. A solid and yet giving warmth, wondrously alive. At the door, he looked back to where his mother still sat on the bench. He knew it was only the way the vines were casting their shadows across her face, but in that moment she appeared strangely stricken and sad.

Chapter Four

The first time Maeve Rourke looked into the eyes of the man who would become her lover, it was over the prostrate body of the Virgin Mary.

Later, she would decide that the moment must have seduced her with its whimsy. For until then she had always arranged her life as it ought to be: laying it out for herself on a road, straight and well marked by signposts, so easy to follow. So true. She was nineteen that day her own heart played a trick on her, teaching her that it had a free will and a sense of direction all its own.

She had been six when she decided that she had better plan her life very carefully, otherwise it was likely to go seriously awry. She'd lived in Ireland then, and though she had grown to womanhood holding little of that time in her heart, she could always remember every warp and weave of one particular morning.

In her memories, turf smoke from the fire fills the tiny *shibeen*, with its solid mud walls and thatched roof. She sits on a stool with a bowl of potato gruel in her lap, gruel so thin she can see through it easier than she can see through the water that collected in the rain barrel in the yard. Her da lies sprawled on his tailbone before the hearth, his mouth pulling on a jar of *poitín*, and in her memories the harsh, peaty smell of it bites at her nose.

And always, in her memories, her mem shuffles across the

43

beaten dirt floor in her bare feet and opens the door, so that sunlight spills inside the windowless hut, warm and white. Chasing out the darkness and the smoke, and the other, brutal memories of the night before.

Her mother lived her life in the dark. It weighed on her soul like a pile of heavy stones put there one by one. Even at six, Maeve could mark the way the stones had mounted. One for every day black crepe hung over the door for another babe born and buried. One for every day her mother dug for potatoes in a stubble field, heavy-bellied with another child that would die. One for every winter night when no turf burned on the fire, and the wind blew cold across the bleak bogs and the black hills. Stone by stone for those other nights when Da, lying on the pile of straw in the corner, rutted and grunted over her mother's body, and her mother wept.

Stone by stone, one at a time, and so her mother was always seeking the sunlight, even on the coldest of days.

But that morning Da had wanted none of the sun. He stared at the wash of light that poured through the door, his mouth hanging slack, his red eyes blinking.

"Shut the bloody door," her da had said, only that, but her mem obeyed with shoulders bowed and her mouth pulled in tight. In the instant before the *shibeen* was plunged once more into smoky murkiness, Maeve had been looking at her father's big hand where it was wrapped around his jar of *poitín*. At the way the wiry red hair curled over his thick knuckles and the dark freckles on his skin might have been splashes of her mother's blood.

And she thought, I will never marry a redheaded, freckled-face man with hands as big and heavy and thick as peat bricks that are always ready and willing to be made into fists.

No, she hadn't really thought such a thing, not in concrete words like that—she had been too young. Yet, still, the promise had been made to herself that morning, arriving full-blown in her heart. Even then she had known the strength of her will, and the shape of it.

She was never going to live her mother's life.

On the day Maeve Rourke first looked into the eyes of the man who would become her lover, she had come into the St. Louis

Cathedral to get out of the bruising summer sun. Four years already gone from Ireland, four summers lived in New Orleans, and she still hadn't become used to the terrible heat.

She sat down on a pew near the altar of the Most Blessed Virgin of the Rosary not to pray, but because her feet were hurting like the very devil. She did say a couple of Hail Marys, though, as penance for what she was about to do. No sooner was the last amen past her lips than she was unhooking her stiff new high-button shoes and wrenching them off, along with her black lisle stockings.

She wriggled her bare toes as she leaned over to rub the ache out of her blisters, and saw a pair of plaster feet hanging off the end of the pew in front of hers.

She half stood up and peered over the pew's high round wooden back. The Most Blessed Virgin of the Rosary lay stretched out the length of the seat, as if she had just climbed down off her marble-slabbed altar to take a little nap.

A heel scraped on stone, and Maeve looked up. A man stood in the aisle and he, too, was staring at the statue lying on the pew. He raised his head, and their eyes met, and they shared a slow smile.

Maeve's gaze fell back down to the prostrate virgin. Her white plaster hands were folded in prayer on her plaster chest, her plaster blue eyes stared up at the vaulted ceiling. She had, Maeve noticed now that she was getting such a good up-close look at her, a rather pink and prissy plaster mouth, but then she had probably never suffered from blisters.

The thought nearly startled a laugh out of Maeve. She bit her lip and swallowed hard. She pressed her hands together as if in prayer and covered her face.

The man in the aisle did laugh, trying at the last moment to turn the noise into a cough. Maeve snorted.

She snatched up her shoes and stockings and her shopping basket, and she ran, banging her hip on the pew arm so hard she would find a bruise a couple of days later and wonder how it had come to be there. She was laughing so by the time she burst back out into the sun-drenched square that she couldn't stand up

45

anymore, and she had to sit down on a wrought-iron bench and grab at the stitch in her side.

He followed her out; well, she had known he would. His face was flushed and slightly damp. His eyes, looking down at her where she sat, gasping, on the bench, were bright with his own laugh tears. It hadn't been that funny, surely, the sight of the Virgin Mary taking a nap on one of the pews. Maeve couldn't imagine why they both had carried on laughing so, two strangers together.

He was still smiling as he waved a hand back at the cathedral. "How do you suppose she . . . ?"

Maeve shook her head and pressed her lips together to keep from smiling back at him. "Oh, the saints do preserve us. It must've been the sight of my bare feet what did her in."

He laughed and that set her off again too, and their laughter mixed with the jingle of streetcar bells, the ring of mule hooves on cobblestones, and the echoing booms of ships unloading bananas at the wharf.

When their laughter died, it seemed all the world hushed as well. The quiet that followed held a weight to it that came from the intimacy the shared moment had stirred.

She slanted a look up at him. He was jauntily dressed in a tight-buttoned linen jacket with a high collar. He had the look of the Creole about him, in his dark hair and eyes, and in the way he held himself—old blood, old money, old name.

She had chosen a bench next to a blooming magnolia tree, and the air around them was cloyingly sweet. Beneath her bare feet, the stones of the square burned hot from the sun. She liked the feel of it, soothing and exciting both at once. "You wouldn't happen to be having a button hook along with you?" she said.

He actually patted down his pockets as if there was a chance he might find one, then he shook his head, smiling.

She smiled back at him this time, and longer than she should have. "Never you mind. I've blisters on me blisters, as 'tis."

She stood up, smoothing down the crisp white apron she'd put on that morning for going to the French Market. In just that instant her smile had gone. She felt a scratchiness in her throat now, and her nose had grown pinched. She was ridiculously close to tears for no reason she could name, and he was looking at her as if he knew what she was thinking, which was so unfair since her thoughts were a mystery to herself.

"I've my shopping still to do," she said.

He tipped his straw hat at her, but instead of turning away he stepped closer. So close his shoulder nearly brushed hers, and she could see the smile creases at the corners of his mouth and a little mole the size of a cinder above the flush of color along his cheekbone.

"May I come along?" he said. "I can carry your shoes for you."

He held out his hand. It was a beautiful hand, slender and long-fingered, and he wore a wedding ring. But then her finger sported a ring as well, and he could see it plain since she'd had to take off her gloves to unbutton her shoes. She thought she would tell him no thank you and send him on his way.

She put her shoes into his hand.

The sky above them was hard and bled nearly white by the relentless summer sun. They walked together through the market, beneath the shade of the scrolled colonnades, past crates of cantaloupes and strawberries and plump Creole tomatoes. Past shallots hung in bouquets and big silver bells of garlic. Past bins of shrimps on ice and pyramids of oysters and latanier baskets of blue-clawed crabs. She carried her own little shopping basket over her arm, but he walked beside her, and so she was too flustered to buy anything.

His presence beside her disturbed her, and not because of the wrongness of the moment—her, a married woman, walking barefoot through the market with a strange man. He disturbed her because he made her want something from him, although what that something was she couldn't even formulate into a thought, let alone put into words.

He didn't cast quick looks at her, the way she was doing with him; he studied her openly. She knew what he was, and she knew what he wanted.

They came to the end of the colonnade, where a Negro woman sat on the sidewalk balancing a big basket of rice fritters on her head. "*Bels calas*," she cried with the voice of an opera singer. "*Bels calas, tout chauds*."

He bought them all a fritter to eat, even the cala woman herself. Maeve thanked him and smiled, and then as if he'd only just thought of it, as if it hadn't mattered before this, he asked her what her name was. She stumbled over the giving of it as if wasn't really hers, or shouldn't have been.

"Maeve," he repeated after her, rolling her name around on his tongue as if tasting it. "How lovely."

She felt another strange smile come over her face at the compliment.

Out on the river a tugboat tooted its horn, and a great flock of seagulls rose up from the market's tiled roof. Together they tilted back their heads and watched the birds fly off between the spires of the cathedral. She thought she should tell him that she had to go back home now, that she was late as it was.

"Some days, after I've done with my shopping," she said, "I go for a walk along the levee."

The levee had always fascinated her, from the first moment she'd set foot in New Orleans. From the road you could look up at the tall grass bank and see masts and smokestacks floating disembodied across the sky, as if the sky itself were a river.

They walked along the spine of the levee for a while and then sat beneath the lime green shade of some willow trees, among a splattering of buttercups. He had taken off his fancy jacket for her to sit on, so then he rolled up his shirtsleeves and rested his forearms on his bent knees. He had taken off his hat, too, and it dangled from his long fingers.

The sheen of his hair was like the purple and black colors of a crow's wing. His mouth looked soft, and full enough to belong to a woman.

She looked away from him, at the gray mud banks of the river. The *batture* was covered with hundreds of little mud chimneys, which were built by mud-divers—those ugly, crusty bugs that turned into locusts and made so much noise she couldn't sleep at night. Some people had fashioned houses out of driftwood among the cane brakes and the mud-divers' chimneys. It seemed a whimsical way to live, in those driftwood houses. She would never have chosen such a way for herself.

His voice broke into her thoughts, asking her what she saw when she looked at the river.

And she said, without thinking, "It's a mud-diver's heaven that I see."

He threw back his head and laughed. She stared at his throat, at the way the strong muscles moved and the sweat glistened on his skin. His skin wasn't olive like so many Creoles; it was deeply golden, the color of apple cider in the sun.

She liked it that she had made him laugh, and when he was done laughing he told her what he saw when he looked at the river. His words sounded like poetry; she didn't try to make any sense of them.

When he asked about her husband and children, she told him about her Mike and their two boys as if she felt no shame. She knew what he was, all right, and what he wanted from her, and still she was letting him steal her innocence and her honor, though he had yet to touch her.

He said, "My wife and I are about to have our first. I hope for a son, of course." He smiled, and his teeth were white and even in the dark gold of his face. "But I will settle for what she gives me."

Maeve wrapped her skirt tighter around her bent legs. She thought she ought to get up and wish him a good day and walk away. She thought that, but she never did it.

By the time she got home, she was so late for her baby's feeding that her breasts ached and were leaking milk. Still she lingered on the stoop a moment. The sky had darkened with rain clouds, but the house glowed golden as if it had saved up the morning's sunshine just for her. The red bougainvillea that clung to the trellis over her front door trembled in the wind.

Her Mike made a good living as a city policeman and he was proud of how he had provided for her. He had provided her with a home, one-half of a shotgun double. He had provided her with shoes so new they gave her blisters, and a colored girl named Tulie to come help with the cooking and the cleaning and to watch her babes for her while she went walking the levee with another man.

In her hand she carried a key, and it pressed into her flesh like a brand. A key to a house on Conti Street. She thought she ought to have thrown it in his face. She thought she ought to go around back now and throw it into the cistern, where it would be lost forever.

She slid the key deep into her pocket.

She walked through the house and back into the kitchen. Her firstborn son, Paulie, had gotten into the dish cupboard and was banging pot lids together. Somehow Tulie's new baby was managing to sleep through the racket in a basket, which had been set on top of the icebox. A pot of red beans bubbled on the stove.

Tulie sat at the pine table with its blue-checked oilcloth and the yellow crock of lard and the shaker of Morton salt that always sat in the center of it. The girl was nursing Daman for her, and her baby son's pink lips were pulling on the girl's nipple. His tiny hand grabbed at her breast, which was round and brown and soft, like a baked apple.

"I'm that sorry I'm late," Maeve said. "I hope he wasn't fussing too badly."

Tulie smiled. She had a big gap between her front teeth, and one day she had shown Maeve how she could whistle through the hole like a boy. And she had beautiful dark eyes, like wells, that always seemed to have been carefully emptied before she raised her thick-fringed lashes to let you look into them. Maeve thought the slaves had probably met their masters' stares with such an emptiness in their eyes.

"Now, never you mind takin' your time, Miss Maeve," Tulie was saying. "I's milk enough for both our boys."

"I went to the cathedral," Maeve said. "And then I went for a walk on the levee. In my bare feet." She held up her shoes so that Tulie could see. She had almost forgotten them, almost left them lying there on the levee. He had run back to the willows for her, to get them.

Tulie smiled to see the shoes, but whatever she thought of them, she kept it to herself.

Maeve's breasts were aching something fierce now and leaking milk. She wanted to take her son back from Tulie, to hold his weight heavy in her arms and feel his suckling, to breathe in his baby smell of milk and talcum and soft, moist flesh. Yet she stood there, saying nothing, watching the way his lips moved in and out as he nursed at Tulie's breast, how his little fist clenched and unclenched. Paulie took after her, but Day was all his father's son: fair, with that ready, dimpled smile. His eyes, too, came from his father. Midnight blue, people said they were, though she'd never understood the expression, since every midnight sky she'd ever seen had been black as pitch.

Later that evening, when her Mike came home for supper, she saw how his eyes were very nearly the same color as his policeman's uniform, and she wondered why she hadn't noticed such a thing before.

As she set the plate of red beans and rice and fried *sac-à-lait* down in front of him, she told him she had gone for a walk on the levee. She asked him what he saw when he looked at the river.

Mike Rourke shook his head at her. "What kind of a question is that?" he said around a mouthful of beans. "I see water. Muddy water."

She stared back at him and she hated herself for what she was thinking, what she was feeling. He was a good provider and a good man, kind to her most of the time and affectionate with his sons. He was always touching the boys, cuddling up to them.

She turned away from him without another word and went into the bedroom. She lay down on the bed but got right back up again. She went into the bathroom, ran cold water in the sink, and splashed it on her face.

Mike's shaving things were laid out neatly on the shelf above the sink: the porcelain mug, the badger-hair lather brush, his warranted Perfection razor.

She stared at her husband's razor and thought of how she would come awake sometimes at night with her husband sleeping heavy beside her, and she would feel such an aching, echoing emptiness inside. Hot tears would overflow her eyes and roll down the sides of her face, into her ears, and she would wonder when Mike Rourke had become, with no warning and with no reason, this thing to run away from, like her da.

She picked up her husband's razor, hefting it in her hand as if to feel its weight. Her mother had killed herself with Da's razor. Mike had told her once that most people didn't do it right—they cut across instead of up. But her mem had known how to do it.

Maeve pulled open the razor and ran her finger along the blade. Her skin split open, and the pain shocked her, and the way the blood welled up so fast and dark. The razor slipped from her hand, clattering on the tile floor.

She looked into the mirror above the sink and saw a strange woman with dark hair and dark eyes and a white face. She said the strange woman's name the way he had said it at the market that morning, rolling it around on her tongue.

"Maeve . . . Maeve . . . Maeve . . ."

She walked into the kitchen with blood dripping from the end of her finger.

"Sweet Jesus!" Mike shouted when he saw her, jumping up from the table, snatching his napkin off his neck, wrapping it around the small, bleeding cut. "What have you done?"

"I wanted to see what it would feel like," she said, but that wasn't exactly true. She had wanted to see if she could feel it at all.

He stared at her. He looked frightened.

"It hurts," she said.

"Aw, darlin'." He tried to kiss her, but she jerked away from him. For a moment she thought she might retch. "I want to be alone," she said.

She went back into the bedroom and lay down on their bed. She brought her knees up to her chest. She took the key out of her pocket and pressed it between her palms, and then she pressed her clasped hands between her bent knees. She thought she would get up later and go out into the yard and throw the key into the cistern, where it would be lost forever.

Chapter Five

From the New Orleans *Times-Picayune*, extra edition, Wednesday, July 13, 1927:

PROMINENT NEW ORLEANS LAWYER MURDERED
Wife Discovers Body
In Pool of Blood

Mr. Charles St. Claire, Esq., a criminal defense attorney known for mounting zealous, if unorthodox, cases on behalf of his clients, was found brutally slain last night in an outbuilding of his plantation house, Sans Souci, in the Faubourg Bayou St. John.

Mr. St. Claire, 30 years old, was married to a famous star of the silver screen, Remy Lelourie St. Claire. It was Mrs. St. Claire who first heard screaming coming from the old slave shack at the rear of the property and went to investigate. There she found Mr. St. Claire lying in a pool of blood, expiring from a cut in his throat. The police recovered the murder weapon, which is said to be a common cane knife, at the scene. No motive has yet been ascribed to the crime, and no arrests have been made.

Grieving Widow

Mrs. St. Claire, who emerged briefly from seclusion early this morning, spoke to reporters with her eyes full of tears bravely held back. "I, this city, and the world have lost a great man in Charles St. Claire," she said. "I loved him with all my heart and I can't believe he's gone."

Mrs. St. Claire, the 29-year-old daughter of Mrs. Heloise Lelourie and the late Mr. Reynard Lelourie, is a native New Orleanian who has enjoyed considerable success of late as a motion picture actress. In February of this year, Mrs. St. Claire returned to New Orleans from her home in Hollywood, California, for the premiere of her latest endeavor, *Jazz Babies*, whereupon she became reacquainted with Mr. St. Claire, a third cousin once removed and a childhood friend. After a whirlwind courtship, they married in a small, quiet ceremony at the Old Church of the Immaculate Conception. They were residing together at Sans Souci at the time of Mr. St. Claire's death.

"They were such a happy couple," said Mrs. St. Claire's sister, Miss Belle Lelourie. "And now this horrible thing has happened."

No Stone Unturned

Mayor Arthur J. O'Keefe, Sr., and Superintendent of Police, Mr. Weldon Carrigan, have jointly called for a vigorous investigation into Mr. St. Claire's suspicious death.

"We will leave no stone unturned," vowed Superintendent Carrigan. "I want to assure the good people of New Orleans that the perpetrator of this foul deed will be brought to justice with the greatest possible dispatch."

The murder victim, Mr. Charles St. Claire, was a member of one of New Orleans' oldest and most distinguished Creole families, but the St. Claires have been haunted by tragedy in recent years. Mr. Charles St. Claire's parents, Jacques St. Claire and Annabel Devereaux St. Claire, were both killed suddenly seven years ago in a train accident outside of Paris, France. Mr. Charles St. Claire's elder brother, Mr. Julius St. Claire, committed suicide eleven years ago at the age of 22, and an only sister, Marie, died of influenza during the epidemic of 1918.

Outside of his wife and her branch of the family, Mr. Charles St. Claire has no surviving relatives, except for distant cousins residing in Mobile.

"One might almost believe in voodoo curses," said a family friend, "the way tragedy and violent death have stalked the St. Claires."

Daman Rourke tossed the *Times-Picayune* onto his desk and went to stand close to the barred and dust-encrusted window so that he could look down on the noisy, crowded street three stories below.

The sun had come up red and hot that morning, baking the streets and sidewalks with such ferocity that you expected at any minute the pavement would start splitting and cracking like dried river mud. Charles St. Claire's mutilated corpse had turned up only a few hours ago, yet already it seemed that every reporter in the state had congregated before the Criminal Courts Building, which housed police headquarters and the detectives squad. The mammoth rusty brick and sandstone edifice looked like a medieval castle with its turrets and clock tower, and the press had put it under siege. The surest circulation booster, next to a gory murder, was a juicy scandal involving a beautiful Hollywood starlet, so this one had it all.

Inside, the squad room was hot and crowded as well. Most of the detectives, even those whose shifts were over, were hanging around and hoping for a personal introduction to the Cinderella Girl. She was supposed to be coming in voluntarily to have her fingerprints taken and to make an official statement as to her whereabouts and actions last night while her husband had been getting himself murdered. Fiorello Prankowski had taken it upon himself to entertain his fellow cops while they waited.

"So I got dead bodies coming out my ears all night," he was saying, "then I drag my aching ass on home at four o'fucking-clock this morning, and that's when the wife hits me with it. She went out and bought a Kimball parlor organ. Now, I'm asking myself—what the hell's a parlor organ and what does she want with one? She can't hum a tune without sounding like a cat with its tail caught in the screen door, and yet she's telling me there's a parlor organ sitting in the parlor and it's all ours for only forty easy little payments. Hell, I'm already making easy little payments on everything in the house—the refrigerator, the washing machine, the bedroom suite." He drawled out the word, saying sooo-eet. "Even the frigging vacuum cleaner's got an easy little payment."

"I was just reading an article about that," said Nate Carroll. He was the youngest detective on the force and he looked like a Raggedy Andy doll. He had orange curly hair and a round, soft face with two blue buttons for eyes and two pink buttons for a nose and a mouth. All morning he'd been drooling over a slick magazine that had still shots of Remy Lelourie's hottest love scenes. One showed her languishing in a sheik's tent wearing nothing but veils, but Nate had so far been the only one to see it. The other detectives were riled at him because he wasn't sharing.

"What it is," Nate was saying, "is one of them new theories has to do with—what's that guy? You know, Freud? When women do that—when they go out and buy stuff they don't need—it means they got these sexual urges that aren't otherwise being satisfied. . . ."

His words trailed off, and the squad room fell into an awed silence as they all contemplated the fact that Fiorello Prankowski, who was an unpredictable Yankee with biceps the size of hams and fists like ball-peen hammers, had just had his manhood insulted.

Fio had been leaning lazily back on the hind legs of his chair, but now he let it fall forward and lumbered slowly to his feet. He ambled over to Nate Carroll's desk. "You saying my wife's new parlor organ reminds her of my organ?"

Somebody snorted and then went instantly quiet. Nate swallowed so hard his throat clicked. He stared down at the magazine in his lap as if it held a blueprint for his salvation. "I was just, you know . . . talking."

" 'Cause you'd be right," Fio said. "Both make them long, deep notes. Do all that throbbing. Vibrating." He whistled softly and plucked the magazine out of Nate's grasp. "Man, is her hand holding what I think it's holding?"

At his vigil by the window, Rourke was now smiling. A sugar wasp had found its way there as well and was bouncing against the glass. A taxicab was pulling up to the curb below, and the reporters were now all running toward it.

So she has come, he thought. He saw her legs first as they came out of the cab. Long and slender and pale. Next came the crown of a black straw hat. The hat had a flared brim and a long pheasant feather that curled down over her shoulder.

She looked up, as if she knew he watched her.

The reporters and the curious had checked for just a moment at their first sight of her, but now they surged around her. They shouted questions and snapped cameras in her face, but no one actually touched her. She moved through them gently, like a minnow swimming upstream, creating little eddies in her wake. They treated her, Rourke thought, as if she were touched by magic. But if she went down, they would tear her to pieces.

They were all waiting for her in the squad room—even Captain Malone had emerged from his office—and the expectancy was like a hum in the hot, heavy air. Rourke turned away from the window and leaned against the wall with his hands in his pockets, his eyes on the door.

The desk sergeant brought her in. She wore a simple black sheath dress that gave her a tragic air. The brim of her hat, with its curling pheasant feather, covered one eye. She looked right at Rourke and her face went even paler, and she looked away just as Captain Malone came up to her.

She gave the senior detective a shy, tentative smile, her white teeth catching on her lower lip for just an instant. The hand she held out to him looked impossibly fragile, and had red-lacquered nails.

For a moment Rourke wondered if she'd miscalculated. No lady in New Orleans would paint her fingernails, let alone do them up a bloodred when she was supposed to be a grieving widow. Remy, though, had always thrived on flirting with disaster. She would want every man in the world believing in her innocence, but only if it cost them a sliver of their souls.

Her gaze went now to every man in the room but him, and Rourke watched her pull them in one by one. She seemed to be searching inside their skins for something she wanted, coveted, craved.

His captain, looking a little stunned, was still holding her hand, as if unsure whether he was supposed to shake it or bring it up to his lips and kiss it. Captain Daniel Malone had careless southern-gentleman good looks to go with his careless southern-gentleman good manners: rumpled sandy-blond hair, dimpled chin, and sleepy brown eyes that always managed to look sad even when he smiled. His wife was the mayor's cousin and that had got him his rank, but such was New Orleans. He was a good cop, and the detective squad liked him.

He mumbled something now about taking care of a few formalities and led Remy Lelourie over to a plain ladder-back chair.

She lowered herself gracefully onto the seat, folded her hands with those red-lacquered nails on her lap, and tucked her feet beneath her. Her shoes, Rourke saw, had little black bows at the ankles.

The captain took a seat beside her. "Miss Lelourie—that is, Mrs. St. Claire . . . may we get you something? Coffee? A glass of water?"

"You are too kind," she said, so softly they all had to strain to hear. "But I'm fine, truly I am."

Captain Malone's hand came up to hover over her shoulder for a moment, as if he would pat it if only he dared. If she wasn't the most beautiful woman in the world, Rourke thought, she was certainly the most photographed. They had lived with her image for years, these cops, been surrounded by it everywhere, and so they had thought they knew her, maybe even thought they owned a little piece of her. Now they were seeing how wrong they had been.

"Mrs. St. Claire, I know this is difficult," Malone said, and his words so intruded on the moment that they seemed cruel, obscene. "But if you could go over one more time what happened last night when you found your husband's . . . when you found him. Please think it over and leave nothing out, no matter how insignificant it might seem. The smallest detail may turn out to be the clue that will break the case."

She nodded, slowly, and then her shoulders straightened bravely, but she kept her eyes demurely lowered on the hands in her lap. "I had gone to bed and just drifted off when I was awakened by screaming coming from that old slave shack in back of the house. Since Charles often spent time there when he wanted to be alone, to think and to read, I immediately became afraid for him. But I sleep in the nude, you see, so I had to stop and throw my dress back on before I could go out there."

"Did you—" The captain's voice broke roughly while each man in the room was still rocking beneath his own image of a naked Remy Lelourie lying sprawled on silken sheets. "Did you see anyone? Anyone leaving the shack?"

"No, I saw no one . . . except for Charles. He was lying on the floor and blood was everywhere, and a knife was stuck in his chest. I think I might have pulled it out—the knife. Charles was still breathing, you see. He had a horrible cut in his throat, but he was still breathing, and the cut in his throat was making this awful gurgling noise and spewing blood. He was struggling to say something. . . . I think it was my name. He was trying to beg me to help him, only I couldn't, I couldn't . . ." She shut her eyes, but a single tear escaped to roll slowly down one flawless cheek.

Somebody breathed loudly; another man sighed. She was playing them like Satchmo played his coronet, Rourke thought, crying up that last sad note until it cut to the bone.

"He died . . . my Charlie died in my arms," she said, her voice bleeding like Charles St. Claire had bled. Somebody, Rourke thought, ought to be applauding. Then, slowly, the brim of her hat lifted as her head came up, and she looked right at him, and he almost fell into her eyes.

The desk sergeant saved him by coming up to stand in front of him, blocking his view of her. "The super just rang up," the sergeant said. "He wants to see you, pronto. He said to tell you he's taking breakfast at the Boston Club this mornin'."

Rourke pushed himself off the wall. "When Mrs. St. Claire is done here, don't let her go out through that mob out front. Take her down to the basement and show her the way up to the alley 'round back."

"Sure, Loot," the desk sergeant said with a winking grin as Rourke brushed past him, heading for the door.

Her voice—soft, sad, sweet—followed after him. "I guess I must have gone into shock then, because the next thing I remember is hearing Beulah scream. And the feel of Charles's body, cold and heavy in my arms."

He was halfway to the stairwell at the end of the hall when he met Roibin Doherty coming out of the toilet, buttoning up his fly. Rourke started to go around him, but Doherty planted himself in the way, and when Rourke made to go around him a second time, he shifted, putting himself in the way again. The man's red-veined cheeks bulged with a drooling chaw, whiskey fumes floated off him like hot off a tar road, and hate burned in his swollen, watery eyes. Hate that had long been festering.

"Pardon me," Rourke said, making an effort to keep his own face flat and empty.

Doherty swayed into him, breathing a reeking laugh, and Rourke almost gagged on a reflex of revulsion and an old, remembered fear.

"Won't be gettin' no pardon from me, boy," Doherty said in a voice as rough as a furnace shaker. "Won't be gettin' no pardon from the gov'ner neither on the day they fry your ass up in Angola."

Doherty's rank was detective sergeant, but he didn't do much detecting anymore. He was supposed to be looking after the property and evidence room, maintaining the archival files, and only occasionally covering a case on the street when the workload was heavy. What he mostly did was drink away the hours, waiting for the day when his pension would kick in and brooding over his conviction that Daman Rourke ought to be picking cotton on a prison chain gang instead of carrying a detective's badge. Usually, though, Rourke could find a way to avoid him, or Doherty's own sense of survival led him into keeping his malice to himself.

Rourke took a step back now and gave the older man a slow once-over, as if cataloging the cotton suit coat, rumpled and stained with sweat and tobacco juice; the wet spot on the front of his trousers; the grimy, thinning, tangled gray hair.

Rourke smiled, showing his eyeeteeth. "Jesus, Sarge. You are like a walking spittoon."

Doherty swiped at the sweat that dripped off the end of his nose and smirked. "You're scared, ain't you, boy? Plumb scared shitless, because it won't be so easy for y'all to get away with it this time, you an' her. Not gonna be no suicide verdict for poor ol' Charlie St. Claire, no sirree bob. Kinda hard to make it look like the man slashed his own throat with a cane knife."

Rourke smiled again, and he was still smiling when he planted his fist deep in Doherty's drinker's belly. It was, he thought, like punching a pillow.

The man doubled over, gasping and wheezing, and Rourke walked around him. He was almost to the head of the stairs when Doherty called out, "Hey, what's the dirty little secret, boy?" and Rourke made the mistake of turning back around.

Doherty stood swaying in the middle of the hall, a pinched, malevolent light burning in his eyes. Behind him, lounging in the open door to the squad room, was Fiorello Prankowski.

"What's the secret, huh?" Doherty said again. He wiped the tobacco juice off his mouth with a fat thumb and grinned. "Jus' what did them poor St. Claire boys have on that lil' witch of a gal of yours, that Remy Lelourie?"

Rourke said nothing. Doherty's smile widened, showing off a mouthful of brown teeth and gray gums. He shot a stream of tobacco juice onto the brown linoleum floor and then tottered off down the hall toward the property room.

"Bastard's been on the sauce so long his brains have turned to boiled grits," Fio said, but Rourke had seen the sharp calculation come into his partner's eyes before he'd covered it with a smile and a shake of his head. "Maybe you shouldn't take it so personal."

Rourke shrugged. It was probably a hundred degrees in that hallway, the air so wet you could wring it out and get bathwater, and yet he felt cold inside. "I gotta go see the super," he said. "I'll catch you later."

Fio touched his forehead in a mock salute. "Yeah, sure. You do that, partner. You catch me later."

Outside, a brassy sun smote the sidewalk like a hammer. City smells—of gasoline and garbage and dust—floated on the thick, motionless air like algae on swamp water.

Rourke walked over to Canal Street, where the Boston Club imposed its presence upon the South with classic white elegance. In a city where two or more folk gathering on a street corner were apt to form a club, this was still the oldest and proudest men's gathering place. If you wanted an invitation to pass through its plain but hallowed front door, it helped if your daddy was a member, and his daddy before him, and yet there were always ways to get around not being born to the proper family. Ways like money and juice.

This morning, a green Pierce-Arrow touring car, all gleaming brass and wood and leather and chrome, was parked alongside the club's front curb. Underneath the shade of the club's upper gallery, the city's official bootlegger stood shooting the breeze with two city-council members and a state legislator. Money and juice. Casey Maguire might have been born poor and Irish, but he'd always possessed a sure knowledge about the privileged and powerful that they barely realized about themselves: He knew all the ways they were for sale.

Rourke waited for the conversation to end, and for the bootlegger to cross the sidewalk toward his car, and then he did what that old drunken sergeant had done with him a moment ago—he planted himself in the way.

Only this time the contest was more even. Casey Maguire boxed daily at the New Orleans Athletic Club; his body was quick and lean and braided with muscle. He wasn't nearly as tall as Rourke, though, and he had to tilt back on his heels and lift his head to meet Rourke's eyes.

"Good mornin', Day," he said. A small smile played around his wide mouth, as if he knew where this was going and was merely amused by it. "It's been a while since we've spoken. I hope I'm finding you well."

Casey Maguire had worked most of the Irish Channel out of his accent, he'd put polish on his manners and sophistication into his dress, but he hadn't been able to do anything about his eyes, which were so pale they were nearly colorless, like spit. When you come from a place where you learn early to do mean unto others before they can do it unto you, it shows in your eyes. Maguire could be frightening, even to those who had come from the same place.

When Rourke didn't say anything, Maguire moved to go around him. Rourke shifted his weight, putting himself in the way again.

Maguire blew a soft sigh out of pursed lips, as if he were mildly exasperated. "If we're going to dance, Detective, maybe we should be doing it to music."

Rourke smiled, and his smile, he knew, could be as frightening as Casey Maguire's eyes, even to those who came from the same place. "Seen Vinny McGinty lately?" he said.

A sadness settled over Maguire's face. His was a strangely austere face, like the martyrs in the missals they'd carried to church with them as boys—handsome in a severe way, fine-boned, drawn. The face of a man who could weep as he killed, and so the sadness, Rourke thought, might even have been real.

"Poor Vinny," Maguire was saying. "He was always talking about taking off north to Chicago, to see if he could make it in the prize rings up there. When he disappeared a couple of weeks ago, I assumed that's where he'd gone. Now I hear he's turned up dead in the swamp. What happened? Did he drown?"

"He was garroted with piano wire."

Maguire's face was full of beautiful surprise. "Oh, really?"

"Yes, really."

Maguire sighed again. "I didn't have him killed, Day, although I know I've little chance of convincing you of that. Lately I seem to have turned into the Devil incarnate in your mind." Now the smile came back, a self-mocking one that invited Rourke to share in the joke. "I'll have to see Vinny gets the best send-off money can buy. After all, he was practically family."

It had become a mobster tradition lately, treating fellow gang members to funerals that set records of extravagance with flowers and ornate coffins. The Italians had started it, but now everybody was doing it.

"I'm sure it'll be one fine funeral," Rourke said. "And I guess we've been to a few of them, you and I. I've been thinking a lot about the old days, remembering things."

What he remembered, suddenly, was one summer's night, he and Case kneeling across from each other over the body of Rourke's old man, who was sleeping off a drunk in the gutter, with the rain pouring down on them all, running into their eyes and mouths, turning the street into a river, and Case yelling at him to turn his father over onto his back so that he wouldn't drown, and Rourke for just that moment not wanting to do it, thinking for just that moment, Drown, you son-of-a-bitch, drown, so that Case had done it instead, and Rourke had just sat there and watched him. Knelt there in the street with rain pouring down and his hands hanging empty and heavy at his sides.

What Rourke said was, "I was remembering how we used to walk through the Swamp on a Saturday night, and you would filch the pennies out of the pockets of all the old bums and winos, even when you weren't hungry. Even when you were flush. You'd do it just to get in the practice."

Maguire let several seconds pass between them in silence, and then he said, "I'm telling you I had no reason to kill the guy, Day."

"But you did it anyway. You'd do it just to get in the practice."

Maguire's gaze shifted to the traffic in the street. A coal wagon and an ancient brougham had locked wheels in the intersection, and a Model T was trying to jostle around them, its horn blaring. A streetcar clattered by in the neutral zone, adding to the din.

"If you want to know who killed Vinny," he said, "why don't you talk to that nigger cock-queen who was selling him the flake he'd been putting up his nose these last couple of months. That boy had gotten to where he would've traded his soul for dope." His gaze came back to Rourke, and the burn in his eyes was like a match flame against the skin. "But then you'd know all about that place, wouldn't you, Day?"

Rourke knew. Cocaine, and the need it bred in you, could be like a heavy, dark cloud you dragged along with you everywhere you went. It rained on you every day, but you just couldn't seem to shake it.

Maguire brushed past him, and this time Rourke let him go. He watched the bootlegger, who had once been his friend, get in the beautiful and expensive green Pierce-Arrow and drive off, and the taste in Rourke's throat was raw and bitter.

Money and juice. The Boston Club's library fairly reeked of both. Roman busts rested in marble niches, between glass-fronted cases filled with books bound in green and gold-blocked calf. Turkey rugs of muted colors covered the parquet floor, and green velvet drapes framed the French doors that looked out onto the gallery, where a lone man stood like a general facing a battleground. Hands laced behind his straight back, graying leonine head up, eyes hard with resolve.

Weldon Carrigan, superintendent of the New Orleans Police Department, had plenty of both money and juice, but it hadn't always been that way. The tenth son of a traveling shoe salesman, he had been born with two talents and a single ambition. His talents were subtle and yet deceptively simple. He had a deep understanding of how leverage could be applied to human nature, and he could make you like him. He could make you like him even when you knew that his single ambition was power, and that he wanted as much of it as he could get, spare no expense, even yours.

But in New Orleans power came from only two frequently overlapping sources: family and politics. So Weldon Carrigan, the son of a nobody, began his career by making the Democratic Party machine his family, and they'd served each other well. Even politics, though, had not been able to do as much for him as had his marriage to Rose Marie Wilmington, heiress to one of the city's oldest and proudest American names. With her had come fourteen-karat respectability, a mansion in the Garden District, and three million dollars.

He had never acknowledged the irony when, twenty years later, he had offered Daman Rourke fifty thousand of his wife's dollars not to marry their daughter.

Yet in spite of that rocky beginning, Rourke and his father-in-law had over the years formed a grudging toleration for one another that occasionally crossed over into a wary respect. They both knew that, as superintendent, Weldon Carrigan had the power to make or destroy his son-in-law's career. That was his leverage. Rourke's leverage was Katie, which was all the Carrigans had left of their beloved and only daughter, Jo.

Now, though, Weldon Carrigan's chiseled face was as stony as one of the Roman busts as he watched his son-in-law enter the room. "I saw you having a heated word with Casey Maguire," he said immediately, before Rourke even had time to say good morning. "If it's not moving, Day, don't poke at it."

Rourke tossed his straw boater onto a nearby marble table and sat down in a maroon tufted-leather chair. He stretched out his legs and rested his folded hands on his stomach. "If it turns out he had that boy strangled with piano wire and tossed in the bayou, I'm going to arrest his ass. It'll give him the opportunity to get his money's worth out of y'all down there at City Hall."

Beneath his hedgerow of thick black eyebrows, Weldon Carrigan's eyes had the dull sheen of gunmetal. He used them to stare down at Rourke hard, letting him feel the threat, and then he smiled.

"You must be feelin' tired this morning. You're usually better at hiding your damn insubordination."

Rourke smiled back at him, finally provoking the older man to laugh softly and shake his head as he settled his solid bulk into a wing-backed chair that looked too small for him. He had the large shoulders and hands of a working man, although he had never really done any hard physical labor. At the moment he was dressed for golf in patterned gold hose, baggy knickers, and bow tie. He would be playing eighteen holes with the mayor later that morning, as he did every Wednesday.

"That bayou floater was already yesterday's ball game the minute after it happened," he said. "It's Charles St. Claire's untimely demise we all ought to be fretting over." He gestured at the morning's extra editions that were spread out on the coffee table in front of him. "You had a chance yet to read through any of this tripe? I swear, that gol-bedamned Wylie T. Jones of the *Morning Trib* has taken salaciousness to new depths. The body's barely cold yet and he's already writing about the Cinderella Girl maybe going into the dock for the Trial of the Century."

"I looked at them," Rourke said. The *Morning Tribune*, the worst of the tabloids, had printed a photograph of the body wrapped in a bloody sheet being carried out to the coroner's hearse. The other papers—the *Times-Picayune*, the *States*, and the *Item*—showed pictures of the grieving widow. She had come out onto the gallery of Sans Souci this morning, shortly after dawn, to talk with all the reporters who had gathered there. In the photographs they'd taken of her, she looked beautiful and tragic. Innocence betrayed.

"I'll be straight up with you, Day," his father-in-law was saying. "This murder last night is going to have tabloids from all over and their hacks like Wylie T. Jones crawlin' out the woodwork like roaches in a fire. If we do have to go and put Remy Lelourie on trial for the murder of her husband, we're going to find ourselves in a three-ring circus swinging by our dicks on a trapeze with no net. For one thing there isn't a jury in the country that would convict her, even if she'd been caught right in the act—"

"She as good as was. Or so it looks."

The superintendent slammed the flat of his hand down on the table. "And I'm telling you that when it comes to this case, justice and guilt aren't going to matter diddly. On the other hand, it can't look as though we're letting the murder of a man like Charlie St. Claire pass us on by without any attention being paid to it at all." He waved his hand at the newspapers. "I don't want some shit-sniffing bastard writing about how my cops're nothing but a bunch of peckerwoods who couldn't take a trip to the outhouse if there wasn't a path already worn in the dirt to show them the way. We've got to get out of this St. Claire mess as cleanly and with as little fuss as we possibly can."

Rourke cut his gaze away to the gallery doors and their view of the heat-hazed sky. Weldon Carrigan was a politician, not a cop. He saw the spilling of blood, the pain and suffering, only as part of a political game to be duked out in the pages of the press and on the polished floors of City Hall, where some deaths mattered and others didn't, and where the best justice was the kind that came easily.

"So an arrest would be helpful as long as it isn't Mrs. St. Claire's," Rourke said.

The superintendent had taken a Havana cigar out of a silver case and was clipping it with a slender silver knife on the end of his watch chain. "Another suspect wouldn't be unwelcome."

"Do you have anyone in mind? Or will just any-old-body do?"

"I heard St. Claire had himself a colored mistress. You hear that?"

"No," Rourke lied. The coldness he'd felt in the hallway of the Criminal Courts Building had come back, worse than before. A deep, bone-breaking cold.

"She's not some parlor chippy either," his father-in-law was saying. "Supposed to be married, in fact. And even though she's a nigger, St. Claire was supposed to've had a real affection for her."

Carrigan lit the cigar with a wooden match, staring all the while at Rourke, who met his eyes but said nothing.

"You don't find that significant?" Carrigan said when the cigar was drawing.

Rourke leaned forward to rest his elbows on his thighs, but he kept his gaze locked on the older man's face. "What I find more significant is Mrs. St. Claire covered in blood and sitting next to a cane knife and the slaughtered body of her husband. You go talking to the press about a colored mistress and you've just given them a motive to put on the wife that's as good as a pair of hand-cuffs."

The superintendent pushed himself abruptly to his feet. "Find out who this girl of Charlie's is, Day. Haul her black ass in for questioning, and make her give you something. Something we can use."

He went to the French doors and then turned back again. His face seemed to have softened, but perhaps it was only the smoke from the cigar, which feathered the air around his eyes. "You and Katie will be coming to my party on Saturday?" he asked. Weldon Carrigan would be fifty-five on Saturday, but when it came to his birthday, he was still a child at heart. He threw himself a big party every year, complete with cake and ice cream and a fireworks display.

"I don't know as how I'll have the time," Rourke said, feeling mean. "Sounds to me like I'll be too busy with the rubber hoses, beating confessions out of anybody that's handy."

Carrigan's teeth tightened around the cigar. "Whatever works."

He took the cigar out of his mouth to stare down at the burning ash, sighing. "Jo told me once—I think it was one of those times when she was trying to explain to me why it was that she just had to have you. She said that to you being a cop was like being a priest, like it was kind of a holy calling from God, and so you walked a tightrope between the way the world was and the way you wanted it to be and you saw nothing but darkness beneath you and no end in sight. Now, my daughter, she thought the greatest act of courage she could imagine was that your honor kept you clinging to that rope, when anyone else would've just let go long ago."

Weldon Carrigan looked back up and his mouth curled into something that was definitely not a smile, and Rourke knew he was about to be asked for something he wouldn't be able to give. "Me, I told her that martyrs usually ended up burning at the stake. I want you to bury this Vinny what's his name—this two-bit

70

goon—and forget about him. Meanwhile, the city of New Orleans would also be very grateful if you could find some way to clean up the murder of Charlie St. Claire without us having to hold a goldamned Trial of the Century. You can start by running down this nigger gal he was supposed to have been banging."

"And to hell with truth and justice," Rourke said, and immediately wanted to kick himself. Honor, truth, and justice. Shit.

The smile Rourke gave to himself was full of self-derision as he stretched to his feet. He picked up his straw boater and sauntered from the room, singing under his breath just loud enough for the super to hear, "In the meantime, in between time, ain't we got fun?"

Chapter Six

She came toward him out of the shadowed, trash-littered alley, a mystery woman in black silk.

"I have a quarrel to pick with you, Lieutenant Daman Rourke," she was saying, her voice as breathless and broken as he felt. "Your captain says you played a lyin', sneaky, dirty trick on me. It seems there is no law that says I had to come down here just on your say-so and roll my fingers on that inky pad. And now you're going to try and hang me with that nasty ol' bloody thumbprint."

He smiled. "Electrocute you."

She laughed, as he had known she would. She had never been afraid of either sinning or dying.

"Dead is dead, and hell is hell, and it doesn't much matter how you get there," she said, her mouth almost singing the words. Her mouth was unforgettable. He had never forgotten the taste of her mouth. "But you shouldn't try and send me there ahead of you, Day."

She had come all the way up to him, to where he leaned against the rakish fender of his Stutz Bearcat Roadster, came up to him so close their bellies almost brushed, and she put her hand to his throat as though she was going to choke him, but gently. "That isn't fair."

"You know what they say about all being fair."

"But which game are we playing at this time, darlin'—love or war?"

He could feel his pulse pounding against her hand. Once, they hadn't been able to keep their hands off each other.

"War for now," he said. "Although we can have a go at love again, if you've the guts for it."

Her fingers followed a sinew in his neck down to the hollow in his throat and paused there, pressing a little. "Is that a dare?"

Jesus, oh, Jesus.

Her hand fell to her side and she took a step back. "I bet you call her 'baby,'" she said.

"What?" he said. He could still feel the pounding of his own pulse in his throat.

She walked away from him, trailing her hand over the automobile's long and sexy hood, softly stroking the canary yellow paint job with those red-lacquered nails.

She laughed at the look on his face. "You *do* call her 'baby.' I bet you take her out on the Old Shell Road and say, 'Come on, baby. Let's see how fast you can go.'"

Rourke couldn't help laughing with her, because she was right. He'd paid the Bearcat's exorbitant thirty-five-hundred-dollar price tag with *bourré* winnings, and he thought that putting the six-cylinder, air-cooled Franklin engine through its paces was almost as good as sex.

Remy had come back to him, close enough to touch him, although this time she didn't. "So take me for a ride in her, Day. And make her go fast."

He had intended all along to take her for a ride. It was why he'd had the desk sergeant bring her out this back way, away from the crush of reporters and her adoring fans. He wanted to take her to a place where he could see how much, if any, she had changed.

He opened the passenger door and watched her climb in, flashing her long legs. As she settled into the Bearcat's low-slung, hand-buffed Spanish leather seat, her black sheath dress rode up to reveal the roll of her stockings and shocking pink knees. Painted nails and rouged knees—she was sure one hot little tomato.

"Mourning becomes you," he said.

She looked up at him, her eyes wide and guileless. "Am I being too subtle, do you think? Should I have wrapped myself up in long black taffeta skirts and a veil?"

He could feel an energy pulsing off her like heat lightning. He knew where that had come from. Even in the little bit of time he'd spent with her there in the squad room, he'd watched her come to possess them all, one by one. Seasoned, jaded cops who'd seen everything and should have known better had fallen into those big, cat-like tilted eyes, and their souls had become electrified.

And she had fed off them, was feeding off them still.

Rourke got behind the wheel and started the engine, but before he put the Bearcat in gear, he pulled a hip flask of scotch out of his pocket and held it out to her. "To soothe the grieving widow's shattered nerves."

"To love and war," she said, taking the flask, touching just the back of his hand, and he despised himself for it, but he felt the burn of her touch low and deep in his belly.

Rourke sent the Bearcat shooting out of the alley in a cloud of dust and a scattering of oiled gravel.

He took Tulane Avenue to Claiborne and turned east. She didn't ask where they were going, not even when they headed toward the river and open country on the St. Bernard Highway. He opened the Bearcat up, coaxing the speedometer up to eighty miles per hour, which was twice as fast as any sane man would drive on that road.

She was drinking steadily from the flask, probably more than was wise for someone about to be grilled by a homicide detective. "You are so mean, Daman Rourke," she said after a time.

"Am I?"

"I walked into that police station of yours scared to death, and you give me this look. Just like some nasty ol' monster would do, before he goes chasing after the girl and growling 'I'm gonna get yooou.'"

He laughed, and she smiled back at him. She had to hold down her hat against the wind they made, and he could see the blue veins on the inside of her arm. Her face shone like a white rose.

This was like a scene in one of her movies, he thought. Drinking bootleg whiskey in a fast car, with the wind in their hair. The gay, irresponsible, tomorrow-we-die celluloid life.

Last night, covered head to toe in her murdered husband's blood, still she had seemed so frightened and vulnerable. So innocent, if you didn't know her. Last night she had tried to seduce him with her innocence.

She was still trying to seduce him. But this morning there was a brittleness, an edgy desperation, to her. She was more believable somehow, this Remy.

He cut his eyes off the road and back to her again. There was that luminescent quality about her that shone through so strongly on the movie screen, a shimmering, like an icicle melting in the sun, but she gripped the flask so hard her knuckles had bled white, and he could see faint black stains left by the fingerprinting.

"Don't you think you ought to be getting yourself a lawyer?" he said.

She took another long pull of the scotch. "That's what Mama told me—well, Mama didn't *tell* me exactly, since we aren't speaking. She had Belle telephone this morning and pass along the wisdom: that I need to get me a lawyer. 'Course, Mama isn't worried about me being arrested so much as she is about me not getting the house. You know how Mama feels about Sans Souci."

"So are you going to get the house? Does it come to you in St. Claire's will?"

"You are such a cop anymore, Day. Now you're thinking I killed him for a house."

She had pushed her lips into a little pout, playing with him, being obvious about it and not even caring that he would see right through her, not caring that he knew she had coveted Sans Souci the whole of her life.

He slammed on the brakes and the Bearcat slewed to a stop,

tires screeching and burning rubber. He stared at her and she stared back at him, unblinking. She wasn't even breathing hard.

Then, as he watched, her eyes slowly filled with tears. She turned her head away, to look across an empty pasture toward an old dairy barn. The barn, once painted red, was now the color of rust. You could see, just barely, the faded image of a spotted cow on the steeply slanted roof.

He gripped her chin and pulled her head around to face him. "My, my, just look at you—the grieving widow all of a sudden. But who are the tears for, baby? For yourself, or for him? Do you want me to believe you're sorry he's dead?"

She shook her head, and he felt a splash of wetness on the back of his hand. "Don't be like this, Day, please," she said, so softly he could barely hear her. "Don't hate me like this."

He let go of her as if she'd suddenly caught on fire. She was setting him up, twisting him inside out, with her truths and her lies. He knew that if he let himself listen to her long enough, he would find a way to believe whatever she told him.

He listened to her cry for a while, until her cheeks were all puffy and wet, and her nose had turned red. He had seen her cry like this before, both for real and in her movies—hard, brutal tears that could make her seem so human as to be almost ugly. That she wasn't so beautiful when she cried made it even easier to believe her. But then she probably knew that as well.

"I am sorry for Charles," she was saying. "For his dying and the horrible way of it, and for all the pain we'd brought to each other in these last months."

She looked at him, with her lips partly open, her eyes so wet and dark and deep. Like her tears, everything about her had the potential to be a lie. He gripped the steering wheel, hard, to keep from touching her, and drove off the road, turning onto a track that cut through the pasture toward the old dairy barn. The barn had been converted into a hangar, where a couple of Spad fighter planes and a Jenny trainer had been relegated as surplus from the war. One of the pastures had been turned into an airfield, although nothing stirred there now but the cattails and the crows. Even the wind sock hung listless in the thick, sultry air.

He had gone to war after she had left him that summer, the summer of 1916. The Great War, they called it, and great it had been from the way it consumed blood and flesh and bones by the trenchload. America hadn't joined in the carnage yet, but there had been a French flying squadron of American volunteers, the Lafayette Escadrille. Daman Rourke had gone to France hoping to die, and instead he had renewed his love affair with danger in the form of tracer bullets blazing out of the blinding sun. He had discovered inside himself new and terrible talents, for fighting and killing and jousting in the sky.

He'd had to stop the killing after the war was over, but he hadn't been able to give up the flying. It was so easy, he had discovered, and so very sweet, to take an airplane out on the screaming edge and dance.

Usually for stunt flying he flew one of the Spads, but he rolled the Jenny out of the barn now and began a preflight check, running his hands over the struts, testing the tension of the flying wires, tightening nuts and bolts. Remy walked around the plane the way she'd walked around the Bearcat, touching it, taking in the fragile contraption of wood and wire and fabric.

"Is it your intention to take me flying in this thing?" she finally said.

"Well, you did allow as how you wanted to go fast. Guaranteed thrills, and your money back if you get killed." He put a whole lot of challenge and just a touch of meanness into his smile. "It's double-dare time, Remy Lelourie."

She only laughed.

He helped her to put on goggles, helmet, and one of his old leather jackets, and then he lifted her up into the front cockpit's worn wicker seat. Even though she wouldn't be doing the piloting, because of her much lighter weight she would have to ride up there to prevent the aircraft from being nose-heavy.

She sat in the cockpit, watching him, and he thought he could feel the excitement in her, the life, like a vibration along the plane's flying wires. She watched his every move as he checked to be sure the ignition switch was off and that both the air- and gas-intake valves were open before he hand-pumped air pressure into the gas tank. He went to the front of the plane and flipped the propeller four times clockwise, then came back to the cockpit and slowly shut down the air valves and turned on the magneto switch. He went around up front again, put his palms on the propeller blade, and heaved.

The engine coughed and roared to life even as he was jumping clear of the flying propeller blades. He swung up onto the wing as the plane began to roll.

He climbed into the cockpit and took the Jenny up. The horizon was strung with wisps of gray clouds, like dirty feathers, but the sky above them glowed with a soft, saffron light. They went up and up, flying, until the palmettos, the water oaks and willows, were all reduced to green splashes on brown earth, and the oyster and shrimp boats looked small as doodlebugs on the water. They flew, soaring high toward the sun, and he widened his eyes so that he saw the whole world below, above and around him.

He cruised for a while, getting the feel of the plane, and then he warmed up with a few barrel rolls and a couple of loop-the-loops. At the end of the last loop, he fell out into a slight dive, then climbed to full power until he was flying completely upside down. At the top of the circle, instead of cutting his engine and diving down to complete yet another loop, he held full power and rolled a half turn to the left and back again into an upright position, and then he twisted the plane around into a long, straight spin, going down and down and down, and he held it, held it, held it, as the ground came rushing up to meet them.

He waited until the last possible second to pull out of the spin, waited until he was a heartbeat away from being too late, reaching for that belly-clenching, breathless place between greased lightning and the sweet spot where it hits.

Any other woman in the world would have screamed. Death was screeching at them on the press of the wind, but Remy Lelourie was laughing.

She hadn't changed.

On the drive from the airfield back to the city, they stopped along the side of the road where a man was selling slices of watermelon off the tailgate of a battered pickup truck. They ate the fruit sitting side by side on the Bearcat's running board, spitting seeds into the dirt and getting their hands and faces all sticky.

Pinpricks of sunlight pierced the black straw of her hat, freckling her ear and jaw. Her lips were wet with watermelon juice. He thought of the way it had been between them once, how they'd been no more than kids, really, and yet there had been something pure and distilled in the fury of their love, like the blue flame of a match before it burns out on its own. Afterward, he had gone off to war, he'd married another woman, had a child by her and then buried her—he had lived and thought himself over Remy Lelourie.

"What are you doing here?" he asked aloud. "You had the whole world to play in, so what have you come back for?"

Her mouth pulled into something that was not quite a smile. "You might find this hard to believe, but there's a limit to how much one can bear of a thing—even champagne baths and tango dancing and petting parties in the purple dawn."

He spat a seed at a fence post. "Yeah, I've had that same feeling myself lately—too much of a good thing. Like too many scotch-and-ryes and *bourré* games that last past two in the morning. Too many dead bodies."

She turned her head and met his gaze, but her face kept her secrets well. He had read once that when you are acting whatever you are thinking, the camera will catch it. But if your thoughts are lies—what then does your audience see?

"I wanted to come home, Day," she said. "Oh, maybe not for forever, but for a little while. Sometimes the past can seem as if it has a powerful hold on you, way more than any future can ever hope to claim. I just wanted to come home for a spell. Is that so hard to understand?"

"No," he said, but that was a lie as well. He didn't understand all of it, not when he remembered how their future had been destroyed by what she had done that hot summer's evening eleven years ago. He had always known why she had left. What he still didn't know was how—brave as she was, reckless as she was—she had ever dared to come back.

"It was double-dare time for Remy Lelourie," she said softly, as if she were reading his mind, and that was impossible, surely, for she couldn't have known what he had seen.

He took her watermelon rind and tossed it, along with his, into the weed-choked ditch. He gave her his handkerchief to wipe her hands, and the juice off her mouth. "We'd better be getting you home," he said.

They spoke only once more on the way back to New Orleans. He asked her where she'd been going with her suitcase all packed up last night, the same night her husband just happened to have got himself carved up with a cane knife, and she said, "It's been so hot lately, I decided to go out to the lake for a spell." But he knew that that too was a lie.

He let her out at the top of the oyster-shell drive and watched her walk away from him through the moss-strung oaks, watched her passing through sunlight and shadow, toward the house with its slender white colonnettes and wide, gracious galleries. Although she was a thoroughly modern girl with her bobbed hair and painted nails, her rolled stockings and rouged knees, she looked as if she belonged only to that house and to the South, to the past.

Once, years ago, when they were lovers, his greatest fear had been that she would give up everything, even him, to possess Sans Souci. She had left him anyway, only she'd left the house, as well.

In the end, though, it was Sans Souci she had chosen to come back to, and not him.

Her mama had been the one to plant that particular obsession in Remy's head. Generations ago, as far back as the 1850s, the plantation had belonged to the Lelouries. It had been lost, in a game of cards or through a duel, or maybe those old stories lied and it had simply been sold to pay off bad debts—the how of it had never been important, anyway. What had always mattered to the Lelouries was getting it back. You had to be from New Orleans to understand that a house like Sans Souci was more than cypress wood and bricks. It was a testimony to past glories and old sins, a bequest wrapped up in pride, honor, and immortality. A legacy of ambition, greed, and deceit. It was *la famille*.

It was a thing Rourke did understand, this obsession with the past and *la famille*. His past and Remy's—it was like a shared sin, not forgotten, but never confessed. For once, years ago, his mother had left him and his father and brother, and had gone to live with her lover in the house on Conti Street.

Her lover, whose name had been Reynard Lelourie.

Chapter Seven

When Daman Rourke was a kid he would hang around for hours outside a certain house on Esplanade Avenue. A raised cottage mostly hidden behind a tall black-iron picket fence afroth with honeysuckle vines.

What he hoped for during all those hours of all those days was to get a good long look at the two little girls who belonged to his mother's lover. He thought that if he watched them often enough, watched how they behaved, watched to see if they sassed the nuns, or hid their butter beans under their plates, or stole licorice whips from Mr. Pagliani's corner grocery—if he watched them often and carefully, then he would come to understand why those little girls' father had left them.

Then maybe, like the detective he was today, he would have been able to piece all his clues together, one by one, and figure out what terrible crime he had committed that had caused his mother to leave him.

They had kept themselves to themselves, though, had Reynard Lelourie's two daughters, but their mother was what folk called a serious recluse. When Heloise Lelourie's husband had left her to go live openly with his mistress—Daman's mama—in the house on Conti Street, she had put on mourning black, as if he had died, and only set foot outside the iron gate to go to Mass on Sundays. Except for when Reynard Lelourie had died for real, from eating a bowl of spoiled shrimp gumbo the day of his fiftieth birthday—then Heloise Lelourie had caused a bit of a stir herself, by going first to her husband's wake and then to the cemetery to see him good and buried.

It was less than half a mile as the crow flies between Sans Souci and the Lelourie cottage on Esplanade Avenue. Rourke drove there now, parking beneath the shade of a giant palm, whose thick green fronds clicked in a breeze that came up from the river, damp and heavy. Sunshine glazed the few puddles left over from last night's rain.

In the early years of the city's history, Esplanade Avenue with its root-cracked sidewalks had been only a muddy road, which wound through French colonial plantations from the river to the Bayou St. John. Eventually the plantations were parceled up, and the muddy road was paved with Belgian blocks and lined with elegant Creole mansions and raised cottages. Then, as more years passed, some of the families died out or moved uptown, and many of the mansions were turned into rooming houses. Others had been allowed to go to seed. But in New Orleans only the appearances of life changed, Rourke thought. The rhythms remained the same.

The metal of the cottage's gate was hot to the touch when he pushed it open. All those hours he had spent hanging around the outside of this gate, and this was the first time he had ever passed through it.

The garden was lush and beautiful, profuse with oleander, azaleas, camellias, and roses. Some animal on a tear had been at the flower beds along the river side of the house, though. Mangled blossoms and shredded leaves lay tossed and scattered in deep furrows of wet, turned-up earth.

The house was in a sad way as well, paint flaking and cardboard patches in the windows where the stained-glass panes had gone missing. The Lelouries had never been rich like the St. Claires and they had fallen on even worse times lately, but their blood was just as blue. Their name was as old as Louisiana itself.

Rourke climbed the steps to the saggy gallery and pulled the bell. A long crack, he saw, ran across the fanlight above the door.

He knew they were home. Still, he waited awhile for the door to be answered. Long enough for a clothes-pole man and a fruit seller's wagon to pass by on the avenue, the two men together making a melodious song out of their shuck and hustle.

"Clothes poles. I got the clothes poles, lady, sellin' clothes poles a nickel and a dime."

"I got watermelon red to the rind."

When the door finally opened Rourke touched the brim of his straw boater and smiled. "Mornin', Miss Belle."

She tried to slam the door in his face, but he put his hand out, stopping it.

"You have your nerve—coming to this house, Daman Rourke," she said. Her voice was dry and brittle.

From within the house a woman called a question, and she half turned to answer. "It's *that woman's* boy, Mama. . . . No, not the priest. The policeman." She swung back around to him, color staining her cheeks, her eyes bright. She'd always had bright eyes, he remembered—golden brown, the color of a candle flame seen through a glass of whiskey. "I'm tellin' him just where he can take himself off to."

"No. Let him come in."

Mrs. Heloise Lelourie materialized out of the darkness of the hallway, standing small and slender and straight-backed behind her younger daughter.

Rourke had never spoken to her before, this abandoned wife of his mother's lover. But he was well acquainted with the sight of her—as a boy, he had often gone to Mass in her church just to observe her, her and her girls. Hers was a French face, petite and sharply boned, timeless. But her coloring was fair, gray eyes and blond hair now faded to the color of old wax.

For a moment longer Belle still kept the door half-shut against him, and her hand that held it trembled. Her short nails were grimed with black dirt, and a band of sunburn circled her wrist between where her gardening glove must have ended and her sleeve began. She saw him looking at her hand, at her nails, and she let go of the door and stepped back into the gloom of the hall.

Mrs. Lelourie led the way into a front parlor that was furnished in black walnut and red velvet that had faded to puce. The large gilded mirror over the mantel was spotted with mildew. The carpeting was so threadbare the floor showed through the nap in places. A dry, musty smell hung around the place, like that of a grave so old that even the bones had long ago fallen into dust.

Mrs. Lelourie waved her hand at a black horsehair settee that was worn bald in places. "Please, will you take a seat," she said, her words blurred by a soft accent, but then she had grown up speaking real French. In her day, her people had seldom married outsiders, and the paterfamilias didn't even like their children learning English in school.

"Belle," she said, as she settled with old-fashioned grace onto a lyre-backed chair, "if you would prepare and pour, please, the *café* for our guest."

Belle stared at her mother and some feeling burned quick and hot across her face, gone before Rourke could read it. She turned on her heel and left the room, and the cheap cotton skirt of her dark blue dress, too long to be fashionable anymore, made a sighing sound as it brushed her legs.

Mrs. Lelourie folded her white, veined hands on her lap and lifted her head up proud. She didn't speak, and neither did he. Long ago, Daman Rourke had learned that the human heart couldn't bear emptiness, and a silent room was emptiness of the worst sort. The heart would ache to fill the silence. All he had to do was wait and listen.

The house was so quiet he could hear Belle way back in the kitchen, making the coffee. He doubted any guest had stepped into this parlor in years. "My mama lives in a grave, and I hate her for it," Remy had said to him once, but even then he knew it wasn't really hate she felt. He understood the tangled layers of shame and pride that had made a crypt out of this house for

Heloise Lelourie, but he wondered now why Belle had chosen to stay and be buried alive along with her mother.

There were many women like Belle in New Orleans, though, Rourke thought—women who awaken one day to find themselves left behind, caring for aging parents and living out their lives in fading rooms behind drawn curtains, where antique clocks measure out the time in years, not minutes, and too much is left unsaid.

The strong chicory smell of the coffee made it out to the parlor first, followed by Belle carrying a tarnished silver tray weighted down by a large gray agate *cafetière* with steam rising from its spout.

The coffee was thick and black as tar. He watched Belle pour it, together with the hot milk, into china cups. He remembered her as a pretty child, with long curls the color of late-summer apricots that would slide back and forth over her shoulders when she walked. She hadn't bobbed her hair, the way all the other girls of her generation had done, and she wore it swept up now in a thick, soft bun. Its bright color had faded some, though, the way a ribbon will do when left too long in the sun.

As she leaned over to hand him his café au lait, a medal on a heavy silver chain swung out from around her neck. It was a St. Joseph's medal, the patron saint of spinsters, and so it seemed that she still had her hopes of escaping, after all.

Belle sat down on the sofa, and Mrs. Lelourie took a delicate sip from her cup. The older woman's gaze met Rourke's, then she looked away. She smoothed the napkin on her lap. "Everyone knows how those Hollywood movie people do all sorts of wicked, unnatural things that no one else does."

"Oh, Mama, you really mustn't say such things," Belle said, although the words sounded forced, as if they'd gotten caught in her throat on the way up and she'd had to cough them out. "Mr. Rourke is going to think you're sayin' that Remy killed her husband."

Mrs. Lelourie took another sip of café au lait. "Stuff and nonsense. He knows I speak of this thing of shame that my daughter

Remy has done after her husband's death. Allowing him to be cut up, butchered in that foul place. There can be no proper wake because of it, no open casket."

The older woman's hand betrayed her for just a moment by trembling and spilling coffee into her saucer, and Rourke had to look away. He ached for her. All she had to fill her days, her years, were the rituals of life and the memories they made—the wakes and weddings, the births and burials. Yet for Reynard Lelourie's wife, it must have seemed as though even the rituals kept betraying her over and over.

"I wish you could have been spared the pain of a postmortem," he said. "But the procedure is always required nowadays, when there's a murder."

"Murder." The sound she made was between a genteel little snort and a sigh. "Charles St. Claire brought his death on himself. It runs in that family, that sort of insanity."

"Oh, Mama, you mustn't say . . . Now Mr. Rourke is going to think you're the one who's gone a little crazy."

Mrs. Lelourie lifted her shoulders in a small shrug, as if murder and insanity hardly mattered anyway. "The important thing, *bien sûr*, is that Sans Souci will be back with the Lelouries now, where it belongs."

"Under Louisiana law," Rourke said, "the husband's property doesn't always pass on to the wife. Especially if she killed him for it."

The smallest of smiles pulled at the corners of Mrs. Lelourie's mouth, and her gaze went to an oil painting of the house that hung in an ornate gilded frame above the mantel. "God will not disappoint us."

Belle pushed herself to her feet in a sudden, jerky movement. She went to the window to stare out at her beautiful garden through lace panels yellow with age.

She crossed her arms over her middle, hugging herself. "As you can see, our mama was just as pleased as can be when Remy married—not that Mama would ever tell Remy so, and she wouldn't go to the wedding either. But later on that evenin' Remy came on over with her new husband, flashing that weddin' ring on her finger, Mrs. St. Claire at last and after all these years, and Mama still wouldn't speak to her. Poor Remy. You should have been here that evenin', Mr. Rourke. You would have felt so bad for her. She thought she'd found the one thing that would make Mama love her again, but Mama doesn't forgive so easily. Do you, Mama?"

"To disgrace oneself is to disgrace the family. My daughter has shamed the name of Lelourie."

Belle swung her head around to her mother. "She has shamed our name, Mama? *She* has?"

Rourke got up and went for a closer look at the painting hanging above the fireplace. The artist had signed his work: Henri Lelourie. It must have been done many years ago. Sans Souci was lovely today, but she had been lovelier then, in her prime.

Mrs. Lelourie's gaze was riveted on the painting as well, and her voice floated through the room's musty silence as if she spoke from a dream. "Sans Souci. Remy understands, and so does Belle. *Mon trisaïeul*, my great-great-grandfather, built her. Once she was the most beautiful plantation in all of Louisiana. Once she was ours, and now she will be ours again."

Her gaze lingered lovingly on the painting, and then it shifted to Rourke's face, and even from where he stood now across the room from her, he could see a hard glitter in her eyes, as if they had been glazed and fired in a kiln.

"Have you heard it told, then," she said, "how we Lelouries came to lose Sans Souci?"

"Something about a duel between a Lelourie and a St. Claire, and cheating going on during a game of cards."

She stared at him a moment longer, and then she looked away, and he got the feeling that what she said next wasn't what she'd been about to say.

"Yes, that is how the story goes. There was cheating at cards and so Sans Souci was lost, and then there was a duel, in which the Lelourie boy died and the St. Claire boy lived. Because of the wicked greed of a St. Claire, our beautiful plantation house has been out of our care for all these years and my husband never knew his granddaddy. So what does it matter who killed him, or if he brought it on himself? Charles St. Claire's dying was justice long past due."

"If you believe the sins of the father should be visited upon their sons. That's a long time to bear a grudge, though, and your husband has been dead for years himself, and long past caring."

Her face was composed, but he could see her pride, and her pain, in the way she drew herself up tall. "I was born a Lelourie, I married a Lelourie, our children are Lelouries. We are family, and none of that changed no matter what came after—not my husband's desertion of me and our girls so that he might go off and live in sin with your mother the Irish whore, and certainly not his dying. Nothing has changed. But then I would never expect a boy like you, come up from the gutter, a son of *that woman*, to have an understanding of these things."

She stood up then, as if that should be the last word on the subject. She inclined her head to him. "Good day to you, sir."

He waited until she got as far as the doorway before he said, "I couldn't help noticing how the umbrellas in the hall tree were still a bit wet. I hope y'all didn't get caught out in that terrible downpour last night."

She paused for a moment, her hand on the jamb. She half turned back to him, although he thought her gaze might have flashed for just an instant to her daughter. Belle had gone perfectly still.

Then that smallest of smiles brushed across the older woman's mouth again. "Doubtless all our neighbors will be pleased to tell you how I have hidden my head in shame and not left this house come an evening in twenty-seven years. But the truth is my daughter and I have been known to take comfort from Mother Church and her sacraments on other days besides Sunday. Belle, will you see this gentleman out?"

Heloise Lelourie turned and walked from the room with her head held high and her back straight, her long black skirt from another era brushing in a whisper over the floor. Rourke watched her go, understanding her more than she thought. He understood how she had fought to keep the past alive by feeding it with the hopes and dreams and desires of her children. He understood, because he himself had never been able to separate his obsession with Remy from the shame they shared over a past they suffered from but hadn't made.

"Poor Mama," Belle said. "But then you know why she is the way she is. And how is your own dear mama?"

The smile Rourke gave to her held more than a touch of meanness in it. "The same. Beautiful, dark, and mysterious. Still wearing black, just like your mama."

He turned back to the painting and stared at it until Belle was moved to leave the window and come to stand beside him. "Is this going to be enough satisfaction for your mama?" he said. "A pretty painting hanging above the mantel? Even if Remy does end up with the deed to Sans Souci, I don't expect she'll be inviting y'all to move on in with her."

"What about my sister?" Belle said after a moment. "Are you going to arrest her?"

Rourke didn't answer. He saw that they had turned a nearby sideboard into an altar. They'd covered it with a crocheted lambrequin and on that sat a plaster statue of St. Michael, patron of *les familles*. Pray to him and he would keep your family safe.

The statue was surrounded by dozens of votive candles, some still burning, and some long since melted down to globs of wax. Dangling from St. Michael's prayerful, outstretched arms was a string of rosary beads. Made out of small red peas, they looked like tears of blood.

They had been praying a lot for something lately, the two women in this house.

Beside one of the puce velvet chairs was a walnut table laden with framed photographs. Many were of Belle when she was a child, but he didn't see any of Remy. Then he noticed that one wasn't a photograph, after all, but a lock of black hair mounted on rose velvet and enclosed in a gold-leaf frame.

He stared at the lock of hair a moment, but what he picked up was a photograph of Belle framed in ornate silver. She had been such a pretty child that everyone called her Belle so often it had become her name. Those thick apricot curls, round dimpled cheeks, a rosebud mouth. Remy had been a dark child, in looks and temperament. Remy had been edgy and fierce, and with the individual parts of her face—her eyes and mouth and chin and cheekbones—all seeming too much for making up the whole of it.

Rourke set down Belle's photograph and picked up another. This one was of a young Charles St. Claire and his brother, Julius, posed arm in arm on the gallery of Sans Souci and dressed for sailing.

"You can't tell them apart, can you?" Belle said, peering over his shoulder to look at the picture along with him. "But they were only alike in their looks. Why, Julius was all the gentlemanly virtues personified."

"And Charles?"

She smiled, pleased that he'd obliged her by asking. "He could be charming too, although he had his mean side. But then you know that."

He knew it now, he supposed, although in the days when this photograph was taken, Rourke had barely ever thought of Charles.

But he sure enough had hated Julius.

"Mama always used to declare that of the two boys, Julius was the sweetest and the weakest," Belle was saying. "But then he was also the oldest, and Sans Souci would have come to him if he hadn't died—not that that ever really mattered to Remy, though. She loved Julius for himself."

She reached around him and brushed her finger over Charles St. Claire's smiling image. "Some people are going to say that's why she killed him, you know. Why Remy killed Charles. For the house, and because she loved Julius best and she must've come to find out that she couldn't wrap Charles 'round her little finger the way she'd done with his brother. She must've come to find out that no matter how alike in looks they were, Charles wasn't really Julius and never would be."

Rourke returned the photograph to the table and picked up the one of Belle again. He turned it around and held it up for her to see. "You were sure a pretty little thing, Miss Belle. Back in those days. Pretty enough to be in the movies."

Her face twitched as though he had struck her. She snatched the picture out of his hand and slammed it down on the table. She leaned close to him, close enough for him to see the fine lines feathering her eyes and catch a faint whiff of mildew that clung to her dress. "It was Julius she loved. He was the one she was going to marry that summer. That summer he died and she ran off."

Rourke went out of the parlor and down the hall, pausing only long enough to pick up his hat from the sofa table and put it on.

"Why, I remember how we used to talk about it, Remy and I. How we carried on, planning her wedding, the dress she would wear, and all the flowers, and how there'd be a champagne fountain at the reception." She had followed him out the front door, onto the gallery with its peeling gray paint. Her face was flushed, and the anger in her voice came as if from a fire raging inside her. "It was Julius that Remy loved. Never you, and not Charles."

The clothes-pole man was long gone, but the fruit man had stopped to make a sale next door, and now he'd just started off down the avenue again.

"Aw-range, so sweet right off the tree, lay-deeee." The fruit man wore a battered top hat; his mule wore a floppy straw one. A big pan scale swung on a chain as his wagon lumbered along, flashing silver in the sun.

"It was always Julius she loved."

Rourke lifted his own hat and gave her his best southern-gentleman smile. "Or so you would have me believe, Miss Belle. But then we all have our own little shuck and hustle."

Rourke left the Lelourie cottage, retracing the way back to Sans Souci, but on foot this time. He crossed the avenue and passed through the scrolled iron gates of the St. Louis Cemetery No. 3, where some of the crumbling old crypts dated back to the turn of the last century. Over a hundred years' worth of Lelouries and St.

Claires had been brought to their eternal rest here in this city of the dead.

The tomb of the *Famille Lelourie* was in the style of a Greek temple with a marble child-angel dancing on top of it. The caskets were kept in vaults, behind a lacy wrought-iron gate, but the names of the Lelourie dead had been carved throughout the years onto the temple's lichen-mottled walls. One of the names, he thought, must belong to the Lelourie boy who had lost Sans Souci in a game of cards and then died in a duel.

One set of deeply engraved letters seemed to stand out larger than the others: REYNARD LELOURIE. There was no inscription to go along with the name, though; no "Beloved Husband of Heloise," no "Beloved Father of Remy and Belle." Certainly no "Beloved Lover of Maeve Rourke." But above the name was a smaller set of letters: MAUREEN, BELOVED DAUGHTER OF REYNARD.

"Maureen," he said, and the name was like a foreign word whose meaning you only half understand.

In his memory it is a warm spring evening when Rourke is seven years old. The sun is gone but the day still holds on to its light, the sky a dusky gold wrapped with black ribbons of clouds, and Rourke is playing baseball with a gang of boys in an abandoned lot across from the wharves on Tchoupitoulas Street. In his memory his father staggers out of a bar in the Swamp and comes for him while he is catching behind the plate, or maybe he is playing shortstop.

His father had been sloppy drunk that evening, his face all red and sweaty, and he'd smelled. Rourke didn't know what he'd done to set his old man off, and he didn't care. All he wanted to do was get out of there and away from the other boys, more ashamed of having a falling down, stinking boozer for a daddy than afraid of the whipping he thought was coming.

The shame was a roaring in his ears, so loud he couldn't hear what his father was saying, and then he did and he knew whatever was coming would be bad, because it was always bad when his father talked about *her*.

" . . . such a tough lil' bastard, always so goddamned tough. It's 'cause you got religion. You got the faith—only it ain't God you pray to, it's her. You got this conviction inside you that she'll be comin' back for you one day, that she's goin' to be savin' your sweet ass. Well, boy, today's the day I'm showin' you different."

That at least is what his father says in his memory, and the grip on his arm is like a shackle of iron, unbreakable, but that probably wasn't true. He could easily have gotten loose from a shambling drunk who was having trouble even keeping his own feet underneath him.

Still, in his memory he is being dragged to a house in the Quarter, on Conti Street, bursting through the front door and into a strange parlor and then beyond, to a room where his mama and a man are lying on the bed without their clothes on. His father and Reynard Lelourie are shouting but he can't hear the words, nor can he see their faces. The only thing in that room is his mother, kneeling up on the bed, and she is crying and holding out her hand to him, and her naked belly is swollen, distended, huge.

He had wanted to run away, but he hadn't been able to tear his gaze from her belly, and though he made not a sound, was barely breathing, in his mind he was screaming, because his daddy had been right—a small part of him *had* believed she would one day be coming home. He was her son, and surely she must love him too much to stay away forever.

A couple of months later somebody told him that the baby, a little girl, had lived only a week or so and then quietly died. For a long while afterward, whenever he imagined the baby lying in her tiny coffin, she would always have his mother's face.

Until this day, though, he had never come to the Lelourie crypt, and so he had never known that his baby half-sister had been named Maureen.

Rourke left the cemetery and walked through a green tunnel of oaks and elms and sycamores, on sidewalks that were buckled and peaked by the roots of the old trees and the passing years.

He paused to talk to those he met: to the maiden aunts who snipped the dead blooms off their mother's prize rosebushes; to the young wives who met at each other's houses for bridge and mahjongg parties; to the colored girls who swept off the porches and rocked the babies on their laps. To the men who delivered the ice and the coal and the gossip from other mouths and places.

The neighborhood lived on its galleries, especially during the hot summers—creaking back and forth in rocking chairs, observing the rhythms of life. Some of these families had resided in their houses for generations. They thought they knew the Lelouries and the St. Claires as well as they knew themselves, but they didn't always know themselves all that well. They saw everything, but they didn't always see it right.

As he walked, Rourke kept an eye out among all the peddlers and hustlers for a knife-grinder, because the murder weapon had looked recently sharpened and it was the wrong time of year for cutting sugar cane. He finally found the old man and his cart a block down from the neighborhood corner grocery.

The knife-grinder had gnarled, palsied hands and a spray of moles across his cheekbones, like dandelion seeds, and he nodded solemnly as Rourke asked his question. He did remember sharpening a cane knife about a week back, but not much about the colored boy who had brought it to him. "I know all the families here 'bout and those that do for them," he said. "This boy I never seen befo'. "

Rourke gave him five dollars in reward money for helping the police in the course of their investigation and then walked the rest of the way to Pagliani's Fine Foods. Mr. Pagliani was always the first to know who was expecting a baby, whose grandmother had died, and whose kid had the measles.

The grocery had a long, wide gallery with ancient, flaking white paint that looked like dried fish scales. Men sat on crates and old ladder-back chairs beneath the shade of a china bell tree, played dominos for a nickel a game, and drank sour mash out of bottles wrapped in brown paper. The place hadn't changed at all since Rourke was a boy, except that the Coca-Cola sign was now electrified.

Inside, the place smelled of bananas, coffee, and the loaves of

French bread piled high on the counter. As he always did when he walked through the door, Rourke looked up to see if the big paper umbrella still hung from the ceiling among the strings of Italian cheese and the coiled links of sausages. The umbrella had pink cherry blossoms and a blue dragon painted on it. From all the way back when he was a boy, Rourke had always wondered how that umbrella had come to be hanging up there, and why.

Next to the cash register, two big-horned loudspeakers were blasting a baseball game out of a crystal set made from an empty Quaker oats box. The Pelicans were playing out at Heinemann Park, and the game was being re-created off the ticker tape by Jack Halliday.

Rourke heard Halliday's scratchy voice say, "That pitch just nicked the outside corner—strike two," and a thought hit him like a fist to the heart. He had promised his Katie he would take her to that game today, and then Charles St. Claire had been murdered last night and he had forgotten all about it. He was always doing that to the poor kid, making promises he ended up breaking, sometimes with barely a thought.

He looked up to find dapper old Mr. Pagliani standing next to the cash register, as if guarding it. The man's dark eyes were piercing, and the mouth beneath his blackened and waxed mustache was frowning. Daman Rourke had stolen a lot of licorice whips out of this store when he was a kid, and Mr. Pagliani still didn't quite believe that the boy he knew as a quick-fingered thief had grown up to be a cop rather than a resident of a cell in Angola.

Rourke smiled. "Evenin' to you, Mr. Pagliani. What inning is it?"

The voice on the crystal set crackled with excitement. Someone had just hit a double against the right-field wall. Maybe there was a chance he and Katie could still catch the end of the game, but he knew, even as he indulged himself with the thought, that it was an easy lie. Katie had probably sat out on their front stoop, wearing her Pelicans hat and with her mitt in her lap, waiting for him to come pick her up and take her out to the ballpark, and she had gone on sitting there and waiting through the opening pitch and the first hit, and then, as the pitches and hits had come and gone, she had finally known her daddy wasn't coming, and Rourke knew there was going to be no making up for that kind of forgetting.

"It is the top of the ninth," Mr. Pagliani was saying in his thick Sicilian accent, "and the Pels, they are ahead with six runs. You think maybe they win the pennant again this year?"

"Can't miss," Rourke said, and smiled again, even though Mr. Pagliani was pretty wise to his tricks. He bent over to fish a Coca-Cola out of a big tin tub, which stood next to the pickle barrel and was filled with shaved ice and bottles of soda pop. The old man had to lean way over to keep an eye on his thieving hands.

When Rourke put a coin on the worn and nicked wood of the counter, the grocer relaxed a little. He even offered to pry the cap off the bottle. "You come nosing 'round the neighborhood because of the murder that happened over at Sans Souci last night, no? Hunh. You was always coming 'round here when you was a kid and getting up to no good."

Rourke took a swallow of the soda. It was crisp and cold and delicious. "Yeah, but now they're paying me to do it. A sad business, that murder."

Mr. Pagliani cast a slow, furtive glance around his store and then leaned forward onto his elbows as if he was about to impart a deep, dark secret. "The wife, she did it. Sliced her man up like he was salami. She was always a wild thing—that Lelourie girl. Up to no good . . ." His words trailed off as if he just remembered that some of the occasions when Remy Lelourie had been up to no good, she'd been in Daman Rourke's company.

He frowned at Rourke and straightened up, cocking his thumb down at the racks of newspapers beneath the cash register. "It says right there in the *Trib* how you cops think she probably did it. Look to the woman, no?"

Rourke bought another soda and went to the back of the store, where the chicken cages were, and where the old Negro who did the slaughtering and the sweeping out had been hovering and casting wide-eyed looks in his direction ever since he'd walked through the door.

"Hey there, Jackie Boone," Rourke said.

"Hey, Mr. Day," the old man answered on a big expulsion of pent-up breath. He lifted the ragged straw hat off his head long enough to wipe the sweat off his brow. "Hot again this evenin', ain't it?"

"Uh-huh. How about a Coca-Cola? It doesn't pack the kick of gin, but it sure goes down cold."

Jackie Boone flashed a smile that was missing most of its teeth. "Thank you, suh." He wiped his hand on his bloody apron and took the bottle of pop from Rourke. He swallowed down a good long drink, then wiped off his mouth with the back of his wrist. "Terrible thing 'bout Mr. Charles, hunh? Him dyin' in that bad way."

"I guess the whole neighborhood pretty much can't talk about anything else."

The old Negro's gaze went from his boss to the men who had set up squatters' rights on the front gallery. He scratched the coils of gray hair on his chest and lowered his voice. "What they papers and some other folk're sayin', though, 'bout how Miss Remy done it . . . She'd never do such a thing, no way, no how. It was probably the *gris-gris* what started it off, and the *loup-garou* what ended it."

You could buy the voodoo charms called *gris-gris* all over New Orleans, but only the most powerful voodooiennes claimed the secret of changing their shape into that of a werewolf and would, for the right price, promise the death of your enemy.

"Some juju woman been puttin' spells on Mr. St. Claire? Some juju woman like Mamma Rae?"

Jackie Boone drank down his Coca Cola and smacked his lips. "Mmmmmm-huh."

"Who she be spelling for?"

The old man's gaze slid away from his. "I wouldn't be knowin' nothin' 'bout that, Mr. Day. No, suh."

Rourke allowed a silence to fall between them while he finished off his own soda. The chickens clucked and scratched in their cages. A breeze came in through the open doorway and set the paper umbrella to twirling.

Jackie Boone finally sighed and rolled his shoulders up high and pulled his head down low, as if he were expecting a blow. "I don't know who be wantin' to put the death curse on Mr. Charles, I swear I don't. But they say his throat was tore open, and the *loup-garou* she always go for the throat. Someone put a cross of wet salt on the gallery of the big house, an' then left a *gris-gris* in the bed in that ol' shack where he was killed. Two, maybe three weeks ago. It was bad *gris-gris*—dirt taken from the grave of a strangled chil', the skull of a one-eyed toad, and drops of blood from a hung man. Didn't scare him none, though, all that hoodoo. No suh, not Mr. Charles. I tol' him he needed to get hisself a frizzled chicken to keep in the yard, to scratch up any hoodoo what might be buried 'round there, but he only laughed.

"Now look at where it got him. His throat tore out by the *loup-garou*."

From the grocery Rourke walked the rest of the way back to Sans Souci, going the long way, by the bayou road. The sun was brutal, the glare from it like a slap across his face. It beat on the sour mud and dead green water, stirring up a smell of rot.

He came around a bend in the road just as a giant garfish exploded out of the bayou, its gills and belly blazing white in the hard sun. The gar was hooked on the end of a cane pole, and the pole was in the hands of a skinny Negro boy, who was wearing a pair of rolled-up dungarees and a big straw hat.

The boy was reaching for the flopping fish. When he looked up and saw Rourke, his eyes grew wide. He dropped his pole and took off running, the skin of his back shining like ebony from his sweat.

"Hey, LeBeau, hold up there!" Rourke called after him, but he had already disappeared into the thick scrub oak.

Rourke looked down at his own shiny two-toned oxfords and his light beige linen trousers and he sighed. But he left the road anyway, climbing the levee and then heading down toward the water.

Gnats and mosquitoes boiled out of the saw grass and canebrakes. His eyes burned in the wet heat. On the bank where the boy had been fishing lay an upside-down pirogue. The log canoe looked well cared for, caulked and clean of algae on the bottom. A couple of small, crude wooden spears were stuck in the ground nearby, and caught on the branches of a dead cypress was a looped line that dangled black hooks like jet beads off a necklace. All that a boy would need for catching frogs.

Rourke picked up one of the Civil War Minie balls the boy had been using as fishing weights. Rourke juggled the ball in his hand a moment, then sent it skipping across the water. He looked back toward Sans Souci. From here, especially from out on the water, you could see the slave shack, and the wide expanse of lawn and trees between it and the house.

He thought of the lantern lights he had seen out here on the bayou last night—boys gigging for frogs in the moonlight. Boys who might well have seen a murderer come and go.

He climbed back over the levee and down to the road and crossed onto the St. Claire land. He passed through pools of shadow made by the live oaks. His shoes crushed the dried husks that lay scattered under the pecan trees. The sharp fronds of the banana trees hung listless in the heavy air.

He walked from the slave shack across the lawn toward the big house. On the bayou side of the house, a huge cistern sat among a tangled bed of ferns and wild lilies. It was shaped like a fat beer barrel, although it was at least as large as two truck beds—bigger around than most other cisterns, but not as tall. It wasn't for the house anymore, not since the advent of indoor plumbing, but it was still used to water the garden. Its staves had once been painted dark green, a long time ago, and its big metal hoops were rusting through in places. On top was a hinged lid and strainer to keep out the leaves and the rats, and to make sure that the neighborhood cats didn't fall in.

He stopped in front of it, his heart beating hard, as if he'd been running.

The hinges on the cistern's lid screamed as he opened it and looked inside, but of course he saw only water, the black-brown color of chicory coffee. When he brought a pool of it up in his cupped hands, though, it was clear and cool. The lid screamed again as he shut it.

A hard stillness came over him as he stood there next to the cistern. A feeling of held breath, of taut waiting. He hadn't heard her come, but he knew she was there.

"Looking for more dead bodies, Lieutenant Rourke?"

Chapter Eight

For a moment he could only stand there and stare at her. He had always been half afraid that she was way more than a little crazy.

"Just a couple of hours ago you were trying to seduce me into believing in your innocence," he finally said. "Now you might as well be challenging me to search the premises for more murder victims."

"No." Remy Lelourie came up to him and laid her hand against his cheek. "If I wanted to seduce you, I would do this." She pressed her mouth against his in a kiss that was almost virginal, and then in the instant before its ending, she ran her tongue along the inside of his lower lip, and he felt the carnality of that deep in the marrow of his bones.

Her hand fell to her side, and she took a step back. She wasn't smiling. "You look hot," she said. "Come inside and I'll fix you something long and cool to drink."

He followed her up the gallery steps and through the kitchen door.

"If I *were* to empty out that cistern," he said to her back, "what do you think I would find?"

She looked at him over her shoulder. "Not another dead body, Lieutenant Rourke. Surely you knew that I was only teasin'."

She'd said that very well, but he thought that if he touched her she'd be trembling.

"On the walk back over here from your mama's . . . Did you know I'd gone to see your mama?"

" 'Course I know. Belle telephoned to tell me I was about to be arrested. Am I?"

"Not yet."

She smiled. "I almost feel disappointed."

"The day is young," he said. "Anyway, I was thinking about grieving widows and matinee idols, and I was remembering that movie you were in where you threw yourself onto your lover's burning funeral pyre. You had every man in the world wishing he could know if only for one night a woman willing to die with him."

"*The Rajah's Secret Wife*. A love so powerful it survived death and flames, and the director trying to get into the leading man's bed rather than mine for a change." She laughed softly and shook her head. "That particular film really was nearly the death of me. One of my veils caught on fire and I got smoke in my lungs and wound up getting pneumonia. The studio sent flowers to the hospital, though."

"And here all this time I thought you were living the glamorous life out there in Hollywood. Champagne baths and tango dancing and petting parties in the purple dawn."

She laughed again, and he realized he was smiling at her, and meaning it, and he made himself quit.

He watched her take a cut-glass pitcher out of the dish safe and pour into it enough bourbon from a bottle with a label to get them both good and soused. She had a languid, boneless way of moving that millions of women the world over had tried to copy. Just as they had tried to copy with paint and pencil the slashing bones, the tilting eyes, the generous mouth.

She added sugar to the bourbon, and a trickle of water, and some mint leaves. She then set about attacking the ice in the box rather viciously with a sharp scraper. He watched the strong, young muscles in her bare arm clenching and unclenching, and the smile playing around her mouth that told him she knew what he was thinking.

She put the shaved ice into two tumblers that were rimmed with sterling silver, and poured the julep over it, and then gave him one of the drinks, making sure their fingers brushed.

She touched her glass to his. "To even more love and war."

He took a small, slow sip, and even then his throat closed up with the kick of the booze. She was back to staring up at him with those wide-open eyes and that vulnerable and desperate look on her face that had always affected him, even when he knew better.

She smiled a sad smile and shook her head. "I've spent the last ten years of my life surrounded by beautiful men, and none of them was you."

"But you made do," he said.

She shook her head again, and he thought her mouth might have trembled a little, but he didn't want to see it because he was afraid she was still acting.

"Belle wrote to me sometimes," she said. "Belle made certain to write me about your getting married. I was sorry to hear later that your wife had died."

Sorry. That was what everyone had said. How sorry they were and what a tragedy it was that God had taken her so young. By the time he got to her she was already dead. He had kissed her mouth, her neck, her ear, and then her mouth again. He hadn't been able to let go of her, even after she began to grow cold in his arms.

He realized Remy was staring at him again and he dropped his gaze down to the glass in his hand, shielding his thoughts.

"You loved her," she said.

Had he loved Jo? He thought he must have, but he could no longer truly measure the shape and depth of what he'd had with his wife. Once he must have believed that she would save him from everything, even himself, but she had died too soon.

He felt a woman's fingers lightly brush his cheek, and then Remy Lelourie was walking away from him, out into the hall and toward the front of the house. She had always walked away expecting him to follow her, and he always did.

She led him upstairs into the parlor they had been in last night. This time of day in most houses the jalousies would be closed against the heat, but she had left them thrown open, and sunlight poured like honey through the windows.

Rourke stood still and looked around him, at the high, corniced ceilings, the *faux marbre* walls, the polished heart-pine floors. "Your mama," he said, "seems to be anticipating with pleasure the fine day this house passes back into Lelourie hands. Maybe once that happens she'll be able to forgive you for letting Julius die on you before y'all could be husband and wife and you could be mistress of Sans Souci. Your little sister Belle, though, now she thinks you didn't marry Charles so much for the house as because you're still in love with Julius, and you hoped his brother was the next best thing, only you found out later that he was just about the very worst thing."

She had been listening to him with her head slightly tilted, that soft smile playing around her mouth. "My heavens," she said. "What frantic detecting you've been doing. No wonder you look so hot and worn out."

He stared at her until her smile began to fade and she turned away from him, and then he came after her, using his cop's voice. "Why did you marry him, Remy?"

She went to one of the tall, narrow windows that overlooked the moss-garlanded oaks and the crushed-shell drive. The long gauzy curtains stirred out over the gray planks of the gallery, but softly, as if they had moved with her sigh.

"Charles was New Orleans," she said. "Like this house is New Orleans, and I did so very badly want to come home. I came here for that movie premiere, already half thinking I would stay awhile, and he was at the party and the next thing I knew he was courting me. It was rather sweet the way he went about it, old-fashioned and gentle. He didn't seem to want—" She cut herself off and gripped her elbows with her hands, holding herself. "I thought that because he'd known me from when we were just kids, then he would know what I was, just little ol' Remy Lelourie, his third cousin from on up the road. I thought he could love me for myself."

She turned back around to face him again. The sharp bones of her cheeks were flushed, her dark eyes bright with unshed tears. Innocence betrayed. "We hadn't even been married a month when I understood just how wrong I had been."

"You made a mistake, but that didn't mean you had to go on trying to live with it."

Her mouth made a wry, twisting movement that might have been regret. "Your mama can tell you—we Lelouries don't believe in divorce."

So you killed him instead. He could have said that, but he didn't. Still, he waited for her to deny it. He realized that neither last night, nor yet today, had she said, I didn't kill him, Day. I didn't kill my husband.

He wanted to choke the truth out of her, even if the truth was raw and ugly. He wanted to take her in his arms and hold her. Once he had done that. Once.

Once he had whispered her name to himself just for the magic of its sound.

This time he was the one to turn away from her. To her it might have seemed as if he wandered the room aimlessly, but he knew what he was after. He'd seen it when he walked through the door last night. It was the second thing he had noticed, after her. An etched, gold-plated revolver mounted on the wall above a pier table that held a simple milk-glass vase of bloodred roses. A French pinfire revolver, over seventy years old but still in prime condition.

He set his julep on the table and took the pistol down from the wall.

Once before, he'd held this gun in his hand, had felt its weight and the awe that came from knowing in his gut that this was death and death was forever. The gun's grip fitted cold against his palm now, slick with oil and the clammy sweat of old fears remembered.

He heard the click of her heels on the floor behind him. He turned with the gun in his hand and looked at her.

"It's the gun that Julius killed himself with," she said. "Charles had it mounted up there shortly after we were married. He said it was to remind himself that he had it all over his brother now—being alive and having me, while Julius was dead."

She was lying. He knew for a certainty that she was lying about the most important part of it, at least, but he didn't care. His mouth had gone sour, as if he could even taste the sweat on his tongue, and it was like the taste of a gun barrel in your mouth, cold and bitter, the taste of death. Death faced down and beaten, the best high he'd ever found.

Beneath the noise of his heart sloughing in his ears, he thought he heard Remy's voice as he'd heard it that day, heard it way too many times for the good of his soul: Do it, Day. I dare you. Her taking him out there on the screaming edge and him loving every dark moment of it.

"For you I would do it. . . ." For a moment he wasn't sure if he was hearing her voice now or only imagining it, remembering it. "For you I would throw myself onto a burning pyre. I would die with you, Day."

Somehow, without his realizing it, she had wrapped both her hands around his hand that held the gun, and she was turning the gun toward herself, bringing it up to her face, bringing it up until the barrel was pressing against her cheek. He looked into her eyes and saw how the wildness had come into them, and he thought of how he hadn't checked to see if the damned thing was loaded.

"Don't," he said. "We aren't kids anymore, and this isn't a game. Your man died a bad death, and if it turns out you did it, then heaven help you, darlin', because I win and you lose, pure and simple. This time the only one who will pay the nasty price is you."

Slowly she shook her head, and the gun's barrel slid across her cheek until the muzzle was caressing her lips. "Nothing's ever been pure and simple between us."

He let go of the gun, surrendering it to her. He realized his mistake when he saw her thumb pull back the hammer, and the barrel swing around and up, until it was pointing at the sweet spot right between his eyes.

He smiled.

She pulled the trigger, and the firing pin fell on the empty chamber with a soft and gentle *click* that had the reverberating impact of a heart suddenly stopping in midbeat.

"I dare you, Day," she said. "I double-dare you."

After he left her, he kept walking on down the road along the bayou, wishing it were possible to walk until he found the edge of the world. He would do a dance when he found it then, oh yes, he'd dance on the edge of the bad ol' world and see if he could keep from falling off.

The trouble with being a gambling man, thought Daman Rourke, is that you're never satisfied. If you're losing you have to keep on playing, feeding the vain and vanquished hope that at any moment your luck is going to turn. If you're winning you have to keep on playing too, because a gambler knows the ride is going to last only so long, and so you got to catch that ride, you got to stay on that train until the end of the line, stay on until you're losing again, and it only ever ends when you've lost it all, when everything is sold or hocked or bartered, including your soul.

As he walked along, he told himself that she had known for a certainty the revolver wasn't loaded, and then he called himself a liar because he knew her too well, knew her the way one gambler knows another. She had been along for the wild ride and she hadn't cared one way or the other whether there was a cartridge in the chamber, just as she hadn't cared which way the barrel was pointed when she pulled the trigger. He knew her. Better than he knew himself, he knew her.

He had left the genteel life behind him now. The road was bad in this part of town, and the only way you could go along it was to walk. It was too potted and rutted for the survival of balloon tires, but then the people who lived in this part of town didn't need a smooth road for an automobile they would never own.

In this part of town the cattails in the ditches and the black-eyed Susans that lined the road were always coated with dust. Dilapidated boathouses floated in the bayou, and squatters' shacks, made of tar paper and driftwood, perched on the levee as if daring a good storm to come along and knock them off. Men with skin colors that ranged from brick dust to olive brown to jet black sat on their porches and decks, dipping home-brewed beer out of lard buckets and wondering what a white man was doing all the way to hell and gone out here, figuring it had to be bad news for some poor soul.

He stopped at a place beneath the railroad bridge and bought three big links of hot *boudin* wrapped in wax paper. A couple of boys were fishing for perch from the bridge. The Black Bridge, where once, long ago, Remy had shown him how death's hot and screaming breath had a kick more powerful than cocaine.

At a place in the bayou where the cypress trees grew thick and the water was a deep moss green, a house floated on rusted oil drums. To get to it Rourke walked across a gangplank that had been laid over a bank of gray mud where crawfish peeped above their holes and dragonflies flitted among the canebrakes.

The young woman who opened the door immediately averted her face from his, but not before he'd seen how her cheeks were puffy and her eyes were red around the rims. She didn't have a telephone out here on the houseboat, nobody in this part of town had a telephone, but the grapevine would have been just as quick.

"Don't look at me like that," she said. "I been sick."

She turned and went back inside the cabin, leaving the door open for him.

It took a while for his eyes to adjust to the darkness after the harsh sunlight. He set the *boudin* he'd bought on top of the galley's sop stone, where the bowl of cush-cush she'd had for breakfast glistened with ants. The cabin smelled of reefer and sour mash.

She stood with her back to him, swaying on her feet. She had soft, very light brown skin, like a sepia-toned photograph. Her hair had a copper glaze, and it fell thickly to her waist in tight dark coils.

"Luce," he said softly. Even so her back flinched as if it had just caught the lash of the whip. "I got to ask you, honey . . . How did you spend last night?"

"I got me a gig in a speak on Dumaine Street. You know that."

He grabbed her by the arm, spinning her around, and gripped the sides of her head with his two hands. Her eyes stared up at him, round and shining like yellow china marbles.

"Stop it. Just stop it," he said, and although the words were calm and quiet, anyone with half an ear could have heard the violence underneath. "I been lied to up one side and down the other today and I'm runnin' out of the patience for it."

He was gripping her too roughly, and so he let her go. She backed up a step, crossing her arms over her chest. "*Here* is where I spent last night. I been sick, which is what I already tol' you. What you goin' to say next? That I killed him?"

Her gaze shifted away from his as she became aware that already she had said too much. She could have witnessed the whole thing, but he'd probably never get it out of her now, and he didn't blame her. She'd have to be a fool to put herself in the middle of the murder of a white man. Put herself within a mile of that slave shack and next thing she knew, the judges, the cops, the prosecutors—they'd all have the cane knife in her hand.

A clay jar of sour mash sat on the floor next to a bed that was a tangle of messed sheets. She leaned over to pick it up and lost her balance, lurching and nearly falling into the bed. He wrapped his arm around her waist, steadying her, and she sagged against him. She was wearing an old pink satin wrapper that had lost its belt, and beneath that nothing but a thin cotton slip. He could feel the burning heat of her skin where she pressed against his side.

"He's dead, Day," she said. "Mr. Charlie's dead."

"I know, honey. Let's get you up on deck where there's some air."

She pulled away from him, trying to walk there on her own and not doing all that good a job of it. She was a little swacked on whiskey and marijuana, but he thought it was more than that. She walked as if she were trying to hold all the broken pieces of herself together.

He settled her in a chair and went back inside. He opened a window and threw the ant-encrusted bowl out into the bayou. On a shelf above the sink, he noticed, was a small packet of coarse yellow powder, the kind you would get from some voodooienne, and next to it three owl feathers bound up together with a string of moss.

He knew what that particular charm was for; he'd seen it often enough the summer he was nineteen and having sex with Remy Lelourie every chance he got. It was supposed to keep a baby from coming.

He went looking for LeRoy's harmonica, found it, and slipped it in his pocket. He rinsed out a couple of tin cups, fetched the jug of sour mash, and joined her up on deck. They sat side by side in ladder-back chairs, leaning against the bulkhead. Gold and scarlet four-o'clocks were opening in the shade along the banks. One of the boys on the bridge had hooked into his supper.

The booze was harsh and potent and it sang through his blood like a strummed guitar. He let it do its work on the both of them awhile before he spoke. "Did Charlie St. Claire ever have you meet him in that old slave shack out in back of his place?"

Her chest rose and fell in a nearly soundless sigh. "You back to harpin' on that? I done tol' you how I spent last night right here on this boat. I bet you be wearin' that po-liceman's badge of yours even when you take a girl to bed. What you do with it—pin it to your thing?"

He took the harmonica out of his pocket and held it cradled in his hand. "Talk to me, Luce. And then I'll play for you."

"Oh, Lawd God," she said on a tired and ragged laugh. "Like that's supposed to make me want to put my neck in the white man's noose." She leaned over, bracing her elbows on her thighs, and pushed her fingers through her tangled hair. "All right . . . sometimes, yeah, he had me come out to the shack. But not last night. I didn't go near that man last night."

"But when you did go was his wife there, up in the big house?"

Her rounded shoulders lifted in a little shrug. "I wouldn't know from that."

"Did he have another girl on the side lately, besides you?"

She dropped her hands, letting them dangle loosely between

her spread legs. She watched a doodlebug dance over the water, and after a while she said, "Couple months back maybe he was makin' it with somebody else. I don't know who, 'cept I think she was white, 'cause he be sayin' things, then, like how I was still his best lay and the blackberry always got the sweetest juice." Her mouth hardened, making her look older than her twenty-four years. "He liked sayin' stuff like that, knowin' how it would make me feel. You would swear he was born from stone, was Charlie St. Claire."

The boat rocked a little on the shifting current, releasing the pungent smell of rotting algae. The constant drone of the insects in the saw grass grew suddenly louder.

"They goin' to say I did it. That what you here for, ain't it? You here 'cause they sayin' it must be his colored whore who killed him."

Rourke looked down at the harmonica in his hand. He rubbed his thumb up and down the mouthpiece, up and down. Behind them a fish jumped at a fly, splashing, but neither of them turned to look. "The best thing you can do for yourself, Luce," he finally said, "is to tell the truth."

"Hunh. There's what happened and then there's what the white man want to say done happened. Which one of them truths you think goin' to keep me outta jail?"

She raised her head, letting him watch the tears form in her eyes and fall, following a pair of tracks over the bones of her face, falling, leaving wet spots on her pink wrapper. "You think I wanted to be lettin' him do to me like he done? Gettin' down on my knees to suck his thing, spreadin' my legs so's he can stick it in me. But he promised me, don't you know? He promised that if I gave him what he wanted, he'd make it so's they got to give LeRoy another trial—two years he been promisin' me that. Mr. Charlie might've been usin' me like a whore, but he been the only hope me and LeRoy got. What I goin' to do now that he gone? What I goin' to do?"

He reached up and slipped his hand beneath her hair to cup her neck. She was trembling now with what she was trying to hold deep inside herself. "Shhh, hush, now. It'll be okay."

"I swear before Jesus, I di'n't go near that shack last night."

"It'll be okay."

She made a small snuffling sound, like a child, and smeared the tears off her cheeks with the pads of her fingers. "We're growing old apart, me an' LeRoy. Him up there in Angola and me down here, doin' things that make my mama cry and the Lord want to turn his face away from me. Every night 'fore I go to sleep I ask the Lord what it was we done to deserve what happened. Why it was the white man had to come along and lock him away for somethin' he never do. Fifty years. Might's well kill him. Might's well kill us both."

He let go of her neck, but she grabbed his wrist before he could pull back, and he felt her desperation in the way her fingers bit deep into his flesh. She took his hand and brought it down, pressing his palm onto the bare skin of her breast where it swelled above her slip.

"I'ma not a whore," she said.

"I know."

"But I do what I got to do." She shifted in her chair, letting her legs fall wide apart and the slip ride high up her thighs, letting her mouth turn soft and inviting. "I would suck your thing, Day. If that's what it took."

He couldn't stop the shudder that went through him. A part of him had always wanted her, even though he'd always known it could never be more than just a wanting. It wasn't only that LeRoy Washington was his friend and she was LeRoy's wife. He was white and a cop, and that gave him a power over her that he would never use.

Gently, he pulled his hand free from her grasp, and then he leaned forward and took her mouth in a soft, slow kiss.

He didn't touch her anywhere else, just on the mouth. He ended the kiss gently, lingering for a heartbeat before he pulled away. "You're free from all that now, Luce. You're free of him."

She tried to laugh, although it came out broken. "Free. Yeah, I'm free of him, sure 'nough. Meanwhile my man's hoein' cane up in Angola, and he ain't never goin' to be free again." Her smile, slow and sad, came to him from out of the day's dying moments. "Sounds like the words to some low-down blues, don't it?"

He smiled back at her, loving her. In a way he had always loved her. "So sing it for me, Luce."

She sang, a song with long drawn-out notes in it, a dark song that came from deep down in her. A raw and rugged song with echoes of field hollers, of slaves picking cotton and cutting cane. A song about bad luck and prison and loving a man who wasn't there.

The sun set, and the sweat that had come from the hot summer and hot desires glazed and dried on his skin. The sun set and left a pink light to linger for a while, caught up in the tops of the cypress trees and in the burned copper curls of her hair. The sun set while Lucille Durand tore open her heart, and her voice bled blue.

When the last of the sun was finally gone the fireflies came out, and it seemed thousands of tiny, twinkling stars had fallen out of the sky. Kerosene lanterns lit up on the nearby houseboats, and soft voices called to each other across the water. He put LeRoy's harmonica to his mouth and played her song back to her, until the song became his, coming from his own dark and deep places and shaking loose the loneliness inside him.

Playing the blues was a lot like loving a woman: They both wound up taking something from you that you didn't know you had, and it hurt every damn time. It hurt so good.

Chapter Nine

Lucille Durand spent a good part of her growing-up years living in a shack held together by tar paper and chicken wire on a muddy road called Pailet Lane. Her mama washed clothes for a living, and her daddy was gone. But then a lot of the kids who lived on Pailet Lane had daddies who were gone. Gone up north to get a job. Gone upriver to do a jolt in Angola. Gone home to Jesus in heaven. Gone.

So it was just the two of them living in that shack on Pailet Lane, just Lucille and her mama. Mama would get up at dawn and take the streetcar uptown to where the white folks lived, and she'd wash their clothes for them out in their backyards in a big tin tub over a little coal furnace for seventy-five cents a day, plus car fare and dinner. They were poor but Lucille didn't know it, because everybody was poor on Pailet Lane.

A lot of her mama's people lived in the neighborhood, so there was always someone around to look after Lucille and plenty of cousins for her to play with. The other girls didn't like her much, but Mama said that was just because they were jealous of her being so smart and pretty and all. The boys teased and pulled her pigtails. They chased her all over the yard, even though when they caught her they didn't know what to do with her, except for Jimmie Moe Jones, who one day tried to pull down her drawers.

Lucille kicked Jimmie Moe Jones in the shin and then she ran off to tell on him to his mama. All the aunts and mamas were at Aunt Josie's that day. They were shelling pecans to bake into pies for the church bazaar and picking what gigs they were going to play in the lottery.

Aunt Josie's sister-in-law, who was visiting from over in Mobile and knew how to read, had brought a dream book along with her. The ladies were all recounting what dreams they'd had lately, and Miss Celestine was looking them up in her book to see which three lucky numbers their dreams were telling them to play. Lucille's mama only ever played the washerwoman's gig—four, eleven, forty-four—and even though those numbers hadn't come up yet, Lucille figured it was only a matter of time. So she wasn't putting much stock into any dream book; she was waiting politely just within the kitchen door for Miss Celestine to stop and take a breath so she could get her tattling in.

Then she realized Miss Celestine wasn't talking anymore about dreams or the numbers, but had gone on to something else entirely, and that something was Lucille herself.

"Wasn't that Augusta's girl I seen playin' out in the yard? Land, she sure is comin' up light."

Aunt Josie dumped a handful of shelled pecans into a tin bowl and dusted off her palms. "Mmmmm-huh, she sure is. But then blood do tell."

"That it do, sister, that it do. Why, with color like she got she might could pass, if it wasn't for that nose and mouf. She got the kinky hair, too, but that can always be straightened. Pity she got that nose and mouf."

Aunt Josie picked up one of those paper fans that come from a funeral home and stirred the air in front of her face, then she said the words that ended all discussion and argument and answered all of life's mysteries on Pailet Lane: "Ain't that the way it is."

The other ladies all nodded and hummed their agreement. "Mmmmm-huh. Mmmmm-huh."

Ain't that the way it is. About the only sentence Lucille had ever heard more coming out of the mouths of the mamas and aunts was "Don't sit like that."

She went back out into the yard and held her bare arms up to the sunshine. They were the color of the café au lait Mama gave her in the mornings, just a little bit of chicory coffee and lots of boiled milk, and she hadn't noticed before that of all the black and brown arms on Pailet Lane, hers was the lightest of all. Well, she'd noticed, but it hadn't meant anything, only now she felt proud and special. I'm comin' up light, she said to herself. Blood do tell.

It was a few years later, though, when she was old enough to ride the streetcar by herself, that a thing happened that should have been no more than a glancing blow to her thoughts, and yet in that one moment she understood at last exactly what her Aunt Josie had been talking about when she'd said how blood do tell.

Lucille got on the streetcar and kept to the very back, standing like a sailor on a pitching deck with the way the floor swayed and rattled beneath her feet. It was easy to remember where she was supposed to sit, for there was a screen—a board a couple of feet long and a few inches high—that fit into slots in the backs of the benches, and separated the colored from the whites-only seats.

She sat in the second seat behind the screen, on the left, because the prettiest houses, she thought, were on that side of the street. She clutched the seven cents for her fare in a sweaty hand. She was excited, but also a little scared to be out on her own like this. But she was ten years old now, not a little girl anymore, and she was determined to do her mama proud.

In the seat in front of her sat a large Negro woman with coal black skin. The woman was wearing a big straw hat whose brim was loaded with a gardenful of straw daisies, and she and her hat took up so much space that Lucille kept having to stick her head out in the aisle to see if the conductor was coming along to collect the fares. So she was glad when the woman reached up and pressed the button and got off at the next stop.

Lucille hadn't noticed the white man who had got on until he was almost on top of her, and then she realized that all the other seats in the car were filled, except for a colored seat—the one where the woman with the daisy hat had been sitting. But the white man simply set down his string bag of groceries, lifted the screen and moved it back a bench, dropping it into a new set of slots with a loud *click*, and then he sat in the empty seat. Right in front of Lucille the white man sat.

She stared over the screen at the back of the man's neck and tried to puzzle out the sense of it. How could it be that with such a simple act the seat had changed from being for coloreds to white persons only? The wooden slats of the bench would still be warm from the Negro woman's body. On the brass armrest by the window, where her hand with its black skin had rested, his white hand now lay. What would happen, Lucille thought, if someone came along and moved the screen from in front of her to behind her? Suddenly she would be sitting in a white person's seat. She could be sent to jail for it, and her mama would never know what had become of her. The motorman would stop the car, the conductor would point her out to the police, and she would disappear. That happened to people from Pailet Lane sometimes; they came up against some trouble in the white man's world and they disappeared.

Lucille looked down at her hands, which were gripped into a fist in her lap. Her hands that were a spoonful or two of chicory coffee darker than that white man's hands, that white man who was sitting on the other side of the screen, in the seat in front of hers.

I'm comin' up light, she said to herself. Only this time the words were frightening to her, menacing somehow, and that was when it clicked in her mind, just as the streetcar screen had clicked into place, magically changing a seat from colored to white. *He* was white. The daddy her mama never would talk about except to say he was gone was a white man, and that was where he'd gone sure enough. Gone back to the whites-only world he had come from, once he was done with her mama.

The summer Lucille turned thirteen a thing happened that was as surprising and wondrous as winning the lottery with the washerwoman's gig would ever have been. Mama got hired on as a live-in housekeeper for a white woman who lived on Conti Street in the Faubourg Tremé.

Conti Street in those days was right smack in the middle of Storyville, that part of New Orleans the law had set aside for a time as the place where strumpets and their fancy men and madams would have the legal right to go about the making of their scandalous living. The white woman herself had led a most scandalous life. She had deserted her husband and children so that she could live with her lover.

Mama had been washing clothes for the white woman for years, since before Lucille herself was even born. The first Lucille saw of her, though, was that day she and Mama came to live in her house. "You come on into the front parlor and say hey to Mrs. Rourke," Mama said, puffing up the sleeves to Lucille's new white dress and tightening the sash. "But, mind, you stay out of that room otherwise, 'less you invited. An' don't you be forgettin' your manners while we in this house."

For this, their first day in their new life, Mama had put on a long white apron that covered her from her toes to the top of her generous bosom and was so stiff with starch it crackled every time she drew a breath. Mama was of a size that was always impressive, but in that apron she looked like a ferry boat steaming up the Mississippi. That morning when she got dressed, along with the apron, she had also put on a red *tignon*, wrapping the scarf around her head until all her hair and the tops of her ears were covered. Once long ago, during the slavery days, there had been a law, the *tignon* law, which said free women of color were only allowed to wear a simple madras handkerchief on their heads rather than the plumes and glittering jewelry they'd preferred—as if such a proclamation was all it would take to stifle their charms. So when Mama put on her red *tignon*, she was making a proclamation of her own.

Mama's response, whenever Lucille complained about the unfairness of life, was to say, "You just forget 'bout that, 'cause ain't nothin' you can do 'bout it." Yet whenever Augusta Durand wrapped her red *tignon* around her head and sailed forth into the unfair world, she was proclaiming: "Might be nothin' I can do 'bout it, but I still got my dignity. I got my pride."

Oddly, *pride* was also the word that came to Lucille's mind as she looked out from beneath her eyelashes at the white woman who sat in the tall, wing-backed chair. She was dressed in mourning black and her face was drawn with grief, but then Mama had said that her lover had died some few weeks before. For all her air of grave sadness, a proud and wary defiance burned in her eyes. It was the defiance of a woman who had lived her life to her own set of rules and suffered for it.

Lucille stood in utter stillness before the white woman's gaze. When the woman spoke, her voice, like her face, was etched with grief. "You've raised a fine girl, Augusta."

At a sharp jab in her ribs from Mama, Lucille curtseyed again. "Thank you, ma'am," she mumbled to the roses on the carpet.

Mama led her from the parlor after that, even though Lucille had wanted to take a closer look at the gilded mirrors and marble-top tables, at the giant vases filled with palms and aspidistra, and the whatnot in the corner with its collection of china ballerinas. She knew white people didn't like Negroes who gaped, so she was careful to keep her eyes on her freshly blackened shoes as they followed Mama out the door.

She ran into the white woman later that day, though, ran smack into her as she was coming out of her new bedroom, full up to bursting with the excitement of having seen the bed she would sleep in, the bed with its spooled headboard and soft white sheets. The woman caught her, steadied them both actually, by wrapping her arms around Lucille's back so that Lucille's face was pressed into her black shirtwaist that smelled of the Octagon bar soap Mama had washed it with.

For a moment the white woman's hands gripped Lucille so tightly that Lucille could feel her fingers pressing into her flesh. "Do you like your room, Lucille?" she asked as she let her go.

Lucille curtseyed. "Yes, ma'am." She dropped her gaze to the floorboards and tried to sidle on past, into the safety of the kitchen, but the woman stopped her with but the cool, careful pronunciation of her name.

"Lucille."

Slowly, reluctantly, Lucille lifted her head. A smile came and went across the woman's face, making her look younger. "If you curtsey every time our paths cross, your poor knees are liable to just wear out on you."

"Yes, ma'am," Lucille said, and nearly curtseyed again.

"And you will call me Miss Maeve. Please."

"Yes, ma—Miss Maeve," Lucille said, and she wondered how they would ever manage to get on, the three of them in this house.

Slowly, though, the awkwardness of the first days eased into the strained familiarity that came when people shared portions of their lives but lived in different worlds. Miss Maeve barely spoke except to give Mama instructions on the shopping and the chores, although her instructions were couched in the politest of phrases. They took their meals separately, of course: Miss Maeve alone in the dining room, at the long and well-polished walnut table; Mama and Lucille at the oak table in the kitchen. When Miss Maeve wanted to speak with Mama, she pressed a button in the floor or rang a bell and Mama would go to where she had been summoned. Lucille never went anywhere beyond the kitchen and her and Mama's bedrooms.

One morning, though, Miss Maeve came into the kitchen to drop off a list of things she wanted fetched at the market and she lingered awhile, and Mama asked her if she wanted a cup of coffee and so Miss Maeve sat at the oak table and drank a cup of coffee while Mama washed the breakfast dishes and they talked about nothing in particular. Only after that it somehow came about that Miss Maeve was spending hours in the kitchen with Mama and even helping with the cooking sometimes. Then one strange day Mama was asked to join Miss Maeve for tea in the parlor, and after that it became a daily ritual they shared, even though they never once shared a meal at the long and shining walnut table.

One time Lucille came upon them in the kitchen, Miss Maeve with a bowl of beans in her lap that she was snapping, and Mama at the sink making clabber, and Mama telling a story about some scandalous goings-on down on Pailet Lane that had Miss Maeve laughing so hard she was nearly choking with it. Another time Lucille looked out her bedroom window and saw Mama and Miss Maeve down in the courtyard, and Miss Maeve seemed to be crying hard over something, for her shoulders were hunched and heaving, and then she turned and went into Mama's arms and Mama held her and patted her back, and although Lucille couldn't hear her words she knew they were soothing by the way Miss Maeve was taking comfort.

It was a strange accommodation the two women achieved, and like so much else in New Orleans it was a thing full of illusions. Somehow Mama and Miss Maeve had invented and defined their own rules, and those rules had managed to give them each what they wanted without destroying the conventions of their separate worlds. Perhaps two other women could not have done it, but Mama and Miss Maeve, so different in so many vital ways, were alike in their obstinacy. Once they both set their minds on a certain path they stayed there, come rain or shine or Jesus.

It occurred to Lucille one day that Miss Maeve was lonely, and Mama had become her friend in every sense of the word but the most public one. She was too much a lady ever to consort with the neighborhood's riffraff, but no respectable woman had had a thing to say to her in years. When her lover had been alive and living with her in this house, he had been enough. But then her man had died and left her alone.

It was the kind of aloneness the mamas and aunts on Pailet Lane would all have understood. The kind of aloneness that could come into your house even when it was full of squabbling relatives and hungry babies. The kind of aloneness that came over a woman after her man had gone.

Lucille went through an awkward stage where she grew up but not out, and was all elbows and knees and feelings. Then it seemed all in one summer she turned sixteen, grew hips and a bosom, and fell head over heels into her first mad crush.

Miss Maeve had two sons by the husband she had left all those years before. The elder, Mr. Paul, was in the seminary and about to be ordained a priest. The younger, Mr. Day, had joined the New Orleans police force not so long ago. He was six years older than Lucille, he'd been a flying ace during the Great War, and he was all man compared to the silly boys she knew.

Neither of Miss Maeve's sons had ever lived with her in the house on Conti Street, but Mr. Day had visited from time to time after her lover had passed, and more often since he'd come home from the war. Lucille was not so foolish as to fancy that he came calling to see her, but he did seem to enjoy her company. Whenever he saw her he would always pause to talk awhile. He would ask about her friends and school, and tease her a little, and her heart would be pounding so hard she was surprised he couldn't hear it.

Although Mama no longer washed clothes for a living, Monday was still washday, and the linens and towels in the house on Conti Street still needed doing. It was a chore Mama had gladly given over to Lucille, while she stayed in the kitchen and cooked red beans and rice for supper.

Even in the early hours of the morning, that Monday was a scorcher, and the charcoal brazier that burned in the back of the courtyard sent more heat waves floating into the air. On top of the brazier an old copper tub boiled and bubbled, and Lucille had been stirring the laundry with a long, soggy wooden pole until her arms had grown tired. She had taken off her straw hat to fan air in her face when she caught a movement out of the corner of her eye.

He was lounging in the open carriageway to catch the little bit of breeze that was blowing off the river. He was wearing his policeman's blue uniform, but he'd taken off his own hat, and his hair was like warm honey in the sun.

She knew he had seen her, had been watching the way her hips moved as she stirred the wash, but she pretended to be oblivious to him. She arched her back and stretched high, thrusting her breasts into the air. She held the pose a moment, then slowly turned. She made her eyes go wide and brought a splayed hand up to her chest.

"Lawd God, Mr. Day. You almost scared me outta my skin."

He smiled at her, knowing her for a liar and a tease but too sweet to say so. He had the most ravishing smile she'd ever seen on a body, man or woman.

It didn't matter either whether he saw through her, because she got what she wanted. He pushed himself off the wall and joined her out in the courtyard. He was tall and he had a sauntering way of walking that caught a girl's eye, like a lazy cat on a hot day.

He came all the way up to her, so close she could see the golden stubble of his beard and the weariness of the night beat in his eyes. His eyes were bluer than his uniform.

"Hey, Luce," he said. "Can I help you hang up these wet things?"

She laughed, pleased with herself, and handed him the sack of wooden pins. She swung the wicker basket full of washed linens up on her hip and led the way over to where the clothes poles had been thrust into the soft dirt at the edge of the flower bed.

She took a pillowcase out of the basket and shook it, sending drops splattering onto the paving stones, and the small space between them was filled suddenly with the smell of cooling dust.

She slanted a look up at him. The brass buttons on his uniform and his Crescent City policeman's badge outshone the sun but not his hair. She thought he could probably tell plain as day how she admired him, but she didn't care. "You sure lookin' almighty pleased this mornin'," she said. "Did you nab yo'self a big bad gangster, Mr. Po-liceman?"

"Not hardly. I spent the night calling 'round to all the gammies and pimps, collecting the precinct captain's bag money."

"Ain't that the way it is."

She'd said the words, Pailet Lane words, without thought, but she saw how now his mouth had tightened and his eyes had darkened as if he suffered from some inner shame. She had noticed that about him before, that he was not only unhappy with the world the way it was, but he seemed to blame himself for all its failings.

He looked as though he needed touching and she wanted to touch him, and so she laid her hand on his arm. "It's not like everybody else don' do it."

His arm tensed beneath hers, but he smiled. "Sure, I know that. My daddy was the kind of cop who drank up what the city paid him. My brother and I would've starved if our old man hadn't been on a pad."

He took the pillowcase out of her hands and turned to hang it on the line, averting his face and allowing her the pleasure of looking at him.

His skin was tanned from the sun but oddly translucent still, even for a white man. When he was younger it had flushed easily, but he had gotten better at hiding his feelings. There was a hardness to his mouth and a tenseness around his eyes that hadn't been there before the war. She had overheard Miss Maeve telling Mama that he had gone off to fight in the war because the girl he'd been in love with had run off and left him with a broken heart. Mama said men suffered through a broken heart worse than women did. Mama said that a man's heart broke the way a seasoned hickory stick did, slow and hard and with a noise like a scream.

Lucille took another pillowcase out of the basket, shook it out, and went to throw it over the line, deliberately losing her balance so that she stumbled into him, and his arms came around her, to steady her, but holding her tighter, surely, than they needed to. She tilted her head back and looked up at him, looked into his eyes, and slowly, so slowly she thought she'd faint for lack of breath, his head dipped until his lips were touching hers.

His lips touched hers only for a moment before his arms fell open and he took a single step back, away from her.

She put her fingers to his mouth, stopping his words before he could even think to say them. "Don't you be sorry for somethin' I wanted."

He took her hand by the wrist and pushed it back down to her side, although he gave it a gentle squeeze before he let it go. "Your mama would chase me out of here with a broom if she caught me kissing you like that."

"I liked it, though, Mr. Day. I liked it a lot."

"I liked it too," he said, and then gave her one of his ravishing smiles.

But although he helped her finish hanging up the wet linens, he didn't kiss her again, and he left soon as they were done. Lucille picked up the empty wicker basket and took it to the house, walking through the kitchen door and right into the flat of Mama's hand as it struck her hard across her face.

The blow sent her staggering into the coal box and brought tears to her eyes. Less from the pain than from the shock of it— Mama had never raised a hand to her before in her life.

Lucille brought the back of her own hand up to her throbbing mouth. "What you do that for?"

Mama pointed a stiff finger at the window with its cheerful daisy-print curtains that overlooked the courtyard. "For the way you behavin' with Mr. Day out there—pushin' your bosom up in the air, wrigglin' your bottom like some two-bit who'. Small blessin' alls he did was kiss you."

Lucille touched her mouth again and then looked at the back of her hand as if she expected to see blood there. "If you was spyin' on us then I guess you saw how it wasn't much of a kiss. We only bein' friendly."

Mama slammed her hand on top of the icebox so hard the dishes in the safe above it rattled. "Don't give me none of that. I seen the way you been makin' moon eyes at him all this summer, and sure 'nough I knew that soon as he opened up his own eyes and got to noticin', there was goin' to be trouble."

"You mean the sort of trouble that happened 'tween you and my daddy?"

Mama's face turned gray beneath her color, and for a moment she actually swayed on her feet as if she would faint. Then she seemed to gather herself, pulling in a deep breath and drawing herself up tall. It was only a different version of the same question Lucille had been asking all her life, and she knew she wasn't going to be given any answers this time either.

"You save yo'self for some nice colored boy," Mama said instead, "and don't you be messin' with the white mens. They only break yo' heart."

"But what about my nose and mouth, Mama? Colored boys want colored girls who look white. What if your nice colored boy don't like my nigger nose and mouth?"

"Aw, Lucille, honey," Mama said then, and enveloped her in her arms. "You such a pretty chil', you know that. But you leave Mr. Day alone. You do that for yo' Mama. You save yo' heart for some nice colored boy."

She pressed her face into Mama's neck, breathing deep the sweet talcum smell of her girlhood, but she was a woman grown now, and so she soon pulled free of the arms that held her.

"Come on, honey," Mama said, and Lucille saw the sheen of tears held back in her eyes. "Sit yo'self down at the table and let me heat you up a bowl of my stewed shrimps."

"I ain't hungry," Lucille said, and she walked out of the kitchen, knowing nothing could have hurt her mama more than not to eat her food.

The colored boy who was to end up with Lucille Durand's heart came into her life a bare month later, and he was not to Mama's liking at all.

She was feeling alone and lonesome the first time she saw him, at a Sunday afternoon dance in a small park called Congo Square. A hundred years before, the city slaves used to gather in the park on Sunday afternoons to dance the calinda and the bamboula to the rattle of beef bones and the beat of bamboo drums. On this day the music was New Orleans tin-panny. Someone had brought a piano outside on a wagon bed and was playing ragtime, and later, rival jazz bands were going to have a bucking contest to see who could produce the best boogie-woogie.

He caught her eye because of the way he was strutting through the crowd and the sycamore trees, strutting like he owned the world and everything in it. She didn't want to admire such a turkey cock, although she had to admit he did look so fine in that white suit and black shirt. His face seemed chiseled out of ebony. His skin was so black it glinted blue in the sunlight.

She thought she'd lost sight of him when, next she knew, he

had grasped her around the waist and was whirling her out among the dancers. "You lookin' at LeRoy Washington, girl," he said, as if she ought to have heard of him, and the truth was she had. He was a club boxer who was already starting to make a name for himself in New Orleans. He fought for an exorbitant five dollars a night—as much as most Negroes could make in a week.

"LeRoy who?" she said.

His teeth were pure white, and he'd had gold rims put around the two front ones, so that they flashed when he smiled.

That first night he took her out to his houseboat on the Bayou St. John and laid her down on his bed and showed her how a man made love to a woman he wanted, hard and rough and hungry. He was the first man to have her, and she knew from that moment she would want no other.

Afterward, in the silver glow of moonlight, she ran her hands over the veins and arteries of his arms where they flowed in ridges just beneath his beautiful dark skin. He had muscles like black iron.

He scared her, though, because he didn't think like anyone she knew. His thoughts were the way he dressed: flashy. He was prideful and he had a streak of the rebel in him and he always spoke his mind, and that was dangerous for a Negro. The white man wanted him to speak only when spoken to, and to look away with humility.

Once they went for a walk through the zoo in Audubon Park, and she got a stone in her shoe. But she couldn't sit on one of the benches to take it off because they were for whites only, and that made her think of that day in the streetcar and the moving screen that could magically change the color of things, and she said, "I could maybe get by with usin' that bench for a minute if you wasn't with me. Light as I am an' with it comin' on to dusk."

They had been walking side by side, with one of his arms wrapped around her waist, but he pushed away from her now with such violence she stumbled a little. "Don't you give me none of that high-yeller shit," he said. He wasn't shouting, but she'd never heard a voice so hard. "You just as much nigger as me, girl. You think you a step closer to heaven 'cause you got some white massa's blood in you?"

She turned away from him so that he wouldn't see the tears that had welled in her eyes over the love she felt for him that was so wonderful and so terrible that to lose him now would be to cease to exist.

"You say that like I should be shamed," she said, so softly she didn't think he'd heard her until his hands came down gently onto her shoulders.

"Come here, baby." He turned her around and gathered her into his chest. "It ain't the nigger in us we should be shamed of, it's what we let them do to us. 'Slong as we fetch an' shuffle an' say, 'Yes massa, no massa, three bags full, massa,' 'slong as we believe the white man's shuck about how we somehow less *human* than they are, then we deserve ever'thing they do to us."

She kept her face buried in his chest and her thoughts to herself. You can't change the world, though, was what she was thinking. You just forget 'bout that, 'cause ain't nothin' you can do 'bout it.

The day came when Lucille knew she would have to take him home to meet Mama, and that scared her more than anything she had ever had to face. One of her cousins had married a black-skinned boy, and the girl's family had had nothing to say to her or her husband since. Lucille didn't want to have to choose between Mama and her man.

She asked him to Sunday dinner at the house on Conti Street, and Mama fixed a chicken in his honor. They ate at the round oak table in the kitchen, and Lucille watched the resistance settle over her mama's face as she took in the size and blackness of him, and his nappy hair.

Mama asked him all sorts of questions about what he did for a living and who his people were, where they came from. The more Mama poked and prodded, the surlier his mouth got, and no sooner had he left through the door than Mama declared him an "uppity nigger," which was the worst condemnation she knew.

Lucille gathered up the dishes in silence and took them to the sink, but Mama wasn't going to let it alone.

"You light-complected and light-eyed, and you come from good stock, girl. You don' want to be throwin' yo'self away on just any-old-body."

Lucille thought about asking Mama what stock her daddy had come from, what stock had given her her light complexion and light eyes, but she knew it would be no use. It didn't matter anyway, because she knew what she wanted and his name was LeRoy Washington, although she thought that if she tried to figure out why she wanted him so much she would never be able to do it.

Later that evening LeRoy came back to the house and took her out for a date, to the Sunday dance again at Congo Square. He still strutted through the crowd, but this time she was on his arm, and she felt proud and happy and in love. He stopped beneath a sycamore tree and gave her a kiss so sweet and deep it turned her inside out.

He nuzzled her neck, pressing his lips to the place where her pulse beat. "You want some jelly, baby? That what you want? Say yes."

"Yes."

He laughed and slipped his arm around her waist and they left the dance no sooner than they'd got there, heading for his houseboat and his bed. They walked down Villere to catch the streetcar, too wrapped up in each other to notice how the road had become deserted, except for a gang of mulatto men who seemed to have come at them from out of nowhere and had them surrounded before she could even draw breath to scream.

There were five of them. Shrimpers by the look and the smell of them, and they were so drunk they breathed whiskey fumes.

She could get a good look at only two of them. The one had a head the size of a watermelon and dull, stony eyes. The other, who was smiling, had turquoise eyes and was the color of old brick. He pursed his lips at her and made a wet, smacking noise.

For a moment all was strangely still and quiet. The hot packed dirt beneath her feet smelled of oil and rust. She thought she could hear a banjo playing, but it seemed a long way away.

Then the man with the turquoise eyes grabbed at his crotch, pumping his hips, and laughed, and his laughter hit her like a hard fist. "What's a peola piece a ass like you doin' steppin' out with this big black nigger?"

"LeRoy," she tried to say beneath a breath that wasn't there. "Don't fight them."

"Honey, I don't think they givin' me much choice."

The shrimper laughed again. "Got to teach you to keep your nigger hands off our women, boy. Uh-huh."

"Run!" LeRoy shouted, thrusting her away from him just as he was enveloped in a flurry of fists.

The force of LeRoy's push carried her as far as the banquette, where she tripped over the curb and went sprawling. The scream that had been lodged in her throat since the shrimpers had come upon them popped out of its own accord.

Her scream brought LeRoy spinning around to look at her just as one of the shrimpers took a swing with a fence slat like it was a baseball bat, smacking LeRoy square across his face. He toppled onto his knees, swaying, blood from a long cut on his forehead running in streams over his eyes. He tried to raise his fists in the classic boxer's stance and get back onto his feet, but they were kicking him now, five sets of hobnailed boots, and from every direction.

"LeRoy!" she screamed, and tried to crawl to him on her hands and knees.

A man came running around the corner, yelling and swinging a long, double-linked chain above his head. At first she thought it was a white man come to join the shrimpers in their nigger-knocking, but then his hat flew off and she caught the yellow flash of his hair.

LeRoy had fought as if he'd been in the prize ring, but Mr. Day was doing it dirty. He had one end of the chain wrapped around his fist and he was going for their eyes. One shrimper's face erupted into blood, and the man screamed and reeled away. Another got a kick between his legs that had him on his knees vomiting up the sour mash he'd been drinking all day. When a third went out cold after the chain clipped him hard behind his ear, the last two took off running, scattering gravel behind them like birdshot.

Lucille felt a strong hand pull her up by the arm. "You all right, Luce honey?"

She nodded, her breath sobbing in her throat. "LeRoy?"

"He's okay. Just dazed. Come on, let's get out of here in case they have friends."

They half carried LeRoy between them, limping their way to the neutral ground on Esplanade Avenue. They leaned LeRoy up against the trunk of a palm tree, while he glared at Mr. Day through his swollen eyes.

"Where the hell you come from?" he said.

Lucille figured she didn't have to introduce them, even if she could find the breath for it. They had met each other in passing twice at the Conti Street house, and both times a pair of alley cats would have behaved friendlier.

"I was parking my bike 'round the block," Mr. Day was saying, "when I heard all the commotion." He had carefully unwrapped the chain from around his fist and now he was sliding the heavy links back and forth in his hands and staring at it with a perplexed look on his face. His knuckles were bruised and bloody. "Shit. I got the blasted thing off, but now how do I get it back on?"

LeRoy pushed himself off the tree. He swayed back and forth on his feet. "I never asked for no help from no white cop."

Mr. Day was still breathing so hard his throat sang, but he was able to convey utter disdain with the lifting of one eyebrow. "I beg your pardon. I guess I didn't notice how you were winning the argument."

"Well, it's won. So you can just be moseyin' along now."

Mr. Day spat a wad of blood into the grass. "I was going to the boogie-woogie contest, but my mouth's all busted up, thanks to y'all. How'm I supposed to play my sax with a busted mouth?"

LeRoy hawked a laugh and spat his own wad of blood. "Prob'ly with the same kinda finesse you showed fighting."

"Finesse? And this criticism is coming from the man who couldn't last one round with Catfish Pruitte when he was having a bad day."

"Hunh." LeRoy tried to look mortally insulted, but the truth was the only fight he'd ever lost had been to the Cajun mulatto, and Catfish had beaten him hollow. "I could whip yo' white ass on one of my *worst* days and not break a sweat."

"You think so."

"I know so."

Mr. Day smiled and shook his head, and let fly with a left jab to LeRoy's mouth that sent blood and spittle spraying into the air.

The surprise punch didn't knock LeRoy to the ground, but it sent him staggering. It was like a fight between a pair of junkyard dogs after that, and it lasted about as long. They ended up kneeling in the sun-browned grass of the neutral ground, facing each other and bleeding all over themselves, which served them right. At first she thought they were choking, and then she realized they were laughing.

She didn't know how it came to be that the three of them wound up on LeRoy's houseboat after that, with her frying up a mess of catfish on the stove and the two of them sitting at the table. She kept thinking about those mulatto shrimpers. How they had wanted to beat up LeRoy for stepping out with a light-complexioned girl. She thought how they'd been so full of hate, and she thought how their hatred was probably mostly for the white man, and for their own brown skin and the Negro in their blood, but they couldn't fight the white man or themselves, so they had gone nigger-knocking instead. She thought how the hatred in their eyes had been thick enough to slice up with a cane knife.

She put plates heaping with fish in front of the men, but she couldn't bring herself to sit down with them. Whites and coloreds just didn't sit down to supper together, and yet there they were, doing it. It was the elusive principle of the moving streetcar screen all over again.

They weren't saying anything to each other, the men, only

digging into her catfish and drinking beer from green quart bottles.

When LeRoy was done scraping his plate clean, he leaned back in his chair, patted his belly, and ran his red tongue over his black, swollen lips. "Man, we showed them fuckin' niggers. We busted they fuckin' nigger asses good."

An hour or so after the fight and Lucille was finally getting her breath back. She swatted him on the back of the head. "You watch yo' mouth, LeRoy Washington."

"Ooo-ee! Listen to the righteous girl." He rubbed away the sting and then craned his head around to grin at her. "You think we married the way she carries on."

"I think you ought to be," Mr. Day said with a face set serious and in a tone she couldn't put a name to except she thought it would surely send LeRoy up onto his high horse again.

Instead, the two men shared a slow smile, and the smile was like a handshake. Or a promise.

Mr. Day didn't play his saxophone that night because his mouth was too sore and swollen, but he came back other nights, bringing his horn along with buckets of fried shrimp and cartons of dirty rice. As fireflies sparkled in the black-green trees and the bream popped in the bayou's dark waters, he and LeRoy would drink wine out of mason jars and pass a reefer back and forth. After a while he would play for them, and pain would be in every deep, crying note. It was as if he had taken out of her own life all the misery and confusion, all the wrongs she'd done and all the wrong done unto her, and put it into his music.

"Where a white boy learn to play like that?" LeRoy asked one night, and he told them he'd learned from the Negro musicians who played in the saloons and bawdy houses of Storyville, and from hours of listening to race records. She thought the music must have been in him before that, and when he played he was only traveling back to a place he already knew, a place of hauntings and of longings for things lost or left undone. For a love and a life that should have been, but never was.

LeRoy had a harmonica and sometimes he would blow along. Lucille didn't know how to play anything, but she could sing. It was how she learned to sing the blues.

Chapter Ten

From the New Orleans *Morning Tribune*, late edition, Wednesday, July 13, 1927:

THE SCANDALOUS LIFE AND DEATH
OF CHARLES ST. CLAIRE
By Wylie T. Jones

The pools of blood are mostly dried now, the body has been carried away, yet the mystery of who killed Charles St. Claire remains.

The gruesome and brutal manner of Mr. St. Claire's death is known: seven deep wounds with a cane knife, including the fatal slash to the jugular. But what every man, woman, and child ought to be asking themselves as the sun sets today on the City That Care Forgot is, Why?

The answer to this question is for the police to discover, of course; however one cannot help but wonder if the motive for Charles St. Claire's death does lie in his life. For in only a few short hours, this reporter has been able to uncover some sordid particulars regarding the victim of last night's heinous murder. Please be forewarned, though, that such a licentious way of life does not make for salubrious reading.

Mr. St. Claire's profession was the law, but his practice was to defend the accused in criminal trials, where for the gratification of what even his friends do say was a monumental hubris, he often attempted to turn a case in his favor on legal technicalities or through theatrical antics before gullible juries, thereby bringing about the release of these men and women—hardened criminals in some cases—back into society where they might continue to prey upon other innocent victims. It should also be noted that many of Mr. St. Claire's so-called clients were of the Negro race.

On late, late nights when decent men had long before retired to their beds, Mr. St. Claire could be seen frequenting this city's most notorious speakeasies and participating in lewd acts and drunkenness. His favorite cocktail is said to have been absinthe and cocaine.

Whole families could live for a year off the sums Mr. St. Claire would wager during a single day at the track or in a night at the *bourré* tables.

Indulging in behavior reminiscent of the days of *plaçage* from the last century, Mr. St. Claire is said to have kept a colored mistress in an apartment on Rampart Street, even continuing with the liaison after his marriage last February to famous film star Remy Lelourie.

Such was the life of Charles St. Claire.

One wonders if in his final, horrifying moments, as the cane knife slashed through the tender flesh of his throat and his red blood splattered over the floor and walls of the old slave shack on the grounds of Sans Souci—did Charles St. Claire understand at last that the sins of the flesh are paid for in death?

From the New Orleans *Times-Picayune*, final edition, Wednesday, July 13, 1927:

BODY FOUND IN SWAMP

The body of a man was discovered in the swampland east of New Orleans shortly before dawn this morning. Police say the body appears to have been in the water at least two weeks, and that the cause of death was strangulation with a length of piano wire. The victim has been tentatively identified as Vincent McGinty, age 20 years, a resident of a boardinghouse on Tchoupitoulas Street.

Daman Rourke looked back once from the end of the gangplank. She sat on the deck of her houseboat, almost swallowed up by the falling darkness, and he had never seen anyone look more alone. To see her that way hurt so, he said her name aloud.

"Lucille."

She surprised him by answering, her voice throaty and deep, as if she sang the words. "You go on home now, Mr. Day. I'll be all right."

He walked back to where he'd left the Bearcat on Esplanade, with only the serenade of the tree frogs and the locusts for company, but he didn't go on home. He drove out to the place on the edge of the swamp where last night they had found Vinny McGinty's strangled body.

Smudges of lemon grass and tobacco burned against the mosquitoes in front of Jack's Place, but they seemed to be doing little good against the insects that boiled out of the marsh like clouds of steam. The smoke was even thicker inside, and laced with the smells of muscatel, sweat, and the slab of ribs frying in grease on the grill.

Jack Jackson, who was tending to his own bar, was a tall, ropy man with a head like a cue ball and shrewd, pale yellow eyes that emptied of all thought and feeling as soon as Rourke walked through the door. He did everything short of shuffling his feet as he slipped into the role of trying to satisfy the white man's illusions about the way a colored man was supposed to behave, and he answered Rourke's questions with the care of someone walking through a minefield, aware at every moment how little it would take to make everything blow up in his face.

Not to his surprise, Rourke got nothing useful out of the man at all.

The musicians, the singer, the cootch dancers, the joint's clientele—they all were careful and polite, and they too added nothing new to the tale of Vinny McGinty's sorry death. Sugar wasn't there, and no one seemed to know where she had got to.

Back outside, he walked down to the bayou, but except for a few broken canebrakes and some matted-down saw grass, there was nothing to see. The water was stagnant and smelled of dead garfish, or maybe of dead Vinny McGinty.

You wouldn't have to walk too far out into the swamp, Rourke thought, to find a tub of fermenting potatoes and an alky cooker. It was possible that Vinny had made a play for a piece of Jackson's moonshine business, or maybe he'd come out to collect a vig on a loan. But Rourke didn't seriously believe that any of these people out here had anything to do with the murder of Casey Maguire's errand boy.

He walked back down the lane, past Jack's Place and a watermelon patch, to one of the shacks, where an old woman sat in the dark in a willow rocker on a sagging porch overgrown with purple trumpet vine.

"I know you's out there, Mr. Day," the old woman said in a voice that broke like a boy's. "So you might's well come on up to the house an' say hey an' eat some of my *filé* gumbo."

Rourke crossed a plank board that lay over a stagnant rain ditch coated with mosquitoes. He was met on the way by an old arthritic bluetick dog, who escorted him up onto the shadowed porch.

"Evenin', *Tante* Adenise," he said.

The old woman got to her feet with the help of a bamboo cane, her body unfolding itself slowly like the leaves on a fan. Her bowed legs carried her precariously across the threshold of her open door. "You come on in and take a seat, you."

It smelled good inside, of *boudin* and gumbo and the steam of chicory coffee rising from a pot on the black, four-lid woodstove.

She went to light a lamp, but he stopped her. "Leave it be, *Tante*. There's a sweetness to the dark tonight."

The shack's two small windows had no glass, or even paper, and enough moon- and starlight found their way inside to put a strange silver patina on the furnishings: a black iron bed, a chiffonier with only three legs, a washstand with creosote curtains. A picture of Abraham Lincoln held a place of honor above the knotty pine eating table. Next to the president was tacked a curling photograph of LeRoy Washington in prizefighter's silk trunks and hose, his gloved fists raised in the classic boxer's stance.

When the four Washington boys were growing up, Adenise Treebaut used to say she'd found them one by one out back in her watermelon patch. The boys liked the story, even though they knew they'd really come to her all at once, when her daughter, their mama, had run off to Chicago with a trumpet player and their daddy had died doing a jolt in Angola. Blind since the age of four from a bout with scarlet fever, Adenise had put food in her grandsons' bellies and clothes on their backs by working on her hands and knees at Jack's Place, scrubbing the floors every morning of the nightly leavings of men's lust and drink.

She was proud of the fine, strapping boys she'd raised, but she was proudest of LeRoy. She had thought to see him go so far, as far as the moon she used to say to him. Instead he had gone where his daddy had ended up, to the Louisiana State Penitentiary.

You couldn't prizefight in New Orleans without a club and a sponsor, and LeRoy's had been the Boxing Irish, owned by Casey Maguire. The Boxing Irish had the best training gym in the city, managed by Maguire's little brother, Bobby Joe. There had always been a bit of a thing going on between LeRoy and Bobby Joe Maguire. Bobby Joe thought LeRoy was a prideful nigger who needed a boot on his neck to remind him of his place. What LeRoy thought he had kept quiet about, except that he couldn't keep it from showing in his eyes. One day, money turned up missing out of the gym's petty cash box, and Bobby Joe said LeRoy had taken it.

That night Bobby Joe Maguire was found lying sprawled in the middle of the sparring ring, after someone had wrung his neck like they do with a chicken's. The police came and they arrested LeRoy Washington for the crime, the trial lasted a day, and the judge— known for being both soft-hearted and soft-headed—had given him fifty years instead of the electric chair. It was the only break LeRoy had caught.

Lucille and *Tante* Adenise had always believed in his innocence. Rourke, being a cop, shouldn't have been so certain—for LeRoy Washington was proud and he had a temper, and he wouldn't have backed away from any man, even a white man, who'd called him a thief. Except that a badly beaten LeRoy had sat in a cell in the House of Correction the morning after his arrest, looked Rourke straight in the eye, and said he hadn't done it. So in the two years since, Rourke had spent as many of his off-duty hours as he could spare looking for another lead, another suspect, another motive for the murder of Bobby Joe Maguire. All he'd found, though, was a big nothing, and LeRoy was still in a cell and likely to die there. Nobody made it through a fifty-year stretch in Angola.

LeRoy's grandmother set a bowl of gumbo and a cup of tar-black chicory coffee down on the scarred pine table and motioned Rourke to a chair. At the first spoonful of the thick okra-and-shrimp stew, Rourke had to shut his eyes. "Oh, sweet, sweet mercy. I do believe you make the best *filé* gumbo this side of heaven."

"Hunh. Don't think I don't know when I'm being buttered up like a hot biscuit," the old woman said, but she was pleased.

She wouldn't sit down at the table with him, so Rourke waited until she'd gone back out to her rocker, and then he picked up his bowl and coffee and joined her out on the porch. The night was still and thick, and the murmur of the insects in the bayou seemed to give voice to the sultry heat.

Tante Adenise sucked on a cold cob pipe and rocked while Rourke ate. "You been up to see LeRoy?" she asked after a while.

"Not since the last time I told you about."

She nodded, hummed, rocked. "I know what you come out here for anyways, you, and it ain't to visit with this ol' blind woman, no suh. You out here lookin' to see what you can see 'bout that poor dead boy the bayou done threw up last evenin'. Did he drown?"

"Strangled."

"That what I thought. I figured that boy wasn't drowned, 'less it was done in a bathtub. Mmmmm-huh." She nodded and sucked on the bit of her pipe. "Wasn't no stranglin' done out here, though, either. He was brought already dead and in the thick o' the night, two weeks ago last Sunday."

"How do you mean 'brought'? In a pirogue?"

"Brought in a truck by two white mens. The truck was a Ford and it been haulin' shrimps before it be put to work haulin' dead mens."

"Well, shoot, is that all you can tell me," Rourke said, teasing her. She would have smelled the shrimp, even all the way up here, her nose was that sharp. So were her ears—LeRoy used to say she could not only hear the angels singing, she knew which ones were off-key.

She made a loud hooting noise now to let Rourke know what she thought of his sense of humor. "I got me country ears and nose, white boy, not like your clogged-up city ears and nose. People look at this old woman, see blind, and think stupid. But ain't never been nothin' wrong with my ears and nose. They creepin' around, they white mens, thinkin' they bein' quiet, but they makin' noise like they unloadin' shrimps baskets at the French Market. White mens from the Irish Channel, like you."

Rourke smiled in the darkness. "Probably more like me than I'd care to acknowledge."

She made a wet sound with her tongue. "They know you, sure 'nough. One of them said somethin' 'bout it bein' crazy to do it this way, 'stead of just lettin' that poor dead boy sink like a stone without even leavin' no ripples on the water. An' then the other said somethin' 'bout you. Said that nigger-lovin' cop Rourke had to be thrown a bone, otherwise you keep on diggin' 'til you found the whole skeleton."

Rourke stopped chewing to think about that for a moment. "They used my name?"

"Mmmmm-huh. I heard yo' name plain. Sounds like they wantin' you to be puttin' a whole buncha things together an' addin' up to a lie 'stead of the truth. You think this got somethin' to do with LeRoy?"

"I don't know." Rourke fiddled with the puzzle pieces in his mind, trying to fit them together. LeRoy had spent the last two years in jail for killing Casey Maguire's little brother, Bobby Joe. When he wasn't collecting vigs for the Maguires, Vinny McGinty had been hanging around the Boxing Irish club—so, hell, he might have even sparred a few rounds with LeRoy before the man was put away.

Charles St. Claire had been LeRoy's lawyer, supposedly working on his appeal while screwing LeRoy's wife a couple of times a week as a retainer fee.

"You said in the thick of the night, two weeks ago Sunday?"

"Don't have no clock, me, but felt like 'bout one, one-thirty. An' I ain't so old yet that I don't remember one day from the next."

Two weeks ago Vinny McGinty is strangled with piano wire, then brought out here and dumped into the swamp; last night someone in a wild frenzy hacks Charles St. Claire to death with a cane knife—two different murders of two very different men, whose only link was that they were both acquainted with LeRoy Washington. But then this is New Orleans—pick any two people at random and you could eventually discover a connection between them. In Rourke's experience with life and crime, wild coincidence often played a bigger role than deductive reasoning was ever able to allow for. What did seem to matter, though, was that Vinny McGinty's body had been dumped out here on purpose, and "here" was home to *Tante* Adenise and the Washington boys.

The old woman's sightless eyes were turned toward the wet and black bayou, but her concentration was focused on Rourke, as tangible as the stroke of a hand across his face. "You a good man, Mr. Day," she said. "You able to get beneath the skin of people, to know their souls. But you shouldn't go blamin' yourself for what-all you find there." She lifted her head, as if she were sniffing out the night like a bird dog. "You best be careful what you do with this bone they be throwin' you. I got me some bad feelin's. I see bats flyin' 'cross the moon, and the bayou's done turned the color o' blood."

Rourke didn't smile; he had a deep and abiding respect for

Tante Adenise's bad feelings. "*Tante*, I got to ask you a favor," he said. "I need you to get your LeBeau to come see me, and the sooner the better."

She didn't say anything for a moment, and her hands, gripping the arms of her rocker, tightened hard. "What he done?"

"Nothing that I know of for sure, but maybe something. Something small that could get made into something big. Also, I think he might have seen something, and he could get hurt if he were to speak of it to the wrong person."

"I don' know what you talkin' 'bout. LeBeau just a boy."

Rourke let it ride for a bit, while he finished up the gumbo and the night settled in deeper. Out in the marsh, a gator flopped. "Y'all hear out this way about what happened to Charles St. Claire?" he finally said.

"White man own the world. Colored people get by knowin' what we got to know. 'Course we hear."

"Then you'd know that when a man like Mr. St. Claire gets chopped up with a cane knife, certain folk might see it as an awkward predicament and they might look to solve that predicament the easiest way they can, and if that means putting that knife into the hands of a scapegoat, well, then they might could find a way to let their collective conscience do just that."

She sat in utter stillness now, no longer rocking, her fear as palpable as the night's humidity. Her two older grandsons had fled New Orleans for jobs in the northern factories, and LeRoy was in prison. LeBeau was all she had left. "Makes it 'specially easy," she said, "for they certain folk to solve their predicament if that goat is black."

The moon rose over the roof just then, flooding the porch with a silver light, and Rourke saw the sheen of tears on the old woman's shrunken cheeks.

"That LeBeau," she said, "he only thinkin' to scare Mr. Charlie a little with the hoodoo. He had nothin' to do with no cane knife." She rubbed the gnarled knuckles of one hand with the other. "He just a boy."

"I know. Tell him to come see me, *Tante*."

"So you can put him in jail, you?"

"No."

"Hunh. An' what 'bout Lucille?"

"She's going to be fine."

She would not be fine. Gossip had been floating around for a good while that Charles St. Claire kept a flat in the Quarter where he brought his colored mistress. Her name wasn't known before this because no one had much cared; but they cared now, the tabloids had already started digging into the scandal, and so Lucille would not be fine.

Tante Adenise had begun to rock and croon her 'termination song in time with the beat of the rocker's slats on the warped floor. *Were you there when they crucified my Lord?* Suddenly her head fell back and she emitted a sharp little cry, like a dying bird. "Lordy, lordy. Looks like I can't get the miseries out of this house no matter how hard I try."

He left *Tante* Adenise, carrying her bad feelings with him.

He didn't want to go home, where he would spend the night alone. No, that wasn't true. His daughter and his mama were waiting there to give him company. What he wanted, though, was to wrap his fists in Bridey O'Mara's long red hair.

He wasn't sure she wanted him. She worked evenings at Krauss Department Store, selling gloves, and she often went afterward to her mama's for supper. Tonight she was staying to help wash up, and so he had to wait for her out on her mama's front gallery. Because of the sin they made, he and Bridey, sleeping together without the blessing of Holy Church, her mama hated the very air he breathed, and he respected her feelings by staying out of her house.

Bridey smiled, though, when she came out and saw him waiting for her on her mama's steps. He stood up and slipped his arm around her waist, pulling her to him. He could smell the sweet powder she'd put on after her bath.

They walked home slowly, stopping at a speak to buy a bucket of cold, sudsy beer. Once inside the house, they started stripping off clothes. He put Gershwin on the phonograph and they danced to "Someone to Watch Over Me," while desire and the heat of the night touched their skin like a moist breath. He held her in his arms, and he thought the giving warmth of her body through her thin slip was what had been missing for so long in his life.

When the record fell into a scratchy silence, she touched the back of his hand and smiled at him with her eyes.

He took her into the bedroom and laid her down on the spooled bed. He kissed her eyes, her nose, her mouth, and finally the sun freckles on the tops of her breasts. He touched her hair and wished that he could somehow touch her heart.

He made love to her, and after it was over he tried to hold on to the moment, the way you cling to sleep so as not to let go of a sweet dream. But the moment faded like a dream, and he rose from the softness of her body and sat on the side of the bed.

She laid her hand on his back and left it there. Only when he heard her breathing fall into the rhythms of sleep did he slide out from beneath her touch and get up. He pulled on his trousers and his shirt, although he left the shirt unbuttoned, and went back out into the night.

He walked out into the middle of the street and looked up. The moon was slender and sharp as a sickle, the sky bursting with stars. There was a sharpness to the silence, so that small sounds became loud: the palmetto bugs rattling around the street lamps, the creaking branches of the crepe myrtle tree that grew next to her front gallery, a ship's horn blowing down on the river.

When he'd married Jo he had hoped he would never be lonely again, but then she had died. He couldn't think of his wife without his heart seizing up, but how much could you really love a woman, knowing her for only a year? He supposed what he mostly mourned now when he thought of Jo was the loss of the hope that she had given him, and grieving had a way of burrowing itself inside you and making itself at home. He had been wanting to let go of the pain for so long now, so long, but it had become as comfortable and familiar to him as an old blues song. He wanted to let go, but he was also afraid.

A car turned the corner. A black Lincoln whose headlamps suddenly went out, and Rourke felt a lick of fearful premonition in the back of his throat.

The Lincoln shot forward with a roar and a squeal of its tires. At first Rourke thought the car was going to run him over, but at the last moment it swerved toward the house, peppering the crepe myrtle and the lamppost with gravel. Something came flying out of the car's side window—a black metal something the size of a baseball, but with the shape and look of a pineapple. It hit the gallery floor and rolled beneath the swing, just as Bridey burst out the front door, crying his name.

Rourke was running now, running toward the house, and the grenade that lay smoking beneath her porch swing.

The Lincoln swerved back into his path. The front grill hit him hard, and he thought he felt a rib go as a pain like liquid fire shot through his chest. The impact sent him flying backward through the air, into the middle of the road. His head smacked into the packed dirt and gravel, and a blinding white light flashed before his eyes.

Bridey screamed.

The light exploded into flames and flying shards of wood and glass and metal.

He came back to a world of noise. The crackle of fire, the wail of sirens, shouts. His own breath rushing in and out of his throat.

Someone knelt over him, touching his shoulder, saying something he couldn't hear because of the noise. Blood poured from his nose, down his shirt and throat. He couldn't seem to catch a deep enough breath.

A body was sprawled at the bottom of what was left of Bridey's front steps. Someone had thrown a blanket over it, but one outflung arm lay exposed, bathed in the ambulance's pulsing red light. It made the blue tattoo on the inside of her left wrist look like a smear of blood.

Rourke's head fell back. He looked up at the night sky, and the sickle moon wavered and blurred and broke into pieces.

Chapter Eleven

Nothing broken on him. A bump on the head, a couple of sprained ribs, but nothing broken. He was alive, nothing was even broken, and the sun had come up on another morning.

A thunderstorm had built up during the last hour, though, and the sky now lay heavy and gray overhead, like a blanket of soggy stove ash. Yet heat still pulsed in cruel waves from the sun-baked stone steps of Charity Hospital where Daman Rourke stood, shivering.

Fiorello Prankowski waited for him out in the street, leaning on the fender of a parked squad car. Rourke stayed where he was, unmoving, his gaze fastened on the crepe myrtle trees that lined the sidewalk. Thunder rumbled, and the clouds darkened and pressed down on him, heavy and hot, but inside he was cold and he could not stop shivering.

"You okay?"

Rourke blinked. He hadn't seen Fio walk up the steps to meet him. It was as if time had done a fugue on him and he'd lost track of the beat.

Fio was looking him over, his eyes narrowed in his haggard face. He looked worried by what he found. "They said you got a concussion and some busted ribs or something. You sure you should be out of bed?"

They hadn't actually released Rourke from the hospital; he'd simply got up, dressed in the clothes his mama had sent over, and walked out. Now here he was and here Fio was, and yet he didn't say anything, just kept on staring at those crepe myrtles. Bridey had had a crepe myrtle growing alongside her front gallery. The grenade had blown it into kindling.

"Nothing's broken," he finally said to Fio, because unlike Bridey he was theoretically at least still breathing and so he had no excuse for bad manners. "I'm just a little bruised and stiff, is all. Thank you for bringing a car around."

Fio shifted his weight, his shoulders hunching. His hands hung at his sides, big, limp, helpless. "Jesus, Day. You're lucky you weren't righteously fucked up. . . ." Fio's face suddenly colored. He took off his hat and pushed his hand through his spiky hair. He cleared the roughness from his throat. "Man, I'm sorry about Bridey. What in hell is this all about?"

Rourke breathed. He felt the pain of his battered ribs expanding, felt his mouth part open, but he couldn't seem to get enough air. There wasn't enough air left in all the world.

"I don't know," he said, or might have said. He didn't see how he could be talking when he couldn't breathe.

"Jesus, I just don't know what to say. Bridey. . . . Man, I'm sorry."

Rourke felt the muscles of his face pull into a smile. He knew it was his bad smile by the way Fio was looking at him. The smile he used to wear when he flew his Spad right at the enemy, his fingers pressing hard and relentless on the triggers of his guns. Long silver barrels hacking bullets, death flying from out of a cold blue sky.

"It takes about ten seconds for a grenade to explode," Rourke said. "She had time to know she was going to die."

"You can't be sure—"

"She screamed."

Rourke started down the steps. Fio stared after him for a beat and then followed.

Rourke went around to the passenger side of the car and got in.

Fio hesitated a moment, looking up and down the street as if he hoped the cavalry would come. Sighing, he opened the door and eased his bulk inside behind the wheel.

He cranked up the engine and turned to Rourke. "So are we going somewhere in particular, or do you just want to take a ride?"

Last night death had come in a fancy black Lincoln, one guy driving and another riding shotgun. The moon and the street lamps had only managed to cast the interior of the car in shadows, and both men had been wearing black fedoras, pulled down low to hide their faces. A professional hit, slick and thorough and impersonal, and most likely aimed at him. Bridey had only been in the way.

If he shut his eyes he could still see her in that instant before the explosion of white light and bursting shards of metal and wood and glass. He was careful not to shut his eyes. There was nothing he could do, though, about the scream he kept hearing in his head.

"I'm hungry," Rourke said. "You hungry?"

Fio gave him a slow, careful look. "Maybe."

Rourke felt his mouth twist into that terrible smile again. "I've a hankering for one of Tio Tony's oyster sandwiches."

"Aw, man." Fio's breath came out in a big gust. Tio Tony's was a low-rent diner and bookie parlor down near the riverfront in the Irish Channel, and two blocks from Casey Maguire's slaughterhouse, where the bootlegger still kept his business offices. Maguire had eaten lunch at Tio Tony's every day for the past ten years.

Fio gripped the steering wheel, then swore and let it go. "Guys like Maguire don't try to kill cops. It just ain't done. And it especially ain't done in New Orleans."

It hadn't been done in New Orleans since 1890, when the Sicilian Mafia had assassinated popular police superintendent David Hennessy for interfering with Mob business, and the city's outraged citizens had retaliated by lynching eleven of them in the courtyard of the old Parish Prison. Since then organized crime had not completely disappeared from New Orleans, but they had learned either to put the cops on the pad or leave them alone.

"You going to drive?" Rourke said. " 'Cause I'm getting hot, sitting here in this car."

"Could be that Chicago pineapple wasn't even meant for you. Could be her husband came back and—"

"He's dead." Sean was dead.

"Maybe not, though. Or maybe, back when he was on the job, he sent somebody upriver who just now got out and doesn't know he's gone missing."

Sean O'Mara was dead, and Rourke was seriously wondering now if somehow, some way, he had gotten close to stumbling on to how Sean had died and why. Maybe the connection wasn't between Vinny McGinty and LeRoy Washington, but between Vinny and Sean. The hit on Bridey's house had been professional, the way Vinny's murder had been professional. Vinny, his bone. It had the stink of Casey Maguire all over it.

Yet to believe that, you would have to believe . . .

One summer's evening when they were thirteen, the four of them had sneaked into the St. Alphonsus rectory and stolen some of the wine meant for the Mass and the sacrament of Holy Communion. They'd all been altar boys at St. Alphonsus in those days—all except for Bridey, of course—and so they knew where the sacramental wine was kept. Dark green bottles with hand-scrawled labels that were tucked away in the back of a closet in Monsignor McAuliffe's office. Afterward, drunk on the wine and the wicked sins of theft and blasphemy, they had taken the streetcar out to City Park, where a traveling carnival had come to town with a Ferris wheel advertised as the biggest portable one of its kind in the world.

It seemed to soar a couple hundred feet or more into the heat-hazed, cobalt sky. Decked with strings of incandescent lights, it spun in the dusk like a giant pinwheel of stars. Brightly painted red and yellow gondolas hung from its thick iron spokes, beckoning. Oh, to fly.

They each paid a nickel and stepped onto the wheel's landing as an empty red gondola swung down to meet them. Being southern gentlemen, they let Bridey climb into the wooden car first, and then Sean and Casey almost got into a fight jostling each other over who would sit next to her. Sean won and, grinning, he slipped his arm around Bridey's waist.

As soon as their gondola lifted away from the earth, though, Sean let go of his prize and put a two-handed grip on the safety bar, and the rest of them started ribbing him bad about his fear of heights.

They floated out over the park, above the dueling oaks, the colonnaded pavilion, the lights twinkling on the new iron-arched Pizatti Gate. Smells and noise rose up from the ground, popping bubbles of laughter and shouts and shrieks of joy, roasting peanuts and popcorn balls.

Their gondola climbed halfway up the arc of the wheel's revolution and then stopped, swaying, and Rourke felt a little light-headed. The wine had been too sweet, and the sin of stealing it was such a wonderfully mortal one. If they died now they would go to hell, damned for eternity. It was a frightening thought, and the fear excited Rourke, making him dizzy, drunker than the wine had.

He caught Bridey staring at him. Her eyes were stark in her face, and one corner of her mouth trembled. She looked scared, but then she could always sense when the hunger, the craving, for trouble was upon him. She'd know that tonight, for him, stealing from Holy Church wasn't going to be enough.

Rourke smiled. Bridey jerked her gaze away from his, hugging herself.

The Ferris wheel creaked into motion, they climbed and climbed, and the landmarks of their world spread before them. River and lake and swamp. Garden District mansions and water-front dives—manna and corruption. The spires of St. Louis Cathedral and the whitewashed tombs of the city's many ceme-teries—death and salvation.

Their gondola swayed to a slow stop at the very peak of the wheel's revolution. They dangled in midair. It was a long, long way down. Certain death, surely, if you fell.

Rourke stood up.

The gondola teetered wildly, and Bridey stifled a little cry. Sean yelled at him to sit down.

Rourke leaned over the back of the car and looked down, at a white oyster-shell walkway and the peaked top of a red and blue striped tent where hootchie-cootchie girls were doing the dance of the seven veils. The gondola below them was empty. It swung as if pushed by a breeze, although the air was hot and still.

"I bet y'all each a dollar I can jump from this car down to the next one," he said.

Sean hooted a loud laugh. "You're blowin' smoke. And besides, who's got a dollar?"

"Day, please don't," said Bridey, who knew him better.

"You might make it," Casey Maguire said after a moment. "But if we start moving once you've jumped, you're dead."

Rourke climbed up onto the back of the seat, grabbing one of the wheel's thick, supporting spokes. The gondola teetered again, so violently this time it felt as though it would flip right over. Sean yelled, threatening to knock him into next week if he didn't get down.

Rourke could feel the throb of the steam engine vibrating through the riveted metal. He could, with just the slightest shift of his weight, make the gondola rock like a cradle. The other car was at least fifteen feet away, but the angle wasn't impossible. As long as, like Case had said, the wheel didn't start to turn.

Make it, you live. Miss and you die, and with the stain of mortal sin black on your soul.

Die and you go to hell. To hell and everlasting punishment.

Yes.

He could taste fear at the back of his throat. The fear quickened his breath and made his blood burn, his skin shiver. He bent his knees and pressed his weight into the balls of his feet and jumped.

Would have jumped if Casey Maguire hadn't snagged his strong fingers in Rourke's belt at the very instant that the wheel jerked into motion again.

Rourke fell back into the seat. The car swayed and tipped and finally settled as it descended. In the breath-held silence that followed they could hear the creak and groan of the wheel's spokes as they flexed and the strains of Turkish music from the hootchie-cootchie tent. One of them laughed, and then they all four were laughing, wild with fear and relief, and they were all still a little drunk on stolen sacramental wine.

And then, as their laughter wound down, Casey Maguire had said it. Right out loud he had said, "God, I love you guys."

They had looked at him in surprise, a little embarrassed at the freight of feeling they'd heard in his voice, then Sean laughed and leaned over, punching him lightly on the shoulder with his fist, and Bridey blew him a teasing kiss. Rourke had stared off to where the horizon of trees and rooftops was rising up to meet them, saying nothing, because for just a moment he had looked into Casey Maguire's face and had caught Case looking back at him with an undisguised and fearful love.

And that, Rourke thought now, had taken more raw courage than he would ever have or hope to find.

Tio Tony's waterfront diner was on Tchoupitoulas Street, tucked between a gray-clapboard colored movie theater and a long brick warehouse. It looked out over the wharf, where banana boats awaited unloading and trucks filled with hogsheads of sugar stood ready for shipping upriver. The smell of roasting coffee beans and boiling molasses hung thick in the air.

Fio was taking his sweet time prying his bulk out of the squad car. "You're going to get our asses fired," he was saying. "Uh-huh. 'Cept you won't be fired 'cause your daughter's grand-daddy is the superintendent of po-lice in this fair city that care forgot. So they'll give you one of them nice offices upstairs in City Hall where you can shuffle papers all day and pick the lint out from between your toes. Me, I'll be fired, and then I won't be able to make the forty easy little payments on my new parlor organ."

Rourke stared at him across the car's scuffed and sun-faded black hood. "You done?"

"Yeah, I'm done. Are you going to kill somebody?"

"Not today."

Fio rolled his eyes, beseeching the thunderclouded heavens to give him a break. "Oh, blessed are the meek of spirit and the pure of heart."

Tio Tony's wasn't big on the amenities. You could sit on a stool at the stained tile counter or in one of the cracked red leather booths. Photographs of prizefighters intermingled with holy cards of the Virgin and her saints on the diner's tired yellow walls. A fan creaked in the pressed-tin ceiling, stirring the floating layers of cigarette smoke. The place smelled of fried oysters and burned coffee, with a faint odor of booze underneath. If you knew how to ask for it, Tio Tony served a first-rate scotch and rye, and some of the best Ramos fizzes in the city.

At the back of the diner, a swinging door with a porthole for a window opened into the kitchen. A door in the kitchen led to a bookie parlor and a room with plank benches, sawdust on the floor, and a rope-ring where boxing exhibition matches were held on Friday nights. In Tio Tony's back room, up-and-comers could make their reputations by taking on all challengers.

For being so close to the lunch hour, the diner was quiet, nearly empty. A man with a bald head the size and shape of a watermelon sat at the counter, paring his nails with an open pearl-handled barber's razor. He was talking to the man behind the counter, who wore only a sleeveless undershirt beneath his grease-splattered apron. The cook—if he was the cook—didn't look armed, but Rourke had no doubt that a Thompson submachine gun was within reach beneath the counter.

As they entered the diner, the door knocked a cow bell into jangling, and the man with the razor turned to look, the stool squeaking beneath his weight. Eyes the size of dimes blinked rapidly as his oversized head processed what he was seeing. Then he shrugged and turned back around, probably figuring Rourke and Fio were just two more cops on the pad who had dropped by to collect. He said something low to the cook, and the cook laughed, his gaze sliding to the booths in back.

It was hot and muggy in the diner like it was everywhere else.

Dark, wet loops stained the armpits of the cook's undershirt, and droplets of moisture clung to the bald-headed man's forehead like rain. As they passed by them, Rourke could smell their sweat.

Only one of the booths was occupied. Two men sat while another stood in front of them with his hat in one hand and a taped brown envelope in the other.

The man with the envelope set it on the table between Casey Maguire's hand and the remains of an oyster sandwich. He ducked his head and turned to leave, paling as he saw Rourke and Fio. He put on his hat, holding on to the brim to hide his face as he brushed past them.

Casey Maguire lifted his hand, but he did not pick up the envelope. He sipped from what looked like a glass of iced tea garnished with mint leaves, and probably was. During the last few years, the city's official bootlegger had become a teetotaler.

Sitting across from him and working on a plate of red beans and rice and fried *sac-à-lait* was Maguire's right-hand goon. Paddy Boyle's head came up as they approached, and his washed-out blue eyes looked them over slowly. His thin lips pulled into a smirk, and he scratched at his neck where the hair curled out of the open collar of his shirt like bronze wire.

Rourke smiled and touched his own cheek, near the corner of his mouth, where on the other man a deep V-shaped scar puckered the skin. It was called a rat mark, put there in prison by a shiv on the face of a man who was an informer.

A flush colored Paddy Boyle's scarred face, and his right hand made an inadvertent movement to the small of his back, where he would be carrying a revolver of some sort, probably a hogleg.

Maguire looked up then, saw them, and slid out of the booth. His face seemed drawn even thinner with a terrible pain. He spread his arms as if he would embrace Rourke, but then he let them slowly fall.

"Day, I heard—Jesus, what an awful thing," he said instead. "Poor Bridey. I still can't believe it."

Rourke's smile turned all down-home southern charm. "Well, try bending your mind to it some more. It's only right you should be able to believe her dead, since you're the one who killed her."

"Day." Blood suffused Maguire's pale face. He closed his eyes, shaking his head, but Rourke thought that deep inside him something had flinched.

"I loved her," Maguire said, his voice thick and gritty. "I was the only one of us never to have her, but I probably loved her the best of either of you two bastards."

"I do believe that, Case. I believe you loved her, only you just went and killed her anyway. Yeah, so maybe that grenade was meant for me and not her, but if that's how it went down, then too bad for you, because she's dead. And I'm not."

Maguire turned half away from him, waving his hand. "How do you like this guy? We were best friends growing up, tight as brothers, and now he's here treating me like I'm spit on the sidewalk."

Something ripped open inside of Rourke then, or perhaps the rent had been there all along and he was only just now feeling it. His gut still told him Case had done it, but now his heart was pleading for it to be a lie, and this weakness of his both disgusted and enraged him.

His hand flashed out and gripped Maguire's left wrist. From the corner of his eye he saw Paddy Boyle pull his gun. Behind him, he heard Fio cock his own .38 Special revolver. The goons at the counter pulled back the hammers on their weapons, and suddenly Tio Tony's sounded like a ditchful of crickets in July.

"Easy, boys," Maguire called out, his gaze fastened hard on Rourke's face. "Nothing's going to happen."

Rourke twisted Maguire's wrist over and shoved up his shirt-sleeve, exposing the small eight-pointed blue star. "You broke the faith."

Rourke felt the tendons in Maguire's wrist constrict as his hand closed into a fist. "Not me, Day," he said, his voice low, aching. "You."

Slowly, gently, he pulled loose of Rourke's grasp. "We were family once, closer than the family God gave us. You think I don't remember how it was with you? You were always wilder than the rest of us put together—Jesus, I swear I used to think sometimes you were certifiably crazy. But we were stand-up, the four of us. Blood brothers for life. Only you went and pinned on a badge and married some Garden District debutante, and suddenly you're Saint Daman and your shit doesn't stink. Sean became a cop, too, but he never did that."

"What Sean did do—he should've known better."

"Sean *did* know better. Unlike you, he had no grand illusions about himself. Before he blew town, Sean O'Mara was a man just like your daddy—a drunk cop who owed his soul to the loan sharks and took his graft in trade in the brothels."

It was all true, and it hurt to know it, to acknowledge it. Rourke took a step, bringing himself close to the other man. He heard Maguire's breath hitch, saw his eyes widen just a little. His own eyes, Rourke knew, had turned heavy-lidded, cold.

"Before," he said, pitching his voice low and soft, "I was figuring on sending you up for a thirty-year jolt in Angola for killing Vinny. But now, if I found out you did Bridey too, I'm going to tear your lying, murdering heart out."

The skin tightened around Maguire's eyes, but he let his breath out slow and careful. "For Bridey's sake, in her memory, I'm going to pretend I didn't hear you say that."

Paddy Boyle made some kind of noise that at the last moment he turned into a cough. He had laid his gun down on the table when he'd figured out there was no mortal danger to his boss. Now he lit a cigarette and dropped the burned match into his half-empty plate. He looked up at Rourke, blue smoke curling out of his nose.

His mouth parted, as if he would say something, but he never got the chance. Rourke seized him by his pomaded hair and slammed his face down on the table. Cigarette, lips, and teeth smashed into the plate, and the cheap pottery shattered into pieces.

Rourke tightened his grip on the slick hair and jerked the man's head back up. Clumps of fish and rice and beans dripped off

Paddy Boyle's face, and his legs flailed beneath the table as he tried to get away. Rourke still had him by his hair and he snapped a couple of hard punches into the man's nose and broken, bleeding mouth. Pink spittle flew from Boyle's lips and blood gushed from his nose like water from a broken pipe. Rourke slammed the bloody face back into the shards of pottery, again and then again, as the rage and grief exploded out of him.

He heard Fio shouting, felt Fio's hands pulling him away. He let go of Paddy Boyle's hair and stepped back, drew in a breath, and then another, nodding to whatever Fio was saying even though he couldn't hear him with the way the blood was roaring hot in his ears.

Paddy Boyle tried to lift his head, his eyelids fluttering as he clung to consciousness by a thread, then he fell facedown in the broken plate. Blood had splattered in fanlike patterns all over the booth, the wall, the floor.

Rourke's gaze went from the beaten man and the ruins of the table and found Casey Maguire. The bootlegger stared at him, his pale eyes jittering with anger, but his hands were quiet at his sides.

Rourke smiled. "Tell your junkyard dog that the next time he pulls a gun on me, I'll ram it down his fucking throat."

Rourke thought he heard a woman screaming, and then he realized it was a church bell ringing. He drew in a deep breath, wincing as his sore ribs pulled, smelling the mud of the river and the damp brick at his back. He was outside, leaning against the wall of a warehouse, although he couldn't remember how he'd gotten here.

Fio stood in front of him, his neck flaming with color, a muscle jumping in one cheek. "You kind of hung me out to dry there, partner."

Rourke's gaze cut away. In a vacant part of the wharf across the street, some boys were playing pitch-and-catch. The smack of the ball into leather echoed in the heavy air. One of the kids—a scrawny thing in ragged knickers—was wearing a Pels cap.

Katie.

Rourke shut his eyes, but what he saw was bad so he opened them again. His ears rang with the memory of Bridey's scream, and his face suddenly felt cold. People he loved had always tended to leave him or die on him, but he didn't see how he could live through losing Katie.

He could still feel the blood singing in his neck, but his hands felt useless and thick at his sides. He tightened them into fists, then opened them, tightened and opened, tightened and opened, and breathed.

He'd have to put the word out, talk to his contacts on the street, see if anyone had a lead on who the fedoras in the black Lincoln were. He could wire the Chicago PD. Mobsters up in Chicago used grenades on each other all the time; that's why they called them Chicago pineapples. And Lincolns were the automobile of choice for Al Capone and his boys. Maybe Sean wasn't dead. Maybe Sean had gone up north, gotten into trouble, and that trouble had followed him home.

He kept playing the moment over and over again in his head. The black Lincoln swerving at the house, the flying grenade, Bridey. The guys in the fedoras would have been wearing hoglegs for sure, would have had machine guns with them. He had been standing out in the open, in the middle of the street, yet they hadn't fired a single shot.

The black Lincoln swerving at the house, the flying grenade, Bridey, Bridey screaming. Bridey dying. Bridey.

No, he still had to believe it more likely that the hit had been meant for him, and Bridey had simply died in his place.

And that brought it back to Casey Maguire and Vinny, the bone.

Or maybe Charles St. Claire.

"Partner," he said aloud. He brought his gaze back to Fio. "Did you ever get around to talking to St. Claire's law partner yesterday?"

The skin of Fio's face was still stretched tight with anger. "Golly, are we going back to detecting? And here I thought we were about to declare war on the local bad guys."

Rourke's hand hurt. He made another fist and looked down at the raw place where the skin had split across his knuckles. He looked back up at Fio and flashed a sudden, genuine grin. "Sweet mercy, that did feel good, though," he said.

Fio narrowed his eyes at him. "You think I don't know what you're trying to do. Go to hell."

"Okay," Rourke said. He pushed himself off the wall and headed for the squad car.

"You're gonna have to wash up and change your suit before we go calling on any uptown lawyers," Fio called after him. "You've got goon's blood all over you." He waited another beat, then followed after Rourke, jingling the nickels and dimes in his pocket. "Detecting. Uh-huh, this is the life. Day I was born, you'd have thought my mama would've seen trouble coming and drowned me for luck."

Chapter Twelve

Raindrops the size of bottle caps were pinging on the hood and windshield by the time they pulled up in front of Charles St. Claire's law offices on Napoleon Avenue. Rourke had stiffened up in the car on the drive uptown, and he got out carefully. He winced as he pulled at his battered ribs while struggling to get into the clean suit coat he'd picked up from home on the way.

The firm was small, just St. Claire and another Creole by the name of Jean Louis Armande, according to the discreet brass plaque mounted next to the door. They worked out of a converted Queen Anne house, resplendent with fluted colonnettes, turned-wood balustrades, carved panelwork, and a turret with fish-scale shingles.

While a secretary announced them, Rourke and Fio waited in a front parlor that was like the overfurnished, overstuffed, overdecorated rooms of the fashionable men's clubs. Fio settled into a plush green velvet sofa and began thumbing through a magazine. Rourke wandered over to look at the artwork, a series of Currier and Ives lithographs depicting history's worst disasters: the sinking of the *Titanic*, the Chicago fire, the eruption of Mount Vesuvius. Maybe, Rourke thought, looking at bad news on such a cosmic scale was supposed to make you conclude that the wreck of your own life wasn't so terrible.

Rourke was studying a lithograph of San Francisco in rubble and flames after the '06 earthquake when the firm's surviving member came out himself to escort them back to his office. Jean Louis Armande's looks belied his venerable Creole name. He was a freckled-faced man with thinning hair the color of dead leaves, a pudgy nose and mouth, and bushy eyebrows that crawled above his seawater blue eyes and rimless eyeglasses like caterpillars.

His languid manners were pure old New Orleans, though. He saw them settled into leather armchairs, asked after their health, and commented on the weather. He offered them coffee, which he poured himself from a rose-sprigged china pot. As he handed around the delicate cups and saucers, Rourke noticed deep, flaming red scratches on the backs of his freckled hands.

He saw Rourke looking and flushed, then his small, pursed lips produced a surprisingly charming smile. "My daughter has a new kitten that thinks it's a tiger."

Armande's spacious office overlooked the garden. A window framing a moss-garlanded live oak tree formed a southern pastoral backdrop for a walnut desk, whose glossy surface bore a Tiffany lamp, a cut-glass inkwell, and an onyx postage-stamp box—but no papers or documents of any kind.

The lawyer sat behind the desk and folded his hands in front of him. Although Rourke had never met the man before, around the Criminal Courts Building Jean Louis Armande was known to handle his firm's prosaic, but more lucrative, civil cases, while his flamboyant partner had amused himself playing the dragon slayer and championing lost causes in criminal court.

"I would prefer," Armande said in that soft, lilting way some Creoles had of talking, "to assist the police as much as possible in their investigation of my law partner's unfortunate . . . demise. However, as I will be assuming most of Mr. St. Claire's cases—provided the clients wish it, of course—I don't know how much information I might be able to venture forth about his professional life without wandering into the area of attorney-client privilege."

"How about his Negro clients?" Rourke said. "You taking them on too?"

"I should hardly think so." The lawyer's small lips pursed and twitched as if he were amused by the question. "I have nothing against *pro bono publico*, you understand, but unlike Charles I've never seen where is the public good in keeping another worthless nigger out of jail."

"Black skin kind of being like the mark of original sin in your eyes?" Rourke said. He was smiling, but it was pure mean, and the look in his own eyes slowly forced Armande's gaze to fall to his clasped hands.

"Mr. St. Claire was working the appeal of a Negro prizefighter by the name of LeRoy Washington," Rourke said. "Mr. Washington was convicted two years ago of choking his manager to death. That ring any bells with you?"

Armande made pockets of air in his cheeks while he thought, or pretended to. "No, I'm afraid it doesn't."

"Where were you Tuesday night between, say, eight o'clock and midnight?"

Armande looked surprised at the question. "At home. With my family."

"You sure about that?"

"Of course I'm sure." The lawyer's voice had broken over the protest, and a flush spread in a slow stain over his cheeks. "We had our disagreements—I will admit to that—but I would hardly kill a man because we didn't always view the world or the law from the same philosophical perspective. Charles St. Claire was not only my law partner, he was my friend."

Rourke could feel his own partner's eyes on him, but he wouldn't look Fio's way. The room fell into a strained silence that was underscored by the hum of the window fan and the click of rain against the glass.

Fio scratched the back of his neck, cleared his throat. "Mr. St. Claire was supposed to've had a colored girl he was banging regular and was said to be rather fond of. Would you happen to know about that?"

"Oh, dear." Now Armande's lips pursed into a supercilious smile as he recovered his demeanor. "You fail to understand:

Gossip has always trailed after Charles like ants at a picnic. He liked women, and because they liked him in return he had a tendency to indulge himself. Indulge and then discard them, and whatever her pathetic hopes I can't imagine how this Lucy's fate would eventually have been any different."

"Lucy?" Fio said. "You do know her then."

"Certainly not. I overheard Charles speaking to her on the telephone once. He called her Lucy."

"Just Lucy?"

Armande's thick eyebrows rose up over the tops of his glasses. "She's nothing but a bit of colored tail. Since when do they have last names?"

Rourke's hand was hurting him. He looked down and saw that he was making a fist, and he slowly unclenched it. The beat of the rain on the window was a roar in his ears, and then the noise faded to a hiss and patter and he heard Armande's slow Creole drawl, and he realized that Fio must have asked another question. Time had done that odd misstep on him again.

"As a matter of fact, I did prepare the will," Armande was saying. "His wife gets all of his assets, including the house and property. Sans Souci."

His gaze lifted back up to Rourke's face, then shifted away again, around to the window this time. He watched the rivulets of rain race each other down the panes.

"There is one thing I should mention," he said. "Although I hesitate to do so, because it might not be either pertinent or germane to the matter at hand, and such remarks taken out of context can be quite inflammatory and misleading—" He drew in a deep breath as if girding himself before plunging on. "But one morning a couple of weeks ago I came upon Charles in the hallway, and he was laughing to himself. When I asked him what he was finding so amusing, he told me that together he and Al Capone were going 'to rock the good ol' Crescent City back on her heels,' but I—"

"Al Capone?" Fio said, sitting up a little straighter.

"As I was about to say, I assumed he was only being Charles—

having his little joke with me, as he was wont to do. It's only in hindsight that I . . . " He turned his head back around, his gaze sliding off Rourke and settling on Fio. "It's just that there were so many things that could set Charles off into speaking and behaving irrationally, and so one learned to . . . A new woman—and there was always a new woman, even after he married. A *bourré* game. And then he was . . . well, he liked to indulge in the occasional cocktail."

"Along with the occasional snort of cocaine?" Rourke said.

Armande's eyelids flickered behind his glasses. "I would know nothing about that."

"I'm sure you wouldn't, sir," Fio put in, smiling and exuding a little southern charm himself. He leaned forward, bracing his elbows on his thighs and turning his hat around in his hands. "But the women, the drinking, the gambling—although regrettable, certainly, I gather they were customary misbehavior, so to speak, on the part of Mr. St. Claire. Do you know of anything unusual that was going on in your partner's life recently?"

"Unusual?" Armande's eyelids flickered again and another stain of color spread up his neck. "No. Unless you mean . . . Oh, it's all probably rather silly and harmless, but about a week ago Charles brought a voodoo charm in to work with him, said he'd found it tucked into his bed. He seemed to think his wife was behind it— he said he wouldn't be surprised to wake up one night and find a *loup-garou* in his arms. Only he was laughing about it. They played games with each other, he and Rem—Mrs. St. Claire."

Fio raised his gaze from the contemplation of his hat. "You would say he was a happily married man, then?"

The flush spread up over Armande's face all the way to his receding hair, and his gaze jittered away from Fio now and back to the window. "In his own way, yes, he seemed to be so. She challenged him and he needed that. Charles craved excitement in his life. He had other women, but then he was never going to be faithful to just one woman, no matter whom he married. And though I can't name names, I always had the impression she dallied with other men. I don't know that Charles minded—

indeed, I think he rather liked hearing about it. The excitement again. It was all part of their game."

"Maybe one of them got tired of it, though," Fio said. "All that playing around."

Armande thrust himself to his feet. He turned his back on them and walked to the window. He leaned over, pressing his fists on the sill. The movement pulled the fine linen of his white summer suit taut across his back and shoulders. He hadn't seemed to be such a large man when seated behind his walnut desk.

"This is awkward," he said. "But Mrs. St. Claire has her own lawyer, and so I'm not behaving unethically if I tell you. . . ." He straightened and swung back around. The flush on his face had receded some, but a muscle ticked beneath his right eye. "That evening of the night Charles was murdered, Tuesday evening—heavens, was it only less than two days ago?" He paused to thrust a hand through his hair, then let it fall. "Charles had been out of the office all that day, but he came in late, about five o'clock, and he was like a man possessed. He started going through the law books in the library, tossing them on the floor when he couldn't find what he was looking for, cursing and ranting aloud. As I said, Charles was excitable, but it wasn't his way to be so . . . so vulgar and outright hysterical."

Armande's words trailed off, getting swallowed up by the splatter of the rain against the windowpanes. It was really coming down now; the oak tree in the garden loomed smudged and hulking in the misty wet.

"What was he looking for, sir?" Fio pressed gently.

Armande drew in a deep breath, letting it out slowly, along with his response. "Annulment statutes and precedence. He said his marriage to Mrs. St. Claire was over and that he wanted out. No, it was stronger than that. He said he *needed* to get out of it, and now."

Rourke felt as if a great empty space had blown up inside him, as if he were back up in the Jenny with the wind pressing against his ears, flying through that white, white, empty space with Remy laughing behind him, talking about the past and telling lies, and somehow getting him to believe in her again, in spite of it all.

"So maybe the thought of her stepping out with other men was bothering him more than he'd been letting on," Fio had said, and Armande was shaking his head. Rourke saw the man's mouth open; he felt the words come at him from out of white, empty space, like the rush of the wind.

"I know this sounds strange, given what I said about his cursing and such—but I don't think Charles was angry that evening so much as frightened. It was all over him, the fear. In his face, in his eyes—I declare you could almost smell it on him. Naked fear."

"Who's LeRoy Washington?"

They stood within the shelter of the porch and watched the rain come down so hard it was dancing and bouncing off the pavement. It sluiced off the balustrade above their heads, making a waterfall. It ran along Napoleon Avenue, overflowing the gutters and forming puddles that would qualify as lakes in some states.

Rourke thought Fio had said something, a part of him had even made sense of the words—but time was segueing back and forth on him again. The headache behind his eyes burned white hot, and the boards of the porch were like shifting sands beneath his feet.

"Day?"

"Who I said. A Negro prizefighter who went to prison for killing his manager. He says he didn't do it."

Another silence settled between them as they watched the rain come down some more. The air had finally cooled some, and it smelled of wet trees and torn leaves.

"Okay," Fio said. "So maybe St. Claire uncovered new evidence that could help this boy LeRoy's case. But who-all's going to care that badly one way or the other that some darkie got railroaded for something he didn't do?"

"Mr. Washington is a particular friend of mine," Rourke said. His voice was quiet, but his eyes weren't. "I care."

Fio continued to stare at him for a slow, hard moment and then he shrugged. "All right."

"The murdered manager," Rourke went on, "was Casey Maguire's baby brother, Bobby Joe."

Fio made a small sound that might have been either surprise or exasperation. Rourke wondered if now was the moment when he should tell his partner about Lucille. Sweet, vulnerable Lucille *Durand Washington*, whom that prick of a lawyer had been "banging regular," and who had no real alibi for where she'd been the night the man was murdered.

He wasn't sure how far he could trust Fio, though. The whole city would so love nothing better than to pin the murder of Charles St. Claire on the man's colored mistress, that the convenience of having her as a suspect would overrule even the fact that her lover had been her only hope of getting her husband out of jail.

"I don't know," Rourke said instead. "The hit a couple of weeks ago on Vinny McGinty, and then last night on me—two guys in a black Lincoln, tossing a Chicago pineapple. Now St. Claire's partner throws us that bone about Al Capone. It's starting to all feel connected in some way, only I can't see how."

Fio thought on that for a bit, while the rain teemed and the water gushed from the spouts and rose another two inches in the street.

Finally he rubbed his bent nose, shaking his head. "I don't know either, Day. This is New Orleans. You meet a guy and turns out his mama knows your mama, or he knows a guy used to work for your brother, or you both got cousins living next door to each other in Slidell. I think you've got a hard-on for Casey Maguire, and you're letting that affect your judgment. You need to be careful—and I'm telling you this serious here. The man's got friends in high places."

"Yeah. He has sure enough bought himself a lot of friends."

Fio clamped his jaw down so hard Rourke heard his teeth grate. "I know you weren't including me in that remark," Fio said. "Otherwise I'd have to hit you, and you aren't feeling so good."

Rourke smiled. He jumped off the porch and ran out into the rain.

They were soaked through by the time they got in the car.

Steam fogged the windows, and the rain pounded like hammers on the roof.

Fio tried to look angry, but he couldn't really keep it up. He rubbed the condensation off the windshield with the flat of his big palm, punched on the ignition, then sighed and turned it off. He twisted around in the seat to look at Rourke.

"Whatever theory it is you're working on, Remy Lelourie don't fit into it nowheres that I can see. I guess maybe your mind was wandering when Mr. Armande got to the part about the other men and the annulment. Call me crazy, but maybe whatever it was that made ol' Charlie St. Claire suddenly think he had to get the Cinderella Girl out of his life, was the very same thing that drove her to kill him. I don't know. It's just a theory."

She had said, among all her other lies, that all she'd wanted to do was come home. Jesus save us, Rourke thought, but she might as well have walked into the St. Louis Cemetery No. 3 and thrown open the doors to all the crypts—where the old sins still lived, not confessed and never forgotten.

"The way I'm seeing it," Fio said, talking through Rourke's silence, "is Remy Lelourie's got herself a righteously ugly secret she doesn't want the rest of the world to know about, and somehow her man doped it out and so she killed him. It's the oldest motive in the book, next to catching him in bed with another broad. The fear of being found out."

Fio started up the engine and slipped it into gear. "That little vamp act she was putting on in the squad room yesterday morning—man, that was scary. Like some dream you find at the bottom of a bottle of whiskey, all mystery and fire and sin. She was seducing every cop in that room, wringing them empty, and by the time she was finished with them there wasn't a one could call his soul his own. They'd have done anything for her. Died for her, killed for her."

Fio's breathing had grown loud and heavy, fogging the windshield again; trickles of sweat ran down the sides of his flushed face, soaking his collar. It made Rourke smile in spite of the cold fear he was feeling inside. "And you're immune?" he said.

Fio popped the clutch, and the car shot forward in a spray of water. "Shit. I'd have to be dead to be immune. She scares me, though. You both scare the hell out of me."

"You scare me," Maeve Rourke said to her son.

She looked up and down Conti Street, at the two uniformed patrolmen who had been put on watch at either end of the block, and then she looked behind her, at the third patrolman who stood within the carriageway of her Creole cottage. Another cop hovered at her right shoulder. He'd been detailed to accompany her to evening Mass, and he was trying hard not to look fascinated. Maeve Rourke had once been one of New Orleans' most beautiful and notorious sinners, a woman who had dared to choose love above all else. She was still beautiful.

"It's only a precaution, Mama," Daman Rourke was saying. "Until we find out what-all was behind what happened at Bridey's house last night."

He'd telephoned his father-in-law from the hospital as soon as he could after the attack, knowing Weldon Carrigan could have a guard put on the Conti Street house within minutes. Then he'd telephoned Maeve and told them all to stay inside, keeping to the back rooms, until he could be with them. He knew it wasn't wholly rational, but he hadn't wanted his family stepping out into the open when he wasn't around, even though it was his presence that probably put them in the most danger.

His mother was staring at him now, a small frown darkening her eyes, as if she longed to understand him but could not. Which was only fair for a change, since he'd spent his entire life trying and failing to understand her and the choices she had made. "Well, if you insist," she finally said. "Although I feel rather like I'm leading a parade." He thought he saw her mouth curve into a fleeting smile before she reached up to her hat and peeled the black net veil down over her face.

Rourke watched her walk away from him down the banquette, the policeman trailing in her wake. A woman in mourning black for the lover she'd lost eleven years ago. She hadn't stepped foot in a church while Reynard Lelourie was alive, but in the years since his death she'd gone to Mass almost every day. Rourke had often wondered what she prayed for—he didn't think it was forgiveness. In all the time since he and Katie had come to live with her, he had never heard her utter one word of regret for what she'd done to him and his father and brother. Or for what had been done to Mrs. Lelourie and her two little girls.

Just then he heard a shriek, and the street seemed to explode in front of his eyes, into white light and fire and wailing sirens, and Bridey screaming, screaming . . . and then he realized it was only Katie laughing.

He turned around, making himself breathe, making himself stop shaking, to watch his little girl at play.

He'd had Fio drop him off at home so that his family could get out for a couple hours, and Katie had joined some of the neighborhood boys in a game of street hockey played on roller skates, with palmetto branches for sticks and a packed wad of newspaper for a puck. At only six and a half, she was several years younger than the other kids, but they didn't seem to mind her joining in their game.

She threw herself into it with a fierceness, though, that kept sending Rourke's heart up into his throat. He watched while his little girl and a towheaded boy almost twice her size spotted the puck at the same time and skated for it. The boy got there first, but Katie charged into him, flinging up her elbow to smack the boy in the mouth. The boy squealed as his skates shot out from under him and he landed on his rump. The puck was all Katie's now, and she was flying toward the goal and the turned-over garbage can that served as a net.

She swung back her stick to take a shot just as the toe of her skate caught in a crack in one of the pavement blocks. The skate twisted off her foot, and she went down hard on her hands and knees.

Rourke took a step, then stopped when he saw her push herself back onto her feet. She was laughing as she came toward him, hopping and pushing herself along on the one skate. She plopped herself down onto their front stoop, where Augusta was already sitting, knees spread, snapping an apronful of beans.

Rourke took the skate and the key Katie kept on a rubber band around her wrist and squatted before her, although the movement pulled at his aching ribs. He wriggled the skate back onto her Converse All Star Ked. It was still such a small shoe, he thought. When she was a baby, just the sight of her tiny booties had always turned him cold with terror. He'd never loved anyone the way he loved Katie—so utterly and unconditionally. Yet she was so small and helpless, so totally dependent on him, and he was so scared, all the time he was scared that he would fail her. Or maybe, Rourke thought, with a derisive smile for himself, he was only afraid that she would somehow grow up ahead of him and leave him behind.

Still, his hands shook a little as he tried to fit the skate key's wing nut onto the bolt. He turned the key, tightening the clamps onto the rubber sole of her Ked, while Katie examined a scrape on her knee through a rip in her black lisle stocking. He looked up in time to catch Augusta shooting him a glare strong enough to curdle milk.

"I don't know what you 'bout," she said, "raisin' that chile to be a hooligan."

"Did you see me, Daddy?" Katie said, oblivious to the trouble he was in, or maybe not. "I smacked that Ernie Parker right in the kisser with my elbow, and he yelped like a stuck pig. Ernie Parker is *such* a pantywaist."

Augusta made a noise that came up from deep in her bosom and shot out her nose. "Huuunnnh, how that chile do talk. She pickin' that up from the radio. You hadn't ought to let her be listenin' to no radio. No tellin' what hooligan slang she might be pickin' up."

Rourke grinned up at Katie. "Holy mackerel, I'm in hot water now."

Katie giggled, but then she slipped her arm around Augusta's waist and gave her a quick hug. The woman made another noise, a softer one, and she shared a smile with Rourke.

He stood, pulling Katie up with him. She balanced herself by holding onto his arms with both hands, while she tilted her head back and looked up, where the sun shone through a break in the clouds, misty and soft in the trees and rooftops. It would rain again before nightfall, and the sun and clouds were casting shadows on her face that made her look oddly haunted.

"Daddy? How long before it gets dark?"

"A while yet. You've still got time for some more cutthroat hockey before we need to go in. Only how about going a little easy on poor Ernie from here on out, okay?"

She clung to him still, running her skates back and forth over the bricks of the banquette now, hard enough for the metal wheels to throw out tiny sparks. "Are those policemen here to make sure the gowman stays away?"

"There's no such thing as a gowman, Katie. You know that." He wanted to tell her of the real threat he had brought into her life, and of how much she meant to him, and how desperate was his need to keep her safe, but the words wouldn't come. She was hanging on to his arms, looking up at him, and still the words wouldn't come. He could feel them instead, all those unspoken words, sliding through his fingers like grains of sand.

"The gowman doesn't come when you're here," she was saying, "so will you stay home with us tonight just in case?"

He grasped her shoulders, stilling her. "I need to stop by the squad room and then I have to go pay someone a visit later on this evenin', but I'll be back before it's even time for you to go to bed, and if it's not too late I'll crank us up some ice cream. You can be thinking of what flavor you'd like."

She pushed her lower lip out in a pout, but he had felt the tension go out of her shoulders. "Who are you going to be visiting that's so important?"

He started to say he was going to see a ghoul, but he caught himself just in time. "He's a man I work with, a doctor of a sort. I'll be back before your bedtime. I promise."

She looked up at him, love and accusation in her eyes, beautiful dark, grayish green eyes with golden flecks. Her mother's eyes. "You don't always keep your promises."

Chapter Thirteen

Rourke sat at his desk in the empty squad room. He put his hands down flat on the old worn and ink-stained blotter, pressed them down hard to keep them from shaking.

He stared at his hands. He stretched his fingers out wide, so wide the veins and bones pushed against the skin. He was so afraid, afraid that if he stopped moving, stopped thinking, then the only thing left would be the sound of Bridey screaming. It felt as if his chest had developed a weak place over his heart, as if all flesh and bone had been stripped away until only the thinnest layer of skin remained, thin as a skein of ice, and if he touched it, if anything even so much as brushed against it, he would shatter.

He heard a step out in the hall and he made one hand pick up his pen; he made the other hand pull out a requisition form and lay it on the desk in front of him.

Nate Carroll came sauntering through the door; he was whistling, his orange Raggedy-Andy curls bouncing with his every step.

Rourke made himself smile. "Hey, Nate."

The young man looked surprised to see him. "Hey, Rourke," he said.

He pushed through the swinging wooden gate in the railing

that separated the working part of the squad room from the desk sergeant's domain. He went to his own desk and sat, fired up a Lucky Strike, picked up his telephone receiver, jiggled the plunger a couple of times, then hooked the receiver back on the cradle again.

He got up and wandered over to Rourke's desk, leaned over Rourke's shoulder. "What are you doing?" he said.

"What does it look like, for chrissakes? I'm filling out fucking requisition forms." Rourke put an X in the box marked Authorized Expenditure and forged the captain's initials. "There's a fucking crime wave happening, and I got to waste my valuable time begging for every fucking pencil and thumbtack."

"Yeah, fuckin' waste of time," Nate said. "So how come you're not over at the Parish Prison?"

"Should I be?"

"Not unless you don't care if it looks to the boss like they managed to collar St. Claire's killer without you."

The nib of Rourke's fountain pen ripped a jagged tear through the paper. He pulled in a careful breath and slowly raised his head. Something bad must have still showed on his face, though, because the other man smiled weakly and took a step back.

"Who?" Rourke said.

The rookie detective cleared his throat. "Uh, the lil' nigger gal St. Claire was supposed to've been banging. It was Roibin Doherty who sniffed her out—who would credit it, huh? He and Prankowski went to pick her up."

The Parish Prison butted up against the rear of the Criminal Courts Building, and Rourke went to it through the connecting corridors in the basement.

He walked down a sloping hallway lined with holding cells—dank, dark cages full of cockroaches and human wretches who howled at him, or sobbed, or shouted obscenities. Half the bare lightbulbs were dimming or burned out, and the peeling walls, unpainted since the last century, were the color of old vomit. They smelled sour: of fear and sweat and years' worth of overflowing piss buckets.

At the end of the long hall was a single interrogation room. Rourke had known grown men to break before they made it that far, almost welcoming the beating that would give them the excuse to confess.

The interrogation room was bare of any furniture, except for a stool in the middle of the cement floor. The stool sat over a drain hole, which was there for when the place needed to be hosed down. The legs of the stool had been sawed off so that anyone made to sit on it would find himself in an undignified and vulnerable squat.

Fiorello Prankowski was leaning, with his hands in his pockets, against the wall next to the door when Rourke came through it. Roibin Doherty was circling the stool, and on it sat Lucille. Her hands had been cuffed together, pulled down between her bent legs, and fastened by a chain to a ring in the floor. Her back was bowed in a taut arch; her head hung heavily, her chin resting on her breastbone. One sleeve of her cheap yellow calico dress was ripped out at the shoulder. He couldn't see her face through the long copper coils of her hair, but he could hear the wetness in her throat when she breathed and swallowed.

"Well, if it ain't Loo-tenant Rourke," Doherty said. "Hey, boy, this nigger cunt claims to know you. Fancy that. And now you're just in time to hear her tell us how she went after Charlie St. Claire's cock and balls with a cane knife."

Rourke's breath backed up in his throat. "Get him out of here," he said to Fio.

When he got no response, he turned slowly and met his partner's eyes, and he lied.

"I was with her that night."

Doherty hacked a laugh. "What? You gonna claim you were balling her too?"

"Get him out of here," Rourke said.

Fio's jaw had locked up tight as a fist; it crunched as he unhinged it. "The whole night?"

"Up until when you sent people out looking for me after the body was discovered. Only it's not what you think."

"He's thinking you're full of shit," Doherty said.

Lucille raised her head. Her face was wet and tear-swollen, and a cut at the corner of her mouth trickled blood. "Mr. Day . . . Tell 'em how I didn't do it."

Doherty swung around and kicked out, slamming the toe of his brogan into Lucille's belly. "Nigger bitch!"

Rourke didn't know he was beating the man until he felt bone and cartilage collapse under his fist. Fio had thrust himself between them, shouting something, and Rourke tried to go around him. Doherty stumbled backward, groping for the door.

"He's fucking nuts." Doherty pulled out his shirttail to mop the blood off his face. "Jesus, did you see what he did? He fucking broke my nose."

"Sergeant, go on back to the squad room," Fio said. "We're done here."

"Fuck this shit." Doherty flung blood and mucus off the ends of his fingers onto the floor. "You got no right—"

"Yeah, I do. I'm pulling rank."

Fio muscled the older cop out the door and shut it. He turned and stared at Rourke for a long, bitter minute, then tossed him the handcuff key. "Talk," he said.

Rourke snatched the key out of the air. He knelt beside Lucille and unfastened the metal shackles from around her wrists. She had vomited after Doherty had kicked her in the belly and she was still breathing hard, almost gagging. He didn't want her talking, and so he said nothing. She wouldn't look at him.

He spoke to Fio instead. "You've met my mama's housekeeper, Miss Augusta? Lucille's her daughter. When we heard that evenin' how Lucille was feeling poorly, my mama sent me over to her houseboat with some gumbo. She and I sat out on the deck and talked, drank some sour mash, and made some music. That was all we did, but we did it while Charles St. Claire was getting cut."

She tried standing up, only to fall against him, sending a sharp pain through his own battered ribs. He wrapped his arm around her waist, half lifting her back onto her feet. She was barefoot, her legs grimy and scratched. He wondered how they had gotten her into this room and onto that stool, if they'd dragged her kicking and screaming down that long, ugly hall.

"Lemme go," she said, but he didn't. He tightened his hold around her, wishing he could pick her up and carry her in his arms as he would a child.

They had to go around Fio to get to the door.

"Don't mind me," the other cop said. "I'm just going to stand here for a while and mull it all over. You know, poke at it like you do a loose tooth with your tongue, and try to figure out where and how-all you've been lying to me."

Rourke made himself take a breath, and then another. He felt close to killing somebody.

"I wanted to keep her out of it."

"Shit. How did you possibly think you could keep her out of it?"

"She's LeRoy Washington's wife and LeRoy is a friend. When he went to prison I made him a promise I'd take care of her." Rourke gave his partner a hard, challenging look. "I would do the same for you and your wife."

"But she's just a—" Fio cut himself off, and a dark flush spread in a stain over his cheekbones to his ears. "You willing to go into court and alibi her under oath?"

"She didn't kill him."

"Yeah. So you say."

The bayou flowed black and thick under a sky that threatened rain.

Rourke wrestled the squad car over the last few ruts and bumps in the road and coasted to a stop alongside the levy in front of Lucille's boathouse. The car's engine ticked away its heat, smelling of burning oil.

They looked together out the windshield at the stand of cypress trees across the water. Clawed branches, like witches' brooms, swept the bottoms of the sagging dark clouds; the wind was coming up.

Lucille looked at the trees, but she wouldn't look at him. After a while she said, "How come you lied for me?"

"You know why."

"For LeRoy."

"And for you."

She shook her head, and then let it fall back. She raised her arm, holding it up to the muted light coming in through the window, turning her arm over and then over again, as if with wonder, as if she were seeing her own arm for the first time.

"When I was growin' up on Pailet Lane," she said, "the aunts and mamas use to talk alla time 'bout how I was comin' up light. But they never 'splained it to me right. They never tol' me no matter how light I'd come up, no matter how much white I had in me, I'd always be a nigger. One drop of African blood—that's all it takes for the white man's world to call me a nigger. For me to *be* a nigger."

"Luce—"

"No." She let her arm fall back into her lap, closing her eyes. "You don't know what it's like. You think you do, but you don't. There's no way you can know how scared I was in that room, squattin' on that stool and chained to the floor. The white man, he still lookin' for ways to keep the colored folk his slaves, an' Angola prison does y'all fine as anythin' else. When's a body with dark skin ever get a fair trial in Lou's'ana? When's the last time you seen a jury believe a Negro's word against any white man's, let alone a cop's?"

She opened her eyes and turned to look at him at last, and he was rocked back by the naked hatred he saw in her eyes. "You got white skin and you a cop," she said. "So don't you be tellin' me you know what it's like."

She started to get out of the car, but he stopped her by grabbing her wrist. "You're right, Luce—I'm a cop, and one who has just put it all on the line for you. Which is why you're going to tell me right here, right now, what got Charlie St. Claire so upset Tuesday evenin' that he went hieing off in a panic, looking to get an annulment for his marriage to the most beautiful woman in the world, only to finish off his very bad day by getting his throat slit with a cane knife. Why an annulment, Luce? Tell me."

"I don't *know* why. I was Mr. Charlie's nigger bed slave, what for would he be tellin' me things 'bout his wife?"

She had put plenty of real passion into her denial, but Rourke had seen the startled fear flash across her face when he'd spoken the word annulment. He tightened his grip on her wrist and made his voice go mean. "Don't make me think about taking you back uptown."

She stared at him, unblinking, and he felt the muscles and sinews of her wrist tighten as she made a fist. "Lawd God, you alike enough to Mr. Charlie to be his brother—made from stone the both of you. He was alla time tellin' me he loved me like a wife, but that di'n't stop him from makin' me into just another whore. Alla time braggin' on the good he doin' for my 'people,' like that goin' to change how I feel 'bout him. 'I'm a champion of the Negro,' he used to say to me, usually right after he got done fuckin' me in the mouf, an' you could tell how he liked sayin' them words 'cause it made him feel like the good massa."

She pulled away from him. She looked down at the red marks on her wrist put there first by the handcuffs and then by his fingers, then she looked back up at him and her mouth curled into something that wasn't even close to a smile. "Is that how *you* feelin' now, Mr. Day—like the good massa?"

She got out of the car and he watched her walk away from him, watched her climb the levee and disappear over the other side. He thought he would never be able to forget the purity of the hate he had seen in her eyes.

Chapter Fourteen

The coroner's laboratory was deep in the basement of the Criminal Courts Building, next door to the colored toilets. You walked into the Ghoul's lair and the stench of formaldehyde and decay would hit you like a blow. The two electric fans only managed to stir up the foul air.

Moses Mueller was at the far end of the room, attempting to pry open a wooden crate with a crowbar. He looked up as the bare electric bulb cast Rourke's shadow onto the wall in front of him— a wall that might have been painted white at one time but was now the color of old vomit, with faded, rusty streaks that Rourke hoped weren't ancient bloodstains but probably were.

"Ah, it is Lieutenant Rourke, I see," the Ghoul said. "Here to discuss the postmortem. Good, good." He held a finger in the air like a professor about to make a significant point. "But if you will allow me just another moment."

He gave the crowbar a hard yank and the wood split apart with a scream. "You will be pleased to know that I have purchased for us two marvelous new inventions: a helixometer and a comparison microscope. We will now be able to conduct ballistic tests in this godforsaken southern backwater."

During the year since Moses Mueller had taken over as the

parish coroner, he had been buying all the latest, most experimental forensic equipment for the lab with his own money—once he figured out he had precious little hope of prying much of a budget out of City Hall. Rourke wondered about the Ghoul's money. The man dressed like a tramp, but there was that chauffeured green Packard, and cash to throw away on a comparison microscope and a heli-whatever.

The mention of ballistics had made Rourke curious enough to come up for a closer look, though, and in spite of the cost to his nose. A lit cigarette was dangling from the coroner's lower lip, but even with the smoke wreathing his head, the slickum in his black hair, and the yellow stains of Lucky Tiger cologne around his collar, he still smelled like something that had just crawled out of a grave.

The Ghoul was panting with the effort it was taking to bend over and pry open the front of the crate. Nails squealed as they pulled free, but all Rourke could see inside was packing straw.

"With these two instruments I shall be able to compare a bullet fired from a suspect's gun with the one found in the victim's body. What do you say to that, Lieutenant? What a pity no firearm was involved in our latest murder."

"You never know."

The coroner tilted his head back and gave Rourke a bemused look. "Well, I do believe we can safely conclude that Mr. St. Claire did not die from a gunshot wound." He straightened up with another groan, laid the crowbar down on top of the crate, and mopped his sweating forehead with a grimy handkerchief. "Have you been engaging in yet another bout of fisticuffs, Lieutenant? You have flecks of blood on the cuff of your shirt, and the backs of the knuckles on your right hand seem to be oozing fresh blood as well."

"They had a run-in this evenin' with Roibin Doherty's nose."

"Ah, splendid. Sergeant Doherty's nose—splendid indeed . . . And now to the photographs. I have pieced together a theory of how the unfortunate Mr. St. Claire spent his last earthly moments on Tuesday night."

He led the way over to a corkboard, his broad backside rolling like a tugboat caught in a heavy wake. They had to navigate around a pair of steel dissecting tables. One had a body covered with a stained sheet lying on it, bodily fluids seeping into the channels that led to a drain clogged with cigarette butts. On the other table lay what was left of Vinny McGinty.

Rourke's step faltered. He came across a lot of dead bodies on the job and he always hated it, but there was something about seeing poor Vinny reduced to a piece of butchered meat on a coroner's slab that cut deep. The kid had been a loser, a vig collector, and a hop fiend, and he didn't have a blue star tattooed on his wrist, but he and Rourke had come from the same place. Rourke looked at Vinny and saw too much of himself.

At least they hadn't brought Bridey here, Rourke thought. He didn't know if he could have stood that.

The Ghoul had turned back around when he realized Rourke had stopped following. "I'm only just close to finishing the preliminary work on that one," he said. "Execution by means of a wire garrote, most likely from a piano, done at least two weeks ago, possibly more. Markers in his digestive tract might help us to pinpoint the actual time of death better, if we knew what he'd last eaten. Lividity suggests the body was moved after the heart stopped pumping. Oh, and his body was meant to be found eventually. That rope around his leg had been deliberately frayed to break."

"My bone," Rourke said as he joined the Ghoul by his corkboard.

The Ghoul blinked against the smoke floating in front of his face. "I beg your pardon?"

"He was meant to be found by me."

"Ah," the Ghoul said, as if he understood. Rourke wondered if he did, because he himself sure as hell didn't.

The photographs, of St. Claire's body and the room in which he died, were lined up in neat rows and covered the entire board. They had been taken with a camera that was equipped with a grid, so that one could measure such things as the distance of the corpse from the door.

"Mr. St. Claire's wounds," the Ghoul was saying, "are consistent with the cane knife found at the scene. The cut to his abdomen probably happened first, as it is not incapacitating and so he would still have been able to attempt to escape his assailant."

He picked up a pencil and pointed it at a photograph of blood-stains on the wall. "Once the bloodletting starts, if the knife is swung back for the next stab, you might see, as we do here, cast-off patterns—these small splatters higher up on the walls and ceiling, which line up in long, narrow arcs. What is occurring is that blood is being flung off the weapon as it is moved through the swing. These patterns tell us the nature of the swing, whether it was up and down, left to right. As I had surmised, our assailant was right-handed."

The Ghoul stopped to draw a wheezy breath and drop his cigarette butt on the floor. "I should note at this point that Mrs. St. Claire's dress bears copious bloodstains, but none in a cast-off pattern."

"Meaning?"

"Meaning either she was not the one swinging the knife, or she was the one swinging the knife but the cast-off pattern happened to fall elsewhere rather than on her clothing."

The Ghoul fired up another cigarette. He sucked in a deep lungful of smoke, held it a moment, then breathed it out through his nose. "So the attack begins. Mr. St. Claire tries to get away, tries to defend himself. His hands are cut, he loses his finger. The knife slashes across his groin, an artery is partially transected, and so you have arterial spurting. These spurts leave trails on the floor. Here, and here and here, for he is still running and the blood is spurting, you understand, producing these numerous spinelike projections emanating from the trail. But then comes the fatal cut—the one across his throat."

The Ghoul pointed to another photograph, this one a close-up view of Charles St. Claire's black, gaping death wound. "He has fallen to the floor by now, thrashing in his agony, and blood is spewing from his mouth."

"Spewing all over the murderer?"

"It would have been unavoidable. Yes, the blood is spewing—gushing, really. He begins to drown in his own blood; he is dying. Still for Mr. St. Claire it is not over. His assailant slashes the knife down one last time, across his chest and with considerable force, with a fury, one might say, and the blade becomes caught, for a moment at least, on a rib bone, a lung is punctured, and Mr. St. Claire continues to die. . . ." His words trailed off as he became lost in the scene he described, as if he were there in the slave shack, living in the moment of Charles St. Claire's terrible, violent death.

He blinked, and his gaze sharpened. He tapped his pencil against the photograph of the murder weapon. "Here is where the evidence seems to point most particularly to Mr. St. Claire's wife: her bloody thumbprint on the knife. The location and orientation of the identified ridges of the print show that it could have been made when the knife's momentum stopped abruptly, as when it caught on the bone, and the hand slipped from the handle onto the blade. The wound she bears on her palm could also have happened in this way. And part of the blood pattern on her dress is consistent with the bloody mist that is sprayed when a lung is punctured."

"So what about her story?" Rourke said. "Could she have got so bloody and cut herself and planted a print on the blade, all the while pulling the knife out of him?"

"Oh, yes. If he was still alive when she came upon him, as she has claimed. And her hand could have indeed slipped while she attempted to pull the knife out of him. The knife was not found in him, after all. It is both the strength of a case against Mrs. St. Claire and its weakness. The blood on her dress, her thumbprint on the knife blade, and the wound on her hand—this evidence, it is all consistent with Mrs. St. Claire being the assailant. However, it is also consistent—although less likely—with her version of the events, and the lapse of two hours' time between the victim's death and discovery by the housekeeper can be somewhat tenuously explained by shock."

Rourke huffed a short laugh beneath his breath. "Now that's something a jury would just love hearing—probably she did it, but maybe she didn't."

One of the Ghoul's almost-smiles flitted across his face. "Juries can indeed be difficult, especially where science is involved. My advice to you, Lieutenant, would be to discover a compelling motive. Preferably one which involves a basic human emotion like jealousy or greed. Juries like motives."

Rourke pushed his hands into his pockets and glanced back at the bodies, and then away again. "Motives I can do. In fact, I seem to have my pick of those."

"And I can give you a couple more." The Ghoul stuck his cigarette in his mouth and wheezed and lumbered his way back across the laboratory to a deep, chipped enamel sink. Alongside it sat a tray of gruesome, bloodstained instruments and a steel pan filled with the kind of horrors that come out of a slaughterhouse. Rourke swallowed down a sigh and made himself look. He really, really hated bloody pieces of dead things.

"The victim's internal organs." The Ghoul waved his hand at the bloody mess with a flourish. "Someone killed Charles St. Claire with a cane knife, but the man was already dying. He was poisoning himself with the wormwood in the absinthe he drank to excess. Furthermore, the inflamed condition of the mucous membranes in his nasal passages and the beginnings of a perforation of the nasal septum indicate a chronic ingestion of cocaine."

The Ghoul was taking care now to keep his gaze on the pan of organs and off the face of the man standing next to him, and Rourke had to give himself a derisive smile. "I take it you've heard about my own little flirtation with the happy dust," he said.

"After your wife died." The Ghoul lifted his head and met Rourke's eyes. "It is hard to lose one's love so young, so soon. But I think the worst is all over with now, yes?"

Rourke let his smile show, although the edge stayed on it. "I still have my bad nights, but I don't go out and wrestle with the gators anymore."

"Mr. Casey Maguire you do not consider an alligator?"

Rourke laughed, wondering how gossip always managed to

spread so fast around the department—he and Maguire had had their little set-to only this morning.

The Ghoul started to laugh himself, only to get caught up in a cigarette-induced coughing fit. "You might have flirted with the cocaine, Lieutenant, but Charles St. Claire went all the way. He was thoroughly addicted to his poisons, the symptoms of which are mental deterioration, confusion, paranoia, severe and sudden shifts in mood, hallucinations. One could say the man would have been misery itself to live with."

"Misery enough to put him out of it?"

"The temptation would arise, I should think." An expression flickered across the Ghoul's face that might have been amusement. "More fodder for the jury to chew over, yes? And I have still one other thing." He gave Rourke a glass petri dish, along with a magnifying glass. "I found this beneath the nail of the finger that was severed."

Rourke peered through the magnifying glass at the contents of the dish, while the Ghoul told him what he was seeing. "A chip of white enamel such as might be used to glaze ceramic. And a purple spangle, measuring a quarter-inch in diameter, which could have come from a woman's party dress, or a costume."

"There aren't any spangles on the dress she was wearing that night."

"No."

"Could he have picked it up earlier?"

"The chip of white enamel glaze perhaps. But the spangle was jammed beneath his nail with considerable force and deeply enough that it pierced the soft bed. It would have hurt—so much that he would have wanted to pry it out immediately. Provided he was not being distracted by other, worse, pain."

There was something vaguely familiar about the purple spangle, but Rourke couldn't place it. It didn't fit with anything else about that night.

Rourke's gaze went from the sheet-draped body on the dissecting table—a piece of bloody, mangled meat now—and then on to the photographs of Charles St. Claire's terrible last moments. It had been a bad death, a bad murder. The act of someone who had no stopping place.

"Why?" he wondered, unaware that he'd spoken aloud.

"If you are asking me rhetorically," the Ghoul said, his gaze also on the photographs, "then I would have to answer, Just about anyone could have done such a thing and for just about any reason. Even in our own hearts we can never really know for a certainty what foul deeds we might be capable of when in a state of fear or rage. Or passion. But surely you, a policeman, would know above all other men how this is true."

Rourke knew. Since his rookie year when he had seen a woman dunk her newborn baby into a washtub of boiling water, he had known that there was no limit to the ugly, cruel, and purely evil things human beings could do, even to the ones they were supposed to love.

"Now, if you were wondering," the Ghoul was saying, "whether I believe the Cinderella Girl took a cane knife and slashed and slashed, again and again, across the naked body of her husband until he died, drowning in his own blood . . . Then I would have to say the forensic evidence suggests that she did."

He looked up at Rourke blinking through the veil of smoke that floated between them. This time the smile came through, although Rourke wasn't sure he liked it. "Others have been hanged on much less."

It was as if she'd been waiting for him. She stood on the upstairs gallery of Sans Souci and watched him come, beneath a sky that looked bruised and hued with a strange and smoky green light.

He drove up on his Indian and stopped beneath the last oak before the house. He looked up at her. She turned and went inside, but he knew she was coming to him, and so he waited.

He heard her step on the shell drive before he saw her materialize out of the shadows. She was all Hollywood vamp this evening, wearing some white slinky tunic decorated with long strings of beads over black silk harem pants, and shoes with heels thin and sharp as spikes. A sequined headband shimmered in her dark boyish hair. She looked tougher since he'd last seen her yesterday, and yet she looked hurt, her eyes wary, as if all the betrayal, the lies, had been his and not hers.

She stopped before him. He could smell the coming rain and the chalk of the crushed oyster shells, and then she climbed onto the bike, straddling his lap with her thighs, and all he could smell was her.

They had come this way before, her riding in front of him on his motorcycle. Through the Pizatti Gate and into City Park, along palm-lined Anseman Avenue, pass the voluptuous bare-breasted statues. Late one night the summer they'd been lovers she had taken off all her clothes and posed for him next to those marble replicas of ancient goddesses. He had thought her body whiter and more beautiful than theirs.

They left the park at Black Bridge, where the railroad tracks cross the bayou, and got off the bike to climb to the top of the levee. Below them, kerosene lights burned in the boathouses against the coming rain. She stood against a plum-colored sky that pulsed with veins of lightning. Thunder cracked, and the wind clutched at her hair and whipped the beaded strings of her tunic around her hips.

"How about another dare, Remy?" he said. "The train will be coming along the bridge soon. We can always see if we can still beat it across."

She stared at him, her eyes wide and stark. Lightning flashed. "You know what's the funny thing about running, Day?" she said as the thunder exploded around them. "Once you start you can't stop. No matter how tired or scared you get, no one will let you stop."

The wind gusted so hard she rocked back on her heels, and the clouds opened up. Large flat raindrops struck the water hard, as if God were flinging rocks from heaven. It wasn't a small rain; it battered Rourke's hands and face, yet she had turned her own face up to the sky, as if she wanted to be beaten.

They had been standing apart, but now he went to her. He laid his hand against her cheek. In the two days since her husband's murder, the bruise had darkened and turned yellow at the edges.

"What did you two fight about that night, Remy?"

She startled beneath his hand, and pulled away from his touch.

"When did he hit you, darlin'? Was it before or after he told you he was going to try and have your marriage annulled?"

He watched her carefully, looking for surprise. What he saw was fear. It gusted across her face with the same force the wind had, rocked her like the wind.

She wrapped her arms hard around herself as if she had to hold herself together. Haunted, her eyes glowed at him.

"Was Charles going around telling people that? Why? Did he tell them why?"

"Suppose you take a wild guess for me."

She closed her eyes and turned away, and her head fell forward as though it were weighted down. "I don't know. I don't even know why he married me in the first place anymore. I thought he wanted me, but I think he wanted other men's envy more. He wanted me to quit the movies, to belong only to him, and he was hoping I would get pregnant right away, but I made him . . . I didn't want a child and I had no intention of giving up on my acting, and then one after another other things just seemed to come between us."

"What other things? His other women? Your other men?" Lightning streaked across the sky, and it was like the flash of a bullet firing out of a gun muzzle, white, deadly. "Was it Julius?"

Her back was curved and taut, the knob of bone at the nape of her neck prominent against the pale skin. "Is that it, Remy? Did Julius's dying come between you?"

He began to measure the lengthening silence with the rough, purring rhythm of the rain. The lanterns in the boathouses flickered. A ball of lightning rolled through the flooded canebrakes and broke into sizzling shards against a pier on the bridge.

Slowly she raised her head and looked at him. "There is no other man."

"That must be a first for you," he said, wanting to stop himself now, afraid that he wouldn't. She hadn't been faithful to him, either. The whole time they'd been lovers that summer, she had been fucking Julius too.

Somehow she had gotten close to him. Somehow she was laying her hands on his collarbone, and he felt the heat of them through the thin wet cambric of his shirt. "Day, please don't. I'm so scared, and I need you, and I can't bear to have you hating me."

He knew her, knew how she could be. She would play him, see how deep she could go into owning his soul, and she was so very good at it, the best he'd ever seen. He told himself he knew her too well, because if he thought for a moment that she really needed him, he wouldn't be able to help himself. He'd start looking for ways to turn every lie she'd ever told into truth.

She brushed her lips against his throat, and he let her, because risk was always so sweet, even when it was cruel. He turned his head so that his own lips could linger in her hair. "I stopped hating you long ago, baby, if I ever did. But what I haven't been so good at is forgetting. I can't help thinking about that last afternoon, the two of us on the willow island, making love, you crying in my arms. . . ." *And all the while Julius St. Claire was lying in that slave shack with a bullet in his head and a gun in his hand, and the taste of your mouth still on his.* "I can't help remembering how the next day you were gone, and without so much as a so long, darlin'."

He felt the whisper of her lips once more, and then they were no longer touching him and it was already a memory. A look of utter sadness shadowed her face, but her words were hard. "Perhaps you ought to be thanking me for sparing you."

He tried to match her with a hardness of his own, but he felt torn up inside and he was hurting. "Why? Because I haven't ended up dead yet?"

"Something like that."

Chapter Fifteen

It was so hot that June evening when they waked Remy Lelourie's daddy that you could practically hear the heat, as if the very air were panting and dripping sweat. Everybody stood around flapping funeral-parlor fans in front of faces that were as red as boiled beets, sweltering in their dark mourning clothes.

Her mama's face, though, Remy thought, was gray. Nearly as gray as the face of the man lying dead in his coffin.

Her daddy.

Well, he had been her daddy in the sense that he'd stuck his thing up between her mama's legs one night and left behind a little token of his appreciation. In New Orleans, whenever you patronized a butcher or a grocer he gave you a *lagniappe*, a little something extra free of charge to thank you for your patronage, like a bit of parsley or a lollipop. That's what she and Belle were— a *lagniappe* from her daddy to her mama. Thank you, my dear, and so long, darlin'.

He had died of eating spoiled gumbo, had her daddy. Or so the doctor was saying, although Mamma Rae could probably tell it differently. If it had been left up to Remy they wouldn't have come within miles of this wake, but Mama had wanted to. . . . She didn't know what her mama had wanted to do. Gloat was what she had thought, but now, looking at the way her mama stared at the man lying dead in his coffin, she wasn't so sure. You saw eyes like that sometimes on women who were addicted to laudanum.

Remy Lelourie looked around the parlor and allowed a sneer to show all over her face. The mirrors and pictures on the walls draped in black crepe; the clocks that were stopped. Daddy's black lacquered coffin balanced on a pair of chairs. A horseshoe of dyed red carnations sitting at Daddy's feet, a holy lamp burning at Daddy's head. There weren't a whole lot of mourners about. Just a few of her daddy's business acquaintances, herself, Belle, and Mama. Oh, yes, and the hostess, of course. Mrs. Maeve Rourke. Daddy's mistress, and the keeper of his house and heart for sixteen years. Lord God almighty, tongues sure were going to wag over this one.

Even with the perfumed candles burning and liberal use of lilac water and cologne, the room was still beginning to acquire a smell. But then that was what came of dying in New Orleans anytime between March and November, when your mourners were likely to work up a sweat. *That woman* was not only perspiring like a steam locomotive, she was looking positively haggard and sallow. Surely, there was no accounting for some daddies' tastes.

Remy was so busy looking at everything else that she missed seeing the boy come in. Suddenly he was just there, standing before the coffin with his hat in his hands, looking down at her dead daddy.

The last time she'd seen him had been about seven or eight years ago. He'd used to hang around outside their house for hours at a time in those days, spying on her and Belle. Remy had hated him, hated the very thought of his existence on this earth, and she decided that the worst torment she could make for him was to ignore him. As a plan it had only been a partial success. She'd ignored him so well he had quit coming around for her to torment.

Since his whole concentration was on her dead daddy, she didn't have to ignore him now. She knew he was a year older than she, which made him nineteen, but he had the body of a fully grown man. She had thought his face too sweet and pretty before, like the picture of an angel on a holy card. She liked it even less now—it was too defined by bold, uncompromising angles. She didn't like his mouth either; it was too sure of itself.

He must have felt her staring, for his head jerked up, and their gazes met and it was the same as that time she'd stuck her finger in a lamp socket just to see what it would feel like, a physical jolt that left her feeling shaken and hollow in her belly, scared and yet strangely exhilarated. She looked away from him, then looked back. He was more daring than she, for he had not looked away.

He stared at her for a moment longer than she could bear it, and then he looked beyond her.

China shattered on the floor, silencing the already dead quiet room, and everyone turned to look. Maeve Rourke stood in the doorway, with shards of a broken tea set and puddles of tea at her feet. For a moment the noise seemed to have stopped not only conversation and breath, but time as well.

"Day," she said, and her voice, too, sounded like a breakable thing. She started toward him, her arms outstretched as if she would gather him to her breast like a child.

"Don't," he said, and that was all. He turned on his heel and walked out of there, loose and confident, careless even, as if he'd just been passing by.

Remy Lelourie went after him, although she'd almost left it until too late. She had to run out the cottage's front door and halfway down Conti Street to catch him up.

"Daman Rourke!" she cried out, using his name for the first time. Even when she'd thought of him to herself before, he'd always been only *that woman's* boy.

He stopped and turned slowly, holding himself stiffer now, and she recognized the look on his face because she had lived with it so many times herself. It was, Swallow your blood and don't let your enemies know you're hurt.

"Where are you going?" she said.

He waved his hand at a motorcycle that was leaning up against the corner lamppost. "For a ride."

"Take me with you," she said, then added, "You know you want to."

There wasn't really room for the two of them on the seat, so she mostly sat in his lap, with her skirt rucked up above her knees. She could feel the thrum of the engine coming up through his body and into hers. His thighs were hard, and the summer wind was wet and hot, and by the time they had rounded the corner of Villere and headed toward Congo Square, she knew she was going to love this one boy and no other, forever.

He drove them out to Black Bridge, where the railroad tracks cross the bayou, and they got off the motorbike. He climbed up onto the steel bridge, leaving her to follow. They sat down on the walkway like the colored boys who fished from there did, feet dangling over the side, looking out toward the lake. Thunderclouds were building in the west, and the sky had turned strange, to the color of old blood. It was so hot the air crackled.

A bream popped the surface of the bayou below, and he leaned forward to look, bracing his palms on either side of his thighs, and she saw how his hands were covered all over with cuts—fresh ones and the scars from old ones.

"Your hands," she said, seizing one of them in both her own. "What have you done to your hands?"

He looked at her, startled by her vehemence, and then he laughed. "What a la-di-da miss you are. Haven't you ever watched anyone shuck oysters? I got me a job on an oyster lugger this summer."

He tried to pull his hand free, but she didn't want to let it go. She turned his hand over, to look at his palm, and saw the blue eight-pointed star on the inside of his wrist, and she nearly gasped aloud at the wrenching sense of loss she felt. Somebody else already owned him.

She released her grip on him. She smoothed her skirt down over her lap. "Why did you come to the wake?" she said.

"To see him dead." He said it matter-of-factly, and with no apology or explanation, and she admired him for it.

"They say he died screaming," she said, and she smiled so that he wouldn't mistake her feelings about the matter either.

He stared at her for a moment, not shocked so much as assessing. "He was your daddy," he finally said.

"So? Why should I care what happened to him? Do you care about *her*?"

"Yes," he said, and it angered her now that he wasn't hiding it, that he was brave enough not to hide it.

Heat lightning flared across the sky. She heard a rumbling and thought it was distant thunder at first, and then she realized the train was coming. A moment later, she saw it: the headlight, and the cowcatcher, and the smokestack belching steam. The tracks behind them began to vibrate and hum.

"How brave are you really, Daman Rourke?" she said. She saw his mouth form the word *what*, but she couldn't hear him, for just then the locomotive's whistle blared. Another sheet of lightning pulsed, making the world go stark white for an instant. "Have you ever tried to outrun a train?"

He didn't laugh at her or declare her crazy as anyone else would have done. He looked at the train that was rocking toward them, and then at the far end of the bridge, considering. "We'd never make it," he said.

"I dare you!" she cried, scrambling to her feet. She climbed onto the tracks and took off running.

The rails sang and shook, and the gravel between the ties rolled and scattered beneath her feet. She caught the flash of his shirt-sleeve out of the corner of her eye and she laughed, and then thought that she must save her breath—the train was bearing down on them, roaring, steam hissing, pistons hammering, rods thrusting and thumping like a dragon's heartbeat.

She snagged the heel of her half-boot on the edge of a sleeper and fell, sprawling hard onto her hands and knees. The whistle screamed; the whole world trembled.

His momentum had carried Daman Rourke past where she had fallen, but he came back for her, and she could see how close the train was by the look on his face.

He grabbed her arm and hurled her onto her feet, throwing her forward and then over the side of the bridge, and her scream of laughter was swallowed by the shriek of the locomotive. She felt the air of the train passing in a gust of wind and a concussion against her ears. Lightning flashed, bleeding the sky empty.

They landed on the levee, hitting the ground hard, and rolled down the grassy slope, ending up pressed together, wrapped up arm in arm like lovers. She could feel through the rough cotton of his sweat-soaked shirt, the hard and taut muscles that encased his rib cage, and the beating of his heart.

He pushed off her and fell onto his back, his chest rising and falling with his harsh breathing. "Aw, man, that was stupid," he said after a while. "Stupid."

She was looking at his face, though, and she could see the wild and unholy joy in his eyes.

The next evening she was waiting for him on the levee where the oyster luggers landed. She watched him unload the day's harvest, wash off at the pump, and then share a bucket of beer with the rest of the crew. She knew he had seen her, but he was making her wait. She didn't care; she would have done the same to him. It was a game. The best game ever imagined, because the risk was so high.

She thought he was going to come to her at last when he stood up from the upturned barrel he'd been sitting on, but instead he looked beyond her and his face changed. She watched, then, while two young men and a red-haired girl came up to him, talked with him, laughed with him. It was obvious the red-haired girl was sweethearts with one of the other boys, but that didn't matter—Remy hated her, vehemently, passionately. She hated all three of them, for the intimacy they shared with Daman Rourke, which was as palpable as the summer heat, and she knew that if she looked she would find that their wrists, too, had forever been marked by a blue eight-pointed star. They were his and he was theirs, and so they would forever own parts of him that she would never even be allowed to touch.

Only after they had left did he finally come sauntering over to her. He stopped, hooked a thumb in the pocket of his jeans, and thrust out one hip in a cocky and blatantly masculine pose that would have made her laugh if it hadn't worked.

"Hey, Remy," he said. "How you doin', girl?"

She stared at him a long time, long enough for him probably to start thinking she was crazy, so she said, "Do you ever wish sometimes that you could just run away? Just hop on a train and ride it to wherever it goes."

"Well, riding a train would sure beat all the dickens out of trying to outrun it," he said, and smiled.

She had seen the smile coming. Even so, when it broke across his face she was unprepared for the intensity of what she would feel. She wanted to scream and beat her fists against his chest. She wanted to kiss his mouth and capture that smile forever, make it hers alone.

She was staring at his mouth and so she saw his lips move and knew that he was speaking, otherwise she might not have heard him with the way her heart was pounding in her ears.

"Where you going to run to anyway, Remy Lelourie? You got to learn how to find the sweet places closer to home."

"There aren't any."

"Sure there are." He smiled again and held out his hand to her. "Come on and I'll show you one. I dare you."

She put her hand in his and let him lead her wherever he wanted to take her. She could feel the strength of his fingers wrapped around hers, and the scars and the calluses.

East of New Orleans was still a swamp, with water that was dark and quiet, and thick with cypress trees. They rode out as far as they could on his motorcycle and then went the rest of the way by pirogue.

The sun was misty and soft in the swamp, bathing the world in a green-gold light. She could tell he knew well where he was going with the way he maneuvered them around the sand bogs and through the flooded canebrakes. The bow sent insects rising up from the reeds and lily pads, and dragonflies dipping and hovering over the water. She saw the armored backs of gars and the black heads of water moccasins poking out of glassy pools beneath the thick overhang of trees.

When they came upon the willow island, she knew that this

was the place. Three ancient weeping willow trees grew together on a spit of sand. Their long, hanging branches, woven and entwined, had made a dry, green cave in the middle of the swamp.

The shadows of the slender leaves moved in etched and shifting patterns over a ground that was soft with mulch and moss. She stood in the middle of the willow cave and turned around in a slow circle. She thought that if the color green had a smell this would be it, pungent and of the earth. She knew without asking that he had been coming to this place for years—to dream and nurse wounds and just to think. To be alone—yes, that most of all.

She had to make him put it into words, though. "Have you ever brought anyone else out here?"

"No," he said, and he reached out and brushed the backs of his fingers across her cheek in a touch that seemed to be both a promise and a regret.

They came back to the willow cave often throughout that summer. Sometimes he would play his saxophone for her, and she would look at the pulse beating in his throat and think that she wanted to put her mouth right there, on the place where his heart beat, and leave it forever.

Once they found a cottonmouth sleeping in one of the lower branches, its brown-and-yellow-blotched body almost blending in with the tree bark, so that they didn't see it at first. Day was going to search for a stick so that he could pick up the snake and throw it in the water, when she stopped him by grabbing his arm. He had his shirtsleeve rolled up to his elbow, and the world seemed to diminish suddenly to nothing but the slick, hot feel of his skin.

"No, don't chase it off," she said. "I can bring it back for Mamma Rae." She had brought along a small wicker basket packed with pork-chop sandwiches, and she dumped those out now and held the basket up to him. "We can put it in this."

He stared at her, and she felt a flutter of excitement low in her belly. Then his gaze went from her to the snake, and she saw him go still inside.

"Mamma Rae says snake's no good for hoodoo if you don't catch it with your bare hands," she said, her voice low and taunting. "Come on, Daman Rourke. I dare you."

He smiled. "You just make sure you have that basket handy."

"Mamma Rae says you got to spell it by staring it down without flinching."

His laugh was a little hoarse, and he wiped his hands on his thighs. "Sweet mercy."

He hunkered down so he was eye level with the snake and he stared. He stared so hard his eyelids slitted half-closed and the veins on his neck stood out against the skin. The snake stared back, its eyes like chips of beer-bottle glass.

The snake's thick, muscular body slithered and uncoiled. Its head darted out, its white mouth opening wide on a hiss that was like water splashing on a red-hot stove. Its tongue flickered back and forth over two venom-filled fangs.

"You're flinching," she said.

"Shit," Day said under his breath. He spread his hands open and rolled up onto the balls of his feet.

Remy had never seen a body move so fast in her life. His hand lashed out, grabbing that cottonmouth by the back of its head and swinging around with it, coming right at her with it so that she let out a little yelp, and the snake's white mouth was open wide and its tongue was dancing and its thick, blotchy body was whipping from side to side. Day yelled something about the basket, but she was already thrusting it at him.

He threw that snake inside the basket so hard it made a *whapping* sound. Remy slammed down the lid and latched it.

They knelt on the floor of the willow cave, facing each other, with the basket jumping around as the snake thrashed and hissed and bit at the gingham-lined wicker. Day was breathing hard as he stared at her, and his eyes were so wide open they were rimmed with white, but there was that unholy look of joy on his face, and a hunger. Already, she knew, he was hungering for more.

She knew how she would make him hers now, how she would

make him hers forever. They were alike, she and Daman Rourke, in all their deepest, darkest places.

A couple of days later when she unpacked the basket it wasn't pork-chop sandwiches she laid out on the ground. She arranged the matching pair of gold-plated French revolvers, one in front of her, one in front of Daman Rourke, and next to each a single cartridge. The light was a murky yellow inside the willow cave. It had rained hard just an hour before and was drizzling still. Drops clicked on the green canopy overhead. The air smelled of wet cypress and moss.

"A St. Claire killed my great-granddaddy with one of these guns in a duel," she said.

He picked one up, running his fingers over the muzzle that shone blue with a thin layer of oil. "They wouldn't have fought a duel with guns like these. They're revolvers."

Strangely, his doubting frightened as much as angered her. "A lot you know, 'cause they did. My great-granddaddy lost Sans Souci in a faro game with a St. Claire and they fought a duel over it—but none of that matters now, anyway. I read about this game in a book. It's like roulette. You put only one bullet in the revolving part—"

"The cylinder," he said. "And you put a cartridge in the loading gate. What comes out the other end is the bullet."

She wrinkled her nose at him. "Well, pardon me all over. Then you spin the *cylinder* around a couple times and put the gun to your head and pull the trigger. And it's either bang you're dead, or bang you're not."

They sat facing each other, knees spread and almost touching. He looked down at the gun in his hand, and she saw his throat move as he swallowed. "You are pure crazy, Remy girl."

"We'll do it together." She picked up the other revolver. Her hand trembled, but she made it go still. "I dare you, Day. I double-dare you."

They loaded the guns and spun the cylinders, then spun them again, and then again, as if as long as the cylinders kept spinning, then so would their world keep on spinning and they couldn't die. Outside the willow cave it had begun to rain hard again. It sounded like a scattering of pebbles hitting the water. Or buckshot.

The hammer made a loud snap under her thumb as she cocked it. She raised the gun to her head, but he stopped her by gripping her wrist and pulling it back down again.

"No, not that way. Put the barrel in your mouth. Otherwise you could end up alive but with only half a head."

She wanted to ask him how he knew that but he had already put the gun's muzzle into his own mouth, and his eyes were somewhere else—in that dark and dangerous and seductive place.

She closed her own mouth around the muzzle. It was cool and greasy and tasted bitter. The rain had stopped again, as suddenly as it had started. It was now so quiet she heard a frog drop off a cypress and into the water.

She watched him, watched his finger, saw it tense and squeeze, and her mind was screaming *No!* as the hammer fell with a soft *click*.

Her eyes had flinched shut and she was already crying when her own finger jerked on the trigger. The *snick* of the hammer falling on the empty chamber sounded loud as a thunderclap to her ears.

She felt his hands take the gun from her and she opened her eyes to his face. She thought, He is going to kiss me, and then he was kissing her.

Rainwater dripped off the willows and the cypress trees and into the still water of the swamp. The ground was soft with mulch and moss beneath her back. He undid the long row of tiny pearl buttons on her shirtwaist, one by one, and his fingers trembled so that she had to help him. He spread open her blouse and slipped his hand beneath her chemise, lifting her breast free, and he lowered his head and kissed her there and then licked her nipple with his tongue, and then he kissed her mouth, and they breathed into one another.

He moved his hand up underneath her skirt, up her leg, past

her stocking and garter, to the bare skin of her thigh, and higher to the slit in her drawers. She arched against him and would have screamed if she hadn't stopped it with her fist.

This is too much, she thought. Too much. This could kill you if you weren't careful.

Chapter Sixteen

From the New Orleans *Morning Tribune*, Thursday, July 14, 1927:

WHY ISN'T CINDERELLA IN JAIL?

By Wylie T. Jones

The rich and famous are certainly different from you and me.

It has been over thirty-six hours since the body of Mr. Charles St. Claire, Esq., was found brutally slain in an old slave shack on his plantation home of Sans Souci, yet the police are strangely reluctant to arrest the most obvious suspect for the crime—Mr. St. Claire's wife, Remy Lelourie.

The Hollywood film star was found drenched in blood and sitting next to the body of her husband, with the murder weapon, a cane knife, lying on the floor by her hand, her bloody thumbprint plain on its blade. Police estimate that she was alone with the body a full two hours after the murder occurred, yet she raised no alarm and has no explanation for the elapsed time, other than "confusion" and "shock."

Furthermore, the colored woman who keeps house for the St. Claires has reported hearing a loud argument take place between the couple earlier that night, and not, apparently, for the first time. Mr. St. Claire's law partner has said that Mr. St. Claire had recently contemplated seeking dissolution of his marriage in the form of an annulment.

You have read on the pages of this newspaper of Mr. St. Claire's libertine excesses in the speakeasies and among the city's colored demimonde. The Hollywood movie sets and mansions where Remy Lelourie recently made her home are notorious for irresponsible and immoral behavior. Indeed, in the past year alone the actress has been blamed for one young man's suicide and named as a correspondent in two divorce cases.

One may perhaps see how within the godless lives of these two people a recipe for tragedy and despair and, yes, even death, might have been brewing. Yet with all this evidence the police remain strangely—and shamelessly—inactive and silent.

The Cinderella Girl's beauty and fame are legendary, and yet that should not make her immune to arrest, especially when the crime is murder, and a bloody, heinous murder at that.

From the New Orleans *Times-Picayune*, extra edition, Thursday, July 14, 1927:

GRENADE KILLS COP'S WIDOW

A grenade, hurled last night from the open window of an automobile, exploded on the front gallery of a house on Prytania Street belonging to Mrs. Bridget O'Mara, killing the 30-year-old woman instantly.

Peace was shattered at 11:25 P.M., Wednesday, on this quiet residential block in the Lower Garden District. Witnesses reported hearing the squeal of tires a few seconds before the explosion and saw a large black automobile with two men inside fleeing the scene shortly afterward. "There was a loud, sharp bang, and then flames and smoke," said a neighbor, who requested anonymity for fear of a reprisal. "The whole street just shook something fierce. I thought the world was coming to an end."

The police admit that the identity of the perpetrators and a motive for the bombing are unknown at this time. However, they believe that the intent of the attack was not to slay Mrs. O'Mara, but rather that it was directed at one of their own, homicide detective Lieutenant Daman Rourke, who was standing in the street in front of Mrs. O'Mara's house at the time.

Lieutenant Rourke, who was unavailable for comment at press time, suffered a concussion, and cuts and contusions. The detective is one of the principle investigators in the Charles St. Claire murder case, but the police are saying that there is no proof of a connection between the two events at this time.

Mrs. O'Mara was the widow of another homicide detective, Sergeant Sean O'Mara, whose boat disappeared during a fishing expedition on Lake Pontchartrain two months ago, and who is now presumed dead.

Daman Rourke was still two scotch and ryes away from being drunk.

Luckily, it was a problem the Swamp could take care of without breaking into a sweat, even deep into a hot July night. It was the toughest part of town, the Swamp—a few blocks along Girod Street near the river, where the flatboatmen did their drinking and whoring. Since Prohibition, the barrelhouses and saloons had withdrawn behind doors with grilles and peepholes, but they were still there, selling their rotgut and heat lightning, and pain.

His father had always descended into the Swamp for his wildest benders, and on the third day or so, Rourke would come to fetch him home. Once, when he was ten, he'd had to walk through a group of women kneeling in the street muck in front of the swinging, slatted doors of the barrelhouse where his father lay inside, sleeping in a puddle of vomit on the sawdust floor. The women, all Garden District matrons by the look of them, were singing about temperance and the light of Jesus and handing out white ribbons as pledges of purity against alcoholic drink. They had tried to give a ribbon to Daman Rourke that day, but he had pushed through them with his head down, pretending not to see. He had wanted to believe that the reformation and salvation they sang of was possible, but he'd already been taught better.

He strolled down that same street now, on legs that were a little too loose and with a head floating thick with illegal hooch and hard memories. He had a particular place in mind he was going to, but first he intended to make himself only one less scotch and rye away from being drunk. One less and no more because he had a stopping place—yeah, he could stop anytime. And if he didn't stop, well, you just have to look for new reasons to hate yourself when you start to wear out the old ones.

Even though the storm had passed, the gutters still ran and water dripped off eaves and spouts. The night sky had cleared, leaving the quarter moon haloed with a yellow ring. Rourke walked down an alley that stank of cat piss, climbed the rickety back steps of a dilapidated Victorian flophouse, and entered a hole in the wall that called itself a concert saloon because it had a dance floor and something that passed for a band.

He went up to the bar, which was nothing more than a crude plank board resting atop stacks of barrels. He caught the eye of one of the beer jerkers, girls who made a penny on every drink they sold and augmented their earnings with three-dollar trips to the rooms upstairs.

The hooch the girl brought him looked and smelled like horse liniment, but he drank it anyway. As he brought the empty glass back down to the bar, his gaze caught his reflection in a mirror advertising Carter's Little Liver Pills. He wasn't surprised to see his father's face staring back at him.

It just wasn't going to be a case of "there but for the grace of God go I," anymore, uh-uh. Instead it was only a matter of time.

It was long after midnight now and Katie would be sleeping. But earlier, before she'd gone to bed, she would have helped her grandmama peel and cut up the peaches for the ice cream while she waited for her daddy to come home. Because she still wanted to believe in promises, did his Katie.

To get to the old corrugated tin warehouse you had to squeeze through a broken slatted fence and cross a vacant lot littered with shattered bottles and rotting newspapers and rat droppings.

A single bare bulb dangled above the open door, where just inside a fat man in a pocketed apron sat on a folding chair and collected your dollar and gave you a ticket he ripped off a roll. Beyond him lay darkness, stifling hot and fogged with smoke. It wasn't until you got all the way inside that you saw the pit, enclosed by bloodstained wooden boards and lit by burning pitch torches.

Crude bleachers ten rows deep rimmed the dark cavern, and crowded together on the rough planks were men of all colors—Negroes, mulattos, redbones and whites—passing around bottles and buckets of beer, betting against the house and one another, and bellowing advice to the two men who knelt at opposite ends of the pit, each cradling a docked and shaved-necked gamecock. The birds, sensing blood, churred low and deep and clawed at the dirt with their fighting spurs.

In a prime viewing spot before the pit was a single chair, and sitting in it as if she occupied a throne was a stately figure in a long white sequined gown. A high, stiff collar flared around her face like the lip of a bell, and her skin caught the light of the torches, holding it with the muted glow of slightly tarnished brass. Her straight black hair fell to her shoulders and framed deep, slanted eyes.

An enormous Negro stood at her back and searched out the crowded, noisy darkness with eyes that gleamed like peeled eggs. A bolo knife hung from a leather cord around his neck and lay against a chest that was slabbed with muscle and glistened with oily sweat.

Rourke knew she'd spotted him the moment he paid his dollar and walked through the door, but she pretended surprise as he came up to her, smiling wetly with her full and painted mouth, batting eyelashes thick as feather dusters. It was only when you got this close to Miss Fleurie that you noticed the big hands and the Adam's apple in her muscular neck.

"Well, if it isn't Lieutenant Daman Rourke, as we all live and breathe. Most men, after they have a brush with death, go to church. I guess you decided to come slummin'."

She spoke in a husky voice that some folk claimed held a trace of the Yankee in it. Bets had been circulating for years on the nature of Miss Fleurie and her origins, but she wasn't saying. She wouldn't even admit to being a man, and if she'd ever taken a lover, he or she wasn't saying, either.

Rourke smiled as he sat down on the end of the bleacher next to her, although drink, the lateness of the hour, and his sore ribs were making him feel weary unto death. "It's always a pleasure seein' you, too, Miss Fleurie."

She pursed her red mouth into a perfect O. "Oooh. Miss Fleurie, she in trouble now," she said, and tossed back her hair with a hand that flashed a diamond ring big as a chickpea.

Miss Fleurie bootlegged the liquor sold in the colored juice joints and barrelhouses and bordellos, and she kept hopheads of all races flying high, supplying the best cocaine, opium, and marijuana to be had in town.

But for kicks she owned and ran one of the more popular speakeasies down in the French Quarter, one that drew the tourists and the college crowd. When she wasn't here at a cockfight or at the track, most nights you could find Miss Fleurie at the Pink Zebra. She had turned her speakeasy and herself into one of the city's main attractions, thrilling her flush customers with a slice of the naughty life: flapper music, gin fizzes, and a flamboyant, flaming drag queen.

She also had one other claim to fame, one that she shared with homicide detective Daman Rourke: They were the two best *bourré* players in New Orleans. They had never played each other, though, but that was only because Rourke had stayed away for years from the Pink Zebra and Miss Fleurie never played *bourré* anywhere else.

At a signal from the referee, the trainers had thrown their birds into the middle of the pit. The two cocks, one cinder gray, one black tipped with gold, leaped into the air and landed with wings flapping, spurs flailing, grappling beak to beak. The gray scored first, sinking its spur deep into its enemy's back. Blood gouted and sprayed in bright drops through the air, glittering like red crystal tears, spattering across Miss Fleurie's face and the flaring collar of her gown.

"They live to fight, those cocks," she said. "If they can't fight they just pine away and die."

Rourke's smile changed, showing a flash of real amusement. "Otherwise they die by fighting."

She made a soft hooting noise deep in her throat; she hadn't bothered to wipe the blood off her face. The black had grabbed the gray by its comb and thrown it into the dust, wings beating, beak stabbing, spurs slashing and impaling.

"Speaking of fighting cocks, you given much thought to Casey Maguire lately?" Rourke said. " 'Cause I think he's got his eye on your little slice of the bootlegging pie. It was a clue I got yesterday, when he tried to finger you for murder."

Her mouth curved into a small smile. "You use what you think might work," she said. She did not, he noticed, ask him whose murder or which murder.

She turned to the giant behind her and touched him lightly on the arm. "Go to the speak next door and get us some drinks, darlin'. A Manhattan for Miss Fleurie and for the gentleman a scotch and rye."

She watched him go and then turned her attention back to Rourke. She crossed one slender, silk-stockinged leg over the other while she fitted a cigarette into an ebony holder that was nearly a half a foot long. She held it out for him to light, leaning into him.

His hand closed over her wrist, holding the cigarette in place while he lit it with a match, but as she started to straighten and pull away, he tightened his grip. "You're going to tell me everything you know about both Vinny McGinty and Charles St. Claire."

She raised her plucked and penciled eyebrows. "Who?"

He squeezed her wrist, hard, crushing flesh to bone. It took a while, because she was tough, but he kept squeezing, harder and harder, until he saw the pain begin to register in her eyes, and even then he said nothing more.

She looked from his eyes to his hand that was crushing her wrist, then back up to his eyes. In the pit, the black cock was trailing a broken wing but it wasn't quitting. It attacked again with a blustery rattle and a flurry of feathers and sharp, flashing spurs. Shouts and screams pulsed and bounced off the tin walls. The hot air reeked of blood and sweat.

"You're being too subtle for Miss Fleurie, sugar," she said. "She thought the whole point of paying for juice was to keep from getting squeezed."

"But I'm not on your payroll. Sugar. So how about I pick a law out of a hat and arrest you for breaking it? Then I haul your sweet ass down to the House of Correction and throw you into a two-man cage with the biggest, meanest cornholer I can find. Or am I still being too subtle for you?"

Derision sparked in her eyes, but her mouth had drawn tight and gray now from the pain he was giving her. A roar went up from the crowd as the fighting cocks sprang again and wrung together. A mist of blood and ripped plumage hung in the dust cloud over the pit.

"They both liked to blow coke up their nose, and Miss Fleurie, she was their snow queen," she said, and then her mouth quirked into a taunting smile. "So arrest me."

He smiled back at her, keeping the mean on it, but he had let her go. "That much I know," he said. "Give me something I don't."

She brought her wrist up and looked at the marks, like a string of purple grapes, that he had left on her golden flesh. In the pit the cocks were really tearing the shit out of each other now. Slashing and beating and stabbing.

"What more is there to say about Vinny McGinty? Step out the door and spit into the gutter and you're likely to hit another just like him. He was a paying customer, though, so I don't know why I should want to go and kill him."

Her hand was steady as she brought the tip of the cigarette holder to her mouth and drew deep. She held in the smoke for two beats before she let it out slowly. "Mr. Charlie, now, he wasn't so unique either. He was just a naughty boy who wanted to be a good boy without having to give up the joy of being naughty. Still, I got to kind of liking him those times I used to bring his coke 'round to that flat he kept down on Rampart Street." Her mouth pulled wryly and she breathed a laugh, along with more smoke. "What you want to go and look at Miss Fleurie like that for? You think you're the only one who's got friends? Mr. Charlie always invited Miss Fleurie up and he'd sit down and have a drink with her like she was white, talk to her like she wasn't some freak show, and we'd both pretend we didn't know what kind of game he was really playing at."

Her gaze went back to the pit. The black cock had been gored through the eyes, but he fought on, trying to slash and impale an enemy he could no longer see. "Lately, though, nothing was mattering to Charles St. Claire much anymore except getting high. He was at that place where he would have sold his soul for the flake going up his nose."

"When y'all did this talking," Rourke said, "what was it about?"

"What everybody else talks about. How hot it's been, buying on margin and selling short." The smile playing on her mouth deepened, became self-derisive. "He was all the time trying to get Miss Fleurie to kiss so he could tell."

"Did he do any of this telling to you, like maybe about who *he* was kissing?"

She brought her gaze back to his face. "You mean besides Lucille Durand?"

"Yeah, besides her."

Her slanted eyes narrowed at the corners, became taunting. "Oh, there was a someone else, sure enough. Only you should know by now that Miss Fleurie, she doesn't give things away. You want it you got to come and play for it. You and me over the *bourré* pot at the Pink Zebra this Sunday night."

She startled a laugh out of him. "What've you been smoking?"

"You give me a game, I'll give you the name. A two-hundred-dollar pot with a twenty-dollar bottom limit."

Sweet Jesus. Rourke felt the blood start to sing in his neck. He could lose everything he owned down to his alligator shoes in one sweet night playing for stakes like that. He told himself he wasn't going to do it, wasn't going out on that screaming edge this time, not this time, uh uh, because it was getting to be too many days in a row now, and it was bad for you, like cocaine. He told himself that he would walk away from it, this time he would walk away, but he was lying.

She was laughing at him now with her eyes. "Miss Fleurie always say, you got to pay by playing."

Rourke smiled. "I'm going to beat your ass hollow, sweetheart."

She pursed her mouth and waved her hand in front of her face like a fan. "Oooh. A girl can dream."

The bodyguard with the bolo knife came up with the drinks, but Rourke was already pushing to his feet. She stopped him by laying her hand on his back. He turned slowly, so that for a moment her hand seemed to cling to the linen cloth of his coat before it fell to her lap.

"I lied," she said. "Sometimes Miss Fleurie do give it away for free. . . . Vinny McGinty was all the time talking about going up north to Chicago, so when he disappeared a couple of weeks ago, Miss Fleurie figured that was where he'd gone. But the last time she saw Vinny that boy was some scared, too scared to even care about getting high. All he wanted was the name of a good lawyer, and so Miss Fleurie gave him the name of a dragon slayer."

He studied her face, but she was giving nothing more away. She drew on her cigarette, blew smoke out in front of her, and looked into it with flat eyes.

"I hope Miss Fleurie didn't bet on the gray," he said.

She swung her head back around to look into the pit, where the black cock stood with one gold-tipped wing trailing in the dirt and one spurred foot buried to the hilt in the neck of its foe. It threw back its blinded, bloodied head and crowed in triumph.

Chapter Seventeen

"He was broke," Fio said.

Rourke had started to bring a hot tamale up to his mouth, but he stopped with it poised in the air and stared at his partner. They were sitting on an iron bench beneath the banana trees in Jackson Square, grabbing a bite of supper in the waning of a Friday that had turned out to be hot and grouchy and long.

Yesterday's edition of the *Morning Tribune* featuring Wylie T. Jones's column "Why Isn't Cinderella in Jail?" had outsold the competition five to one. As a result, the city's other four newspapers had woken up this morning simultaneously struck with the same revelation: Their street circulation would go up more every day the saga of the matinee idol and her brutally murdered husband dragged on, and a Trial of the Century would milk that baby for all it was worth.

Today's first and extra editions, taking their cue from Wylie T. Jones, had been full of editorials on how all the evidence pointed to the wife having done it, and how nobody, no matter how famous or beautiful, should be above justice and the law. Inflamed by printer's ink, public opinion had turned on Remy Lelourie like a rabid dog, and suddenly the mayor and the city council and the city prosecutor's office and the police department were all asking each other why she hadn't been arrested yet.

"Charlie St. Claire was broke up until Cinderella came along, that is," Fio said. The big cop seemed to be taking things nice and easy today, but Rourke could sense an undercurrent of constraint now riding between them. It would be a long time if ever, he thought, before he could regain his partner's trust, and the lies and the omissions hadn't even all come out yet.

"St. Claire had been dropping gambling markers on every bookie in town," Fio went on. "And he'd been playing *bourré* most every night, stuffing the pot like there was no tomorrow. He'd get hopped up on the happy dust, I guess, and start thinking he was invincible. Near as I can figure it, he's gone through over a hundred thousand dollars of her money in the five months since she said 'I do.' Paying off old debts and new ones."

Rourke tilted his head back, his gaze resting on the cathedral spires. He was hot, aching, and tired, because he'd been run over by a big Lincoln, it was summer in New Orleans, he hadn't slept in years, and he'd spent all day crawling through the city's underbelly trying to find out what had had Vinny McGinty so scared, and what he'd hoped a dragon slayer like Charles St. Claire could do about it.

And, coming up later this evening, there was Bridey's wake to be endured.

"Maybe he made Cinderella marry him so he could get his hands on all her dough," Fio said. "Maybe he had something on her, was putting the bite on her, and then maybe she turned the tables on him, got something on him, and he got scared and saw the annulment as a way out and—hell, I'm making my own self dizzy with this shit."

Rourke opened his eyes and leaned forward over his spread knees to bite into his tamale. "You got it wrong, anyway, Fio. She just wanted to come home, and he was being so nice and all. Courting her so sweetly."

"She tell you that?"

"Among other lies."

Fio lit a cigar and flicked the spent match at a pigeon that had come begging for crumbs. "She had so many reasons to kill him, makes you wonder what took her so long. The colored lady who does for them, Miss Beulah—she says they had a bad spat that night, lots of wailin' and shoutin'."

"That fits with the bruise she's wearing."

"Yeah. The happy couple. Oh, and the day before, some kinda owl, a lee-boo—"

"*Le hibou.*"

"Yeah. Well, it was out there hooting in broad daylight, which is a sign someone's gonna die." Fio made his eyes go wide. "And goldarned if that didn't just happen."

Rourke laughed and shook his head, then winced as the movement knocked loose the scotch-and-rye hangover that had settled behind his eyes. He might have stopped last night one drink short of being drunk, but he was still suffering.

A hard white sun beat down on the square. The hot, wet air vibrated with the blaring of horns, the clatter of streetcars, drovers' whistles, and hawkers' shouts. Rourke watched a pair of street dips boost the wallet of a man in a striped jacket, who was being distracted by a girl selling little bouquets of violets in paper cones. It was too hot to give chase to some penny-ante pickpockets, and it wasn't his lookout anyway. He had murders to solve. Truth and justice and honor and all that shit.

"For all his faults," Fio was saying, "this St. Claire seems to have been one helluva lawyer. The story goes he once floated a defense that had his client pulling the trigger accidentally not just once, mind you, but a dozen times. The guy had to stop and accidentally reload, and still St. Claire got the jury to buy it."

A spasm band had formed up on the corner across from the French Market and was starting in on their slap-foot dancing. A washboard, pot covers, and tin cans banging out "Way Down Yonder in New Orleans." The bottle caps on the bottoms of the boys' flying shoes tap-tapped on the brick banquette, striking sparks. Their mouths opened wide, singing hi-de-hi, ho-de-ho. . . .

"I'm figuring," Fio said, "what the Cinderella Girl did was hire some colored boy to take the cane knife to that scissors and knife sharpener you talked to. We find that boy, we can show premeditation, and then we got her nailed."

The boy with the washboard had set it down so that he could throw his whole body into his slap-footing rhythm. This time Rourke didn't holler his name. He stood up and started walking toward him, casual, a hand in his pocket, not looking at the boy at all.

The boy spotted him, though, and took off running.

The boy tried to cut through the market and slammed into a woman who was carrying a wicker tray of coconut pralines. Pink, white, and brown candy went flipping through the air like tiddly-winks. He careened into a stand pyramided with cantaloupes next. Rourke, in pursuit, leaped over the rolling melons, his arm swinging wide and knocking into a mountain of okra, setting off an avalanche.

The boy looked over his shoulder and saw that Rourke was gaining on him. He darted across the street and into the fish market. Rourke could follow him by the disaster he left in his wake: the man waving a scaling knife and bellowing curses; the set of jangling, swaying scales; the giant loggerhead turtle broken out of its crate and making his ponderous and steady way toward the open door and freedom.

Rourke chased the boy back out of the market and into the street. He heard a shout, the frantic clanging of a streetcar bell, then smelled the hot electrical scorch of brakes skidding on the tracks. The boy dodged in and out among cars and trucks, horse-drawn carts and buggies, dashing around the corner onto Royal—a street of secondhand furniture stores and curiosity shops.

The boy made the mistake of looking over his shoulder again and ran smack into a sidewalk table full of alligator skulls, stumbling, his foot thrusting into a pair of gaping jaws, coming down hard on sharp, jagged teeth. He screamed but he didn't stop, although he was limping badly now. He lurched down a service alley, with Rourke hard on his heels.

"Dammit, LeBeau," Rourke tried to shout through his sawing breaths. "Will you stop now?"

The boy didn't stop, so Rourke threw himself forward, tackling him around the waist. They hit the flagstones hard, with Rourke on top, and he heard and felt all the breath drive out of the boy with a *whoosh* like a punctured tire. Rourke's own battered ribs shrieked with pain.

He turned the boy over onto his back. His thin, shallow chest jerked worse than a speared catfish, his eyes bulged, and his mouth pouched as he tried to suck in air. About the time Rourke started to worry that the kid was going to croak on him, the scrawny chest spasmed once, hard, and then he drew in a deep, wheezing, gagging breath.

Rourke gripped him by the arm, hauling him to his feet and down a narrow set of steps that led to the kitchen door of a restaurant. The air was cooler, almost dank within the brick-enclosed space. Smells of fried *panné* and shrimp gumbo drifted through the screen door.

The boy's gaze met Rourke's, slid away, then came back again. LeBeau was LeRoy's brother and so Rourke knew him to be fourteen, although he looked closer to twelve with his slight build and round, pug-nosed face.

"I oughta hit you upside the head," Rourke said. "What in hell possessed you to run like that? Didn't you see that other cop with me? You could've wound up with a bullet in your back."

LeBeau's right eye was twitching, but he got his lips to curl into a pretty good sneer. "So what you goin' to do? Put a bullet in the front of me?"

"Don't tempt me."

The boy's face remained defiant, but the tic in his eye picked up a beat.

"Let's start," Rourke said in his meanest beat-cop voice, "with what you think I know that's got you runnin' scared."

"Man, I don't know what you talkin' 'bout."

"I'm talking about how I know you were out gigging for frogs on the bayou the night Mr. St. Claire was killed."

"I wasn't out there that night. Must be somebody else you thinkin' of."

"Did you see someone come running out of that old slave shack in back of Sans Souci?"

"I tol' you I wasn't out there that night."

The used-clothing store at the mouth of the alley was opening up for the afternoon. Someone came out front and unwound the rope that fastened a roll of canvas awning, and it fell with a snap like a gunshot. The boy nearly leaped clean out of his skin.

Rourke smiled. "And they say you never hear the shot that kills you."

The boy swallowed so hard his throat made a clicking noise, and his gaze broke away from Rourke's. The tic was so bad now it pretty much had his whole body shaking.

"LeBeau—"

"Didn't go giggin' for frogs that night, I'ma tellin' you."

Sometimes it was like trying to slip a noose over the head of an alligator. Sometimes you had to come at the knotty problem from the other end. "You heard from your brother LeRoy lately?" Rourke said.

LeBeau's shoulders sagged with relief at having the subject changed. He wiped his damp palms on his overalls. "He writes Grandmama ever' now an' then, and she gets me to read they letters for her."

"Did your brother hear something bad about Miss Lucille, something that made him angry?"

The boy's gaze flickered at Rourke, then away again. "Don't know what you be on 'bout. Lucille ain't done nothin'."

"Did LeRoy write and maybe ask you to go pay a visit to Mamma Rae, maybe ask her to be putting hoodoo spells on Mr. St. Claire?"

LeBeau shook his head, but the denial was puny this time, and slow in coming.

Rourke took out the pack of cigarettes and box of matches that he always carried around in his coat pocket, even though he didn't smoke. He offered one to LeBeau, and while the boy lit up, he talked to him, feeding him the line.

"You ever been up to Angola to see your brother? He ever tell you what it's like? Working from can't-see to can't-see in the cane and sweet-potato fields, the sweat burning in your eyes and the sun so hot on your head it fries your brain like grits. Then one day you look at the gun bull a bit cock-eyed, or maybe you don't duck your head and call him sir quick enough, and he whips you bloody for it, and then gives you a week in the Hole with nothing but a biscuit and greens, and a cup of water a day."

The boy's hand trembled a little as he took a drag on the cigarette. "Why you sayin' . . ." He choked. "What you gettin' at?"

"Well, I guess I was sort of preparing you for the eventualities of your actions. You see, I happen to know for a fact that you put *gris-gris* in Mr. St. Claire's bed and a salt cross on his gallery. I got all the proof that me and a jury are going to need, and the law doesn't look too kindly on that, uh-uh. It's called breaking and entering, and whether it's for putting something in, or taking something away, it doesn't much matter, you can still get fifteen years for it. Maybe if you're lucky they'll put you into the same dormitory with your brother and he can protect your cherry ass."

The boy sucked on his lower lip, then took a swipe at his mouth with the back of his hand. "But I didn't know 'bout that law. Breaking and . . . what's-it. I didn't know nothin' 'bout that."

"No, I don't guess you probably did. I don't expect your not knowing will cut much ice with the judge, either."

Rourke took off his hat, surprised he still had it with him. He fanned his face with it, bracing his hip against the stair rail, not looking at the boy anymore, reeling him in now. "Lord, I'm telling you this summer heat sure is brutal. It's got me so wore out and frazzled I don't know whether I'm comin' or goin'. It's getting to where I can up and forget something that just a minute ago I knew for a fact."

Slowly, he turned his head and pinned the boy to the wall with his stare. "On Tuesday—two nights past at about nine o'clock, when you were out on the bayou—what did you notice was going on up at Sans Souci?"

Rourke could practically see the scales tilting back and forth in the boy's head, the scales he'd learned from birth to use when dealing with the white man, weighing what he had to give up against what he hoped to get away with.

"I heard this screamin'," he finally said. "Seemed like a screech owl. But then I saw this thing go runnin' 'cross the yard from the shack. I don' know what it was, suh, honest I don', 'cept it wasn't no human bein'. It was all white and it kinda floated in an' out the trees, an' it had snakes for hair."

"You sure this thing you saw was running from the shack, and not to it?"

"I'ma sure. Came flyin' right out the do' and went floatin' 'cross the yard."

"Did you see anything else after that then—say, someone running from the big house out to the shack?"

"No, suh. But then I wasn't stickin' 'round to do any more lookin'."

Rourke slipped a sawbuck into the boy's overall pocket. "One more thing. Did anybody give you a cane knife recently and ask you to get it sharpened by the knife-grinder who works along Esplanade?"

LeBeau's face wrinkled with genuine puzzlement. "Huh? What for would anybody do that? It ain't the time of year for cuttin' cane."

Rourke gripped the boy's shoulder. "Thank you kindly, LeBeau, and now get lost," he said, then gave him a little shove when he didn't move his feet fast enough. "Go on, get. And leave the hoodoo alone."

LeBeau disappeared out of the back end of the alley a few seconds before Fio came trotting around the corner from the front end. The big man's chest was heaving, his face wet and flushed from the heat. His .38 Policeman's Special was in his hand.

He stopped in front of Rourke. He had to suck in air for three beats before he could talk. "Man, you southern boys are full of fun. Chasing jigaboos all over to hell and gone, and during the hottest part of the day—"

"His name is LeBeau Washington," Rourke said. "My friend LeRoy's little brother."

Fio looked away, drew in a breath and then let it out slowly.

"Okay. LeBeau Washington. So you going to tell me what that was all about?"

"LeBeau was in a pirogue out on the bayou across from Sans Souci gigging for frogs the night our man bought it—probably with a couple other boys but he'll never give up their names without a beating. He says he heard screaming and saw something white floating in and out among the trees, coming from the shack. It had snakes for hair."

"No shit?" Fio put his revolver back into his shoulder holster, snapping shut the flap. "Case solved. The gowman done done it."

"Colored gossip has it that Mamma Rae was the one putting those spells on good ol' Mr. Charlie. She could have been out there that night—"

"Killing him? A little murder to drum up the voodoo business?"

"Or maybe she was making a *gris-gris* delivery and she saw something."

"Aw, Jesus." Fio rubbed the back of his neck, shaking his head. "Don't say it, don't fucking even think it. I don't want to go see that witch-woman. You heard about what happened to the last cop who tried to roust Mamma Rae? She put some kind of spell on his cock and he went to take a whiz, and the damn thing came off in his hand, just fell right off, and—what're you laughin' at?"

"That never happened. That's just a New Orleans story, like the one about the hurricane that blew an old woman clean through the slats of a fence without breaking a bone in her body. And the baby that was supposed to've been born with the head and feet and tail of an alligator."

"The gator baby never happened either?"

"Nope."

"Hunh. So you say. But then you lie. You lie with a smile, but you still lie."

They could feel and smell it, the warm brown breath of the river. And a tugboat's horn blew a sad, deep note, touching on lonely places. The evening sky was just starting to turn a dusky pink by the time they made it out to the *batture* settlement where Mamma Rae lived. *Traiture*, voodoo witch, juju woman.

In the years that she had been New Orleans' most powerful *tanton macoute*, she'd probably made a fortune off her black magic arts, but her house was indistinguishable from the other driftwood houses sharing space on the mud flats with the willow trees and flatboats, the dead garfish and the rotting canebrakes. They were watched as they walked along, eyes peering around doorjambs, through rotting window curtains. The air reeked of somebody cooking cracklins outside in an iron kettle.

She stood, as if waiting for them, in what passed for her front yard—a patch of jimsonweed and crabgrass. She was an ageless woman with eyes like beads of jet and tightly coiled black hair with dead blue lights in it. Her thick upper lip was pushed out with a wad of snuff.

"I expected y'all sooner," she said in a voice that was full and husky. The cicadas, Rourke noticed, had suddenly stopped their fierce humming.

"And here," he said, "the very last thing I told that LeBeau was to stay away from the hoodoo."

She stared at him with eyes that were at once both empty and hot, then slowly her gaze went to Fio, to his crotch, and she made a wet sound with her tongue. "You can take yo' hands outta yo' pockets, white man. If I done decided to spell your thing, yo' hands sure wouldn't save it."

She laughed then, and took a step back and planted a fist on her hip, posing for them. She wore a plain black skirt with a red sash around her waist, and a man's white shirt that was open at the neck, displaying a necklace made of snake bones. From it, nestling between her breasts, hung an alligator's fang encased in silver. The fang stirred and trembled, even though she wasn't breathing hard.

"If you've come callin'," she said, "then no sense to standin' out here with the skeeters." She turned and led the way through the mud and canebrakes, following a path only she could see. Her figure was still good, and she showed it off in the way she moved, hips swaying, her arms swinging slow and easy.

Mamma Rae's shack was set up high on stilts. She led them up rickety steps to a warped door with an old-fashioned string latch. It was murky inside, lit only by a half-dozen rancid black tallow candles set in saucers of water on the altar. In the old days slaves would have come to someone like her asking for the gift of domination over the minds of their masters. Now it was for help with a lottery gig, a powder to prevent a man's seed from taking root, a potion for taking that man away from his wife.

But she was a healer too: She could douse the fire in a fever and ease the cramp of a bellyache. She could make warts disappear.

She poured a syrupy homemade wine into a couple of jelly glasses and gave one to each of them. She might have been a hostess in an uptown parlor, except this front room was furnished with gourds, a white horse tail, broken bits of horn and bone, dried lizards and toads. A crude human effigy fashioned out of black wax sat in the middle of the altar.

The juju woman's mouth and eyes weren't smiling as she looked at them, but still her whole face gave an impression of laughter. "I figger you po-licemens want to ask me where I was the night that white Creole man got hisself killed."

"Then you probably got your answer all figured out too," Fio said. He had come no farther than just inside the door, and he'd set his jelly glass down on the window sill without touching it.

"I was right here. Had me some supper, went to bed."

"Uh-huh." Fio rocked back and forth on his feet and shifted the matchstick he was chewing on from one side of his mouth to the other. "People say you were putting voodoo spells on Mr. St. Claire."

"People ax me to do things for 'em sometimes. Me, I'ma obligin' soul."

"Yeah, a regular Sister of Charity you are," Fio said. "And those things people ask you to do—what might those be?"

"The things people wants, Mr. Po-liceman. I only give people what they wants."

She made that wet noise with her tongue again and rubbed the thumb of one hand over the knuckles of the other. She wore a ring fashioned of copper—two snakes entwined, mating with each other, killing each other. Rourke remembered it from that day, as a boy, when she'd given him the tattoo. Then, for some strange reason, it had made him think of the rings the nuns wore to symbolize their marriage to Christ and their faith.

Rourke could feel Fio's gaze on him, but he said nothing. He would let his partner ask the questions that he knew Mamma Rae would never answer. She would tell him things, though. People always told you something, even with what they didn't say.

As if she had read his thoughts, she turned to look at him, her eyes like two burning coals now in her face, and he felt her power that he knew came from that dark place inside himself.

"You don' like my wine?" she said, and Rourke smiled because he had never met a dare he didn't take.

He expected the wine to be sweet, but it wasn't. It tasted of the black earth of a grave, of blood spilled in rage. Of the hot, wet spot between a woman's legs. One swallow and already he felt it burning in his own blood, melting him from the inside out.

Her voice was low and taunting, and strangely echoing in the small and crowded room. "What you afraid I put in that wine? Some woman's *cassolette*, uh-huh. You afraid I goin' make you crazy to death with love?"

Rourke smiled again and drank some more. His skin was on fire now. His heartbeat was like a wild riff inside him. "At least I'd die happy," he said.

She laughed and nodded. "Mmmmm-huh. Make you crazy in love." She twisted her head around and called out to Fio, who was still standing by the door and watching Rourke now with troubled eyes. "How 'bout you, Mr. Po-liceman? I could give you some horsemint. Make that thing you so worried 'bout stand up stiff as a beanpole."

Rourke thought he would go take a look at her hoodoo altar, but rather than walking he seemed to float there instead. Bowls of holy water, plaster statues of saints, a sacred sand pail. A cotton-mouth coiled around a piece of brain coral. He thought it was dead and stuffed, and then its belly undulated and its mouth stretched open. The forked tongue flickered and the fangs glittered in the candlelight, and for one wild moment he almost reached out to touch it, to capture it and feel its poisonous bite. The old ones claimed the voodooienne got her powers by mating with a snake.

She had come to stand close beside him. There was a strong musky smell to her, like what you find in cheap bawdy houses where they don't change the sheets on the beds for days on end.

He felt himself turning, almost against his will, to look at her. She picked up a tin can from off the shelf by his head and spit the snuff into it. He noticed that next to where the tin can had been was a small shallow bowl filled with the same kind of red peas that had gone into the making of Heloise Lelourie's rosary beads. He picked up the bowl for a closer look.

"You want those love beans, you can have 'em. Make a bracelet for yo' lady."

"I haven't got a lady anymore."

Mamma Rae leaned closer to him. The smell of her was overpowering. "You take these love beans away with you anyway, only best to know what you might be lettin' yo'self in for. They can be pretty, used fo' a bracelet or necklace or rosary beads. But they poison, too, love beans are, if they all crushed up and put in somethin' real sweet to make 'em go down easy."

She reached up and ran her finger down the length of his cheek. Her nail was long and sharp and painted black, and she pressed just hard enough to score the skin lightly. "Feed love beans to a man and he'll die screamin'."

He took her hand by the wrist and pulled it away from his face, then wrapped her fingers around his empty jelly glass. Slowly, she pulled her hand out from beneath his, allowing him to feel her flesh. It fanned the fire in him like air from a bellows.

He stared at her hand, wanting her to touch him again, wanting her to rake his back with those nails. Yet the silky feel of her skin had also released a gentle memory. The black hands of the smiling, gap-toothed woman who had raised him. His mama in all but blood and name.

He had to work to get the words out, and when they came he

was surprised at how sane they sounded. "I'd heard it said you make the best blackberry cordial in all New Orleans. It wasn't a lie. You have yourself a good evenin', Mamma Rae."

Fio seemed to figure they'd done what they'd had to do, because he was already out the door. Rourke stopped at the top of the stairs and turned back to her. "You had any news from that LeRoy Washington lately?"

"LeRoy up in Angola. 'Sides, you think I'ma ever tellin' you who I was spellin', and what for?"

Slowly, he smiled. "You just did tell me."

She came out onto the steps with him. Within the shadows cast by the deep eaves of her shack it had grown too dark to see her face, but he could feel a tension emanating from her now that was like heat waves off a tar road. It wasn't part of her juju game. In anyone else he would have thought it was fear.

"Then might be I'll go on an' tell you more than you want t' know." Her voice was soft and low now, even though Fio was too far ahead to hear. "Might be I'll tell you 'bout a white woman alla time sendin' her two lil' girls to me for spells against their daddy. She had them girls hating their daddy like nothin' I ever did see, that white woman did. Then come a day one of them lil' girls, she come to me and she say, my daddy's dead now, Mamma Rae, but I found me a wild yeller-haired boy, an' I want t' make him love me fo'ever. Fo'ever is fo'ever, honey, I says back to her. What if you want rid of him later? But she only laugh."

She leaned close to him and laughed herself, and he could smell the snuff on her breath. "Now why don' you tell me somethin', if you smart as you think you is? You still love that lil' gal? You still crazy in love with that Remy Lelourie?"

Chapter Eighteen

In New Orleans the past is no decaying memory. It lives in the beat of your heart, a constant echo in syncopation with your soul of all the yesterdays and lives that came before you. The sins of fathers, mothers, and their mothers and fathers before. *La famille.* For it is the sins committed that are most remembered, better than any blessings bestowed. So you take your sinful past and you bury it alive in crypts like the ones in the St. Louis Cemeteries. Elaborate, aboveground, but tombs nonetheless. You keep the sins secret, you keep them buried, but you keep them still, within heart and soul, for the sake of yourself, and *la famille.*

The secrets came down through the years in whispers, and rarely were their names spoken aloud. The whispers only spoke of "he" or "she," yet names were not needed for passing down the lessons learned. Heloise Lelourie had listened to the whispers even before she was old and wise enough to understand the truth and the lies that shaped the words. It was the nameless, whispered ghosts of the past that Heloise remembered most of her growing-up years. The sins confessed, but not forgiven or forgotten.

She suffered from the Lelourie affliction. So delicate down below, she was, the poor thing.

She said he was a gentleman when it came to things like that. He hardly ever bothered her after the boy was born.

He had the Lelourie grit, that one. Pulled up sweet potatoes out of the ground like some darkie, but he said there was no shame so awful that couldn't be borne if God wills it, and no damn Yankee was going to see him beaten.

Every bit of it went into the bourré *pot. Lost in a single night. She had to sell her mama's jewelry and it like to have broke her heart.*

She married an American and moved uptown and her mama never spoke to her again. Then, at the funeral, her eyes shed blood. . . . No, it was blood, sure enough. My own mama saw it. They say she still has the handkerchief with the stains on it, tucked away in her first communion missal.

He had the Lelourie coloring, but that nose, oooh, Lord. That nose could have been cut right off his daddy's face.

She held her head up proud and lived with it in silence. What else was she to do?

The stories Heloise most loved to listen to, though, were about Sans Souci and how it had come to be lost. When she grew old enough she pestered her mama and aunts for the details they didn't like to give. She read the old letters, the legal documents, and the yellowed newspaper clippings. She studied the photographs and daguerreotypes, and slowly the whispered ghosts began to take on faces, names. One face, one name, in particular came to haunt her—Henri Lelourie, who was granddaddy to her second cousin Reynard, which made him, then, her own great-uncle. Henri Lelourie, the man who had lost Sans Souci and had died so young and so tragically.

One day, Heloise began to make pilgrimages to the places where it all had happened, for she wanted to imagine how it had been. Not how it had *really* been, but how it had been told, passed down from generation to generation as secrets whispered over blackberry cordials and cups of café au lait.

Carnality and betrayal and murder.

It was Sans Souci she always went to first, that lovely house with the deep galleries and graceful white colonnettes. The first

Lelourie to come to this land of swamps and yellow fever and hot nights had built her, and so she would have been special for that reason alone. It was Sans Souci's beauty that charmed and enthralled, and seduced.

Heloise would stand on the bayou road and look up at the house and imagine she could see a line of ladies, mamas and their daughters, generation upon generation, walking along the gallery, their fans fluttering before their faces, their wide-hooped skirts swaying like bells. The truth was that only one generation of Lelouries had made Sans Souci its home. Within twenty years the family had moved onto a bigger plantation upriver, into a house with wide Grecian columns, marble floors, a spiral staircase. They were rich, for a time, those Lelouries, with ten thousand arpents planted in sugarcane.

But they had kept Sans Souci; they thought they would always keep her, for she was in their blood. It was a matter of practicality, too—she gave the Lelourie fathers and sons a place to stay when they came to New Orleans to eat a bowl of Alvarez's famous Louisiana gumbo and drink a glass or two or three of *le petit guoave*. To sell their crops of cane and molasses, and buy slaves off the block at the City Exchange. To dance their cares away at the quadroon balls in the Salle d'Orleans.

The Salle d'Orleans was the Convent of the Holy Family now, an order of Negro nuns. A place of worship, with its faded green jalousies and stone portico, overlooking the garden of the St. Louis Cathedral. On her pilgrimages to the past, Heloise would go and sit on the stone bench in the garden and look up at the convent's balcony and imagine those years long ago, when dark beauties had stood there instead of nuns. Dark beauties enjoying the night breezes and hiding their smiles behind fluttering, coquettish fans.

Then from these quadroon balls of her imaginings, Heloise's pilgrimage would inevitably lead her to the house on Conti Street, and to what had happened there three generations ago, in the winter of 1855.

In the old days they had called it *plaçage*: the carnal union of a white man and a colored girl. He would meet her at the quadroon ball, beneath a crystal chandelier, and he would dance with her to the scrape of a fiddle, across a floor bright as glass. She would be seductive in her colorful silks and satins, resplendent in her plumes and jewelry, and he would make the proper arrangements with her mama, buy her more silk dresses and a cottage in the Vieux Carré, and there he would visit her until he married, and sometimes afterward, too.

A man has his urges—they can't be helped. But she says he was a gentleman when it came to things like that. He hardly ever bothered her after the boy was born.

She would have been raised a lady, that planter's colored mistress, as much refined as the white Creole girl he would someday marry, and her dreams would have been the same: to attract a man rich enough to protect and provide for her, and who would have a care for her heart. Only unlike the white Creole girl, the man of her dreams could never take her for his wife, and if there was a love between them it would only have been acknowledged in the heat of the night.

Henri Lelourie, though, he had fallen in love, that winter of '55. Henri Lelourie, in love with a colored girl.

No, a love-madness it must have been, and not with a girl who danced a cotillion with her brown shoulders bare, her red satin ballgown rustling, her dark eyes inviting. Henri Lelourie had fallen in love with a slave who worked barefoot in his brother-in-law's sugarcane fields. Henri Lelourie had been a married man, with a babe on the way, and still he had to have that little Nigra field hand, or so that is what the whispers said.

It was as though she'd bewitched him, heart and soul. He lost his honor, he lost his mind, he lost Sans Souci. But he had to have her.

His plantation struggling, desperate for capital, he had sold Sans Souci to his brother-in-law, whose name was Pierre St. Claire, for money and that one slave. "A mulatto female, approximately sixteen years of age, skin medium to dark brown, with all of her teeth, her limbs and back strong and of good conformation."

A mulatto slave, and yet Henri Lelourie had dressed her in silk and set her up in a cottage on Conti Street. There he stayed with her, night after night, as if he had no plantation to manage, as if he had no pregnant wife. Even after his heir was born, a sickly boy, still he stayed in New Orleans with his slave girl, neglecting his home, his wife, his son.

The house on Conti Street sat empty and shut up all the while Heloise was growing up, but she would still try to imagine how it must have been with them—with Henri Lelourie and his colored mistress, his slave, whose name, never recorded, had long since been forgotten. Her name had been forgotten, but not her sin. Behind the gauzy mosquito netting, on that bed of twisted silken sheets, what had she given him that his wife had not? Savage and unbridled pleasure? Or had she been pliant and yielding as she bore his weight and took his body into hers, her master, her Michie Henri? They say, those who are not of *la famille*, that the house was lost, the duel was fought, over a game of faro, but that is a lie.

Sans Souci was lost for love of a slave girl.

Oh, she was a bewitching girl, that Nigra. And well, you know how they can be—like cats in heat. So it was no wonder that Pierre St. Claire decided he had to have her too, even though she wasn't his for the taking anymore. That's why that duel was fought under the oaks. Not for cheatin' over cards, but for cheatin' at love.

The dueling oaks were still there for Heloise to look at and imagine how it had been. Gauzy like a shroud, the dawn light filtering through the gnarled and twisted branches. Shawls of gray moss floating in the mist. Coats lying on the grass, and two men walking away from each other, their boots sinking deep into the wet earth, pistols hanging heavy in their hands. A shout sending startled birds into flight, the men turning, firing. A white shirt blossoming with scarlet flowers.

Henri—unable in the end to kill his friend, the man who was brother to his wife and uncle to his son—had raised his arm at the last instant and his shot had gone high. Pierre, drunk or afraid, or driven mad by lust for the slave girl, had aimed to kill. They say Henri's dying words were *Promise me you'll take care of her.* Whether he was speaking of his faithful wife or his unfaithful mistress, that was one secret that went to the grave untold.

Or so went one story, but there was another: That Pierre St. Claire had waited for Henri early one morning, hidden behind the dueling oaks, and then shot him in the back when he came riding by. Murdered him in cold blood with one of a pair of matching gold-plated French revolvers.

But whether it was murder by stealth or a duel, whenever Heloise would imagine what came after, it was always the slave girl waiting in the cottage on Conti Street. She would imagine the girl hearing a step on the front stoop, a knock on the door. A voice saying one word, a name, and the girl beginning to weep. Had they been tears of grief, though? Or of joy?

The crypt Heloise would save for last on her pilgrimage. The Lelourie family crypt in the old St. Louis Cemetery No. 3. That whitewashed monument of stone, where you came to bury your secrets and your sins. The bones of five generations were housed in the Lelourie crypt, including those of Henri, the granddaddy her Lelourie cousins had never known. Murdered by a St. Claire in the winter of 1855.

Heloise's own grandfather—Henri's younger brother—had been in Paris on his Grand Tour when the tragedy happened. He had returned home months later to find Sans Souci lost and the upriver plantation in debt on the next crop to the hilt. His brother buried, and his brother's wife caught up in a wild grief that was near to madness. His brother's baby son already cutting his first tooth.

That year an early frost destroyed the cane, and a few years later the war and the Yankees came along and destroyed what was left.

There had been ten slave shacks out in back of Sans Souci in those bygone years, but only one was left standing by the time Heloise came along. It disturbed her to look at it, so that she always had to be reminding herself how the shack had nothing to do with her. It was too frightening to imagine that destiny was merely an accident of birth. That the distance between being born in that shack and in a bedroom up in the big house was no wider than the yard one had to cross to get from the one to the other.

It disturbed her, the shack, frightened her, and yet she would lose herself sometimes in looking at it when she made her pilgrimages, and the family thought her peculiar as it was.

That is Livia's girl for you. Always worrying her poor head over that old tale.

Livia's girl. She wasn't Heloise so much as she was Livia's girl, because in New Orleans when you ask about a girl's family, you ask first about her mama. Who is your mama? Oh, you're Livia's girl. In New Orleans a girl never loses her maiden name, not to those who know her. The name she is born under is hers for life, and for Heloise it hadn't mattered anyway, for she was destined to marry another Lelourie.

Reynard Lelourie. She had known him forever. Their mamas had been best friends from the cradle, gone to school together at Madame Picard's, and married in a double wedding to two boys who were cousins. Lelouries. When Heloise had been christened at St. Stephen's it had been in the white linen gown dripping with Irish lace that had been worn by Reynard a year before.

It had been what their mamas wanted, their marriage, and it never occurred to either one of them that they might have wanted something different for themselves. For Heloise, such an eventuality was impossible—her heart would have taken her to the ends of the earth for Reynard. She loved him, both for himself and because he was grandson to Henri Lelourie, whose sad story had so fascinated her as a child.

Heloise was the one who had been born with the Lelourie coloring, the blond hair and gray eyes—like stones under water, Reynard had told her once. His own eyes were dark, and heavy with deep blue moods that made him seem romantic. She never had any thought that the blue moods might have something to do with her.

Even knowing him all her life had not prepared her, though, for how much she came to love him after they were married. She hadn't been prepared for how her body could burn, how her heart could shiver. She pruned the roses in their garden and she loved him. She knelt on the prie-dieu for evening prayers and she loved him. She tatted a lace cap for their coming baby and she loved him. He was so solicitous when she became with child. I won't bother you, he said, and she thought, in spite of her disappointment, Of course he won't for the Lelouries have always been gentlemen when it came to things like that, and she loved him.

Heloise suffered from the Lelourie affliction—she was delicate down below. You have a descending womb, her mama said. Your daddy's mama suffered from it terribly, as you know, and *her* poor mama, she died from it. Yes, Heloise thought, the baby growing inside of her was surely killing her. One morning she would retch up the baby along with her descending womb, and then she would die.

She didn't learn about the Irish woman until after the *accouchement*. The baby had been so long and hard in coming, and it hadn't been how she imagined it would be. The baby looked like a red and wrinkled old pod, and when they put it in her arms she felt nothing for it, nothing. All she felt was tired and heavy all over, in her body and her heart, and then she heard the whispering.

She's Irish. And married herself, so they say. But you know how these little flings never last for long. A man has his urges, and at least he won't be bothering poor Heloise for yet a while.

She never spoke of it to him. She held her head up proud and she lived with it in silence. When she wept it was always alone, and each time she checked her handkerchief to see if they were tears of blood.

She lived with it for two years, lived with it through the sickness of another pregnancy, the hard birth of another daughter. Lying in bed, weak and feverish, she dreamed of herself and her two daughters walking along the broad gray boards of the gallery at Sans Souci.

When she opened her eyes, it was to see her husband's face looking down at her. He was sitting with his hands clasped and dangling between his spread knees. His shoulders were hunched a little, and that made him look oddly vulnerable, like a small boy who is about to be punished. It occurred to her that between them there had always been too much held in, too much unacknowledged regret and silent brooding. An inbreeding of the soul.

Yet even as she thought this, he stood up and turned away from her, was speaking. About the Irish woman. She had a name, the woman. Maeve. It was shocking to hear that name on her husband's lips, like ripping the bandage off a bleeding, putrefying wound.

The woman, Maeve, had left her husband and children. He had set her up in the house on Conti Street, and now he was going to live with her there. Not visit with her as he had been doing two or three times a week. No, they would live as husband and wife, Reynard and that woman. Maeve. Even though that was impossible, for *she* was his wife. She was Heloise Lelourie, Reynard's wife, Livia's girl.

"Why?" she said, and the word seemed to echo in the room as if she had screamed it.

She watched tears form in his eyes and fall like tiny chips of broken crystal. She couldn't tell if his pain was real. He could weep so easily, and over the smallest things. She had known him to shed tears over the death of the diva in an opera. Yet he could kill a woman's heart without remorse and so simply, just by shutting her out of his life.

He spread his hands, a helpless gesture. "I want her."

Something tore loose inside Heloise then. She could feel it bleeding, leaking her life's blood into her chest. "You *have* her," she said, and she would have shouted the words if she'd had the strength, even though ladies never shouted. "Nights, I have lain in this bed waiting for you to come to me, when instead you have gone to her. Evenings, I have sat downstairs at your table, staring at an empty chair. I have given you my . . . my . . ." What had she given him? Only her heart, her dreams, the whole of what she was, and all that she might have been. "What more do you want of me? What more can I possibly give you?"

He had turned his face away from her, but now he turned it back again. It was wet with tears, his face, shining in the weak winter sunlight that came through the window. Yet there was a hardness behind his eyes, a purpose.

"You don't understand," he said. "I don't want you."

There could be no divorce, of course. That went without saying. He left and she tried to tell herself that in spirit he had left long ago. You live with it, she told herself that as well. You just go on living with it. There is no shame so awful that couldn't be borne if God wills it.

She went to Mass, she lit candles before the statues of the Virgin Mary and St. Michael, keeper of families. She set up an altar on her black walnut sideboard, and in the flickering light of vigil candles, she prayed for the strength to bear it. In moments of weakness, in her many moments of weakness, she prayed for Reynard to fall in love with her again. Then one day it came to her, not with a sudden thunderclap of thought, but rather in a slow awakening:

He has never loved me.

Still, she taught Remy, and later Belle, how to make pralines because that was his favorite thing, and she sent their girls to him bearing sweet gifts. Every holiday and birthday and special occasion, she sent them, and each time she hoped that shame or guilt or duty would bring him back to her. It stopped mattering anymore whether he loved her; she wanted him back.

She wasn't sure how it happened that over the years her prayers changed, how her purpose changed. How she went from praying that God would bring her husband into the light to praying that God would leave him to wallow in the misery of the dark. No, more than that. She wanted him to suffer as she had suffered, she wanted him to know the gnawing ache of loneliness that comes from a life wasted, a heart bled empty. She wanted him to awaken screaming in the night from a soul-pain that couldn't be healed or cut out or soothed by anything but death.

Then one day even those bitter prayers ceased to be enough.

So she went to Mamma Rae, the voodooienne, who gave her some love beans. She strung most of the beans into a rosary that morning, and that evening she and the girls made up a batch of pralines because tomorrow was their daddy's birthday.

And while she stirred all the nuts into the boiling sugar, Heloise prayed for death. First for his, and then for hers.

Chapter Nineteen

From the New Orleans *Morning Tribune*, extra edition, Friday, July 15, 1927:

NEW CRIMES, OLD SCANDALS
By Wylie T. Jones

Another day draws to a close and still no arrest has been made for the Tuesday night murder of Mr. Charles St. Claire, Esq.

The floor and walls of the old slave shack on Sans Souci have been scrubbed down hard with lye soap and water, and yet the stains remain. As well they should, for they stand as testimonial that a grievous crime was committed there and yet justice remains unserved. As the evidence mounts against Mr. St. Claire's wife, movie actress Remy Lelourie, still the police dawdle in carrying out their duty.

What do they fear? Remy Lelourie is young and beautiful, and adored the world over, but justice ought to be deaf. Justice ought to be blind. Is it the scandal they fear—the shame of having one of "our own" held up to the world as a murderess?

Yet shame and scandal have never been strangers in the life of this idol of the silver screen. The wild and sordid Hollywood parties, the affairs with her leading men, the extravagant waste of her wealth and youth and beauty have all been recorded over the years in the pages of countless newspapers and slick magazines. Even her days as an innocent child here in New Orleans were tarred by the brush of scandal, when her father deserted home and family to live openly in sin with a married woman, a woman who deserted her own husband and children in turn. They say the sins of the father ought not to be visited upon the children, and apparently homicide detective Lieutenant Daman Rourke agrees, for it was his own mother who became the paramour of Mr. Lelourie.

Perhaps Lt. Rourke can explain, then, why Mr. Charles St. Claire's brutally mutilated body will be buried tomorrow for all eternity, while his slayer still walks the earth—beautiful, rich, famous, and free.

Bridget Mary Kinsella O'Mara lay in a black-lacquered casket in her mama's parlor. Vigil lights flickered on the mantel before a plaster statue of St. Michael, and a brace of candles draped with rosary beads burned at Bridey's head. At her feet rested an enormous wreath of white magnolia blossoms cut from a tree in the backyard and woven together by the loving hands of her mother and sister.

The two women had also draped black crepe-paper streamers over the mirror on the walnut sideboard and along the lintels of the doorways, and tied black crepe-paper bows around the doorknobs. As they'd worked they thought of all the friends and family who would be coming to the wake, to see the wreath and the house in mourning, and so they had wanted it all to seem just right for Bridey.

Doris Kinsella sat stiff-backed now in a chair next to her daughter's casket, her hands gripped together around a handkerchief to make a fist in her lap. She wasn't weeping; she would seem for long minutes not even to be breathing, but then she would draw in such a shuddering gasp of a breath that the crucifix she wore would jump on her breast.

She shook hands and accepted kisses on her cheek from those who came to offer condolences. An empty chair sat beside her. One at a time friends and family would come to fill it, speak to her, and then depart. They all took care to see that she wasn't left alone for long.

Her older daughter, Abby, passed around platters of cheese and soda bread and served tea and coffee and blackberry cordials to the women, who clustered in groups and talked about food and babies and all the rain they'd been having this summer and how it was rotting the roots of the flowers in their gardens. They waited until Bridey's sister had passed out of earshot before the gossip began to unfold in whisperings, like drapery.

It had to be a closed casket. They couldn't make her look right, the poor thing.

He was with her, at her house in the middle of the night, and y'all know what that means.

I still say that husband of hers didn't drown in no freak squall. He ran off with some juice-joint floozie, you mark my words.

Mmmmm-huh. And I wouldn't be surprised if he was the one come back to her house in the middle of the night tossing bombs. When he found out what all she's been up to with Daman Rourke while he was away.

The men had all drifted back through the bedroom and into the kitchen, where a beer bucket sat cooling in chipped ice in the sink and a plate of clay pipes and a bowl of tobacco had been set out on the table. The men dipped tin mugs into the bucket and passed around the flasks of hooch they'd brought along with them, and soon the air became thick with smoke and the malty smell of beer and whiskey.

In New Orleans no occasion, no matter how solemn, passed quietly, and Bridey's wake was no different. People surged through the open door of her mama's house on wings of speech, and were met with a flapping of shouts and exclamations and greetings. Yet when Daman Rourke entered, the noise slowed and died with barely a rustle. They didn't all stare exactly, for that would have been bad manners, but he felt the weight of their collective attention like a slap across his face.

His gaze went right to the casket, then sheered away. He so desperately didn't want to be here, but he'd had to come and so he concentrated on placing one foot in front of the other, to bring himself to Bridey's mama so that he could pay his respects and be gone.

Mrs. Kinsella had her whole attention focused on the handkerchief she was clutching in her lap. Too late he realized the man sitting in the chair next to her, holding her hand and speaking gently into her ear, was Casey Maguire.

As had happened yesterday in the diner, Rourke felt as if the tissue of his self were being torn, twisted between his certainty that Maguire's mind and will had been behind the lob of the grenade that took Bridey's life and an almost desperate need to be proven otherwise.

This evening, though, Maguire's face showed him only grief and a certain wariness. Rourke stared at him for the space of two slow, hard heartbeats, and then his gaze went to the bent head of Bridey's mama. He was struck by how white was her scalp where it showed in the part of her dark red hair.

She looked up as he came to stand before her, but she said nothing. Grief had dragged at her eyes and blanched her skin gray, like coal that has been burned to soot.

He knew if he tried to kiss her cheek she would probably spit in his face. He wasn't sure she would even accept his hand, and so he decided at the last moment to spare them both by not offering it.

He had to say something, though. "Mrs. Kinsella," he began, but he was unable to find more words. His thoughts kept getting tangled and disconnected, and there weren't words for this, anyway. He could tell her he was bruised and bleeding and broken with guilt and grief, and for her it would never be enough.

He felt Casey Maguire's pale eyes burning into the side of his neck, while Bridey's mother looked up at him, out of tear-sodden eyes that were unforgiving. She would never betray bad manners by asking him to leave her house, but her eyes told him how much she wanted to.

He turned away from her and almost knocked into Bridey's casket, and he had to grab the candelabra to keep it from falling over. The cloying sweetness of the magnolias caught at his throat.

He wanted to leave the parlor and the casket, but it was too soon to go back out the front door, and the kitchen was full of his fellow cops. He could see Roibin Doherty through the sliding double doors. The aging sergeant was talking loudly, laughing and gesturing with his hand like an umpire calling a batter out on strikes. He wore a big piece of sticking plaster on his nose, and as Rourke watched he hooked one hip on the table and tucked into a plate of cornbread and cabbage. For once the man didn't look half in the bag, but Rourke still wasn't going near him.

He went instead to the fireplace mantel with its makeshift altar. St. Michael, who was supposed to have kept the family safe, had done a piss-poor job of it.

The saint's statue seemed to be melting before his eyes, dissolving into a pool of black blood. Something let go inside of him, and he was floating away again. He told himself it must be the wine he'd had earlier that evening. Mamma Rae's mischief. He felt as though he were dead himself, one of the walking dead. As if all his bones, like St. Michael's, had dissolved and his blood had turned foul.

Someone touched his arm and he turned slowly, for he was still dizzy and dazed, to look down into red-rimmed, swollen gray eyes. The woman who looked back at him was both someone he knew and a stranger. A slightly older, more worn down version of Bridey.

"Abby," he said, trying to get hold of himself, but his words still kept getting lost somewhere.

She was holding a glass of blackberry cordial in a hand that was chapped red from housework and mothering. She was married to a bricklayer and had five children and lived two doors down in an eastlake shotgun double identical to this one.

She saw where he was looking and tilted the wineglass in his direction. "Would you like some?"

"No," Rourke said, unable to keep himself from shuddering. "I'm . . . No, thank you."

Her mouth trembled, trying to smile. "Well, it *is* ghastly." She took a sip anyway. "I was just telling my cousin Joyce from Slidell? I was telling her about that pet alligator you used to have when we were kids. How you and Bridey once took it for a walk on a leash down St. Charles and like to've scared all the rich ol' biddies there half to death. Whatever did happen to that gator?"

"I took it out to the swamp after that and let it go."

He was pleased that he'd finally gotten out a whole, coherent sentence. Now he wanted very much to leave.

He tried to make a polite sideways shuffle, but she stopped him by touching his arm, although she let go as soon as she felt him shudder again.

"Day," she said. "Mama hasn't been herself since Daddy died—"

"Don't." He drew in a deep breath. "Don't feel you need to apologize for something that needs no excusing. Your mama's right to feel about me as she does. I should've left Bridey alone."

She shook her head, hard. "My sister loved you, all of you—her 'blue star soul mates' she called y'all. She chose Sean, but she used to say that if she could have she would have married all three of you."

He really had to leave. He couldn't seem to stop himself from shuddering.

"Sean was lost to her," Abby was saying. "Whether he drowned or he left her, he was gone from her life. She needed you, and you were good for her."

He must have just up and walked away from her without another look or word after that, for now he found himself standing outside, alone on the narrow gallery. The night was alive with locust-song, the magnolia trees so full of fireflies it looked as if they'd netted the stars right out the sky. Only two nights ago he had sat out here on these steps, waiting for her. He had walked home with her, made love to her, lost her.

His head fell back and he looked up. The trees had left some stars in the heavens, but there were black holes now where the rest had been. His eyes burned, and so he closed them, but it didn't ease the pain.

Bridey.

She had been a friend to him all his life, through everything. He would love her forever for that.

Wood creaked behind him, and he spun around, startled. Roibin Doherty came swaggering out the door, laughing over his shoulder, but he stopped when he saw Rourke. Fiorello Prankowski came out the door after him.

The sergeant was smiling as he looked Rourke over. Half sober, he seemed meaner, more dangerous. In the shadowed light spilling out the door, his eyes glittered as if made of milk glass. "You're like the friggin' plague, Rourke," he said. "The way folk're all the time comin' up dead around you." He took a step, pushing his face in close. So close Rourke could see the gray stubble of beard in the creases of his cheeks and the bellowing of his nostrils as he breathed, the red wetness of his lips and tongue as he spoke. "You're sweating, boy. I can smell it on you."

"We're all sweating, Roibin. It's hot," Fio said. He laid his arm across the older man's shoulders, steering him down the steps, past Rourke. "Come on, I'll buy you a beer."

Rourke watched them go off down the street together, toward the speakeasy on the corner. He closed his eyes again, feeling suddenly tired beyond death. "Shit," he said under his breath.

He felt rather than heard another noise in the doorway behind him. He turned more slowly this time.

Casey Maguire stood at the threshold. The black crepe paper framed his head, accentuating the pale austerity of his face. He seemed to be holding himself too still, as if he were afraid to move. As if his guts had all caved in.

Daman Rourke stood with his head bowed before his wife's grave.

The stars and moon burned hot in the night. Beyond the cemetery, the roofs and chimneys and treetops looked etched with acid out of a sky the red-black color of tarnished copper. Nothing stirred, no breath of wind. Still, shadows lurked and capered among the rows of white-painted brick crypts and granite sarcophagi. A city of the dead.

In the first couple of years after Jo's death he would come out here to the old St. Louis Cemetery No. 1 off Basin Street and trace the letters of her name where they'd been cut into the marble of her tomb, and it would hurt so bad, as if he were carving their replica onto his heart. Yet even then a part of him had known that more than Jo, he had been mourning every woman who had ever left him.

So when she came to him on this night, a woman in black silk, walking though the high peristyled tombs, she looked like something he had dreamed.

"I knew that I would find you here," she said.

"Remy," he answered, her name barely a whisper. He thought he was probably still flying high on Mamma Rae's wine. His blood felt on fire and the world seemed bright and jagged as shards of glass. He wanted to touch her, to run his hands down the curve of her breast, to press his lips into the hollow of her throat.

He wanted her to touch him and he waited for it, but she turned away, toward Jo's tomb.

"How did she die?"

"She had a defect in the walls of her heart," he said. His voice sounded strange, even to himself.

"And now you've lost another love. Mrs. O'Mara. I read about her in the newspaper. . . . Read between the lines." She turned back to him, and starlight caught at the sheen in her eyes. He sensed a deep sadness in her, dark and dreadful. He saw her hand come up, as if through the mists of a shattered mirror. She traced the bones of his face with her fingertips, touched his mouth.

"People don't change," she said. "Especially from up close. They only seem more elaborate."

He grabbed her wrist and thrust her hand down between them, and then somehow his fist was in her hair and his mouth was coming down over hers.

He almost couldn't stop. He tightened his grip on her hair,

pulling her head back, pulling her mouth away from his. "Sweet Jesus. What do you want from me?"

She rubbed her breasts against his chest, rubbed her belly against his, rubbed slow and sensuous. "Do you dare to love your women without conditions, Day? Or do you judge them by the worst thing they've ever done?"

He let go of her hair, his hand sliding around her jaw, his fingers brushing her wet and open mouth. He knew that, no matter what, she would always be his obsession.

"I can't save you, Remy," he said.

Her breath caught, then she laid the palms of her hands on his chest and gently pushed herself away from him. Her mouth moved into a smile that was horrible in its pain. "Oh well, some other time, maybe."

She left him, then, to become a wisp of a shadow flitting among old cracked and sunken crypts, brushing along the crumbling cemetery wall, becoming lost in the wet, black velvet of a southern night.

The sun was bleaching the sky white as bone the next morning as the cortege bearing the earthly remains of Charles St. Claire turned off Esplanade Avenue and drove through the big iron gates of St. Louis Cemetery No. 3.

The pallbearers lifted the casket out of the hearse and carried it down a narrow brick path toward the St. Claire family crypt—a flamboyant affair with miniature columns and capitals and pediments, and double bronze doors with big wrought-iron handles. The priest and altar boys led the way, and the widow walked within the shadow cast by the coffin. A long line of mourners followed her, wending like a slow, sun-drugged snake through the raised and narrow whitewashed tombs. The tabloid reporters crowded close, snapping hundreds of photographs of the coffin and the widow's tragic face.

Only the two cops stood watching from a respectful distance.

"One thing about being your partner," Fiorello Prankowski was saying, "is that you're always full of surprises. Is it a fact what was in the *Morning Call* yesterday evening about Remy Lelourie's daddy running off to live in sin with your mama?"

When Rourke didn't say anything Fio went on, the growl in his voice deepening. "And did this fact just slip your mind, or does it qualify as one of them southern secrets that keep springing up around this case the way mushrooms do down here after a hot, steamy rain?"

"It was a long time ago, is all," Rourke said.

"Uh-huh." Fio's glare burned into the side of Rourke's neck for a moment longer, and then he looked away. He took off his hat and fanned his face with the brim. "Jesus, it is friggin' hot."

It was hot. Rourke could feel the heat from the bricks rising up through the soles of his shoes. This cemetery was only a couple of blocks from Bayou St. John, and they could smell the sun-cooked algae and hear the frogs croaking.

"I'd like to meet the dumbfuck who came up with this rule," Fio said.

He waited a beat, then carried on, as if Rourke had obliged by saying, What rule?

"The rule that says us hardworking homicide dicks've gotta drag our asses out to a cemetery on a hot Saturday morning in July just because the stiff's killer might decide to show up for his funeral. Since most victims get done in by somebody they know, it oughta go without saying that that somebody's gonna be there when they bury him, right? But have you ever known a killer to break down and confess at a funeral?"

"Back in my grandmama's time," Rourke said, "a banker killed his wife, confessed at the cemetery when the priest got to the part about this vale of tears, shot himself in the head, and fell into the open tomb. They just sealed the family crypt up right then and there. Buried two bodies with one funeral."

Fio was glaring at him so hard his eyes looked sore. "That's one of them made-up New Orleans stories, isn't it?"

New Orleans funerals, Rourke thought, were even further complicated by the belief that if the dead person was a relation of any sort, no matter how distant or removed—if you'd gone to school with him, or with any of his siblings, if you were a friend of his mama, or of his grandmama—then you went to his funeral. If the dead man was well connected, half the city could show up to send him off.

Marry a beautiful Hollywood starlet and get yourself gruesomely murdered and they might as well sell tickets.

Remy Lelourie was beautiful, in a simple black dress that made her seem impossibly pale and frail, and a hat with no veil. But then she'd want the world to see her face. To see innocence betrayed. To see grief inconsolable yet subdued, for she was of the Creole aristocracy. No weeping and wailing and tearing of hair.

Last night her hair had smelled of sweet olive. She had been no drug-induced hallucination. He could still feel the imprint of her body against his, still taste her mouth.

He knew why she had come, what she had wanted from him. She was like a wolf caught in a trap, gnawing off its own leg to get free. He'd told her he couldn't save her; he'd made her think he didn't want to. If she could lie, then so could he.

"Some families have designated mourners," Rourke said.

Fio was wiping the wet from the inside of his hat with a splayed thumb. "Huh?" He looked up at Rourke, blinked the sweat out of his eyes, and slapped the hat back on his head. "No, don't tell me. I don't want to hear it."

"Someone in the family, like a maiden aunt. She watches the newspapers to see who's died and is getting waked and buried, and then, if the acquaintance is only a slight one, she'll go as a representative of everybody else in the family. That way the proper respects get paid, but without a lot of undue inconvenience."

"Well, if that isn't just peachy keen. Now we gotta consider that maybe the killer's got some designated family mourner coming here in his place. Nope. Uh-uh. I'm gonna stick with my conviction that the Cinderella Girl did it. She's the widow, so we knew all along she'd show up, and this way we won't be getting any surprises."

The casket had disappeared through the doors of the crypt, which was nearly buried itself beneath a mound of wreaths and bouquets of flowers. It took a long while for the mourners to disperse. Fio left to have a word with the priest, who ministered, they'd been told, to both the Lelourie and St. Claire families.

Rourke sat down on a small green wire bench, beneath the pathetic shade cast by the cemetery's whitewashed brick wall. He'd told Fio he wanted to rest awhile, coddle his aching ribs, but he had his own rule about funerals. Once the dead was good and buried, he liked to see who-all came back.

The first one to come was Miss Fleurie.

Rourke hadn't seen her among the mourners, and he doubted he would have missed the long purple dress decorated with black-dyed egret feathers. She had brought a single white rose, but she didn't lay it down with the profusion of other flowers. Rather she tucked it into the outstretched, prayerful hands of a marble Madonna. She stood for a moment as if in silent salute, and then walked away.

The widow came next, but if she had wanted a moment for private grief or gloating she wasn't given the chance. Jean Louis Armande must have been lingering out of sight behind the crypt, for he appeared as soon as she arrived. The lawyer bent over her hand, kissing it, holding it for just a little too long. He spoke and she listened, and then she reached up and gently, lightly, touched his cheek. He spoke again, pleading perhaps, for he spread his hands as if in supplication. She listened, shook her head. He seized her hand again, kissed it hard, and turned away, and almost stumbled over the raised edge of the crypt.

She watched him walk away from her and then she turned back to the tomb. She laid her hand on the open bronze door but didn't go inside, where Charles St. Claire now lay, where Julius St. Claire had been lying these past eleven years. He wondered how much of them she still carried in her heart; he wondered if you can mourn the ones you kill.

A movement deep at the back end of the cemetery caught Rourke's eye. He watched, his gaze burning with the heat haze and filming over with his sweat, while a woman in a shapeless, faded black dress made her slow, tentative way down the narrow brick path.

Her steps faltered when she saw Remy. For a moment Rourke thought she might turn away, but then she came on. Remy saw her and seemed to be waiting, although when she arrived they neither spoke nor touched. Minutes passed while they stood side by side before the St. Claire crypt, while the sun burned mercilessly and the humid air thickened. Just when Rourke thought they might stay that way forever, they seemed to turn of one accord and go into each other's arms.

From where he sat beneath the cracked and crumbling cemetery wall, it looked to Rourke as though Belle Lelourie was the one who needed and was taking the most comfort.

Chapter Twenty

All her life Belle Lelourie had wanted to be a Mardi Gras queen.

She would spend hours imagining how it would be. Someday, someday, someday. Someday she would be standing, there, on the white balcony of the Boston Club in a pink satin dress and a wide-brimmed hat with a long, trailing ribbon, Queen of Rex. The crowd below would look up at her with admiring eyes and say, Why, there is Belle Lelourie, the most beautiful girl in New Orleans.

She loved the parades. Each float was a sparkling confection of gold leaf and silver tissue and rainbow silks and satins, a magical kingdom pulled along by unicorns. "Those aren't unicorns, you silly ninny," Remy always said. "They're mules dressed up in white robes and their horns are made out of papier-mâché. They're the same mules that'll be back to pulling the garbage trucks come morning." Belle, though, would just shut her ears to her sister's sour words.

The krewes on the floats would throw beads and doubloons out to the crowd, and Remy would always make such a spectacle of herself, jumping up and down and waving her arms, shouting, "Throw me something, mistah!" Belle didn't care about catching those cheap throws. She had no need of glass beads when someday she would wear the real thing.

One Mardi Gras night, though, when she was twelve, a thing happened that was both marvelous and scary.

She always loved the night parades the best, when even Remy could not deny the magic. The Negroes in their red robes carried the flambeaux to light up the floats, their torches bobbing and flaring as they danced and strutted to the beat of the bands. Great wreaths of black smoke swirled up into the night and the floats rode by on rings of fire. The pounding rhythm of the drums, the undulating dancers, the whirling flames—it all stirred something inside Belle.

That night, though, that night was special.

That night the King of Comus came floating by on a gauzy white cloud, wrapped up in a glittering double rainbow. Remy, who was being hateful as usual, laughed and said, "Why, look at the silly old fart. He's as drunk as a peach orchard sow," when the king did the most astonishing thing. He leaned over from his perch high atop his golden throne and pointed his diamond scepter right at Belle, and he smiled.

She stared, with her mouth and eyes open wide in surprise and wonder, and she didn't see the man who was standing next to the king throw the string of purple beads at her until it was too late. The beads struck her in the chest and fell to ground, and the crowd surged around her, trying to get at the special trinket. They knocked her into the float, and she almost fell beneath the flatbed's iron wheels. She stumbled and reeled and got too close to the siz- zling oil being flung from the whirling flambeaux, and her coat caught on fire.

Suddenly Remy was there, tackling her around the waist and throwing her into the street, which was littered with mule and horse droppings and crushed beads. Remy beat out the flames with her hat and hands, and Belle would have been grateful if her sister hadn't been laughing so crazy and saying, "Sakes alive, Belle. You nearly got burned to a bacon crisp, just like Joan of Arc," and with that strange look she could get in her eyes sometimes. It scared Belle, the things Remy did and said, and that look she would get in her eyes.

Every year on Mardi Gras night when the last parade was over—even that year she caught on fire—Belle would go stand outside the French Opera House on Bourbon Street and watch the Queens of Rex and Comus, and their courts, all arriving for the ball in black lacquered carriages. She would say the words like a chant, a prayer: Someday, someday, someday that will be me. Someday, she would wear a gown of seed pearls and French lace and white satin dancing shoes on her feet—and, oh, wouldn't those thin little shoes be plumb wore out by the end of the night? The most exciting moment would come at the stroke of midnight, when a young man wearing the beautiful jeweled and spangled mask of a prince would lead her out onto the floor. She would pretend not to know him, of course, but she would know. Her gloved hand would tremble in his, and his arm would be strong around her waist. He would whisper in her ear a confession: I have loved you all my life, pretty little Belle Lelourie, and now it is time that I made you my wife. It is time you came home at last, to live with me at Sans Souci.

And she would know joy. Absolute joy.

It didn't come to Belle like a thunderclap out of the blue. Rather it came slowly—ominous rumbles, way off in the distance, coming from behind sneaky ol' black clouds that could all of a sudden bring rain upon you when you didn't even see them coming: the realization that not only would she never be chosen queen, she would never even be invited to the ball.

Because of the Scandal, of course. The Scandal, which no one ever spoke of, yet which lived in their house like an invisible mold, decaying things, rotting and befouling the air. Never mind that she was a Lelourie and as pretty as can be. Her father was living in another house with a woman not his wife, her mother was a recluse, and her sister was running wild and crazy. No girl with such a background would ever be chosen Mardi Gras queen.

And then came a worse betrayal. Remy stole her prince.

When Julius St. Claire started coming around to the house, she thought it was because of her. She would get herself all prettied up for him and put on her party manners, even though whenever she was in his presence she got all fluttery and so tongue-tied she could barely manage a breath, let alone a word. It took her a while to realize that it was to Remy his gaze always went whenever she was around, that it was Remy he was always talking about, Remy he was charming for, Remy, Remy, Remy.

Why, if Julius St. Claire had had his way, it was Remy who would have wound up with Sans Souci. Only before that could happen, Julius had killed himself, and Remy had run away, and Belle was the one who'd been left all alone.

Never mind that it was she, Belle Lelourie, who had been raised for something different, raised to be both a queen and a lady, and a wife. She knew which of the five forks sitting beside her plate to use on the oysters, which on the terrapin, and which on the mango—should she ever be invited to a dinner party, which she never was. She could play "Variations from the Operas" on the piano, and "The Grand March of Napoleon," and yet with no one in the house to hear but herself and mama, the music always got swallowed up by the moldy silence. She never went uptown without her hat and gloves, even during the hottest days of summer. Only she had no girlfriends to meet her under the clock at D. H. Holmes for lunch and shopping, and that salesgirl at the perfume counter always gave her such a pitying look, and so she quit going uptown at all after a while. She would work in the garden instead. She would push her hands through the soft, loamy earth, stirring up a strange restlessness inside of herself, and she would wonder how she could be so full up with feelings and yet be so empty inside.

In the evenings she would sit with Mama in the parlor, tatting lace and doing cross-stitching, prettying up pillowcases and sheets and tablecloths for her trousseau. She had a cedar hope chest up in her bedroom, where she would put each piece of linen after it was done. One day she saw that the chest had become so full she could no longer close the lid. She cried that day like the child she no longer was, pushing her face hard against her knotted fists, beating those fists on top of the cedar chest that wouldn't close, and wishing she were dead.

She had cried before, on the day Julius killed himself, even though she'd been wishing misery on him for a long while, praying for him to suffer the way they'd prayed for Daddy's suffering. She had wanted Julius to be sorry for all he'd done to her, picking Remy over her, and he must have been sorry, to go and shoot himself like that. After it was done, though, she kept feeling as if all the hope she'd been putting in her hope chest had been about him and now he was gone for good, forever, and so the chest might as well be empty. Then Remy had run off, leaving her alone with Mama, leaving her alone.

It was a late summer's afternoon a couple of years later and she was in the garden, deadheading the roses, when she realized a whole parade of cars and carriages was passing by their house and slowing down to stare. Some people were even pointing and waving at her, and she couldn't imagine why. It couldn't be the Scandal, surely, not after all these years and with Daddy dead and buried.

It was starting to scare her, the way those people were behaving, and she was about ready to run on back into the house when she spotted Ruthie, the colored girl who did for the family next door, coming out onto the gallery to see what the ruckus was about.

Belle waved her hand and called out soft little yoo-hoos to Ruthie, but Ruthie, the silly girl, was gaping at the traffic in the road and not paying the slightest attention, so that Belle practically had to shout, even though ladies never shouted.

The girl finally sauntered down off the gallery and took her own good time coming over to the fence, so that Belle was in an agony of nerves by the time she got there. "Hey there, Miss Belle," the girl said, "what you doin' hidin' behind that tree like that?"

Ruthie had a scattering of tiny black moles going across her cheekbones and wide-open, Raggedy Ann–like eyes, and Belle was beginning to wonder if those eyes were laughing at her. Only she'd never known Ruthie to forget her place before.

She didn't care at this point, anyway; she was too fretful over what was happening with all those people passing by the house and slowing down to stare. "Do you know who are all those people, Ruthie? What are they all doing? What are they looking at?"

"I 'spect they only be comin' 'round to get a look at y'all and y'all's house 'cause you family of the Cinderella Girl."

Belle forced a laugh. "Oh, what nonsense, Ruthie. Cinderella is a fairy tale. There is no such person."

"Yes'm. I mean, no'm. They done wrote all 'bout her in the newspaper this mornin'. Ain't you seen it? You just wait right here and I'll get it for you."

Before Belle could even say, Yes, please and Thank you, the girl had run on into the house and was back in a few moments with the *Times-Picayune* folded up in her hand. "You go on and keep that, Miss Belle," she said, passing the newspaper over the fence. "We-all's done with it over here."

Belle had a hard time getting the paper unfolded, so that she became impatient and almost tore it.

The headline made no sense to her at first: NEW ORLEANS GIRL LIGHTS UP THE SKIES OVER HOLLYWOOD. But the photograph that was spread over four columns hit her like a blow to the chest. Surely it could not be, and yet it was. Remy, her sister Remy. Remy, who appeared to be going to some sort of a ball, for she was wearing an evening gown with a long train and a tiara in her hair. It was hard for Belle to see the newsprint, her hands were shaking so. Then one passage seemed to leap right out at her:

After only a few moments in her presence, while one stares speechless, enraptured, at those stunning bones, the flawless skin, that luscious mouth, one must conclude that Miss Remy Lelourie is undoubtedly the most beautiful woman in the world.

She took the newspaper into the house, went back with it to the kitchen, and buried it deep in the garbage, beneath the coffee grounds and the eggshells and the fish bones. She felt better then, once it was out of sight, her belly not so queasy, her chest not so hollow.

So her sister had gone and acted in some movie—well, Remy was always doing wild and crazy things. No real lady would ever make a spectacle of herself in public that way, and one day Remy would probably be really sorry for having done it. No nice New Orleans boy would ever marry a girl who had gone and done something like that. As for what that man wrote about Remy being pretty, well, the newspaper had just gotten his words wrong, that was all. No one would ever even think to say such a thing about her sister Remy. Why, when they were little, she herself was the one everybody was always making a fuss over. She was the one they called Belle.

After that it seemed Remy's face was everywhere. Mama said it was a shameful thing, what Remy was doing, flaunting herself in those moving pictures. Vulgar, low-class things. Belle told Mama how people were saying that Remy was near to naked in that one movie, the one where she was in a harem of all things, the slave girl to some Arab sheik, a darkie no less. Shameful, utterly shameful. Remy would be sorry someday, sorry, sorry, sorry. It made Belle feel better to think how someday Remy would be sorry. For a moment Belle would fell better, not so empty inside, thinking how sorry Remy would be.

The night Remy came home to New Orleans for the premiere of *Jazz Babies*, Belle couldn't stop herself from going to the old Union Street station. The size of the crowd shocked her—why, as many people were there as you would find at a Carnival parade. They all started screaming as soon as the train pulled into the station, Re-my, Re-my, Re-my Le-lourie, and went on screaming and whistling and calling out her name, and the screaming only got louder when the train's door slid open and she was framed there in a wash of light, and flashlamps were popping off everywhere, and Remy was smiling and lifting her hand in a way that seemed at once both gracious and shy.

Belle watched it all through a wash of tears that scalded her eyes. How had this happened, how could it be that Remy had become something so much more splendid than a Mardi Gras queen?

Chapter Twenty-One

From the editorial page of the New Orleans *Times-Picayune*, Saturday, July 16, 1927:

LET JUSTICE BE DONE

While our colleagues of the competition inveigh against the officers of law and order for their seeming reluctance to arrest and try matinee idol Remy Lelourie for the crime of murder, we at the *Times-Picayune* believe the time has come for a moment of calm reflection. A heinous act was committed last Tuesday night, an act so bloody and savage one can only shudder to contemplate the horror of Mr. Charles St. Claire's last moments. Just as poverty and ignorance should not result in too swift a leap to judgment, neither should beauty nor fame preclude any judgment at all. Yet it is a serious matter for the state to bring one of its citizens before the bar to answer for a capital offense, a matter so serious it must be undertaken with great care and thoroughness, but above all with fairness. Evidence must be gathered and witnesses questioned. Charges must be filed, and then the innocence or guilt of the duly charged must be weighed by a jury of peers. If in the final judgment Remy Lelourie is innocent of the charges brought against her in the court of public opinion, she has nothing to fear in a court of law, for it is there that the truth will out and justice will prevail.

You always hope, thought Daman Rourke, that the story will have a happy ending, even if it won't ring true. Yet whenever he set foot back into his dead wife's champagne-and-silk-stockings world, he felt as though he were caught in an unfinished fairy tale. He and Jo, two wedding-cake figurines trapped forever beneath the glass dome of a bell jar. She hadn't even lived long enough for him to imagine what might have been.

He parked the Bearcat in front of his in-laws' antebellum mansion, underneath the dark green shade of a live oak tree. He cut the engine and the world descended into the silence of gentility and elegance that was Rose Park. If you strained your ears you might make out the occasional tinkle of a piano or the splash of someone diving into a swimming pool, but you sure wouldn't know it was a summer's Saturday afternoon by this part of town.

Rourke half turned in his seat to look at his Katie. She was adorable in a white dress with a big square sailor collar trimmed with yellow stars and blue anchors—all sugar and spice and everything nice, the picture of femininity if you overlooked the grungy baseball cap on her head.

He smiled at her and she sent a marvelous smile back at him. "You have your paw-paw's birthday present?" he asked.

She rolled her eyes at him since she was holding the present, plain as day, in her lap. She had gotten Weldon Carrigan, superintendent of the New Orleans Police Department, a water pistol.

"Don't you go eating so much ice cream this time that you end up puking in the hydrangeas," he said.

She rolled her eyes again. "Daaaaddy! That happened ages and ages and ages ago, when I was just a baby."

"Be that as it may," he said, deliberately echoing every southern woman he had ever known. "And see if you can get through the evenin' without giving your cousin Gordon a bloody nose."

"But Gordo *asks* for it, Daddy. He's always ratting on everybody and he's just so full of hooey."

"That's no excuse for trying to knock it out of him. And don't go giving your cousin Annabel another case of the hysterics."

The picture of femininity made a rude noise with her nose. "Can I help it if she is such a dumb Dora that she believes every little thing I say?"

Rourke laughed and gave the bill of her cap a tug. "Right. What was I thinking? Come on, let's go before they start the party without us."

As he went around to help Katie climb out of the car, he noticed an old dusty Model T parked along the curb of the broad, landscaped neutral ground, deep within the dark green shade cast by the oaks. It was not the sort of automobile one usually saw on Rose Park, which was why it caught Rourke's eye. As he was looking the flivver over, he saw a man hurrying along the side of the Carrigan mansion, on the path that led to the trade entrance.

The gray-hatted head was turned away from them, looking back toward the house, but there was no mistaking the slouching, rolling walk of a man half-tanked on the hooch. He spat a stream of tobacco juice into the gutter before opening the door to the Model T and getting behind the wheel.

Rourke watched the Model T's smoking tailpipe and bouncing spare tire until they had disappeared around the corner onto St. Charles. He was, he thought, going to have to sit down later this evening and have a heart-to-heart talk about old times with homicide detective Roibin Doherty.

Katie decided to practice singing the Happy Birthday song as they walked through the tall scrolled-iron gate and down a flagstone path toward a house with thick stately columns, a deep marble gallery, and a door glittering with leaded beveled glass. A Negro in evening dress and white gloves met them at the foot of the stairs. He escorted them around to the porte cochère and through an arched carriageway guarded by a pair of stone lions.

Rourke heard the shout of "My service!" coming from the tennis court, and the pat of the ball against the strings. They emerged onto a lawn shadowed from the full heat of the sun by a canopy of oaks and palms. The air smelled festive: of roses, freshly watered dirt, and the whole pig that was roasting on a spit.

Waiters dressed all in white strolled over the clipped grass, carrying trays of lemonade. If the party was true to form—and in this part of town everything always ran true to form—then the glasses with the silver trim would be spiked with bootlegged gin.

Katie had spotted her grandmother and ran pell-mell to greet her, dancing in her excitement to present the bouquet of jasmine she had decided on her own to pick and bring along with them, because as she had said, Paw-Paw shouldn't be the only one to get presents today. The flowers had gotten a bit crushed and wilted on the drive uptown, but Katie's grandmama Rose Marie exclaimed over them, smelled them, and then added the scraggly offering to the perfectly arranged celadon vase of yellow roses displayed on a wrought-iron table among a grouping of wicker lawn furniture dressed in starched white coverlets.

Cousin Annabel, the dumb Dora, skipped up to Katie and grabbed her by the hand, dragging her off to a game of shuttlecock that was being played next to the swimming pool. A couple of drowned birdies, Rourke saw, were already floating feathers-up in the bright blue water.

He walked up to his mother-in-law as she turned to greet him, still flushed from the whirlwind that could be Katie in a passion of excitement. Rose Marie Carrigan was a small woman, all white and pink and soft, like a strawberry meringue. He often thought of her as being soft in the center of her too, but that was probably unfair. In her world, ladies learned early on to blunt all their sharp edges.

"Good evenin', Mama Carrigan," he said, taking both her hands and bending to kiss her cheek. It was as smooth as a doeskin glove, her cheek, and smelled faintly of jasmine.

"Day, my dear. How splendid it is to see you." She stared up at him, and her hands trembled once in his before she pulled them free. He had always made her nervous, even when he wasn't trying to. "Weldon is most anxious to have a word," she said. "I am to send you to him the very moment you arrive. . . ." Her voice trailed off as her gaze searched the yard for her husband, a crease of worry appearing between her pale eyes like a thumbprint.

"I'll try and take it like a man," Rourke said.

Her gaze flew back to him, the worry between her eyes deepening. "Oh, dear."

"I was only teasin'. I'm sure it's nothing serious." He looked around him, admiring the splashes of color that were like a messy painter's palette: yellow jasmine, pink camelias, orange azaleas, lavender wisteria growing on a trellis. "Your garden is looking lovely. I don't know that there's a prettier one in all New Orleans." He brought his gaze back to her face and gave her his most brilliant smile. "Mama says to say hey."

Color rose up to stain Rose Marie Carrigan's cheekbones, and she made a fluttery movement with her hand. "I do hope your poor mama isn't feeling too terribly awful. Summer colds can be so debilitating."

"Mostly she's disappointed to be missing the party," he said, playing his part in this ritual of southern manners. Any invitation to him and Katie always politely included his scandalous mother, and she always politely declined. Thus feelings were spared while propriety was still served, rudeness and awkwardness both neatly avoided.

More guests arrived and Rose Marie Carrigan turned to greet them, freeing Rourke to go look for his father-in-law. He took his time about it, walking out to the fountain beneath trees that were strung with Japanese lanterns for when it grew dark.

Jo was everywhere here, and it hurt, in the way an old wound could sometimes ache years later during stormy weather. Water splashed from an angel's marble trumpet, and he heard her laugh. A dark-haired girl in a picture hat turned her head, and for the skip of a heartbeat the face beneath the wide straw brim was hers.

The dark-haired girl was talking to someone on the other side of the fountain. He watched her through a rainbow spray of water and waited for her to turn her head again.

When he realized what he was doing, he turned away and almost walked into his father-in-law. The two men spent a moment staring at each other, tasting the memory of an old and sour antagonism, then Rourke smiled and held out his hand. "Happy Birthday, sir."

"I'm getting a water pistol," Weldon Carrigan said in a mock whisper as he shook Rourke's hand. "Only I'm not supposed to tell anyone 'cause it's a surprise."

"She tried it out for you on a pantywaist named Ernie this morning. It surprised him, too."

His father-in-law was laughing as he took a cigar out of his vest pocket, but Rourke thought the eyes beneath the thick, black hedgerow of eyebrows looked tired and troubled. The dark-haired girl in the picture hat was glancing over her shoulder now, laughing and waving to someone behind him; she didn't look at all like Jo or anyone else he knew.

Weldon Carrigan had gone through the ritual of lighting his cigar, and when he looked up now the eyes he fastened on his son-in-law were hard. "I want you to know that we're taking what happened to Mrs. O'Mara the other night very seriously—"

"So am I," Rourke said, his smile as sharp as broken glass.

Carrigan punched the air in front of Rourke's chest with his finger. "There is to be a full investigation because *nobody* gets away with killing one of ours. But I want you staying out of it, goddammit. If her husband has—"

"Sean O'Mara's dead."

Carrigan sighed and backed off a little, nodding. "I can understand why you had to believe that he's dead, given that y'all were friends. Hell, I'm not blaming you for sleeping with the woman," he added after a moment. "Jo's been gone a long time."

Another silence fell between them, and Rourke waited now for the chewing out he was due for rousting the Maguires at Tio Tony's.

"In the meantime, we'll still put a couple of flatfeet to watching your mama's cottage 'round the clock," Carrigan said instead, his gaze going to where Katie was trying to whack the bejesus out of a shuttlecock. "Christ, this is turning out to be one long, hot summer."

Jo had died on a day in October. In his memory, white clouds are tumbling over the treetops and she is wearing a yellow dress and a big picture hat. She had a little heart-shaped mole on her neck, right below her ear. Sometimes when he made love to her, he would try to suck it off.

". . . had a conversation with the DA this morning," Carrigan was saying. "He believes he has enough to go on for a warrant and an indictment. He'll be doing it on Monday—Remy Lelourie for the murder of her husband in the first degree."

Rourke took a silver-rimmed glass off the tray of a passing waiter. It was spiked all right, and so cold it made his head ache. "Are you sure y'all are up to it?" he said. "Last I knew you were runnin' from the idea like a nun from a brothel."

"Do you think this is amusing?" Carrigan snapped back. "Because it isn't amusing."

It wasn't amusing.

She had been standing right over there, underneath the mimosa tree, laughing. In his memories Jo is laughing, and turning toward him with his name on her lips, laughing, the brim of her hat slowly tilting up, laughing, and he almost sees her face, almost, and then her heart stops. She had been laughing, turning and laughing, and her heart, full of holes no one could see, had been beating and then it had stopped.

"No, you're right," his father-in-law said, and the weariness was back on him, pulling at his mouth and eyes and making him look older than his fifty-five years. "We got the forensics. We got means, motive, and opportunity. But in spite of all that smug advice the *Times-Picayune* was handing out this morning, we aren't ready for a trial and we probably never will be. The Cinderella Girl is going to have it won the minute she walks into the courtroom."

"Maybe that's why she killed him," Rourke said. "To see if she could get away with it."

Her heart stops and she dies, and the record you are dancing to ends before you are through, and only afterward do you realize that the music had barely begun. She has left you before you can ever come to know her.

She dies, but the stars go on shining and the sun still comes up hot in a Louisiana July morning. She dies and it doesn't change the way the wind feels in your hair, or the need you have for a drink or a woman, or the occasional wild dance on the edge of the moon.

The sky was the deep purple of a ripe plum and promising more rain later that evening when Rourke pulled up behind the old dusty Model T where it was parked on a particularly bad block of Rousseau Street in the Irish Channel.

A single, scraggly palm rattled in the light breeze as he crossed the weed-choked yard, and a strong, sour whiff of boiling cabbage floated from the open kitchen window next door. Roibin Doherty's bargeboard house was built from the scavenged wood of old flatboats that had broken up and drifted downriver, and it looked it.

Rourke knocked three times and got no answer. He was going to jimmy the lock, but he didn't have to. The door swung open beneath his hand on a groan of rusting hinges.

The shades were pulled down in front of the windows, and so the room was darker than the falling night outside. Rourke closed the door behind him and stood just over the threshold. He listened and heard the locusts singing in the weeds out back and a faucet dripping in the kitchen sink. The house smelled sour, of a drunk's sweat.

He took three slow, careful steps and tripped over a body lying heavy and still on the floor.

Chapter Twenty-Two

Rourke landed on his knees and stayed there. He slipped his gun from its holster, but he still heard nothing more than the water dripping and the locusts singing. Out in the street a voice started hollering shrilly for Jimmy to come home.

Rourke's eyes had adjusted enough to the dark that he could see the gray outline of a lamp sitting on a table by a sofa. He fumbled beneath the lamp shade, found the chain and gave it a yank, and a weak yellow light filled the shabby room.

Roibin Doherty lay sprawled on a stained and unraveling rag rug, next to a brown upholstered armchair, which was all naked springs and burst stuffing, and an overturned spit can filled with chewed Red Man. His tangled, graying hair was greasy with sweat and dirt; his small mouth drooled a river of spit and tobacco juice, and blood.

Which wasn't surprising, considering the bullet hole in his right temple and the .38 Policeman's Special clutched in his right hand. Rourke pressed his fingers to Doherty's neck. The flesh felt cold, dead.

Rourke eased back onto his heels, breathing fast and deep. Sweat filmed and stung his eyes.

He stood up slowly, looking around the small and littered parlor,

269

at empty Red Man pouches and bottles of rotgut, a stack of porno-graphic postcards, an unopened box of poker chips. The coffee table, though, was clean of debris; it even looked recently dusted. Squared up in the middle of it, as if for display, was a battered crime case file that had *Julius St. Claire* written in black ink across the front of it and was stamped with the seal of the Crescent City police.

Rourke flipped open the file folder with the barrel of his gun. Stapled to the inside was a cellophane envelope containing a spent bullet and a shell casing, and underneath it a coroner's report. *Indi-cations are of suicide or accidental self-inflicted death by gunshot. There was a smell of burning in the wound and signs of powder blackening. The revolver in the hand of the deceased had been recently fired. . . .* Rourke flipped the folder closed again.

In the kitchen he found chicken bones, a fry pan white with congealed grease, and a lot of roaches.

He walked back into the bedroom and was hit with the sour smell of old and unwashed sheets, and was hit again when he saw what was on the wall opposite the rusting iron bedstead.

The wall was papered with newspaper clippings, cracked and curling photographs, and notes scrawled on stained and torn pieces of paper. Some of the clippings and photographs were of Remy Lelourie, but most were of him: of his high-society wedding and the notices of Katie's birth and her first communion just last month, and press write-ups of the more notorious cases he had worked on. The most recent ones, having to do with Charles St. Claire's murder, had been thumbtacked on top of old ones that went back to his first year as a detective.

Rourke stared at the wall, feeling unclean. He had started to turn away when one of the newspaper clippings caught his eye.

He'd reached for the tack, to take it down, when out in the front room the door creaked open.

Rourke pulled the tack out of the clipping and he had to catch the piece of paper as it fluttered toward the floor. He quietly folded it and put it in his trouser pocket. He was easing back the hammer on his gun when he heard a match strike and smelled the smoke of a Castle Morro.

Rourke put up his gun and walked back out to the front of the house, not being careful anymore about the noise he made since his bright yellow Bearcat was parked right out front. He stopped in the doorway between the kitchen and the parlor and leaned against the jamb with his hands in his pockets.

Fiorello Prankowski was on his haunches, squatting next to the body.

"Somebody ought to call the cops," Rourke said.

Fio thumbed back his hat and looked up. His lip curled around the cigar he was crushing in his teeth. "You see, that's the trouble I've been having lately. I thought we *were* the cops."

"He was dead when I got here."

"Yeah, yeah, that's what they all say." Fio took the cigar out of his mouth and looked down at the body again. "Bullet hole in his head, gun in his hand. It's suicide as I live and breathe."

"So it would seem." Rourke pushed himself off the doorjamb. "You'd better go take a look in the bedroom."

"Aw, man. What?" Fio lumbered heavily to his feet, and Rourke stepped aside so he could pass. "If it's another dead guy, I'm quitting."

He was gone for quite a while, and when he came back his face seemed to have new cares worn into the old grooves. "I know the guy didn't like you and we can't all be Miss America to everybody, but Jesus, that was spooky." He looked around the room, turning a circle in place. "This whole place is spooky. I mean, a detective sergeant's pay is no chicken feed, as we oughta know, and after all the years he's got on the job he's got to be pulling in some righteous juice. So how come he's living like a bum?"

Rourke shrugged. "He played the horses and wasn't either smart or lucky. I heard that lately the sharks had their teeth in his balls."

"Yeah, I heard that too." Fio looked down at the body again, his hands on his hips. "I don't think it was a vig collector did this, though. It ain't their style. When they cap a guy, they like to make it look like a lesson, not suicide."

Rourke leaned against the wall with his hands in his pockets, staring down at the milky caul that was forming over the dead cop's eyes, and saying nothing.

"Hey, come on, partner. I'm spinning tales all by myself here," Fio said. "Let me hear who you think did it."

"I don't know," Rourke said, telling for once the unvarnished truth.

Fio gave him a slow, careful look, then his gaze finally went to the crime case file carefully centered in the middle of the coffee table. He put on an exaggerated surprise to see it, but he didn't make a move to pick it up.

It was, Rourke thought, what Fio had probably been invited here to see. "Go on and take a look," he said.

Fio scrubbed at his nose with the flat of his big thumb. "Naw, I don't need to. I got a good idea what-all's in it. Doherty and me, we had us a few brews after the wake last night. We talked about old times. He had a lot to say about the summer of nineteen sixteen."

In the summer of 1916 Rourke had been nineteen, working a double shift—mornings on the banana boats, evenings on an oyster lugger—making money so that he could someday go to college, maybe be a lawyer instead of just a flatfoot cop like his old man had been. In the summer of 1916, he had been desperately, hopelessly in love with a girl who had been maybe more than just a little crazy. A girl who was feeding all the craziness in him.

"The Red Sox took the Brooklyn Dodgers in the World Series that year," Rourke said. "Four games to one."

"Yeah. And to hear Doherty tell it, that was also the summer you shot Julius St. Claire in the head in the bedroom of that slave shack back of Sans Souci and then fixed it to look like a suicide."

In the summer of 1916, Sergeant Roibin Doherty and a couple of his fellow detectives had taken Rourke down into a room in the Parish Prison and beaten him so badly with sap sticks and socks full of marbles that he'd pissed blood for weeks after. He had kept himself from telling them the one thing that might have stopped the beating, but he hadn't been able to stop himself from screaming.

Fio was staring at him hard now. Rourke met the other man's eyes, but said nothing.

"Are you fucking Remy Lelourie?" Fio said.

"Lately?" Rourke smiled. "No."

Fio rubbed the back of his head and heaved a deep sad sigh. " 'Cause Doherty thought you were fucking her back in the summer of nineteen sixteen. You and Julius St. Claire both, until you got tired of sharing. Or maybe y'all decided to settle it the old-fashioned way—like a couple a quick-draw cowboys. You see, this revolver in Julius's hand, apparently it was one of a matching pair, which means, lo and behold, that there were two of them. One of them ended up in Julius's dead hand, and the other disappeared that very same day. Amazing, huh?"

Rourke went to the coffee table and picked up the case file. He ripped off the cellophane envelope and tossed it at Fio. "Here's the shell casing that was found in the chamber of the revolver Julius St. Claire had in his hand and the bullet that tore open his head. The gun is on the wall in the front parlor of Sans Souci this very day. So why don't you just give it all to the Ghoul and see if he can make something out of it with his fancy new ballistics equipment."

Fio had snatched the envelope out of the air. "And what'll that prove? Somebody with a cop for his old man might be smart enough to know you can tell if a gun's been fired and do some switching."

"Yeah, but if there *isn't* a match, at least you can rule out one suspect. You'll know that Julius didn't kill Julius."

"For what it's worth," Fio said, "I don't think you did it. You might go in with guns blazing, but you wouldn't try to get away with it afterward. I've never seen you take so much as a free cup of java—you're just so fucking pure. Naw, if you committed murder, they'd find you next to the corpse, already braiding the rope to hang you with."

Rourke's mocking smile was all for himself. "I'm touched you think so highly of me, Fio."

"Don't get too full of yourself, though. You might not be

fucking her now, but I think the two of you are playing some deep sick game, you and Remy Lelourie. Heads she gets away with murder; tails you put her away for it. I'll bet you don't even know which way you're hoping the nickel lands."

He knew. Never mind what lies he'd been telling to her and to himself, he knew.

He pushed his hand in his pocket, his fingers closing around the newspaper clipping. He thought of the way she'd looked in the cemetery last night, while she'd been so desperately trying to seduce him. He thought of the sadness in her, so dark and dreadful.

I can't save you, Remy.

"What?" Fio said, having seen the look on Rourke's face.

Rourke pulled his hand out of his pocket. "This was tacked up on the wall in the bedroom. It's a photograph of Remy Lelourie at a Mardi Gras ball about a week after her marriage last February."

You wouldn't have known it was Remy without the caption to tell you, because she was wearing an elaborate Mardi Gras mask, of Medusa, who had snakes for hair.

The girl up on the screen, larger than life, was doing the Charleston on top of a grand piano, legs flying, beads flapping, her painted mouth blowing kisses to the world. "Get hot!" a man in the audience yelled at the celluloid girl, and as if she'd heard him, she laughed, and he laughed back at her. "I love my wife, but oh, you kid!"

Jazz Babies. It was the last movie Remy Lelourie had made before her marriage, a fun but strangely empty story about a fun but strangely empty girl living the glamorous life in Hollywood. Daman Rourke watched that beautiful face as it was caught in quick, revealing flashes by the camera's lens. He thought how it wasn't truth but sweet seductive falsehood that audiences craved.

The movie wasn't over yet, but he got up anyway and left through a door hung with heavy velvet draperies. He walked down a carpeted staircase lined with crystal sconces and into a lobby brilliant with the refracted light from a massive chandelier reflected over and over in huge mirrors on yellow velvet walls, and between the mirrors was her face.

Studio publicity shots, posters from her films, newspaper clippings. Recent ones, of the bereaved widow on the steps of Sans Souci. A photograph of the night last February when she had come home to New Orleans, stepping off the train at the old Union Street Station, wearing a black cloche hat and a gray coat with a fur collar. It had been a real winter's night, cold and drizzly, cold as only New Orleans can be, a damp cold that seeps into your bones. Yet hundreds of people had been there to meet her, even more than when Valentino had come a couple of years before. Rourke had stood at the back, at the far fringes of the crowd that cold winter's night. She hadn't seen him.

The next night, in the Blue Room of the Roosevelt Hotel after the premiere of *Jazz Babies*, she had danced the tango with her future husband, and then she had thrilled the crowd by dancing the Charleston on top of the piano, a jazz baby come to life. There was a picture on the wall of that moment as well.

There was another clipping that Rourke always had to stop to look at, this one from a French newspaper, taken on a beach on the Riviera. She is in a bathing suit, scandalous by American standards, baring not only her arms but most of her breasts, and all of her legs clear up to the tops of her thighs. She is trying to jump out of the way of the splashing breakers, and she is looking back over her shoulder, laughing. A man, nearly out of the frame, is watching her—some film director, the caption says. On his face is the haunted, desperate look of a man who shares her bed but knows he will never have even the smallest part of her that really matters.

The movie was ending now, and the organ was playing a wedding march. Rourke pushed open the glass doors of Loew's State Theater and stepped out onto the wet sidewalk of Canal Street.

He turned up his collar against the rain that fell out of a misty indigo sky. He crossed over to the neutral ground and walked along the streetcar tracks. The rain ran down the store windows like tears; the waving palm fronds made shadow puppets on the grass. A gust of wind picked up a piece of newspaper and slapped it against his leg. He bent over to peel it off and saw her face.

The streetcar tracks began to tremble and hum from a car he couldn't yet see. He stood as if lost, with the rain dripping off his hat brim, until the streetcar came rattling past him from out of the night. It stopped at the corner and a couple got off. He could tell by the way they were looking at each other that the streetcar was bringing them to a bed somewhere. They were young, young enough for this to be their first time.

He watched them walk off arm in arm, leaning into each other to get under one umbrella, bodies cleaving so close they might as well already be one flesh. Rourke closed his eyes and saw the face of Remy Lelourie. Not the face of the flapper girl on the movie screen, or the face of the widow drenched in her husband's blood. It was the face of a girl-woman, flushed from lovemaking, with the sun-dappled shadows of willow leaves floating over the pale skin of her breasts.

He wondered if that boy, who was on his way to getting laid, understood how the first woman you fucked, you might never forget her. But the first one you loved, she would always own a piece of your soul.

Light spilled out the tall windows and pooled on the cedar boards of the gallery at Sans Souci. He looked at her through rain-slick glass. She sat on the sofa with her legs drawn up underneath her, reading, with her head slightly bent, her profile to the night. Yet she seemed less real to him than the celluloid image he'd just been watching up on the screen.

She looked up and saw him—a man standing in dark shadows, watching her. Any other woman in the world would have screamed, but not her.

She stood up, slowly, and came to him. He heard her fumble with the latch, but his gaze was on her. She was wearing a thin wrapper of white silk. He could see the dark shadows of her nipples and the hair between her legs.

At last, at last, the window was opening. She took a step back, and then another, and another. "Day," she said, only that, and he stepped over the wide, low sill and into long ago and far away.

He came all the way up to her, so close and yet not touching. He looked down at her, and it was like staring into the dark side of the moon reflected in the water at the bottom of a deep well. She was mystery—unfathomable, unseeable, unknowable.

"What if I killed him, Day?" she whispered, taunting him, daring him. "What if I did it?"

"Baby, I don't care," he said, and then he laughed and crossed over with her, into the night.

He took her there on the floor, with swift, rough lust. Or she took him. Hunger moved in flashes, pure white strokes of lightning flaring across her face, in her eyes. There was beauty in destruction, seduction in fear.

He breathed in gasps, his body shuddered. He felt the skin draw tight over the bones of his face. They kissed and it was as if they were trying to suck the life out of each other, trying to touch each other everywhere, mouths, tongues, hands, all touching, stroking, tasting all of her everywhere, her breasts, her belly, his hair brushing over her belly, his mouth finding the sweet spot between her legs, his mouth finding her.

He spread open her thighs, and she lifted her hips as he drove into her, hard, and he caught her cry with his mouth. She wrapped her legs around him, sucking him deeper. He laid his open mouth against her neck, tasting her skin, feeling the wild and plunging riff of her blood. He came high and hard and long in her.

He came back to himself with his face wet against her hot and shuddering belly. Her fingers tangled in his hair.

He remembered the moment all those years ago, when she had left him. How he had lain still for a long time, staring at the willow leaves above his head, sweating in the wet heat of the bayou, the taste of her in his mouth, the smell of her on his fingers, in his hair. His body aching all over, as if she had left bruises on all the places she had touched, bruises inside and out.

He might have cried, lying there after she had left, although he didn't think so. He had been much younger then.

Chapter Twenty-Three

The smell of curdled milk filled the kitchen of the Conti Street house as Augusta whipped at the clabber, making Creole cream cheese. She stood at the sink, with her back to the room, and she whipped so hard her skirts swayed around her ample hips and the spoon banged against the bowl, performing an angry counterpoint to the sweet peals of the bells that were ringing for Sunday morning Mass.

Katie dunked her *beignet* into a glass of milk and grinned across the table at her father. He winked back at her.

"You got somethin' in yo' eye, Mr. Day?" Augusta said. "You hadn't oughta be goin' out to no Fair Grounds with somethin' in yo' eye. Wind blowin' today. Might could blow up dirt in yo' face. Make yo' eye worse."

Rourke opened his mouth to answer back, then got smart and filled it with grits instead. He was off the clock, he was going to spend the day with his Katie, and he was going to stay away from trouble even if it came chasing after him.

"Miss Katie, you tell yo' daddy how he ought not to be goin' to no Fair Grounds with somethin' in his eye."

Katie, who would believe the moon was made of clabber if Augusta told her so, was looking intently at his face now to see if he really did have something in his eye.

"There's nothing wrong with my eye, honey. Miss Augusta is of the opinion that the racetrack is no place for a daddy to bring along his little girl and she's letting me know about it. It's called being as subtle as a freight train."

Augusta sniffed. "Nothing there but trash and gangsters and mens who gamble away the food right out they poor chillen's mouths."

Rourke scraped back his chair. "And the day's not getting any younger. So go fetch your hat, Katie, and give Grandmama a good-bye kiss."

Katie jumped from her chair and skipped out of the kitchen, laughing in her excitement. Augusta kept her hands busy with the clabber, her back to Rourke.

"Augusta."

She wiped her hands on her apron and turned. Her strong African features were empty of expression, but her eyes were soft with worry.

"I've got some broken promises I'm trying to make up for," Rourke said. "I'm only taking her where she said she wanted to go."

"An' she only sayin' what she think you want t' hear—she love her daddy that much. But you know it not only that. You haven't been doin' good by her, Mr. Day. Not good at all."

Rourke was spared having to answer to that cutting truth when Katie came running back into the kitchen with her fat brown braids flying behind her, her mouth wide with a laughter that was laced with mischief. Sometimes he loved her so much it hurt just to look at her.

They went out the back door, into the courtyard, and through the carriageway. Conti Street was alive with activity that morning. The prostitutes were out on their front stoops, scrubbing them down with pee and throwing red brick dust on the sidewalk, all of which was supposed to bring them luck for the coming week. The pimps and gamblers, barefoot and in their undershirts, lounged under the shade of the galleries playing poker and cotch.

A young blind man sat on the banquette, beneath the corner

speakeasy's tin canopy, blowing some sweet jazz on a trombone. Rourke gave Katie a dime to throw in the musician's hat. The man turned his head toward her, smiling his thanks, and sunlight flashed off the lenses of his dark glasses.

They picked up Rourke's Stutz Bearcat speedster at the garage where he parked it around the corner on Basin Street, and drove out to Lake Pontchartrain along the Old Shell Road. On the right the canal bustled with shrimp boats, oyster luggers, and barges hauling bricks and coal. To their left the oleanders rioted with pink and white blossoms. The wind was sun-warmed and soft in their hair, and it was hard to tell which was brighter, the day or her smile.

He rented a small daggerboard sailboat and they took it out on the lake. The wind sent the bow slicing through the dark green water, tossing up bubbles that chuckled and broke into a song that was nearly as sweet as Katie's laughter. Rourke tilted his head back to watch the pelicans and egrets fly through the sky on sun-gilded wings. He allowed his eyes to drift closed, feeling the sun deep against his eyelids, deep inside himself, imagining how it would feel to let it all go, to float on the wind, floating free.

Last night he had let go. Loving that girl again, that crazy, wild girl, had been like plunging your fist into a fire and not feeling the pain, even as all the flesh melted off your bones. Delirious heat and a terrible price to be paid later, but he would not think of that now. Now was for Katie.

After their sail, they bought oyster sandwiches and nectar soda from one of the restaurants along the lakeshore and picnicked beneath the shade of a mimosa tree, sharing bits of bread with the shorebirds. Rourke watched her every smile, every tilt of her head, he listened to her laughter, let himself bask in the joy of her, and he wondered how it was that when he was with her, with his Katie, he could feel moments of happiness so intense and pure that they were almost unbearable.

They got to the Fair Grounds in time for Rourke to use his cop connections and give Katie a tour of the stables, so that she could pet the horses and meet some of the jockeys and trainers. When it grew close to post time they took their seats in a box by the finish line. The fronds on the palm trees and the flags on the grandstand fluttered in the breeze. The noise of the crowd ebbed and flowed around them like sea surf.

Rourke closed his eyes for a moment and breathed in the smells of horse sweat, manure, and oats, the loamy sweetness of the freshly raked and dampened sod. It was a perfume that could fire up his blood as quickly as the heat from a woman's mouth touching his.

He gave Katie a program and asked her to pick a favorite for them to root for in the first race. She pointed to number eight, and he had to hug her for the sheer craziness of it.

"Katie honey, that nag has never finished in the money in her life."

"But her name is Lucky Charm, Daddy."

Lucky Charm had the luckiest day of her life, winning by a nose. She paid out eighteen to one, for those few lucky fools who had actually bet on her.

He handed Katie the racing program and challenged her to pick out the next winner. Trying to ignore the money burning a hole in his pocket, the train leaving the station, the fire in his blood as hot as a woman's kiss. No hotter.

"Hotsy-Totsy," she said.

He laughed, feeling a little crazy now. "Hotsy-Totsy probably wouldn't recognize the finish line if he stumbled over it. And besides, what kind of a name is that to stick on a racehorse?"

"It's hep, Daddy. Don't you know anything?"

The laughter fled, and a gentle pain took its place as he looked into her shining, upturned face. His Katie. I know I love you, he wanted to say. What he had never known was why those words always came so hard.

Damn if Hotsy-Totsy didn't come home a winner too. By the time the horse crossed the finish line they were both jumping up and down, shouting as if they'd had a hundred bucks riding on its sleek bay hide. Rourke swept Katie up into his arms and swung her around, singing, "Oh! Oh! Oh, what a gal!" Embarrassing her so that she punched him in the belly—pretty hard for a girl—and told him, "Don't be goofy."

She didn't pick any more winners after that, but she didn't seem to care. She took her joy from the horses sweeping around the last turn, thundering down the home stretch, jockeys' silks flapping, torn sod flying.

Katie laughing, laughing.

He was too happy and it scared him. Already he could feel it coming, like a cloud floating across the empty blue bowl of the sky on its way to swallowing up the sun. That dark edge of melancholy coming to swallow up his happiness because he knew, he always knew, that anything so good couldn't last, that he didn't deserve for the good things to last.

With his mood beginning to darken, he didn't realize the sky was darkening as well. The smell of rain was on the wind now, the air growing thick and heavy. Thick purple clouds were building up in the west, swallowing up the sun, swallowing up the day, swallowing up the good moment.

Katie slid her hand into his and leaned against him, as if seeking the solid weight of him for comfort. "Is it getting to be nighttime already, Daddy?"

"Not for hours yet, darlin'. It's only a bit of a rain blowing in," he said. Yet she leaned closer to him still.

"I don't want the night to come," she said, so softly he barely heard her.

He looked down at her, at the button on the top of her Pels hat. The hat was bleached from the sun and grimy with dirt. "Katie, have you grown scared of the dark?"

"No." She stared at the ground, pushing her foot through the litter of bet slips and sandwich wraps.

He put his hand under her chin and tilted her face up. She was trying to look brave, but her mouth trembled. "I'm scared the gowman's going to come back."

"Listen to me, baby." He squatted down alongside her so that she could look him in the eye and he could rest his hands on her shoulders, steadying her, comforting her. "There's no such thing as the gowman. It's just a myth. A made-up story."

"But I saw him, Daddy."

He tightened his grip on her shoulders, drawing her closer. He kissed her forehead, her cheek, her fat braid where it curled around her neck. It smelled of the sun. "It was a bad dream you had, is all. I know they can seem real sometimes, a body's bad dreams, but if you face them down they go away."

And so you lie, he thought, you lie to make a little girl's monsters go away, and you dread the day she's old enough to see all the monsters you haven't faced, all of your own worst failings. Even more, though, you dread the day she discovers for herself that some monsters demand more courage than anyone can bear to give.

A soft, fragrant rain fell out of the purple twilight as they walked home from the garage. Light leaked out of the slatted blinds and doorways. Where a window had been left open, lace curtains stirred like a beckoning hand.

As they turned onto Conti Street, they heard the crack of billiard balls and the low strumming of a banjo coming from the corner speakeasy, but the block was mostly deserted. A lone cop stood in the carriageway of their cottage; the other must have been lured into the kitchen for a cup of Augusta's coffee and a plate of her red beans and rice.

The blind trombone player was packing up for the day. He knelt on the banquette, huddled close under the leaky canopy, trying to keep himself and his horn dry while he pocketed the coins from his hat and unlatched his instrument case.

The smoky incandescent sign of the speakeasy pulsed blue light onto his face. He turned his head, and the light glimmered in his eyes.

His eyes.

Rourke snatched Katie around the waist and dove, rolling as he hit the bricks so that he bore the brunt of the fall while he struggled to pull his .38 out of its holster. The trombone man reached into the instrument case and came up with a machine gun, firing, and the bullets streaked at them from out the dusk, like heat lightning jumping across the sky.

Chapter Twenty-Four

The machine gun hacked fire. Bullets bit into the banquette bricks, shattered glass, and ripped into a pile of garbage cans with a ringing, pinging racket.

A door banged in the house across the street, and a man in a black fedora ran out onto a sagging upstairs gallery, sparks flashing from the hogleg in his hand, and more bullets stapled the wall above Rourke's head.

He crouched lower. He had wedged Katie into the corner, between their neighbor's wrought-iron stoop and the brick wall, so that he could shield her with his body. Rourke braced his gun on the railing and shot at the trombone man, who was running toward them, his tommy gun still spewing metal. The man's head exploded in a gout of blood and bone.

Rourke twisted around and fired up at the gallery, once, twice, at the same time as the cop who'd been in the carriageway dropped to one knee and also emptied his gun at the man in the fedora. The man's head snapped on his neck, and his back arched as red blossoms burst open on his chest. He pirouetted on his toes and fell over the gallery railing, through a rotting canvas awning, and onto a box of geraniums that splintered beneath him.

Running steps slapped on the wet banquette, and another man in a black fedora charged around the corner from Burgundy Street, the tommy gun in his hand roaring, its barrel lifting. Street lamps and windows exploded in a hail of glass.

Rourke and the cop in the carriageway were already both twisting, spinning, firing. The man whirled and ran back toward Burgundy, but not before he let loose one more burst with his machine gun.

The cop jerked once as a red mist sprayed from his throat. He seemed to hang suspended in the air before he sagged, as if falling gently asleep, onto the banquette.

Smoke drifted slowly through the air, thick with the smell of cordite and brick dust. Glass tinkled, a garbage can rolled and banged into a lamppost. All was silent for a moment, and then the cathedral bell began pealing the Angelus.

Katie had yet to make a sound. Rourke was running his hands all over her body, feeling for wet blood, for ripped and broken flesh and bones. Her eyes stared wild and wide, then they focused on his face and she screamed and went on screaming.

The second patrolman burst out of the carriageway at a run, his gun drawn, and Rourke came within a reflex squeeze of his trigger finger from killing the kid.

The young cop skidded to a stop and looked around him, his eyes bulging white in the falling dusk. "Jesus," he whispered. "Oh, Jesus, oh, Jesus . . ."

On Burgundy Street a car revved its engine and tires squealed, spewing dirt and gravel. A horn blared.

Rourke thrust his screaming daughter into the other cop's hands. "Get her inside. All the way in the back. And get more men over here."

Rourke waited only the seconds it took to ensure he would be obeyed, then he whirled and ran down the street, snatching up the machine gun from the hand of the dead trombone player. He rounded the corner and saw a black Lincoln driving off, its tail-lights disappearing into the misty rain.

The fleeing Lincoln had sent a cherry-red Cadillac touring car up onto the banquette and into a fruit stand. Rourke ran up to the car and snatched open the door.

The driver—a college boy out slumming by the look of him—popped the monocle out of his eye, opened his mouth, and squeaked. Rourke grabbed him by the wide lapels of his knickerbocker coat and dragged him, still squeaking, out into the street.

Rourke got into the Cadillac, threw it into reverse. Berries and peaches rolled off the roof and bounced on the hood. He spun the steering wheel one-handed while slamming the door closed with the other, sending the car into a violent, fishtailing U-turn and clipping a pyramid of empty milk cans. The rear bumper snagged the handle of one of the cans, and Rourke dragged it along behind him for a half block, trailing sparks.

The Lincoln had turned right at the corner of St. Ann, heading for Jackson Square and the river. The man at the wheel was good. It was Sunday evening and traffic was light, but automobiles, buggies, trucks, and horse carts still crossed back and forth on the narrow, cobbled streets of the Quarter. The wheelman not only expertly swerved in and out and around these obstacles, he was using them as shields, putting them between himself and Rourke's pursuit.

Rourke smiled and pressed the Cadillac's accelerator to the floor. The faces of startled pedestrians looked up as he sped by, engine screaming, wheels howling. Rain clicked flatly against the windshield and slanted through the headlamp beams. Street lamps cast intermittent light into the fleeing Lincoln, silhouetting two heads.

One of the heads moved, thrust out the car's open window, followed by shoulders, arms, and a firing tommy gun. Rourke zigzagged, bullets ripped into the Cadillac's right side, and its rear window exploded in a shower of glass.

The black Lincoln crossed Royal Street and barreled into Jackson Square, darting between the closing gap of a streetcar and a black-plumed hearse.

Rourke hurled the Cadillac after them but the gap was closing fast—with a space of seven feet at the most now between the streetcar's cowcatcher and the hearse's flying-horse hood ornament. The streetcar swayed and rocked and rattled.

Six feet.

The hearse's black plumes bobbed and dripped in the wet.

Five feet.

Rourke gripped the steering wheel hard, stood on the gas, and hummed "Toot, Toot, Tootsie, Goodbye" hard under his breath.

He slewed between the streetcar and hearse so fast the car whipped back and forth like a water moccasin, shaving it so close he saw the conductor's teeth as the man's mouth fell open in a scream. Rourke shot the Cadillac into the open square, leaving a chaos of locked bumpers and blaring horns in his wake, but he'd brought part of the streetcar's cowcatcher with him.

The metal got caught up between the Cadillac's wheel and fender, acting as a brake. The car bucked and jerked in Rourke's hands, riding up onto the banquette toward the colonnaded corner of the French Market, which was closed up and empty of people, thank God. The jolt knocked the piece of metal loose out from under the fender, and the car surged with a roar of released speed through one of the markethouse's arched set of columns and out the other, crashing catercorner through the butchers' row along the way. Bloody sides of beef smacked into the windshield before he was back on the cobblestoned street, pointing toward the river and the dead end of the levee, where masts floated disembodied across the dusky, rain-swept sky.

Another burst of machine-gun fire spewed from the Lincoln's open window, bullets shredding the sweet olive trees in the square, before the getaway car whipped a right at the levee. It took the rainslick corner at a skid and headed uptown on the river road, with Rourke on its tail.

The Lincoln had come out of its skid on the wrong side of the road and nearly smacked head-on into a flat wagon stacked with hogsheads of sugar. The wagon's team reared in its traces and swerved into another wagon piled high with bananas just off the boat. Barrels tumbled and rolled and broke apart, spilling sugar, and the banana bunches slid and flopped as the two wagons crashed into each other, blocking the road.

With brick warehouses on one side of him and the levee on the other, Rourke had only two choices: either plow into the tangle of horses, shattered wagons, sugar barrels, and squashed bananas or sprout wings and fly over it all.

He jerked the wheel hard toward the levee, gunning the engine. The Cadillac careened, tilting so far over, impossibly far, until Rourke thought it must be driving on only two wheels, driving up, up, up onto the grassy bank until it seemed he would either flip right over or shoot like a rocket straight up into the sky.

The Cadillac's front tires spun, clawing at the empty air, until gravity won out and the chassis slammed into the ground with a bone-rattling jar.

Rourke drove as fast as he dared along the narrow spine of the levee, digging grooves through the wet green grass and buttercups and dodging the *batture* willow trees. Below him on one side spread the immense swell of brown Mississippi and mud flats. On the other, railroad tracks and a river road that was filling up with the trucks and mule-drawn wagons of farmers bringing their produce into town for tomorrow's market. Ahead—way ahead, too far ahead—was the black Lincoln.

Which veered suddenly toward Howard Avenue, away from the river.

Rourke twisted the steering wheel and floored the accelerator. The Cadillac flew off the top of the levee and he thought, Sweet Jesus, I'm going to die.

The car plunged through a gauzy curtain of cobalt rain, over the railroad tracks, and barely missed landing in a pickup truck full of seaweed-lined baskets of bluepoint crabs. It hit the road so hard Rourke's head nearly banged through the roof and the rear bumper fell off with a loud clang, but by some devil-induced miracle the tires didn't blow. They caught at the wet gravel-and-tar surface, Rourke poured power into the sputtering engine, and the Cadillac veered right, following the curve of the train tracks.

Ahead of him, he saw the Lincoln's taillights leave the road, bouncing and bounding over the spiderweb of rails and crossties at the Union Station terminal, disappearing in the clouds of billowing steam that spewed from the locomotive smokestacks.

Rourke cut hard right through the station's red-brick arcade to head them off, sending a taxicab swerving into a telephone pole. The Lincoln responded with a tracery of bullets and the stuttering *pop-pop-pop* of the tommy gun. Rourke kept on their tail, clattering over the railroad tracks. The machine gun hacked again and a locomotive's headlamp blew in a flash of white light.

Rourke chased the Lincoln a couple of miles through the streets of midcity, past corner groceries and diners, past shotguns and Queen Annes and Creole cottages, whose families would be just sitting down to a quiet Sunday supper. They sped down the rain-slick dirt and gravel streets toward the lake, until the houses gave out and they were on the Old Shell Road, where Rourke had driven with Katie that morning. Lights from the boats on the New Basin Canal blinked by on the right. On the left the banks of oleanders had become hulking shadows. Roadhouse speakeasies rushed by in bursts of light and sound.

Into marshy cypress groves and marshland now, and it seemed the road would go on forever, into the night. It had an end, though, as all things did. At a bridge over the canal and the lakefront resort of West End Park, where you could leave the hot city streets behind and listen to a Sousa concert in the bandstand or watch a movie played on a giant outdoor canvas screen. Dine at Mannessier's overlooking the lake, or take a ride on the *Susquehanna* steamboat and dance the Black Bottom beneath a summer moon.

They tore through the park now, on a winding road, tires grinding and spraying shells and pebbles. In the center of the park an electrical fountain shot rainbow-hued jets of water high into a smoke-gray sky. Even on this rainy Sunday evening a few families had gathered to watch the kaleidoscopic display, and the Lincoln was headed right for them.

At the last possible instant it cut across the horseshoe of grass that ringed the fountain. Rourke, following close behind, responded just a hair of a second too late.

He didn't run over the young boy in a yellow slicker who was tossing a ball up into the air for his dog, because he flipped the wheel hard over and stood on the gas, just managing to pull out of the inevitable spin. Ruby, sapphire, and emerald drops of water showered the windshield. Ahead of him loomed the bandstand and the back of the enormous canvas movie screen.

No concert played tonight, and the bandstand was empty. But the movie projectionist was in love with Remy Lelourie, and although he'd been showing her films over and over, ever since the murder, still he could not get enough of her. Hour after hour, he would send her image out into the night, even when there was no one but him to see.

Rourke didn't even try to stop. He aimed the Cadillac straight at the giant screen's rear supporting struts, riding it like a ramp and hitting the canvas at seventy miles an hour. The car's pointed grille burst through the stiffened cloth, ripping open the beautiful face of Cinderella.

The Cadillac soared twenty feet through the air and hit the ground right in the Lincoln's path.

The Lincoln's brakes screamed as it veered off the road. The face of the man in the black fedora got caught in the beam of the projector's light, and he threw up a hand to protect his eyes. The steering wheel jerked out of his other hand, and the Lincoln swerved violently toward the lake.

The Lincoln's speed took it up the sloping seawall steps, across the embankment, and onto the wide pier. A tire blew but the brakes must have given out, for it kept on going, toward a bathhouse whose steeply pitched roof touched the weathered boards of the pier, and still it kept going, on up the roof, to be launched like a rock from a slingshot out over the lake, where a steamboat rolled, its paddle wheel idle as it eased up to the dock. The Lincoln sheared off the top of the steamer's tall smokestack and sailed another ten feet through the rain-shrouded sky before its gasoline tank exploded in a ball of red and yellow and blue flames.

By the time Rourke had walked to the end of the pier, what was left of the Lincoln had sunk into the deep, green-black water. Out on the steamboat a calliope was still playing ragtime, but the smell of scorched metal and gasoline floated thick over the gently lapping water.

A flapper who had been watching all the excitement from the restaurant window came out to stand next to Rourke. Rain dripped from the silver fringe of her skirt and off the ends of her sheared hair. She smiled at him with a mouth that was red and tipsy, and offered him a drink from a flask she took from under her black lace garter.

Casey Maguire hadn't let the wet weather ruin his Sunday shrimp boil at his camp out on the lake. It was summer, after all, and so he'd prepared for rain. He'd set up a huge red-striped tent on the front lawn, with sides you could roll and tie up to let in the breeze. He'd strung the tent with Japanese lanterns, covered picnic tables with newspaper, and laid out piles of spicy shrimp and crab, loaves of French bread and thin slices of *boudin*. Slabs of pork ribs were put to barbecuing on top of a tin barrel.

The hooch, of course, was the best a bootlegger could smuggle. Labeled, uncut, and straight off the boat.

The camp wasn't really a camp—that was just what folk in New Orleans who could afford one called their summer cottages. Casey Maguire's cottage was built on stilts out over the water and approached by a long, slatted pier. It was a rambling two-story affair, with a wraparound screened porch filled with cots for sleeping and rocking chairs for dozing, and littered with cane poles, crab traps, and fishnets.

Rourke drove up on the lawn in the bullet-riddled, smashed, and dented red Cadillac. Metal grated against metal as he shoved open the door and got out. He brought the machine gun with him.

His shoes flattened the tall wet grass and crunched over fallen banana leaves and palm fronds. He walked into the open-sided tent and, just as at Bridey's wake two evenings ago, he entered on a rush of startled silence. Many of the faces were the same. Most of the guests Casey Maguire invited out to his summer camp shrimp boils were from the old neighborhood. Once, years ago, he had told Rourke that he liked remembering where he had come from.

At Bridey's wake, Maguire had worn a dark blue silk suit and tie. Tonight he had on fashionably floppy white Oxford bags, a snappy hat, and saddle shoes. Yet he stood alone, and with a raw stillness, as if he'd been waiting.

His eyes clicked from Rourke's face to the gun in his hands and then back to his face.

Rourke pointed the submachine gun at Maguire's belly. "You lousy, cocksucking bastard," he said, his voice grating in his throat. "I had my little girl with me."

"Day." Maguire lifted his hands, spreading them a little. "I don't know what this is about, but you've got a tommy gun in your hand and there are innocent people here. Women, children." The black shine was there, deep in his pale eyes, but it seemed born more of pain than of anger or fear. "I swear to Jesus, whatever it is you think I've done this time, you're wrong."

Slowly, Rourke brought up the barrel of the machine gun and laid it against Maguire's face, softly rubbed it against Maguire's cheek before pressing the muzzle hard into the bone. "Your goons missed me, Case, but I did for them. All of them, and the only reason why I don't rip a fucking hole in your guts right here, right now, is because she came out of it without a scratch."

"No, that's not the reason," Maguire said, and the words came out wistful. "You won't kill me yet because you're not sure I'm guilty, and you're much too honorable a man for murder." He wrapped his hand around the barrel of the machine gun and gently pushed it aside. "Let it go, Day. Let it all go."

Rourke shook his head, smiling, showing his teeth. "When we're dead."

He took a step back, and then another. He turned and flung the gun away from him, throwing it out the open side of the tent with a hard violent motion, and the gun flew end over end, in a wide, high arc.

He walked out of the tent and across the lawn, past the wrecked Cadillac and down to the lake where the ragged palms clacked in the salt breeze and a heron was feeding in the edge of the cattails. Rain sparkled over the water like spun glass.

He began to shake. His ribs ached like hell and he felt tired beyond bearing.

He brought his hands up to his eyes, pressing hard enough to leave an impression on bone. Katie, Katie . . . She was all right, though. Not hurt, thank God, not a scratch. She hadn't even made a sound until she looked into his face and then she started screaming. What in sweet, sweet mercy had Katie seen in his face to make her start screaming so?

"Suh?"

Slowly, Rourke dropped his hands and looked up. A tall, thick-shouldered colored man stood in front of him. The man was dressed like a fisherman, but he had the flattened eyebrows and gray scar tissue around the eyes of a former prizefighter.

"Mistah Maguire be wantin' to talk to you tomorrow," the man said. "Mistah Maguire—the man whose place you at here now," he added, misunderstanding the utter lack of comprehension on Rourke's face. Rourke's mind was still back with Katie. He thought he would go home now and hold her if she would let him, hold her until she fell asleep.

"Fuck it," Rourke said. "I've nothing more to say to him."

The fisherman shifted his thick weight, his gaze drifting to the tent and then back to Rourke's face. "Please, suh. Mistah Maguire, he say to tell you he be at the Flying Horses tomorrow at straight-up noon."

Rourke nodded, hardly listening. The Flying Horses was a carousel in Audubon Park—a relatively safe place to meet amongst a crowd in the middle of the day. But that was for tomorrow and tomorrow was an eternity away. Right now he just wanted to go home, to hold Katie, to feel the giving warmth of her living flesh and smell her sweet little-girl breath, and he felt weary beyond belief, because later on tonight he still had to go over to the Pink Zebra and play *bourré* for ruinous stakes against a clever and ruthless Miss Fleurie, who might or might not have something to tell him that he needed to know.

One o'clock in the morning in the Pink Zebra and the music was wild, booze was flowing, and the shebas were easy. They drank Manhattan cocktails and gin fizzes and smoked cigarettes from long, rhinestoned holders, while dancing to a band with a frantic tin-panny beat, their fringed dresses jittering, bare legs flashing, twirling their long beads from fingers that had painted nails. They puckered their red lips and blew kisses to their sheiks, who were dropping dollars like confetti at the bar and gaming tables.

In an earlier incarnation, the Pink Zebra had been an ordinary Bourbon Street saloon with a couple of minor attractions: the games of *bourré* that went on nightly in its back room, and the pair of large zebra skins that faced each other across its gold-flocked walls. Then Prohibition came along, and Miss Fleurie followed. The *bourré* games became brutal, the zebra's white stripes were painted a shocking pink, and the ordinary had been reborn into the Pink Zebra.

Before it became the Pink Zebra, though, back when it was just another Bourbon Street dive, it was the place where Daman Rourke had met his future wife, on Mardi Gras night in 1919. She might have arrived with someone else, but she had left with him.

Although they had never spoken before that night, Rourke had known who she was, for he had seen her for the first time only a few weeks before. He had been out to the Carrigan house on Rose Park, because a pearl-and-diamond bracelet had gone missing during a king cake party. Weldon Carrigan had yet to be appointed superintendent of the police force, but he still had big juice, and so the captain had sent four cops to answer the call— three detectives and Rourke, who was just a few months home from the war and new to the job.

The whole neighborhood had turned the cold, gloomy day festive by stringing lanterns in the oaks that lined the quiet, exclusive street, and the air was filled with the smell of yardmen burning discarded Christmas trees. Rourke and the detectives stood in the front hall while Mrs. Carrigan flounced and fluttered and explained that a silly mistake had been made. The bracelet hadn't been stolen, after all, only lost, a broken clasp, you see, and it had since been found, and so sorry to have been such a bother to y'all. . . .

From where he stood in the wide hall with its molded ceiling and vine-stenciled walls, and its polished floor that shone like pond ice, Rourke was able to look into the front parlor where the party was going on, and there among a group of college boys in fraternity sweaters and debutantes in gloves and pearls, one girl caught his eye. She was laughing, and she wore a white camellia in her dark hair.

He watched her pick up an engraved silver knife and cut into the king cake, watched her lick purple icing off her fingers, and heard her teasing her friends about who would get the piece with the china baby doll and be crowned king or queen for the day. He hadn't realized he'd come up to the parlor's open doors for a better look at her until she glanced up and her gaze met his. They stared at each other long enough for a flush of color to rise in her cheeks, and then she had looked down, veiling her eyes with her eyelashes. Her small smile had lingered for a moment, though.

She was used to being admired, he thought, used to being wanted. That she was supposed to be untouchable and not for him just made him want her more.

The next time he saw her it was across a *bourré* table in the back room of a Bourbon Street saloon. She and her uptown boyfriend had left their Mardi Gras ball to come slumming, looking for excitement. Rourke had been there for the game and the money he could win if he was lucky, and good.

She stood at her boyfriend's shoulder, still wearing her fancy ball gown, watching Rourke deal the cards, her face flushed, her eyes looking a little scared, for she was way out of her debutante depth in this place and she knew it. Then she looked up, and their gazes met the way they had in her father's house, and he knew then that he would have her and soon.

A month after that *bourré* game in the Pink Zebra, they were married. One year and a baby later, she was dead.

Daman Rourke was leaning against the mahogany bar, resting on his elbows, with the heel of one alligator shoe hooked on the brass rail, and watching the girls dance the Black Bottom. He hadn't been here since Jo had died, but he realized now he hadn't needed to stay away. The memories living in this sheik and sheba playland weren't his.

Out of the corner of his eye he saw Miss Fleurie making her way toward him through the crowd. Her beaded and spangled dress was the color of the painted stripes on the zebras.

She leaned into him close, kissing him full on the mouth. "I hope you brought along your balls with you tonight, sugar. 'Cause scared money never wins."

She motioned to the bartender, who poured two glasses of champagne from a bottle with a French label. She took a delicate sip then cocked her head, arching one finely plucked eyebrow. "You aren't drinking?"

"I'm saving myself."

Her head fell back in laughter, brass-shaded lamplight burnishing her muscular throat. "Oooh. And here Miss Fleurie hasn't even showed her teeth yet."

She drank down her champagne in two swallows and picked up the glass she'd had poured for Rourke. Her gaze, full of wry amusement, went to one of the nearby tables, where a flapper had just dropped a pickled cherry down her own dress, and her sheik was trying to rescue it without using his hands. Her friends were all shrieking and laughing over her daring. Her face was flushed as red as the cherry from too many Manhattans, and from the feel of the boy's lips and tongue on her bare skin.

Miss Fleurie finished off the champagne and picked up the bottle. "The poor pathetic, frenetic things," she said. "Let's show them how the game is supposed to be played."

The game of *bourré* has a fearsome reputation, because if you keep losing, you can end up losing so big. It is a cutthroat game, and to be really good at it, you have to know no limit and no fear, and you have to have no stopping place.

It was a game best played with at least five people, and Miss Fleurie had no trouble enticing three uptown boys whose daddies had deep pockets to round out the table. The table was nothing special, just cheap pine covered with faded green felt, and the chairs around it were rawhide-seat Cajun chairs. A tin lamp hung suspended over the table from an old anchor chain.

They each anted up twenty dollars, and Miss Fleurie dealt five cards down, one at a time, to each player, and turned up her own fifth card to determine the trump suit: a five of clubs. One of the uptown boys bowed out right then, but the others stayed and the betting began. Rourke threw away a non-trump ace—a move few players were either brave enough or knowledgeable enough to do— and got lucky by drawing a trump card in exchange. Since Miss Fleurie had drawn two cards herself, he made another risky move by leading with his highest trump, a queen, hoping to flush out her only trump early. The gamble paid off, and he *bourréd* her on the first hand. Now she would have to fill the pot for the next game herself, covering everyone's ante and bets equal to the last hand played. While Rourke had just become seven hundred dollars richer.

He could lose big himself on the very next hand, though, and so Miss Fleurie laughed, for it might be one in the morning on Bourbon Street, but the night was still young, and her blood, like his, Rourke thought, was flying high.

"Oooh, baby," she cooed, pursing her lips at him in a mock kiss. "I knew you were going to be good, but nobody told me just *how* good."

Early morning mist crept along the narrow cobbled streets. Daman Rourke's heels struck against stone, grating raw against his jittering nerves. He never felt fear during a game, but afterward it would take him hours to come down.

He walked to Jackson Square and sat on a bench beneath the banana trees. He braced his elbows on his spread thighs and bent over, covering his face with his hands. His face felt rough and tired and sore, as if the bones had been bruised.

He had won nearly ten thousand dollars and a name from Miss Fleurie.

Chapter Twenty-Five

Charles St. Claire had been married to Belle's sister for a month when he came around to Esplanade Avenue calling on them that first time.

Mama was in bed with one of her sick headaches, and so Belle was left to entertain him alone. She hadn't much to offer him, only effervescent lemon, but he said that would be just fine. She felt strange going back into the kitchen to stir up the citric-acid crystals and chip some ice. All fluttery inside, as if she'd swallowed a mouthful of butterflies.

She didn't remember him much from when they were children. It was odd, now that she thought about it, that after Julius had proved such a disappointment, she hadn't set her cap for Charles. Why, she'd hardly ever thought of him. Julius was always coming around to moon over Remy, but they'd never seen much of Charles. The St. Claires as a family, although distantly related, were always a bit standoffish because of the Scandal and that old business about the duel, and anyway, Charles had always struck her as a rude and sullen boy. She wondered now, though, if perhaps she had misjudged him.

When she returned to the parlor with the effervescent lemon, she blushed to see that he was looking at the painting of Sans Souci that Mama had framed and hung above the mantel. "Remy must be so happy to be living there with you now," she said, mostly for lack of anything better. "She always did so love that house."

He startled her by laughing. "Dear Belle, dear *genuine* Belle. I notice how you don't claim that she always so loved me, and you would be right in your surmise of what each of us is getting out of this marriage. Your sister has Sans Souci, and I am the proud owner of the most beautiful woman in the world."

Belle didn't understand him, how he could say such a thing and laugh. She didn't know what to say to him, so she offered a small, tremulous smile. The smile he gave back to her was sweet and warm and touched her in all her empty places.

He came calling once or twice a week after that. Sometimes they would sit in the parlor with Mama, and it was sweetly hurtful for Belle to see how her mother, so starved for the simple companionship of another living presence in her house, would open up like a tulip in the sun under his easy compliments and smiles. Usually, though, Belle would entertain Charles St. Claire alone in the garden, and as she became more used to his presence, she would sometimes work while they talked. Or rather he did the talking and she mostly listened.

She thought there was a wound he carried around deep inside him that he showed to no one. She could catch glimpses of it sometimes, in the way he held himself as if he hurt all over when he spoke of certain things: his memories of growing up at Sans Souci, and of Julius shooting himself with that old French revolver all those years ago. Yet she thought the pain in him went beyond those things to something unnamed and unacknowledged, an amorphous shadow that went unseen and unheard even by himself.

He said to her once, "For so long things just happened to me, without any thought on my part, or will, or desire, and I don't care anymore, I just don't care." She wondered if the world must seem for him as it was for her, like a house empty of people, of furniture, of light and life, even of memories. She wondered if, like her, he found himself wandering from room to room in that dark house with no sound in his wake, no air disturbed.

She began to live for those hours in the garden, and life stopped on the days he didn't come. Time became an interlude between when she had seen him and when she would see him again.

One day in May, when she was kneeling on the ground planting some chrysanthemums in a clay pot, she stood up too fast and he was there, looping his arm around her waist to steady her, and she wanted to stop breathing. She knew they were wrong, her feelings, but they were there and she was permitting them to stay. He was the someday she had been waiting for the whole of her life. Or not so much him as the feelings he evoked in her.

He kept his arm around her waist, although he should not have, and he said, "You need to get out more often, Belle. Why don't I take you to lunch at Antoine's tomorrow? Would you like that?" And just like that it was done.

She had been waiting for this moment ever since he'd started to come around, waiting for the moment without knowing she was waiting, and at some point the waiting had turned into something deeper, and now the waiting was over. It was done.

He took her to Antoine's, and they went through the back entrance, the one for gentlemen entertaining ladies they didn't want to be seen with. She knew then for certain what he meant to do and she thought once again, It is done.

They sat in a red leather booth, so close she could feel her leg against his and smell his shaving cream. He dropped a raw oyster into a glass of bourbon. It is an aphrodisiac, he told her, smiling, and she felt sophisticated and naughty just hearing the word. She was being reshaped by him, invented anew.

Afterward, they walked through the narrow streets of the Quarter in the rain, sharing an umbrella. She wondered if the house he was taking her to was like her daddy's Conti Street house, come down to him from fathers to sons, from the days of *plaçage*. She wasn't going to feel bad about Remy, she wasn't going to think about this man being her sister's husband. Remy had taken Julius from her, and then Remy had stolen all her dreams. It was only fair that she have something of Remy's in return.

They entered a courtyard through an iron gate, passing under a domed brick walkway. She could smell the river and the damp brick walls, and the molding pecan husks that had fallen from the trees last fall. They climbed the stairs to the top flat of a converted porte-cochere townhouse, and no sooner did the door close with a whisper behind them than he had taken her into his arms.

They kissed and she felt the brush of his cheek, a little rough, and she smelled his warm neck.

"Your hair smells like rain," he said.

"Oh," she said, her voice breathy, frightened. "Well, it's raining."

He laughed and kissed her again, his mouth on hers, and she felt too much to stop now. So deep inside was the feeling that there was nothing to do but give in to it.

She was twenty-eight years old and yet she knew nothing of what to expect—Mama had never been able to mention the word *pregnant* above a whisper, and she certainly had never spoken of what went on between a man and a woman in bed. After it was over, he held her and stroked her hair and told her he was sorry, but it always hurt a girl her first time.

He got up then, and slipped on his trousers and a paisley silk dressing gown. He lit a cigarette and went out on the balcony and leaned his elbows on the railing. It had stopped raining.

She watched him smoke. The sheets were damp, from the rain in the air and from them, from what they had done. The sheets smelled of the patchouli oil he wore in his hair, and of something earthy that reminded her of the loamy dirt in her garden.

I have a lover, she thought, and she felt joy. Perfect joy.

She expected him to call around to the house the next day, but he didn't come and didn't come and didn't come. A hysteria grew inside her, like steam trapped in a bottle.

After two weeks she could bear it no longer. She dressed in the clothes she had bought for him: a green silk crepe dress with a shawl collar, snakeskin shoes. She had got herself a gray cloche hat because it was the style, but she couldn't get it to sit right on her head. It was her long hair, which had to be pinned up and wouldn't fit underneath. She would never cut her hair, though. Hadn't he told her how he didn't like these latest fashions of bobbed hair and flat chests that made women look like boys?

She took the streetcar down to the Quarter. It was raining again, teeming so hard the streets were flooded in places, over-flowing the low brick banquettes and running into shops, lapping at the stoops of the Creole cottages. Rain poured down gutters, along the galleries, and shot in waterfalls off the ends of the sloping roofs. The wet palms and branches of the pecan trees flapped in the wind.

Not until she was knocking on the door to the flat, soaked and trembling like a half-drowned cat, did it occur to her that there was no earthly reason for her to have thought he would be here, in this place, at this moment. So she was surprised when the door opened right up, as if he'd been expecting her.

Opened to the kind of silence that falls after a funeral bell has stopped tolling.

She started to speak, but he held up his hand. "I don't know what has possessed you to drop by uninvited," he said in a voice that should have matched the cruelty of his words, but did not. "I'm afraid, though, that I must ask you to leave. I am expecting company."

She tried to breathe, but her lungs felt thick and wet. "I-I'm sorry," she said. "But I . . . You haven't been 'round in a while and I . . ." Only he was already closing the door and there was some-thing terrible about his expression in the uncertain light. There was no sorrow in it, or pain, or regret. There was nothing on his face at all.

The next thing she knew she was standing in the middle of her garden with the rain cutting her hands and face.

She fell to her knees in the mud and began to rip up by the roots all the flowers so lovingly planted and tended over the years, ripped and ripped, and she thought how sorry they would be, he and Remy. Sorry, sorry, sorry.

She opened her mouth, and the scream inside filled it so she couldn't breathe, and so she tried to rip it out, rip out the scream, only it wouldn't come, and after a time she shut her mouth and leaned back on her heels with her muddy hands resting in her lap and the rain still coming down, and she had the most horrifying thought that this, this one moment out of all her life, was all there would ever be.

Belle had been talking for a long time now, and crying, and so she'd grown hoarse. She knelt in the dirt, and her hands worked the flower bed along the front of the house she shared with her mama, the mangled, savaged bed, digging deeper and deeper into the dirt, until her arms were buried in it up to her elbows.

"Yet you went back to him," Daman Rourke said softly. "Last Tuesday evening. The day he was killed."

Belle pulled her hands out of the wet earth to pound it with her fists. "You are mistaken, I'm afraid. Charlie was hateful to me. Hateful. I never wanted to see him again."

Rourke was sitting next to her, on the bottom two steps of the gallery, although still within the shade cast by the roof. It was barely eight in the morning, but the air was already hot and breathless and dense with humidity. He hadn't had time to go home for a shower and shave after the *bourré* game, and he'd had no sleep, no sleep for years, it seemed. His mouth felt cottony, his body aching and battered.

"It rained hard that evening, so hard your umbrellas were still a little wet the next day," he said, his voice gentle still. He had his forearms braced on his spread knees and was running the brim of his hat through his hands, as if he had only a small concern with what the woman who knelt in the flower bed was saying. He wasn't even looking at her. "Your mama said y'all had gone to church, but my partner asked your priest if you'd been to Mass that evening and he said you hadn't." Rourke's head came up, then, and his eyes found hers. His smile was full of charm, a little teasing. "It's an awfully bad sin to lie about something so sacred as going to Mass."

Her mouth parted, and the skin around her eyes and nostrils went white. He thought she would cry out or rage at him, but she laughed instead. The laughter surprised him, for the wildness he heard in it, yet at the same time it gave her face a dreamy look, showing him flashes of the girl she once had been.

"Oh, I know what you're thinkin'." She pushed away sweaty hanks of her hair, leaving behind a smudge of mud on her forehead. The earth she'd turned up had a raw, damp odor, like an old cellar. "I slept with my own sister's husband. Lordy, how much worse a sin can there be? Well, there's worse. Oh, worse, worse, worse." She thrust her hands hard and deep back into the earth, then pulled them out again, thrust and pulled, thrust and pulled. "It's worse, don't you think, to be an unmarried old maid who's going to have a baby?"

Out on the avenue the vegetable man was making his morning rounds, his donkey's hooves clip-clopping on the pavement, his scale jingle-jangling, singing, "Try my okra and my beans, lay-dee."

A baby.

A flock of mockingbirds flew into the yard to feed on the insects in the grass. She'd planted a gay bouquet of flowers, had Belle: white jasmine and lavender wisteria, yellow and red hibiscus, blue and pink hydrangeas.

A baby. Miss Fleurie had said nothing about a baby, but perhaps she hadn't known. Perhaps Charles St. Claire hadn't known himself until the night he was killed.

"I have a hope chest full of such pretty things for a bride," Belle was saying, "but nothing for a baby."

Rourke drew in a deep breath, choosing his words carefully. "You told Mr. St. Claire that," he said. "On Tuesday, when you went to see him. You told him about the baby."

Her mouth had gone slack, her breathing shallow, and her hands were clawing through the dirt now, almost frantic. "I was sick in the mornings—I didn't even know why at first. It was mama who figured it all out, about me bein' sick, and how I hadn't needed the rags for a while. I was so excited after Mama explained it to me, because I knew Charles would be just thrilled when I told him the good news. Every man wants a son, and he'd told me more than once that Remy wouldn't give him one. She was hateful to him, Remy was."

A breeze had come up, but it was only blowing hot. Rourke could feel the sweat running down his sides, making his shirt stick to his skin. The sun had risen over the roof enough now to catch her in its merciless heat and light. Her face bore dark grooves around her nose and mouth, as if they'd been drawn there in charcoal. Harsh red color streaked her neck, like welts. He thought how he'd never really liked her much and now he felt bad for that, as if his liking her might have saved her.

"It must have been a shock for Mr. St. Claire at first, though," Rourke said. "When you told him."

"He laughed. He just laughed and laughed and laughed, and pretty soon I was laughin' too, just to hear him go on like that." She laughed now, a shrill, bird-like cry. Her hands stilled in their frantic scrambling through the soil.

She cocked her head and a small furrow appeared between her eyebrows, as if she was struggling to understand something. "Then suddenly he turned all mean," she said. "Just like before. He told me I had to leave, that I was to leave him alone, and he said such hateful things to me, he really ought to be sorry. Somebody should make him sorry."

"And how did you do that? How did you make him sorry?"

She was smoothing out the dirt now, patting it down with her hands, as if she felt driven to repair what she had done. "Remy. Remy was going to make him sorry."

The palm trees out in the neutral ground clicked dryly in the hot breeze, but a coldness had seeped so deep into Rourke, he actually shivered. "You told your sister about Charles and about the baby," he said.

Belle nodded, smoothing and patting, smoothing, patting, her body rolling with the motion. "Mama and me, we went to Sans Souci together, to see Remy. Oh, and I remember now, it *was* raining. Mama explained to my sister how there was a way to fix things. She said we could all go away together for a while and when we come back Remy will tell everyone the baby is hers."

Belle drifted into a taut silence for a moment, and then she frowned, her mouth pulling down hard and a little mean. "She's always snatching things away from me, Remy is. She made Julius kill himself and then she made everyone believe she's the pretty one. She took Charles first so I couldn't have him. It's cruel and wicked of her to be taking my baby, too."

Rourke put on his hat and got slowly to his feet. "Is that what she said she would do, take the baby and raise it as her own?"

Belle looked up at him, her eyes squinting against the sun. It gave her pale, sweating face a shrewd look now that didn't match her dreamy, singsong words. "Sorry, is what she said. Sorry, sorry, sorry. She said she'd make Charles sorry for sayin' all those mean, nasty things and hurtin' my feelin's like he did."

Rourke felt a tugging in his gut, the uncoiling excitement that came when the puzzle of a case finally began to fit together. Only this time the excitement had an edge to it that cut, sharp as a cane knife.

He was a cop, and so he'd always had to make himself allow for the possibility that Remy Lelourie had killed her husband, especially knowing her, knowing, fearing, remembering, *If she'd done it once . . .* Until this moment, though, he hadn't realized how desperately he wanted for her not to have done this one, how, deep down, he had *needed* to believe in her innocence this one time if he was going to go on living with the truth of how much he loved her.

It hadn't been jealousy, Rourke thought, not the jealousy of a wife over a cheating, lying scoundrel of a man. It hadn't anything to do with Julius, or being found out, or the house or money. The Cinderella Girl had gone after Charles St. Claire with a cane knife for a reason only New Orleans would understand. He had seduced her baby sister, planted a bastard on her baby sister, and then cruelly rejected and abandoned her. Family is what you are born into, not what you marry. A girl is known by her maiden name until the day she dies, and after, long, long after. Heloise's girls they were, Remy and her baby sister, Belle.

If Remy Lelourie had killed her husband, it was because he had hurt *la famille.*

Chapter Twenty-Six

The red lights were on above both doors of the confessional box, and so Rourke sat in a pew to wait.

The Old Church of the Immaculate Conception was cool and smelled of damp stone and candlewax and holy water. He leaned his head back and closed his eyes. He felt battered, as if his bones had been taken out of his body and used for baseball bats.

He was desperate for sleep, but he still had to meet Casey Maguire at the Flying Horses, and later this evening he had an arrest to make: Remy Lelourie, for the murder of Charles St. Claire in the first degree. He had talked the captain into letting him wait to serve the warrant until after it grew dark and tomorrow morning's first editions had already gone to press. He didn't want her dragged off to the Parish Prison in handcuffs with flashlamps popping in her eyes and reporters shouting their questions in her face.

They had done their jobs too well, he and Fio, building the case against her brick by brick until they had her sealed up behind a jail-cell wall. Throughout it all he had clung to his faith, the credo he worked by: that the murdered ones mattered, that they deserved the dignity of having the world know why they had died and who had killed them. It was his job to speak for the dead, but that didn't mean that this time it wasn't going to hurt.

One summer, long ago, he had fallen in love with a girl full of passion and fear, who had been maybe more than just a little crazy, a girl who had thrived on feeding all the craziness in him. He had been hooked deep by her that summer, and she'd kept her hold on him through time.

But maybe something else had a deeper hold on him, he thought, an excitement, a rushing high he always got from tempting hell. They were alike, he and Remy Lelourie, and so she should have known. *What if I killed him, Day?* she had said, taunting him, daring him. *What if I did it?*

She should have remembered that he never met a dare he wouldn't take.

Rourke heard the hinges of the door to the confessional box creak and he opened his eyes. A nun in a simple black habit with black beads swinging from her waist came out. She went to the bronze statue of St. Peter, knelt, and added the brush of her lips to the thousands of lips that had kissed the saint's foot during the last seventy years, lips that had nearly worn it away with their faith. Rourke couldn't imagine what sins a nun would need to confess, and on a Monday morning, but then he supposed even nuns were not beyond the temptation of evil.

The nun went to the altar rail, where she knelt again and began to make her penance. Rourke got up and went into the confessional where she had been. A faint scent of rosewater lingered within the dark, enclosed space.

He could hear the murmur of the priest's voice giving absolution to the sinner on the other side of the box. He waited in the dark, and it seemed for a moment that he could hear his own heart beating, could hear it skip and stutter. Then the wooden door slid back, and he was looking at the priest through the wire-mesh screen. The priest sighed and stirred, impatient perhaps, for the confessional hour was nearly over. The gold embroidery in his green sacramental stole glittered in the bit of light seeping through the seam around the door. The light defined the priest's face: the round Irish chin, high forehead, short nose.

Which was so unlike his own face, as was everything else about

Father Paul Rourke. They were so unalike, he and Paulie, and yet so close. In the scalding, searing way that people who have shared disasters, such as hurricanes and train wrecks, are close.

In the warm, close silence, he suddenly couldn't speak. There were no words.

"It's hard to begin sometimes, I know," said the shadow on the other side of the screen, fatherly understanding mellowed by humor. "Why don't you ask our Lord for His blessing and then we'll see what happens next."

Bless me, Father, for I have sinned.

There were no words. He could pile up confessions like a drunk on a pity binge, but he wasn't going to feel shriven.

"Never mind," he said. "It was a slow week."

"Day? Is that you? . . . No, don't run off this time," his brother added quickly, because Rourke was already fumbling for the door latch.

He couldn't get the door open and he almost put his fist through the mahogany panel. "Day, you got to quit doing this to yourself," his brother was saying. "Someone else has already died on the cross for all the world's sins."

Rourke stumbled out of the confessional box and nearly ran down the aisle, banging his hip into the end of one of the pews. He pushed through the bronze-studded doors and staggered to a stop, nearly blinded by the white harsh blaze of the midday sun.

The Flying Horses lived in a fanciful white wooden building with stained-glass clerestory windows and a cupola. Rourke unsnapped the flap of his shoulder holster and came through the wide arched doorway on the balls of his feet. He felt like Tom Mix, meeting the bad guy for a showdown at high noon. All he needed was a horse named Tony.

The carousel's calliope was playing "The Man on the Flying Trapeze." Shrill notes piped out of the steam whistles to float through the heavy summer air. Children filled the building, their laughter piping louder than the whistles. He spotted Casey Maguire sitting alone on a bench next to the hamburger wagon.

Rourke studied the people around the bootlegger. Standing at the hamburger wagon was a little girl with bright red-yellow curls, like orange peels, holding the hand of a boy wearing a Mardi Gras mask—the head of a grinning red devil with purple horns and yellow fangs. Next to the bench was a trio of nuns, Sisters of Charity in their dusty blue-wool habits, white starched bibs, and the white starched creations on their heads that looked like a fleet of ships sailing by. Their faces glowed pink with excitement as they watched the wooden horses gallop around.

Rourke's gaze scanned the rest of the building, over and then over again, as he walked slowly to the bench and sat down next to Maguire. They had a short staring contest, and Maguire was the first to look away.

"You look like hell," the bootlegger said.

Rourke thought Maguire wasn't looking so hot either. Whisker stubble dusted the man's jaw like soot, and his skin hung pasty and loose. His eyes were red-veined and blurry.

A muscle ticked in Maguire's cheek as he watched the carousel. "You got to understand that this conversation, us being here—it's not happening," he said.

Rourke looked out the open doorway. The moss on the oaks hung limp in the heat. The sun beat upon the grass and the flower beds and the gravel path, but a native could tell you it would rain again by this evening.

"I got the juice to make it so, Day."

Rourke turned his head and studied Maguire's averted face. "Are you in bed with the Chicago outfit?"

A wry smile full of self-derision pulled at the corner of the other man's mouth. "Why would an Irish boy from New Orleans do business with that Yankee wop Al Capone?"

"Yeah," Rourke said. "That's what I thought." He felt no surprise, only a bone-deep, hollow-gut weariness. Casey Maguire's first job had been plucking chickens at the slaughterhouse he now owned, but he had never really been on the straight and narrow. His racketeering had been all nickel-and-dime stuff, though, until the Volstead Act became the law of the land.

Then suddenly, within six months, he had a fleet of boats, warehouses, cutting plants, and the bootlegging business for the whole Gulf Coast in the palm of his hand. He couldn't have come up with the money for an operation of that size and scope on his own.

"You remember that time on the Ferris wheel," Rourke said, "when I went to jump and you saved my ass? I figure you went up on a wheel and then you jumped just as it was starting to turn, and now you're on that long fall down."

The smell of burning onions floated to them from the hamburger wagon. The boy in the red devil's mask was now chasing his little sister, and she was screaming and laughing, both.

"Sometimes," Maguire said, "you can end up crossing a line you don't even see until you're already over on the other side."

"What line did Vinny McGinty cross?"

Maguire exhaled a deep, sighing breath, like someone who had been waiting a long time for a dreaded pain and now finally it was here. "My brother Bobby Joe had Vinny working the gate for the Boxing Irish club fights, and it turned out Vinny was skimming the receipts. Bobby Joe must've caught him at it, and so Vinny killed him. Up until a couple of weeks ago, I thought it was that nigger boxer who'd done it. When I found out it was that little prick Vinny, I did what I had to do. Bobby Joe was my baby brother, for God's sake. You going to tell me you wouldn't kill the man who killed your brother?"

"Not to mention that the Chicago outfit was due a big piece of those gate receipts that got stolen. Yeah, I can see how a guy like Mr. Capone, a guy with a certain reputation to uphold, wouldn't be too happy if he somehow heard that one of your boys had been fucking him in the ass and that you had let it happen."

"Like I said, I did what I had to do."

"And Bridey? Was she something else you had to do?"

Maguire's only reaction was to allow his eyes to briefly close, yet it affected Rourke more than a sob would have done. "Bridey's dying was an accident. One of the Chicago boys was down here collecting their bag money and he heard me blowing off steam about how I had a cop on my case, giving me grief, and the next thing I know these wop goons show up in town to help me out."

Rourke could see how and why this could happen. Ever since they'd gotten kicked out in 1890, the Mafia had been trying to buy, woo, and finagle their way back into the heart of the City That Care Forgot. Casey Maguire was the closest thing New Orleans had to a genuine mobster, so having a man with Maguire's connections and juice deep in their debt—*owning* the man inside and out—would be one way the Chicago outfit could guarantee themselves a nice, fat piece of the local crime business.

"I tried to convince them it would be better for business just to scare you off," Maguire was saying. "Just lob a grenade or something up onto the front gallery of Bridey's house." He braced his elbows on his knees and bent over his clasped hands as if in prayer. "Y'all were supposed to be back in the bedroom. What in hell was she doing out on the gallery? What were you doing out in the goddamn street? Jesus."

Rourke stared down at the top of Maguire's head. "Goddamn goons with tommy guns were firing at me and my little girl last night."

Maguire pulled his hands apart with a sudden, violent motion and raised his head to meet Rourke's eyes. "I know, I know, Day. What can I say? I'm talking to you like this, brother to brother like from the old days, so I can tell them you're going to be laying off me and then they can lay off you and then maybe the both of us can get out of this mess without getting our asses handed to us."

"Fuck 'em."

Maguire laughed. "I knew you'd say that."

"What about Charles St. Claire?"

"What about him? I admit to killing one guy who fuckin' deserved it and now you want to lay off every corpse you've got on me? How come the whole world knows the Cinderella Girl killed Charlie St. Claire but you?"

Rourke felt a burning in his wrist and he looked down. He'd been rubbing the tattoo so hard the skin around it was red and inflamed.

Maguire had pushed himself to his feet. "You know what-all went down now and why," he said, "and that's just going to have to satisfy this fucking unnatural need in you to always be a cop. You're going to have to let it go. For your own sake, Day, let it go."

Rourke let the other man take a couple of steps away before he spoke, pitching his voice loud enough to be heard over the shrieking children and the steam calliope. "Case."

Maguire turned back around. The stained-glass windows cast splotches of red and blue light onto his face, making him look eerily bruised and bloodied.

"Bridey matters," Rourke said. "The murdered ones all matter—even guys like Vinny McGinty. One way or the other I'm taking you down."

"I believe he told you that," Weldon Carrigan said. "And I believe that's probably more or less the way it happened, but it ends right here. We got other fish to fry."

The police superintendent sat behind his mahogany and ormulu-mounted desk in his office in City Hall, surrounded by polished woods, plush leather, and a wreath of Havana tobacco. Rourke stared down at him, saying nothing.

"In a few hours we're going to be arresting a frigging movie star for murder," Carrigan went on, "and then all hell is going to break loose. I don't need you out there chasing down a case I told you to forget about."

Rourke still said nothing.

"Come on, Day. Nobody gives a rat's patootie about Vinny McGinty. He didn't even measure up to a two-bit loser, and for killing Bobby Joe Maguire he deserved what he got. What we don't need is any more of the Chicago outfit coming down here with their grenades and tommy guns wanting to even up scores over some penny-ante gate-receipt fiddle. You hear what Al Capone did to that one guy who he caught crossing him? He beat in the goon's head with a baseball bat in front of twenty other goons, for chrissakes."

"He, at least, appears to have something of a grasp on the concept of crime and punishment."

Weldon Carrigan's thick black eyebrows furrowed together above his narrowed eyes. "Don't you crack wise with me, boy."

Rourke turned away from his father-in-law. He crossed the thick-pile Turkey carpet to a green velvet—swathed window that offered a view of the statues and palms in Lafayette Square. Blue jays and mockingbirds flitted in and out of the sun-bleached light. In the distance the spires of St. Louis Cathedral trembled in the heat.

"What about LeRoy Washington?" he said.

"What about him?"

Rourke almost put his fist through one of the French panes. He spread his hand out flat against the glass instead, feeling the burning heat of the sun. "Sweet Jesus. The man is serving fifty years in Angola for something he didn't do."

The superintendent's red leather chair groaned softly as he leaned over to pluck a cigar from the cedar humidor on his desk. "It isn't going to matter to the Chicago outfit that Maguire settled the score with his vig boy Vinny, because he did it later rather than sooner. He let it happen. Hell, Al Capone'll probably figure Maguire was in on the skim from the get-go and only decided to bump off poor Vinny when things started getting dicey, and for all we know he could be right. This is a big and ugly sleeping dog, Day, and we got to let it lie. We're not going to subject New Orleans to the threat of a gangland bloodbath just because some worthless nigger is getting a bad break."

Rourke breathed a bitter laugh, turning away from the window. He had to put his hands in his pockets to hide their shaking. "Then what about Bridey O'Mara and all those fine and honorable words you spoke about how nobody gets away with killing one of our own?"

Color stung his father-in-law's cheeks like a sunburn. He averted his gaze from Rourke's, busying his hands with peeling off the cigar's silk wrapper and clipping the end with the slender silver knife on his watch chain. "You told me how Maguire said that all went down. Bridey was an accident. Sometimes we got to go along to get along, Day."

Rourke took a quarter out of his pocket and tossed it onto the spotless green felt blotter, between a mother-of-pearl letter opener and an onyx postage-stamp box. "Here," he said.

Weldon Carrigan picked up the coin, flipping it over in his palm. "What's this for?"

"Two bits." Rourke smiled. "I figure that's just about what your honor is worth."

Chapter Twenty-Seven

Daman Rourke had rolled around in the street getting shot at, he'd chased goons with tommy guns all over the city, he'd played wicked *bourré* in a speakeasy until dawn, but it was his visit to City Hall that really left him feeling filthy.

He went home to scrub himself off in the shower and then to his favorite barbershop for a shave. He felt as though he were doing a death spiral in his Spad, free-falling through space with his knuckles white on the joystick and the roar of the engine and the wind pressing against his ears. Yet his mind was strangely scoured of thoughts and he welcomed their absence—not to think about LeRoy Washington chopping cotton with a gun bull standing over him, not to think about Remy Lelourie, who, like LeRoy, would be seeing tomorrow's dawn coming from behind the bars of a cell.

A damp breeze blew in through the open door of the barbershop from off the river, smelling of coffee, bananas, and more rain. He leaned back in the big black leather chair and shut his eyes, listening to the barber's patter and the blade snicking back and forth over the leather strop.

"I'ma tellin' you, you put your money on that Candy Dancer to win in the eighth, and you be rollin' in the dough, you. You be swillin' *beaucoup* champagne and sailin' a yacht on Lake Pontchartrain."

Rourke opened his eyes and looked at the big mustachioed Cajun through the spotted mirror. Jean Baptiste Mouton was Rourke's bookie as well as his barber. "If I bet any more on that loser," Rourke said, "I'm going to wind up on the corner swigging rotgut and selling pencils."

Jean Baptiste pushed out a laugh from deep in his belly that made his long black mustaches flutter. He wrapped a hot, steaming towel around Rourke's face. "You be wearing more diamonds than Carter's got pills, you. They be seein' you comin' before you've even stepped out the door."

"They'll see me coming because I'll be wearing a sandwich board advertising 'Joe's Eats.'"

A shoe heel scraped across the threshold, and a shadow crossed the mirror. "Day, my man. How're they hangin'?"

"Still loose and feelin' good," Rourke said after a moment, for he had heard the edge in his partner's voice.

Fiorello Prankowski's lips pulled back from the butt of the Castle Morro he had clamped between his teeth. "Yeah. Yeah, I'll just bet they are." He jerked his head at Jean Baptiste. "Get lost for a while, will you?"

"I'm goin' to get a cup of coffee, me," Jean Baptiste said, and left whistling.

Fio set his cigar down on the stained marble shelf beneath the mirror and picked up the straight razor that Jean Baptiste had been sharpening. He tested the hone of the blade with his thumb and then sliced the razor through the air as if it were a toy sword— and barely missed Rourke's nose.

"You feelin' okay?" Fio finally said as he whipped a lather brush around a shaving mug, working up a thick foam. "I'm only asking 'cause I come whistling on into the squad room this morning, after spending a nice quiet Sunday evenin' with my wife and kids, enjoying our new parlor organ, and everybody's talking about my partner. Talking about how last night he went and got shot at and how he took offense, and now half of New

Orleans and all of West End Park is looking like the morning after a hurricane."

He peeled the towel off Rourke's face and began to brush on the lather. The badger bristles were soft, the soap smelled of cedar, and steam floated through the air, warm and moist, mixing with the river breeze. Rourke allowed his eyes to drift closed as he listened to Fio's aw-shucks routine.

"Funny thing about putting a flatfoot on to watch a suspect's house and make sure she doesn't pull a Houdini in the middle of a homicide investigation—if you can see 'em going, then you can see 'em coming. All I can say is I hope you kept an eye open while you were banging her."

"Maybe we shouldn't go down that road, Fio."

"Sure, let's never mind the righteousness of a homicide detective sleeping with the prime suspect. Let's go somewhere's else. We finally got some answers back on our California inquiries. She gives a whole new meaning to the phrase *femme fatale*, does the Cinderella Girl. There was the up-and-coming leading man, who drove his car off a cliff when he found out she was two-timing him with something called a gaffer. And there's the woman now doing time for trying to blow off her husband's dick with a shotgun after he told her he wanted a divorce so's he could marry guess who."

Fio wiped the razor clean, folded it and set it carefully down on the white marble shelf, next to his smoldering cigar, and turned to look at Rourke.

"There. All done and just in time, 'cause we got us a busy Monday afternoon ahead of us. Things to do, people to see, arrests to make."

Rourke sat unmoving and watched Fio through the mirror as he left. After a moment he got up, put on his hat, tucked a dollar bill beneath a jar of pomade for Jean Baptiste, and left, himself.

Fio was waiting for him just outside the door, with his hat fanning his face and his thick shoulders and one foot braced against the brick wall, next to the barber's red-and-white-striped pole. Rourke stopped and half turned to look at him. Fio's hair stuck out in sandy spikes all over his head, and the bags beneath his worried eyes were sagging down to his cheekbones.

"She slits your throat," Fio said, "or you put a gun in your mouth. Either way, she's killed you, partner."

Rourke smiled. "Yeah, I know. In the meantime, let's go have some fun. Let's go see the Ghoul."

The blast from the gunshot concussed and echoed in the room. The blue chambray shirt tore, and the chest underneath it twitched and jumped. The cotton-stuffed man would have fallen to the floor if he hadn't been strapped to the post.

The Ghoul retrieved the bullet from the dummy and brought it over to the two detectives. Rourke still held Roibin Doherty's .38 Special in his outstretched hand and, to his horror, he saw the barrel tremble, and then the trembling was in his hand and he couldn't stop it.

He dropped his arm and glanced at Fio to see if he had been found out, but his partner's attention was all on the Ghoul.

"The comparison microscope," the Ghoul was saying as he puffed a wreath of cigarette smoke around his head, "will tell us if there is a match between a bullet fired from the gun found in the sergeant's hand and the bullet found in his head. Two halves of separate bullet images can be joined together under the same lens, enabling us to compare closely the marks of each."

The Ghoul picked up a hollow probe-like device, which was fitted with a light and a magnifying glass. "We begin, however, by examining the inside of the revolver's barrel with the helixometer."

Rourke had forgotten that he still held the .38. The grip was hard and round and cool against his hand, but the trembling hadn't stopped. It had just gone deeper.

"You will note," the Ghoul said, leaning in close, and Rourke held his breath against the raw, damp odor of the man's body, "the spiral grooves—the rifling—on the inside of the barrel. And the lands, the raised parts between the grooves. They are what will leave the distinctive markings on any bullets fired from this gun."

Rourke used the instrument as the coroner showed him, but

although he looked, he wasn't really seeing. Sweat burned in his eyes, and he thought at times that he could almost feel his heart beating against the wall of his chest. Just get through this evening, he thought, and it would all be over.

He handed the gun and the helixometer to Fio and allowed the Ghoul to usher him over to the comparison microscope. The coroner's round, sweating face shone with his excitement.

"See the distinctive rifling patterns on the image of the bullet on your right—six lands and a right twist—and compare it to the image on your left. Now, the image on your left is that of the test-fired bullet; on your right, the bullet which I have dug out of Sergeant Detective Doherty's brain. As you can see, there is a distinct difference. And there is more."

The Ghoul levered his flabby bulk upright, groaning and creaking with the effort. He replaced the images in the microscope with others. "When a gun is discharged, its firing pin strikes the back of the brass casing, which sets off a detonator inside the cartridge, as I'm sure you know. What you might not know is that the pin leaves a distinctive and individual imprint on the casing. If you will look, please, on the base of the casing image to your right—which came from the spent cartridge recovered from the cylinder of Sergeant Doherty's .38—there is a tiny raised imperfection, the result of a faulty breechblock on the gun that fired it. The image on the left is of the test-fired cartridge and bears no such imperfection."

"So," Fio said, "all this hocus-pocus is tellin' us that Roibin Doherty didn't shoot himself."

The Ghoul squinted up at Fio through a blue veil of tobacco smoke. "Not with his own .38 Policeman's Special, he did not."

Fio was being careful not to look Rourke's way, but new lines of worry were already digging into his face. With suicide officially ruled out, Roibin Doherty's death had just gone from "under suspicious circumstances" to murder, and Fio's partner had just become the prime suspect.

"The trajectory of the bullet through his brain is inconsistent with suicide," the Ghoul said. "It was a contact wound, however.

There were powder burns and stippling visible, and a circular pattern around the bullet's point of entry. The barrel of *a* gun was certainly pressed against his head behind the ear and the trigger was pulled, execution style. The attempt to make it look like a suicide was, in my opinion, quite sloppy."

Fio rolled his eyes. "Well, golly. I guess the killer wasn't figuring on us having Wonder Coroner to point out all the places where he fucked up."

The Ghoul gave Fio a long, unblinking look, and then he said, "As per your request, Lieutenant Prankowski, I also ran comparisons on that old case of yours. The suicide of Mr. Charles St. Claire's brother, I believe you said it was? Now, mind you, a French pinfire revolver was among the first to use a self-contained cartridge in which bullet, powder, and cap were all held in a brass case. Circa eighteen fifty-three, I would say."

Fio's gaze flashed to Rourke and hot color crept up his neck. "Why don't you just cut to the chase, Mr. Mueller?"

"The 'chase,' Mr. Prankowski, is, Yes, there was a match. The revolver you gave to me almost certainly fired the bullet which you also gave to me."

"So I guess Julius could have killed Julius, after all," Rourke said, his gaze on Fio but his voice as blank as he was keeping his face.

"Yeah, well . . ." Fio waved his hand at the Ghoul's comparison microscope. "If you can believe that hocus-pocus."

Rourke smiled, but this time only with his eyes. "I heard it said once that faith is mostly a matter of desire."

Fio held his gaze a moment longer, then he stuffed his hands in his pockets and looked down. "I guess I'd better go break it to the captain that somebody besides Roibin Doherty put that hole in Roibin Doherty's head."

The Ghoul waited until the door to the laboratory closed behind Fio's broad back before he turned to Rourke. "You will also be wanting to know about that plant matter you sent to me for analysis. It is the *Abrus precatorius*, commonly known as the paternoster pea or love bean. Not a native plant, but it can be found in Florida, and is sometimes used in the making of jewelry and rosaries. It is also a highly toxic poison, although as a method of inflicting death it would be difficult. The pea would have to be first crushed into a powder and mixed with something edible, preferably sweet, to be effective."

"Pralines," Rourke said, thinking of his mother's lover lying in his coffin the day after his fiftieth birthday, and of the rosary strung with paternoster peas still hanging from the arms of St. Michael in the Lelourie women's front parlor.

"Ah, yes, pralines," the Ghoul said. "A sweetly nasty death to be sure."

"He died screaming."

That evening the wind came up strong with the fall of darkness. At Sans Souci it shook the black branches of the oaks and rattled the banana trees. Thunder cracked, loud and harsh, and a brutal rain slashed against the windowpanes. The black sky trembled with lightning.

The electricity had gone out. Remy Lelourie stood in the dark with her back toward the door, watching the storm. She was dressed as if she expected company, in long black velvet, and in the cobalt light he saw only the radiant white flesh of her back and shoulders and neck. It was more erotic than if she'd been naked.

He had come to her, as before, without knocking, but she must have sensed his presence, for she turned, saying, "Day?" just as lightning struck again outside, and a white light cut jagged across her eyes like the broken shards of a mirror.

Then she got a look at his own eyes, and the blood drained away from her face, leaving it the gray color of bone. She knew, then, what he would say, and she feared what he would say, perhaps she had been fearing it for years. It was why she had left him that first time. She should, for her own sake, have stayed gone.

"I saw you kill Julius," he said.

Chapter Twenty-Eight

In the summer of 1916, he had been both in love and in misery.

Remy Lelourie.

Her soul was wild, and her heart was free, and her body was giving—but she was damaged, deep down. She had no stopping place, none at all. She would dare anything.

He knew he hadn't been her first lover. She acknowledged her past and she indulged her appetites, that was her way. She'd been fucking Julius St. Claire before she'd met him, and he had a real mean and ugly suspicion that she was fucking him after. It was that house, or so he told himself. Sans Souci. She had some sort of crazy obsession over that house, planted like a poisonous seed in her heart by her half-crazy mama. When she left him it was going to be for Julius St. Claire and Sans Souci.

So on that miserably hot and muggy summer's evening, after he had lugged the last crate of oysters over to the truck, he looked over at the water pump where she usually met him and she wasn't there, and he knew, oh yeah, he knew all right where he would find her.

He drove out there on his motorcycle, going the back way, along the bayou road. He left his bike in the ditch and walked through the scrub pine and canebrakes. The locusts were singing so loud they made the air vibrate. The heat was like a hard slap on the back of his shoulders and neck.

He was walking past the old slave shack when he heard a sharp little cry, that little cry she always made during sex, and he hated himself for doing it and he hated her for making him do it, making him love her more than pride and honor, but he went around to the shack's bedroom, to the open window.

He shielded himself behind a thicket of bamboo and looked inside—

Saw a muzzle flash, saw the back of Julius St. Claire's head explode into a red cloud, and pieces of skull and brains and blood go flying, splattering. A shred of a second later came the sounds: the crack of the bullet firing, the slap of the gore as it hit the floor and walls and furniture, the thud of Julius falling with half his head gone.

Rourke flinched and shut his eyes, as if a sudden blaze had blinded him. He jerked away from the window, flattening his back against the bamboo thicket, his breathing hard. Already, though, his mind was trying to grasp and assimilate what he had seen— like sudden images lit by lightning—in that instant before the muzzle flashed and Julius St. Claire's head exploded.

Remy, naked and kneeling on the bed, and Julius St. Claire on the bed with her, facing her. Julius is crying, making whimpering animal-like noises, and he is holding one of the old gold-plated French revolvers stiffly at his side, with the barrel pointing down. Remy's face is white, so white, but her eyes are burning hot, and the other, matching revolver is in her hand, her hand is coming up with the gun, pointing the gun at Julius, coming up, coming up, and firing point-blank at Julius's face. The muzzle flashes like heat lightning in the sky.

Rourke heard her moving around in there now, heard her harsh breathing and the creak of the floorboards. He smelled cordite and the blood, really smelled the blood. Oh, sweet Jesus. What had she done?

He didn't want to look again, but he had to.

She had her clothes back on and she was bending over Julius's body, where he had been knocked off the bed by the impact of the bullet and onto the floor. She began crooning to him, in a moaning singsong, Sorry, Julius, I'm so sorry, Julius, so sorry, please, oh, please, and all the while she was crooning she was carefully taking the revolver out of Julius's hand and replacing it with the one she'd shot him with. The other, unfired, gun she shoved deep in the pocket of her skirt. When she straightened he saw how her face was slimed with tears and blood.

She parted the beaded curtain in the doorway and then froze, half turning, and looked out the window. She must not have seen him standing behind the bamboo thicket, though, for she turned around again and pushed through the clattering beads.

He saw her walking fast toward the big house, with her hand still deep in the pocket of her skirt. She disappeared from his sight in the trees. A moment later he heard a splash and the bang of wood slamming down against wood. He took one more look at Julius through the window, but there was no doubt the guy was dead, with half his head gone. Rourke knew better than to go into the shack himself; he was a cop's son, after all.

He went out to the willow cave because she would come to him there, eventually. It was part of the game, the risk, the danger, the taste of death, and then the sex, and it had all become inseparable. He thought that before he touched her he should say to her, I saw you kill Julius, but he knew he never would. He wanted her to love him enough that she would come to him for help, for comfort, for absolution. She would come, but for none of those things.

When the smoking light of dusk was in the tops of the cypress trees, she came. She didn't speak, and he could not. She had cleaned herself up, and yet he was sure he could smell Julius's blood on her, and it was as though his own heart's blood were fouled. He felt a violent revulsion for her, for what she had done, and a desperate longing, a hunger, for her that was so great he thought that if she touched him he would fly all apart, fly into a million bloody pieces and chips of bone.

Only she did touch him, and he didn't fly apart. They came together on the floor of the willow cave, undressing each other slowly as if trying to make a lie out of their sawing breaths and racing blood. She pressed him down onto his back and straddled him, raising herself up on her knees and then slowly lowering herself down on top of him. He felt her flex and tighten around him, and he looked into her eyes that were hot and too bright, and although he tried to keep them away, still they came, fragments, lightning images. Julius's foot trembling in his death throes on the floor, his heel rattling on the wood. Julius's blood splashing on her bare breasts. Julius's curled white fingers letting go of the revolver. He saw the gun exploding in her hand, saw her killing Julius, over and over, killing Julius, and he felt all the hopeless love he bore for her, and all the fear he had of her, rise up inside him like a dark, wet bubble, rise and swell and burst into a release between her thighs.

After she was gone, he lay on his back with the smell of swamp water and cypress and blood in his throat, the smell of her in his throat.

He had wanted to save her, but he didn't know how. He couldn't even save himself.

"Why?" he said, eleven years later, as lightning jumped across the shrouded sky and thunder cracked like a gunshot. The pain in her face was too much to bear, even if he didn't quite believe it. "Why did you do it?"

She only shook her head, although she was crying. At least she was crying, even if he couldn't trust the tears to be real.

"You both had your guns pointed down," he said, "but then you brought yours up and shot him in the face. If it was a game, then you cheated badly, darlin'. But it wasn't a game, was it? It wasn't a game."

Her eyes flinched closed. "No. It wasn't a game."

"For God's sake, Remy." He took a step toward her, as if he would force it out of her—the truth, the lies, anything.

She whirled away from him.

He hadn't seen the crystal pitcher of mint julep sitting on the fireplace mantel until she picked it up and smashed it against the yellow marble. Whiskey and ice, chips and slivers of crystal rained on the floor. In her hand was left a raw and jagged piece of glass. Lightning leaped again, turning the oak trees white.

"You are so wrong about me, Day." Blood dripped from her hand that held the deadly shard of glass. "So wrong, so wrong. What do I need to do to prove it to you? Kill myself?" The glass flashed, slashing across her wrist, and a line of bright red blood welled on the paleness of her flesh. "No, that is way too easy. I'll destroy what I am."

He had already launched himself at her but he wasn't able to grab her wrist, so he wrapped his hand around the shard of glass just in time to keep it from slicing into her cheek. The glass cut deep into his fingers, and such was the living force of her will that she kept on cutting him for two more heartbeats before she cried out and flung the shard away.

He stared at her, his hand bleeding a river onto the floor.

She shook her head hard, splattering tears. "I can bear it if the whole world hates me, but not you. Not you."

Sweet mercy. "Remy, don't—"

She covered his mouth with her hand, the one she had cut, and he tasted her blood. "I looked up and there you were," she said, "standing at my daddy's coffin—the bravest thing I'd ever seen. I wanted to cut out your heart and eat it."

His lips moved in the blood on her hand. "You did."

"Did you cry for yourself when I left you?"

"No."

"Then don't you go cryin' for me now."

Because he had been expecting it, waiting for it, he heard it first—through the rain and wind and thunder, the crunch of tires on the oyster-shell drive. Lights from an automobile's headlamps shot out of the wet and smoky night and into the darkened room.

Her eyes widened, caught for a brief moment in the squad car's lights, before she lowered her head. Her hand fell from his mouth and she turned away from him.

He waited with her in silence, through the front door crashing open and the tramp of feet in the hall.

"Christ," Fio said when he saw Rourke. "Did she try to kill you, too?"

"No. It was an accident." Only it hadn't been an accident, or an act. She would have mutilated herself to prove to him . . . what? That she was innocent?

Yet he had seen her, with his own eyes he had seen her kill.

It wasn't a game.

If she did it once . . .

He went outside, onto the gallery, and a few moments later they brought her out. Someone had bandaged her cuts with handkerchiefs and put handcuffs on her wrists.

She stopped in front of him, and she was looking up at him as if he were already a memory. She reached up with both hands, the links of the handcuffs rattling, and she touched her fingers to his throat.

"We can bear this, Day. It will be like the snake—all we got to do is stare it down without flinching."

The next morning he went back out to Sans Souci with a couple of patrolmen dressed in bathing suits. He showed them where the cistern was and watched them climb in.

The thunder and lightning had blown away with the night, but it was still raining hard, the drops pocking and dimpling the cistern's black water. He could smell the wet earth on the wind.

It took them only a few minutes to fish out the white-enameled, purple-spangled Mardi Gras mask. Medusa with snakes for hair. Seen through the slanting rain, it looked as though the snakes were alive.

Then, because he knew it was there, he told them to climb back in the cistern and look for a French gold-plated pinfire revolver.

Chapter Twenty-Nine

A brutal rain streamed against the window where Remy Lelourie stood looking up at a ragged scrap of dirty gray sky. In the greasy light she was too thin and frail, like a waif in the shapeless brown cotton shift and her cropped, shingled hair.

She turned when the door closed behind him. Her face was blotchy, wet, and red, her eyes puffy with tears. She had not just been weeping; she'd been bawling.

Rourke stared at her too long, and her mouth pulled into a painful smile. "You're looking at me like you would a butterfly pinned to a board, waiting to see if my wings will flutter."

He tried to smile back at her, but he didn't think he'd quite managed it. "Sorry." He realized he was still standing with his back against the door and his bandaged hand wrapped around the knob. He took a couple of steps into the small interrogation room, bringing himself closer to her. "Are you making it okay?"

She looked down at the Parish Prison garb she wore. "Cinderella before the prince."

"Remy—"

"Thank you for coming, Day. I was afraid you wouldn't." She lifted her head. A bright, painful light glittered in her eyes. "I wasn't sure of the protocol—how a woman should go about asking favors of the policeman who arrests her."

He tried to keep everything he felt and thought off his face. "Anything you say to me is fair game for your trial, Remy. You shouldn't be talking to me without a lawyer."

She blinked and nodded. "I just . . ." Suddenly, she emitted a sharp little despairing cry and bent partway over, hugging herself.

He took a couple of steps toward her and almost didn't keep himself from touching her. He waved at the battered oak table and four metal chairs that filled the room. "Maybe you'd better sit down."

She chose the chair beneath the window and he sat across from her. The room smelled of stale smoke and years worth of rancid sweat that came from fear and clung to the peeling beige walls. She'd laid one of her hands down flat on the table in front of her, the one that had been cut like his and was bandaged now. The table was stained with water rings and pocked with cigarette burns; the fingers of her bandaged hand looked ephemeral, luminescent, as though they were being lit from within.

She was trembling as if she had a chill. He watched as her eyes filled with tears, then went on watching as they fell.

She drew in a deep, hitching breath. "Oh Lordy, Day. I am so scared."

"Did you kill him, Remy?"

She made a strangled sound, then her head jerked, hard, and tears splashed her hand. "Yes," she whispered, and the breath left him so hard it was as if he'd been punched in the chest.

She had her chin tucked so close to her chest that all he could see was the top of her head. "I shot him out in the slave shack, with the French revolver," she said, the words barely audible. "You saw."

His breath came back, shuddering into him so fast it left him feeling queasy, like a seasickness.

"Yes, I saw," he said softly. "But I'm talking about Charles now. Did y'all have a fight that night over what he'd done to your sister?"

She flung up her head. "How do you know about—?" Her eyes looked so frightened they bulged. "Oh, God. It was my fault, all my fault. I couldn't be what he wanted, and then we just started hurting each other, back and forth, a horrible, ugly game. He used Belle to get back at me—he could be such a bastard. Such a mean, cruel bastard."

Her shoulders bowed and she bent forward again, cupping her elbows, rocking a little. "You're not going to think Belle killed him now, are you?" she said softly. "Belle could never do such an awful thing."

Rourke rather thought Belle could, but he said, "No, Belle could never. But you did it for her, you killed Charles for Belle. Because of Belle and the baby he gave her."

She looked up at him again, stared at him, her eyes roaming all over his face, and she might as well have been touching him with her hands, her mouth.

"The world can be a lonely place, don't you think so, Day? Even when you ought to be feeling on top of it. When it got real bad I used to close my eyes and picture our willow island, and then when I had it just right in my mind, I would put you there, and undress you and lay you down, and then I would lay myself down with you and you would hold me close, just hold me."

"Remy—"

"No." The word had the force of a shout, even though she spoke softly. "Don't tell me something I can't bear." She reached out and touched his hand where it lay on the table. Lightly, her fingers barely brushing his knuckles and the edge of the bandage. "They say the Indians had special places, places where they would go alone to worship the Great Spirit and no lies would be allowed. It's a sacred place to me, Day, our willow island. The only thing I do hold sacred. I swear to you on that place, I did not kill Charles."

Her fingers stroked the bones of his hand. He was terrified of the truth he thought he heard coming up from her heart and saw in her eyes, because he was so certain of the lie. Because to let himself believe and then to be disappointed would be more than he could bear.

He knew what lived inside of her, and it was dark. Dark and sad and crazy. She could run a race with a train, and put a loaded gun to both her head and yours. She could make you so crazy with lust-desire that you'd strip yourself down to guts and bone to have her.

He had watched her kill Julius. Kill him and then be cold-blooded enough afterward to remember that the cops would know if a gun had been fired, and so she'd switched the revolvers to make it look like suicide.

She had murdered that boy and then she had run away and made herself one of the most famous people in the world, because she could hurl the million faces of Remy Lelourie through a camera and onto a movie screen, until she was everyone's fantasy come true.

She could be anything you wanted her to be.

She could be innocent.

God help him, but he believed her.

Outside, it was raining now as if a hole had been ripped open in the sky. The rain rushed in the gutters and along the galleries, shooting off the ends of the sloping roofs. In the Quarter, the water had already overflowed the low brick banquettes to lap at the stoops of shops and cottages.

Rourke walked down Canal Street to the river. He climbed the levee and stood there in the relentless downpour. Clouds pressed down on him, heavy and swirling with mist. Below him the river flowed, high and fast and yellow with mud. Branches and small logs trailed in the current, forming little eddies that foamed and bubbled.

One week ago today, Charles St. Claire had been hacked to death with a cane knife in the old slave shack in back of Sans Souci. Most times you just do your job. You look at the body and ask some questions and you either figure out who did it or you don't, but you speak for those murdered ones if you can, because that is your job. He felt as though he'd lived ten lifetimes since Charles St. Claire's death, most of it hard and cruel, as most of life was. He kept thinking he ought to be learning better, but he never did.

If she was innocent, then someone else was guilty.

So, come at it like you do with a snapping alligator, come at it from the other end.

Heloise Lelourie. Who had probably killed once before, poisoning the husband who had deserted her with pralines laced with love beans. She would see Charles St. Claire as another such man—deserter, adulterer, a man who had damaged both of her daughters, cheating on the one with the other, a man who had planted a St. Claire bastard on a Lelourie. *La famille Lelourie* was everything to her. *La famille*, Sans Souci, and all the sins of the past buried with the dead, in their houses of secrets.

Belle. Ripping up her beloved garden in pain and fear and fury. The woman used and scorned, the woman left pregnant and alone, and no Mardi Gras king would be toasting Belle Lelourie as the parade passed her by.

Lucille. You might as well call it rape, what Charles St. Claire had been doing to her these last two years. Lucille, who hated her rapist with a soul-scouring purity, and who was supposed to have been home, sick and alone, the night he'd been killed.

Mamma Rae, voodooienne and *loup-garou* if you were so inclined to believe, putting hoodoo spells on Mr. Charlie for LeRoy. LeRoy up at Angola finding out how his wife had been whoring for him these last two years. LeRoy and LeBeau and Mamma Rae. Lucille.

Makes it 'specially easy for they certain folk to solve their predicament if that goat is black.

Tante Adenise, with the miseries in her house and her bad feelin's, seeing bats flying across the moon, and the bayou turning the color of blood.

A thought clung there, deep at the back of his mind.

One of them said somethin' 'bout it bein' crazy to do it this way, 'stead of just lettin' that poor dead boy sink like a stone without even leavin' no

ripples on the water. An' then the other said somethin' 'bout you. Said that
nigger-lovin' cop Rourke had to be thrown a bone, otherwise you keep on
diggin' 'til you found the whole skeleton.

Vinny McGinty, his bone.

The steel stairs rang beneath Rourke's feet as he took them two at
a time to the holding cells, where Remy Lelourie had been put
until her arraignment. He waited, impatiently, leaning against the
stained, damp wall among the shouts and sobs, and the clattering
and banging noise of prison life, for the matron to open the barred
door.

The whole place smelled like a jail, he thought—sweat and fear
and desperation.

The cell, lit by a solitary caged and naked bulb, was shadowed
in the corners. She'd been sitting on the slab of concrete that
passed for a bunk, with her legs drawn up under her chin. She
stood up when the door rattled and clanged open.

She looked bruised around the eyes, and the skin about her
mouth was taut and gray. She stood up slowly as he entered her
cell, her eyes searching his. It broke his heart to see hope flicker
briefly across her desperate face.

After running all the way back from the river in the pouring
rain, now he could only stare at her. In the silence he could hear
the water dripping off his coat and hat brim.

He couldn't believe how he had ever doubted her, how he had
once thought to hurt her.

He glanced outside the cell to be sure the matron was out of
earshot. "One way or the other, darlin', I'm getting you out of this
place." It wasn't what he'd come here to say, but it felt right. He
hadn't been able to save her eleven years ago, but he could save her
now. "You just cling to that belief through whatever comes,
because all I got to do is flash my badge to get you out of this cell,
and it'll be easy enough after that to get you out to a boat in the
Gulf that could take you down to Mexico or South America somewhere."

She came up to him until only a hand-space separated them.

Her face was cast in a strange sadness, as if the mystery she carried inside her had at last worked its way out. "Don't you understand yet how much I love you?" She reached up and touched one corner of his mouth with her fingers. "I would never allow you to ruin your whole life for me. And, besides, you're forgetting who and what I am. Where ever could I go where no one would know me?"

He wrapped his fingers around her wrist and held her hand in place so that he could turn his head and brush his lips across her knuckles. "Some places don't have extradition, and it might not come to that, anyway." He kissed her hand again, then let her go. "Did your husband ever mention a client by the name of Vinny McGinty?"

She tilted her head slightly to one side in that way she had that showed she was thinking. "No, I don't think so. Not to me, anyway."

"How about a man named LeRoy Washington, then?"

"LeRoy Washington," she said after a moment. "A Negro prize-fighter who went to prison for killing his manager? I think Charles might have driven up to Angola to talk with him a couple of days before he was killed. I remember that evening because it was a good one, and we'd had so few good ones for so long. He was all excited when he came home, Charles was, and he wanted to drink champagne. We had a couple of glasses and then we put a record on the phonograph and danced."

"Did he tell you anything about what had got him so excited? Think, Remy. It might be important."

Her teeth sank into her bottom lip and she closed her eyes. When she opened them again she was shaking her head. "It just wasn't Charles's way to talk about his work. No, wait. . . . We had lit the candles in the sconces by the fireplace and he held up his glass and looked at the light through the champagne, like you do, to see the bubbles, and he laughed and said something about Cain having a lot to answer for."

The sugarcane and rice fields unfolded beneath a sky that was thick with clouds early that next morning, but, unlike yesterday's, these clouds wouldn't rain. Rourke was driving his own Stutz Bearcat speedster rather than a squad car, and he had the pedal to the floor. Fiorello Prankowski sat hunched over in the passenger seat, staring wildly out the bug-splattered windshield, with his jaw knotting and his hands gripping his knees.

"You aren't going to slow the 'Cat down," Rourke said, "by pressing a hole through her floorboard. The brake's over here."

Fio showed his teeth. "What's that expression y'all use down here? Brassy ma . . ."

"*Brassa ma chu.*"

"Yeah. Well, *brassa ma* Yankee *chu.*"

Rourke smiled and started singing "Ma, He's Making Eyes at Me." Fio made a growling noise deep in his throat.

A few more miles clicked by, fast, and Fio said, "You ever gonna get around to telling me why we're on this little joy ride?"

"They claim Al Capone's outfit pulled in a hundred and five million last year."

Fio whistled. "Man, that buys a lotta parlor organs."

"So where does he make his dough?"

Fio gave Rourke a look. "Golly, let me think. The rackets? Bootlegging, prostitution, loan sharking, protection and extortion, the numbers. Little stuff like that."

"Prizefights," Rourke said.

"Yeah, he's got his fingers in that sticky pie all over the country."

"So if you were all the way down here in New Orleans, running a club, sponsoring a few contenders, maybe you figure you could skim a little off good ol' Al's take of the gate, maybe even fix a few matches to give yourself a break, and what with the way good ol' Al is rolling in the dough, he isn't going to miss it."

"We aren't talking chicken feed here, though," Fio said. "Even way down yonder in New Orleans, those boxing matches can produce a couple-hundred-thousand-dollar gate. Guy like Al Capone didn't get where he's at overlooking the details. And nobody likes being made into a patsy."

"So a smart guy," Rourke said, "wouldn't get greedy. He'd take his own cut of the prizefighting pie and give up the rest, nice and easy, just like he was supposed to do."

"If I was Casey Maguire," Fio said, "and already making myself a fortune running rum, I would give up whatever else I had to to get along."

"Only it didn't happen that way. The Chicago outfit got short-changed on their bag money—Maguire told me that himself. He put it all on poor Vinny, but what if it was his baby brother, Bobby Joe, who was skimming the gate and fixing fights? A couple of days before he was killed, Charles St. Claire drove up to Angola to talk with LeRoy Washington, who happens to be doing fifty years' hard time for killing Bobby Joe Maguire. When St. Claire came home that night, he told his wife that Cain had a lot to answer for."

Fio stared at the side of Rourke's face, then finally said, "Are you saying Casey Maguire killed his own brother?"

"Cain's sin—brother killing brother. Bobby Joe was stealing from the bag money meant for the Chicago outfit. When he found out about it, Casey Maguire probably got visions of Al Capone swinging a baseball bat at his head, and so in a fit of rage and panic, he wrung his baby brother's neck."

A boy bouncing over a fallow field in a tractor gave them a wave. A hay truck rattled past, going south. A flock of starlings rose up from the telephone wires and trailed across the gray sky. "Only somebody saw him do it," Rourke said.

Fio pointed his finger like a gun and made a clicking noise with his tongue. "Vinny McGinty."

"Two somebodies." Rourke stepped hard on the gas and the Bearcat's engine roared. "Vinny—my bone—and LeRoy Washington."

Chapter Thirty

Rourke turned the car onto an oiled road that cut through thick, almost impenetrable scrub oak and pine. Fio made pockets of air in his cheeks, then blew them out in a sigh. Rourke was feeling the same way himself. He couldn't pass through the Tunica Gate with PENITENTIARY spelled out in wrought iron without experiencing a primal fear that he was looking at the end of his own road.

They passed a chain gang breaking a field down by the river, swinging axes and shovels into the roots of tree stumps. The line of slaving, sweating men was surrounded by convict-guards on horseback, carrying sawed-off, double-barreled shotguns propped on their thighs. The guards had to serve the time of any inmate who escaped while on their watch, so no warning shots were ever fired. The guards always aimed straight off to kill. The cons working the field were the bad stripes, anyway, the dangerous ones, marked out by their black and white striped jumpers and straw hats painted red.

Rourke pulled to a stop at the prison entrance, beneath the shadow of the wooden gun tower. They showed their badges, the iron-barred gate swung open, and they were waved on through, the low-slung Bearcat bumping over the cattle guard.

Rourke parked under the shade cast by an old stone building

that was the Negro camp. He stayed where he was for a moment, though, with his hands still wrapped around the wheel. Beneath his suit coat, his shirt was sticking wet to his back. The smell of stewing collard greens drifted over from the Old Camp Kitchen.

"You expect this nig—this LeRoy Washington is going to answer your questions with anything close to the truth?" Fio said.

Rourke looked out over the wide flat fields of the prison farm, fields of sugarcane and sweet potatoes. A line of prisoners was walking down the rows, carrying hoes over their shoulders. Their backs were bent and their heads were hanging, their eyes on the ground.

Fio pushed the door open and pried himself out of the car. "Well, he sure as hell isn't gonna spill his guts with me there, 'cause nobody ever tells me anything. I think I'll go shoot the breeze with the warden. I'll bet he's got a bottle of homemade lightning in his desk drawer. This being a prison and all."

A trusty convict with gnarled brown teeth escorted Rourke to a guardroom next to the dormitory. The whole place reeked of stale sweat and the ancient toilets that had to be flushed out with buckets. The trusty seemed to take relish in warning Rourke that the man he'd come to see was a bad stripe. "Gonna have to break 'im or kill 'im, that's what the Boss said. He's been in the Hole this time goin' on fifteen days. Might've broken the record if you hadn't come along."

The Hole couldn't be seen from where they were, but Rourke knew what it was like. Three iron sweatboxes sitting in a vacant field on a concrete slab, too small to stand up or lie down in, so that all you can do is sit with your knees drawn up and with a slop bucket between your ankles. Just sit and bake and try to breathe enough to stay alive through an air hole the size of a quarter drilled into the iron door.

The room the trusty took him to was closer to the size of a closet and furnished with a wooden table, two wooden chairs, and a butt can. Its puke yellow walls were streaked with rust and speckled with mildew.

It was some time before LeRoy was brought in, shuffling

between a pair of hacks, his legs cramping so bad he could never have walked on his own. His hair dripped sweat, and his striped trousers were stained with dirt and sweat and dried blood. He wasn't wearing a shirt, and raw insect bites covered his bare chest and arms, some so infected they bled and wept pus. Rourke had heard about them staking convicts out on the ant hills up on the levee for punishment, but he'd never believed it was really done until now.

One of the hacks left right off, but the older one stayed and gave Rourke a surly look. He had a flat face pitted by deep acne scars, and pale slitted eyes, like pumpkin seeds. "Here's the dinge con you was wantin' a chat with," he said. He slapped LeRoy hard enough in the small of his back with his black Betty to make the man grunt. "And you, boy—you mind your party manners or your nigger ass'll be goin' back in the Hole for so long the only way you'll be coming out'll be feetfirst." He smacked LeRoy in the back again with his black leather sap, only harder. "What you say, boy?"

"Yes, suh, Boss," LeRoy said, the words cracking rough from thirst. He looked at Rourke out of eyes that were so purple and swollen they were like the pulpy bruises on rotting fruit. He was sucking in air as if the world was about to run out of it.

Rourke tried to keep what he was feeling off his face so that he wouldn't shame the man. "Go fetch a bucket of water and then get out," he said to the gun bull. "Do it," he added when the man didn't move fast enough. The threat of violence was raw in Rourke's voice.

As soon as the hack was out the door, LeRoy sagged against the wall and began rubbing the cramps out of his legs, his face wincing with the pain he hadn't let on to before. Rourke went to look out the small, barred window. It was open, to let some air into the room, but the air it let in was hot and dank, and dead.

The hack came back again with a dripping bucket and then left, as far as the other side of the closed door, anyway.

"Better go easy on it at first," Rourke said as LeRoy gulped the water down almost too fast to swallow. LeRoy gave him a look, but drank only a bit more and poured the rest of it over his head.

He wiped the sweat and water out of his eyes with the flat of his fingers and then nodded at the stack of books Rourke had brought with him and set on the table. "If you brought those along for me, Day, you just wasted your time and money. I lost all my reading privileges and I don't expect to ever be getting them back." His voice changed, became drawling and empty. "Camp captain complained I forgettin' my place. Said that what happens when niggers get a bit of book learnin' in them. They forget their place an' so they gotta get sent to the Hole to be reminded of it."

Long, long ago, in the good old days, they used to sit on the deck of LeRoy's houseboat arguing philosophy and logic into the night. Rourke had been a flatfoot on the night shift and going to college during the day, but LeRoy had read books Rourke had never heard of. When he wanted to, LeRoy could "talk educated white," as he liked to put it. "White as any friggin' member of the Boston Club." White men, LeRoy had told him once, grew uncomfortable when their colored help and field hands sounded smarter than they were, so Negroes had learned from bitter experience that they ought at least to give a good impression of knowing their place in the world.

Most of the time, around whites, LeRoy spoke the language of his people, remembering his place, but out of pride and not fear.

"I'll talk to the warden," Rourke said. "Call in some favors and see if you can't get your reading privileges back."

LeRoy's lip curled. "Yeah, you do that."

LeRoy picked up the box of ready-mades and the matches that were lying on top of the books. He tapped out a smoke and then carefully split a match in two, because in prison they were worth almost as much as the cigarettes themselves.

"A couple of them are weed," Rourke said. "So be careful when and where you do your smoking."

LeRoy hooted a laugh. "Man, you are something else. You come waltzing into prison carrying dope in your pocket—they could just decide to keep you here."

They shared a smile, and then LeRoy slowly subsided into one of the chairs. He set the cigarette and match back on the table untouched. His hands clutched his thighs, and he stared at the floor.

When he lifted his head again, his face had the look of a man who was drowning. "You haven't come all the way up here twice in one month, and on a day that's not visiting day, just to say hey. Is it Lucille? Something bad happen to Lucille?"

"She's fine. I talked to her for a quick minute just this mornin', before I left to drive up here. She sends you all her love."

LeRoy had managed to get some of the prison-hard back into his face. Rourke knew he couldn't bear hearing about Lucille's love, couldn't bear thinking about it, when he wasn't going to have her for another forty-eight years.

"Charles St. Claire is dead," Rourke said, delivering the bad news on the chin, where LeRoy would want to take it. "Somebody cut him up with a cane knife, slit his throat. I figured since he was your lawyer, you'd better know."

LeRoy stared straight ahead with his palms still gripping his thighs. A hard, black shine had come into his eyes.

"I asked Luce this morning if you knew about her and Charlie," Rourke said, hitting the man again and hating himself for it. "She told me you did."

LeRoy breathed a harsh laugh. "What you think—that she tellin' you 'bout it all this time an' never tol' me? If knowin' 'bout it means I pimped for her, then that's what I done." He pointed a stiff finger up at Rourke's face. "That's what *you* done."

"All that she's ever done was for love of you."

LeRoy's eyes squeezed shut, and his lips pulled back from his teeth in a grimace. "Man, I *know* that. But if I gotta let some sumbitch of a lawyer poke my wife so I can get outta here, then I do that. I do that," he said, his head nodding so hard the veins in his neck stood out like ropes.

He pushed himself out of the chair with such force that it skidded across the floor. "Shee-it. Crack you open, Day, and you're still a cop inside. What you think I done, huh? That sumbitch was my only ticket to ride, what for would I want to have someone rip him up?" LeRoy's mouth twisted into a hard, mean smile. "Save that for later, yeah. After I'm out. When I can do it myself."

"I know you didn't have anyone kill Charles St. Claire."

LeRoy had been pacing the room, walking away from Rourke, but now he spun back around. "Then what you come up here for?"

"The truth about who strangled Bobby Joe Maguire."

LeRoy threw back his head in a laugh that was prison mean. "The truth! Y'all think a nigger won't never tell a white man anything close to the truth, and you'd be right, uh-huh."

He stared hard at Rourke a moment, then his shoulders sagged. He turned and went to the window. He reached up and grasped the bars with his two big hands, as if he could bend the bars open with a force of will.

"The other day they brought a new fish into the camp—some pathetic, skinny kid couldn't've been older than seventeen. He asked me if I was the LeRoy Washington who knocked Ricky Martson out cold in the seventh round of the Carnival of Champions, and I told him no. Just some scared kid making conversation and hoping I wouldn't eat him alive, and I looked him right in the eye and I lied to him for no good reason." He breathed a sour laugh. "You find yourself lying about everything in here. There just ain't any truth to be had."

Rourke had nothing he could say to that that wouldn't sound like a lie in itself. It had come to seem to him lately in his life that if you're blamed and punished long enough, you eventually become guilty of all the sins charged against you. You own those sins, then, as surely as if you had committed them.

"There's a woman facing a life in prison, maybe even the electric chair for a killing she didn't do. The truth," Rourke said, "might save her."

LeRoy's back stiffened, but he didn't turn around. "Is she white?"

"Yes."

"Then why in hell should I care?"

"The truth," Rourke said, relentless.

LeRoy's head fell forward, pressing against the bars. The silence strung out between them.

"I went back to the gym that night," LeRoy finally said, "to have it out with Bobby Joe over him accusing me of stealing—and, man, I don't know what I was thinking." He pushed out an empty laugh. "Like I was gonna change that white man's mind 'bout anythin'. But it didn't matter anyway because there was already a big rumpus going on. Bobby Joe and his big brother going at it over the flimflam Bobby Joe had been running with the Boxing Irish. Next thing I know I'm watching Boss Maguire wring Bobby Joe's neck with his bare hands, and all I'm thinking about now is getting my black ass outta there. But when I go to run, I smack right into that homeboy of Mr. Maguire's, who was always hanging around the gym. Vinny something or other."

"Vinny McGinty."

LeRoy straightened up and let go of the bars, his hands falling to his sides. He turned and looked at Rourke. "I suppose you're going to tell me he's dead too."

Rourke nodded and LeRoy nodded with him, confirming the inevitable. Then he waved a hand, brushing the inevitable aside. "Anyway, I just gave that Vinny a push and ran on outta there, went home to my boat. I spend the rest of the night lyin' in bed next to Lucille, sweating and thinking I'm a dead man for what I've seen, and the next thing I know the po-lice are knockin' on my door and sayin' I the one killed Mr. Bobby Joe."

LeRoy limped back to the table. He stood looking down at the books Rourke had brought. He ran his hand lightly over the one on top of the stack and then turned aside. "When they brought me down to the jail, I asked if I could talk to you, and they all said sure, nice and friendly as can be, and I'm thinking, man, it's lucky I got me a cop for a friend. But you never came and after a while those two bulls who arrested me took me down to the basement, into the colored toilets. They chained me to the pipes, locked the door, and then they set about hurting me like nobody's business."

"These detectives—did you know them?"

"I knew the one, because he liked the fights, was always sitting in the front row and betting heavy, coming over to the corner to shoot the shit afterward. A mick cop name of Doherty. I didn't know the other." LeRoy's head swung around, and Rourke thought he saw hate flare in the other man's eyes, the same pure hate he'd seen in Lucille. "But the son of a bitch was left-handed, and I saw his blue star every time he hit me."

Rourke put his own hands in his pockets and sagged against the wall, shutting his eyes. A wrenching guilt ran through him, twisting his guts inside out. "I would've come if they'd told me," he said, his voice thick. "You know that."

"I didn't know it that night—what with all those blue stars I was seeing. Yours, the other cop's, Boss Maguire's. I only knew it the next morning when you came into my cell and I looked into your eyes, but by then it was too late." LeRoy's mouth tried to smile, but it came out horrible, a death's-head grimace. "Because by then I'd already given up your precious truth."

"I tell those two bulls—Doherty and your homeboy with the tattoo—all that I saw happen at the gym the night before," LeRoy was saying. He was sitting on the hard wooden chair, staring at the floor, his hands fisted together and hanging loose between his knees. "I tell them it was Boss Maguire himself who'd killed his brother. When I'm done talking, they go out and leave me chained to the toilet, and I'm bleeding like a headless chicken all over the floor. A couple hours pass in hell, and then the two bulls come back, only this time they have a boss cop with them, and he was the one who told me how it was all going to go down."

Rourke pushed himself off the wall where he'd been leaning with his hands shoved in his pockets. "That was sure some swell deal you cut. You keep your mouth shut and in return you get fifty years' hard time."

"Beats the electric chair, and no white man's judge and jury was ever going to believe my version of the truth. No truth I saw was going to keep those white cops from proving I killed Bobby Joe Maguire if they wanted it that way."

He twisted his hands together, then pulled them apart, staring at his clenched fists. "They started in on telling me what-all they could do to my family. Grandmama thrown out of her house. Lucille put to turning tricks on the streets. My own baby brother, LeBeau . . . Lordy, they'd just lynched an eight-year-old boy over in 'Bama a couple of weeks before. I knew what they could do to us all and, besides, I was going to be sent up the river anyway for doing that killing. There was no stopping it—and those are the truest words I've spoken yet."

"You must have told Charles St. Claire some of the truth last time he was up to see you."

"I never told him nothin'. That was part of the deal I made to keep my family safe—not to tell anybody. I ain't seen Mr. Charles St. Claire, Esquire, in over a month, man. All he ever done for me was file appeals that weren't ever goin' to happen, while he passed his own time fuckin' my wife."

Rourke kept thinking that he should have seen, that he should have known, that he had let all the lies and injustice go on around him and he'd done nothing.

"When I came to you that first morning you were in jail," he said, and his voice broke rough, "you should have told me. I would have found a way to make it right."

"I keep tellin' you, there *was* no way of makin' it right." LeRoy lifted his head. His face had gone gray, as if drained of blood. "An', besides, I'd've had to give up to you my own ugly part of the truth then—'bout how I'd been throwing fights for Bobby Joe for years, and winning some that were thrown to me. You and Lucille were coming to my matches, lookin' at me like I was someday going to be Champion of the World, puttin' your money and your faith on me. I *cared* about that, about the pride you and her took in me— man, I cherished it in my heart—and all that time I knew in my heart I was no better than the rest of them."

His gaze broke away from Rourke's. He pushed himself to his

feet and went back to the window. The prison yard was empty, and the air had gone eerily still, the way it could get sometimes right before a hurricane.

"You know how I was on the outside," LeRoy said. "How I despised other black men for hating the color of their own skin, blamin' themselves for all the misery it brings them. You get treated like a nigger, I said to them, then you actin' like a nigger, and soon enough you goin' to *be* a nigger.

"I thought I had it all figured out, thought I knew how I could make things be. Promised myself I'd grow up different from my daddy, that I wouldn't run off and desert my woman and kids like he done. But what I done to Lucille—it amounts to the same thing. I promised myself I'd never crawl to the white man, but I've crawled. Jesus, I'm crawlin' in here every day of my life."

"No," Rourke said. "What I saw come out of the Hole just now was a man."

LeRoy turned, and Rourke saw that his eyes were as flat as glass with the effort it was taking to keep all that he was feeling bottled up inside. "You got a way of thinking, Day, that's like no white man I have ever known. And you got a way of feeling inside your heart like no *man* I've ever known. But you and I aren't going to change what is, and there's never been a white man born yet who thought every other man born was really the same as him underneath the skin." He nearly broke then. His eyes brightened and shone wetly, and he had to blink, hard. "I'm sorry to have to say this to you, and I'm not blaming you for it, you mind—but I've never been able to get over the fact that when I'm looking at you, I'm seeing a white man."

Rourke wanted to tell him that he was wrong, but he could find no words inside him to show it up for the lie it ought to have been. No words and no hope. Maybe, he thought, if you were told a lie often enough by enough people, you would come to believe it and then it became the truth. Maybe truth was nothing more than an act of faith. If you believed the words, whatever they were, then after a while the words will have turned the lies into the only reality left to you.

Maybe there wasn't any real truth to be had anywhere.

Rourke heard someone bark an order, and the hacks began making noises outside the door. The scuffle of boots on stone steps, the rattle of a key ring. "I'm going to put Casey Maguire away for murdering his brother," he said. "Once that happens you're going to walk out of here a free man."

LeRoy's mouth pulled. "Free, huh? How you goin' to do that? The only ones who could swear to the truth of what happened that night are me and Vinny McGinty. He's dead and I'm a nigger, and courts of law down here in Lou's'ana don't take testimony from dead men and niggers."

"I'll get him, one way or another. In the meantime you hang loose with the bosses. Don't get yourself put back in the Hole."

LeRoy was slowly shaking his head back and forth. "I'm done with crawlin', Day."

"That's not crawling. That's living to fight another day."

"No, suh. I'm done."

The door opened and the bull hack sauntered in, hitching his trousers up over the sag of his belly. He gave Rourke a look of pure disgust, and a mean grin to LeRoy that promised hell to pay for later. "Come along, boy," he said, and slapped his black Betty on his palm. "You got out the Hole, but that don't mean you gettin' out of work."

Rourke held out his hand, and LeRoy shook it. The guard hawked up a glob of phlegm from deep in his throat and spat it on the floor between them.

Rourke's eyes never left LeRoy's face. "You take care."

"That promise you made when I got sent up, 'bout takin' care of Lucille—I'm holdin' you to it," LeRoy said, and then he let go of Rourke's hand and walked out of the room ahead of the hack, even though he was never supposed to pass through a door ahead of any white man, let alone one of the boss men.

The hack glared at LeRoy's back with hot, angry eyes, and Rourke thought that if the man so much as breathed in LeRoy's direction, Rourke would kill him. Then the hack's gaze flickered over to Rourke's face, and you could see him deciding to let it go. He spat on the floor again, hitched up his trousers, and let it go.

The Bearcat bumped over the cattle guard and the gate clanged shut, locks tumbling into place with a rattle, and the Louisiana State Penitentiary was behind them.

"Man, I'm always glad to be back on the sweet side of them bars," Fio said, although mostly to himself.

The sky had grown darker, the air heavier, and yet it wasn't going to rain. Rourke kept thinking that there was something he had left undone with LeRoy, words left unspoken.

A puff of dust floated on the road ahead of them, and they caught up with it quickly enough—a truck carrying prisoners out to join the gangs hoeing grass out of the sugarcane. One of them, sitting on the tailgate with his legs dangling over the side, was LeRoy. He had been given his shirt back, and a straw hat.

He was looking toward the scrub oak and the river, with his hands braced on the bed of the truck, and there was something about the set of his body—like a guitar string tuned so tight it would break with a single strum.

"No," Rourke said aloud, as though the man could hear him. "Don't do it."

"What's going on?" Fio said, then swore as Rourke shoved the Bearcat into higher gear, flooring it.

Rourke's thought was to put the Bearcat between LeRoy and the prison truck, maybe even drive the truck off the road, making it harder for the guards to shoot. Only LeRoy didn't jump toward the levee and the river as he'd expected, but toward the cane fields.

LeRoy landed in the ditch at the side of the road, hitting the dead water with a splash. He ran down the ditch a few yards, until the bank flattened enough that he could scramble up it. His feet and hands clawed at the dirt and weeds, and then he was up and crashing into the thick rows of sugarcane. The guard who had been on the flatbed of the truck with the prisoners shouted and fired, but the truck was still moving and his shot went way wide.

The cane stalks were as tall as LeRoy's shoulders, but he didn't try to bend down or hide—he just ran. One of the guards, who was out with the chain gang in the middle of the field, half stood up in his stirrups and fired first one barrel of his shotgun and then the other. LeRoy's shirt jumped and twitched and tore and bled red, and still he ran. Then the other guns were all firing, and it was like a string of firecrackers popping off at once, and a smoky haze settled over the field.

Rourke had slewed the Bearcat to a stop and was out and running too, hitting the ditch after LeRoy and then diving into the dense rows of cane, with their stiff, sword-like leaves. He heard Fio shouting "Don't shoot! Don't shoot!" as shotgun pellets sprayed around him, tearing into the tall, green stalks and throwing up dirt, but he kept running, as if all he had to do was just get to LeRoy and they would both be saved.

Maybe it was the impact of so many shotgun pellets slamming into his back, or maybe it was LeRoy Washington's fearsome pride that just refused to quit—but whatever it was, he kept on running for a good ten feet after he was surely dead.

Chapter Thirty-One

The swollen purple clouds trembled with heat lightning, and a hot wind pushed through the thick green fields of cane. The stalks rustled and the sharp leaves flashed in the stark, white light like knives.

Rourke had driven twenty miles on the way back to New Orleans before he pulled off to the side of the road. He got out of the car and then sat right back down on the running board because his legs wouldn't hold him. He folded his arms over his belly and bent over, holding himself as if he'd just had his guts flayed open with a blade.

He kept seeing LeRoy's bloodied face and empty, staring eyes, kept seeing flashes of it, intense, bright, like a lighthouse beacon, flashing, flashing, washing out everything else. A fly had been crawling around LeRoy's open mouth.

"Why'd he do it?" Fio said, after a good while had passed. He was leaning against the Bearcat's fender, with his arms crossed over his chest. "The poor bastard never had no chance in hell of making it."

Rourke slowly straightened, until he sat with his hands hanging loose and heavy between his spread knees. His eyes burned and his throat was sore, and he couldn't catch a deep enough breath. "Maybe he wanted to go down shooting."

"Yeah, I can see that," Fio said. "I wouldn't have had the guts for it myself, but I can see it."

Fio pushed himself off the fender and went to the ditch that ran along the side of the road. He measured it with his eye, swung his arms back, and then jumped across. He went a few rows back into the field, where the stalks were sweeter, and cut off a piece of cane with his pocket knife.

"It won't be ripe enough," Rourke called out to him, but Fio either didn't hear or didn't care.

Rourke watched him come back to the car with the cane in his hand. He watched Fio cut off a lower joint and peel it and then cut off a round and pop it into his mouth. Fio chewed it, and the juice leaked out of the corners of his mouth, and his eyes shut at the sweetness of it, the way a child's would do.

It was part of a Louisiana childhood, Rourke thought, eating a piece of sugarcane fresh from the field. He had done it, and LeRoy would have done it, but it was one of the many things they had never done together.

"So I guess we had it figured right," Fio said as he wiped the sticky juice off his mouth with his handkerchief. "Little brother Bobby Joe was fixing the fights and skimming the gate receipts, and Maguire caught him at it. Maguire lost his temper or he just decided to solve his problem the easy way. He knew he had to clean up the mess and keep the Chicago outfit from hearing about what'd been going on down here in New Or-leans, or his ass was gonna be chopped liver. He did tell you the truth about that part of it, anyway—only the mess was of Bobby Joe's doing, not that poor sap Vinny McGinty's. All Vinny did was see it all go down. . . . Him and LeRoy Washington."

Lightning pulsed again on the horizon. The wind smelled of hot tar from the road and fresh-peeled sugarcane. "Vinny was already one of Maguire's goons," Rourke said, speaking partly to Fio but mostly to the God who sent lightning flashing across the heavens and shotgun pellets slamming into a man's back. "So with Vinny everything was *bonaroo*, at least for a while."

"If that's New Orleans for 'hunky-dory,' then, yeah," Fio said.

"And LeRoy Washington was just another worthless nigger whose word don't count. Somebody who could be tapped to take the fall."

Rourke's hands clenched together, making a fist. "And who told the cops who'd arrested him what-all he had seen—that Casey Maguire had killed his own brother." It was probably always going to hurt that LeRoy hadn't trusted him with the truth, hadn't trusted that Rourke would try to save him.

Fio shrugged. "Yeah, he told Sean O'Mara and Roibin Doherty. It was your friend's bad luck that those were two cops Maguire could buy down to their badges."

"He already owned them." Rourke's wrist began to burn. He realized he was rubbing the tattoo and he made himself quit.

Fio cut off another round of sugarcane and flipped it from the knife blade into his mouth. "But somehow in the last couple of months it must have all started to unravel."

"Miss Fleurie said Vinny had been scared bad by something and was asking about lawyers," Rourke said. White light strobed across the sky again, quicker than a heartbeat. "She sent him to Charles St. Claire."

Fio threw the last of the cane into the ditch. "Charles St. Claire, the dragon slayer, who got slayed instead, and there you have it. That feeling you had about it all being connected somehow—the hits on you and Vinny McGinty, St. Claire's getting cut—it was Casey Maguire all along, and man, are we fucked. We went and threw the Cinderella Girl in jail for a killing she didn't do."

Something tugged at the edges of Rourke's thoughts and was gone. Images strobed in his head like a movie reel, in black and white flashes and silent, jerky movements. LeRoy running, falling, dying, lying bloody in a cane field, with a fly crawling in his open mouth.

Fio blew a hollow laugh through his nose. "I was just remembering . . . St. Claire said that together he and Al Capone were gonna rock the good ol' Crescent City back on her heels, and they did. Oh, mama, that they did."

It had grown dark as dusk. The air was crackling and smelled of sulfur. Rourke got up and walked into the middle of the road. It cut through the cane fields like a black mourning ribbon.

He felt Fio come up behind him.

"I was supposed to be his friend."

He heard Fio stir, breathe, then a moment later he felt a heavy hand clamp down on his shoulder. "You were."

The sheets of lightning were dancing across the sky now, one right after the other, fast and frenetic, like a flapper doing the Charleston. Get hot.

"Let's go roust Maguire and his goons," Rourke said. "Ask him how it feels to kill your own brother."

"Aw, man," Fio said.

Rourke smiled.

It still wasn't going to rain. It could get like that in New Orleans sometimes, when the black clouds stacked up one on top of another, pressing down on your head, and the heat built up inside you until it felt like your blood was about to start boiling in your veins, and it still wasn't going to rain.

Hell on earth, Daman Rourke had always known, was a state of mind of your own creation, but if you were of a mind to turn the abstract into the physical, then hell on earth would be a slaughterhouse. A slaughterhouse in New Orleans on a July evening, when it should have rained but wasn't going to.

They stunned the cows before they killed them by hitting them on top of the head with a sledgehammer. You could hear the cows hit the floor, hear their legs thrashing about, and sometimes they screamed.

They would hang the cows from great hooks to butcher them, sending them upside down on conveyor belts to men in aprons stiff with gore, who hacked into the beasts with curved knives that were black and pitted from use. They would cut the jugular first, and the hot blood would spray in great fountain arcs, then slow to a trickle, and then an ooze. The butchers would slit the cow open from crotch to throat, then, and the knife would cut through hide and muscle and fat and bone with a ripping sound. Glistening white and pink guts would spill out onto the killing floor, blood would run in the gutters, and the smell of death would be strong.

It was from a small, glass-enclosed office in such a place that Casey Maguire ran his many businesses. The legal ones, like the slaughterhouse itself, and the illegal: the racketeering and the bootlegging. Maguire wasn't by nature a terribly cruel and sadistic man, but he understood that by bringing a man within the sight and smell of blood and death and butchery you put him face-to-face with fear. Being cut, hacked into pieces, sliced up, bleeding, dying in terrible pain—it was primal, this sort of fear.

Rourke didn't even notice the bloody carcasses as they swung past him and Fio on their creaky hooks. He saw only Casey Maguire, who was standing outside his glass-paned office that overlooked the killing floor, talking to a man in a bloodied butcher's apron. The taste in Rourke's mouth was the cold, oily metal of a gun barrel. His blood was singing a long, high, blue note, and the world had taken on a heightened clarity, all sharp edges and bright colors and pulsating movements.

Paddy Boyle and four more rodmen were hanging about inside the glass-walled office, playing cards around a large gray metal desk. They glanced up to take mild note of the cops' presence and then went back to their game.

The floor beneath Rourke's feet vibrated with the racket made by the conveyor belt. A cow squealed in its death throes. Even with the giant fans blowing, it was hot as misery.

Rourke thought his fury was a living, breathing thing, but then Casey Maguire turned his head and their gazes met, and for a flash of a moment a look crossed over the other man's face; Rourke tasted sweet sacramental wine and felt the dizzying motion of a Ferris wheel.

Rourke made a staying motion with his hand telling Fio to hang back, and he went to meet Casey Maguire alone, halfway across the killing floor. Rourke had filled his smile with good-ol'-boy charm, but now his horizon kept tilting, and he was feeling that queasiness again, like a seasickness.

"Hey, Case," he said. "How's your day goin'?"

Maguire's mouth held a faint answering smile, but that white light was in the backs of his eyes. "It was going fine until you bad-ass cops came 'round to roust me again. What is it that I'm supposed to've done this time?"

Rourke kept his smile as his gaze went over the other man's head to the pair of skinning vats. He watched, seemingly fascinated, as a beef carcass swung around on its hook and plunged into the scalding water with a loud hiss.

He brought his gaze back to Maguire's face, so that he could watch the man's eyes. He felt the tension building inside him, like a fall off a high wire—a long, thin scream.

"I came here to tell you you're a lying son of a bitch," Rourke said. "And that you killed your brother."

Maguire's eyelids flickered as his gaze slanted away. "Jesus, have you started blowin' the snow again? I told you how it was Vinny who killed him. Whatever new story you're peddling now, I don't think you're going to be getting a lot of takers."

Rourke smiled again. "I can try Al Capone. Give him my story along with a brand-new ball bat to play with."

A muscle flexed hard behind Maguire's jawbone, as if he'd suddenly bit down on a nut with his back teeth, but the gaze he turned back to Rourke was full of an odd bewilderment. "Always the goddamn cop, Day. Why couldn't you have just let it alone?"

Rourke stared back at this man who once, long ago, had been his friend, whom he'd once loved like a brother. "Because they matter," he said. "Bobby Joe, Sean, Vinny, Charles St. Claire . . . our Bridey. The dead matter."

"Bridey." Maguire's eyes closed for a moment, and when they opened Rourke saw genuine anguish in their depths. "Bridey was never supposed to have happened—the Chicago outfit did that. What I told you was the truth. Except for the part about why I had to kill Vinny."

"And the part you left out about you killing Bobby Joe because he was the one skimming the club's gate receipts and fixing fights."

Paddy Boyle had left the glass-enclosed office but he was hanging back, waiting to see if the boss needed him. Rourke spared him a glance and then brought his attention back to Maguire. He was aware of Fio's presence behind him, ready, but still far enough back to allow the bootlegger to feel unthreatened.

"Vinny was my bone," Rourke said. "You fixed it so his body would be found because I wasn't leaving Bobby Joe's murder alone. You *wanted* me to think you'd killed Vinny, but for the wrong reason—that you'd done it in revenge for your brother. *La famille.* You knew you'd never stand trial for a murder like that in this town, and you were always more scared, anyway, of Al Capone and the Chicago outfit finding out how you'd let your little brother steal 'em blind."

Maguire's head snapped back a little with the sudden hard clenching of his fists, and Rourke heard Fio stir, coming a couple of steps closer. "The stupid little fuck. We had it made and he was about to blow it with a nickel-and-dime con."

"Yeah, y'all sure can't say that crime don't pay down here in N'Awlins," Rourke said, drawling the words.

Maguire actually laughed. He looked down and saw that his fists were still clenched and he relaxed them, spreading his long fingers out wide. "Would you believe I never killed anybody before Bobby? Maybe if I'd had more practice, I'd've known not to do it in front of witnesses, 'cause then it gets to be like fucking dominos. That nigger and Vinny see me do it, and that nigger tells two cops, and the next thing I know I got a fucking payroll of guys I'm buying off to keep quiet about what they know."

"And then they got greedy," Rourke said.

"Sean got greedy. Vinny got hopped up to the eyeballs and then he got scared. That prick Roibin Doherty offered to get rid of them for me, and he was too stupid to figure out that once he did that he had to be the next to go. Fucking dominos."

A smile, part irony and part mean, pulled at the bootlegger's mouth as he looked at Rourke, and he shook his head as if there were no surprises left. "But smart as you are, I don't think you'd have found your way here without help. I'll bet I owe that all to your little childhood sweetheart, Remy Lelourie."

The horizon tilted beneath Rourke's feet. He fought, putting it right by sheer force of will. "What does she have to do with it?"

Maguire smiled and shook his head again. "I'm surprised at you, Day, that, knowing her as you do, you wouldn't think to wonder who she was screwing once her marriage was over. As small as New Orleans is, we were bound to find each other, don't you think? Me and the Cinderella Girl? That way, I could fuck fame and she could fuck trouble."

The horizon tilted again, hard, and Rourke had to blink the dizziness out of his eyes. "You're lying," he said.

"Am I? One day we're lying in bed together, Remy Lelourie and I, and she's got this wild look in her eyes and this humming going on inside her that's like a live electrical wire. Does that sound like the Remy Lelourie we both know? So she dares me to tell her the worst thing I've ever done, and like a chump I say I killed my brother. Then I ask her what was her worst thing, and she says loving Daman Rourke."

The edge was rushing at Rourke now, like a freight train roaring. A part of him was aware that Paddy Boyle was coming toward them at last, and he could hear Fio's breathing, smell Fio's sweat, as the other cop closed the distance between them, coming up now to stand beside him.

Maguire spread his hands out from his sides and took a step back. "She's been setting us up," he said. "Playing us one against the other, Day. Can't you see it?"

Paddy Boyle had brought his tommy gun with him, but he stopped to lean it up against the wall of the skinning vats, which meant that he, at least, still wasn't expecting trouble. The .45-caliber Thompson submachine gun, with its fifty-round drum magazine, had the weight of a sledgehammer and was a pain in the ass to lug around.

"Setting us up . . . setting it all up," Maguire was saying, backing another step. "I take the fall, you bring me down. And she's home free."

Paddy Boyle scratched a match on a piece of sandpaper that was tacked to the wall and lit a cigarette. He flipped the match into a puddle of blood and it hissed as it hit. He turned and his gaze met Rourke's, then skittered away. Boyle's face looked bad—swollen and crisscrossed with black stitches, his mouth purple and blood-blistered, his front teeth broken off jagged like an alligator's.

"Don't do this, Day," Maguire said. "Don't do it."

Rourke put his hands in his pockets slow and easy. He heard Fio take a step behind him and he shifted sideways, closer to the skinning vats.

He smiled. "Hey, Paddy. I sure did a good job of making you ugly. Didn't I do a good job of it, Fio?"

"Ugly as a hog's butt," Fio said.

Rourke could feel Maguire's eyes clicking back and forth now between him and Fio, but he kept his gaze focused on Boyle. "Ugly as a jailhouse rat."

The only thing that surprised Rourke was that the man tried to hit him with the flat of his hand, a slap, the way a woman would. He caught Boyle's swinging arm at the wrist and brought his own right hand out of his pocket and with it a small leather bag filled with lugs and ball bearings. He brought his arm up from his side, hard, thrusting the whole weight of his body behind the blow, and smashed the sack of lugs and ball bearings square into Boyle's already wasted face. He felt and heard the bone and cartilage in the man's nose collapse and the rest of his teeth break off with a noise like sticks popping.

The force of the blow knocked Boyle sideways into Fio, who grabbed him around the neck by his tie, swinging him up and around, using him as a shield, just as one of the rodmen burst out the door of the office with his tommy gun blazing.

The first of the .45 slugs caught Boyle in the small of the back and stitched a line up his spine to his head as the tommy gun's muzzle rose into the air, lifted by the backthrust of the firing rounds. Boyle's body jerked like a marionette, and then his head exploded.

Casey Maguire had drawn a hogleg from the small of his back as he screamed Rourke's name, and Rourke was down on the floor, rolling toward the skinning vats, ripping his .38 Special from his shoulder holster, firing, and three red blossoms exploded on Maguire's chest.

Rourke came back out on the other side of the skinning vats at a run and snatched up the tommy gun from where it still leaned against the wall, his hand wrapping around the pistol grip, his finger squeezing the trigger, even as he was bringing it up, aiming it at the goon framed in the office doorway, and the man danced as the .45 slugs tore through his chest and guts and blood misted in a cloud.

The other rodmen had taken cover behind the wall beneath the windows and the metal desk. Fio fired his .38 from behind the shield of a beef carcass, while Rourke kept his finger on the trigger, and the heavy machine gun rattled his whole body, and the explosions roared in his ears like a cannon going off.

The rounds hit and blew out the windows. Flying shards of glass and metal and splinters of wood zinged and ricocheted off the walls. The men in the office fired back, and their slugs bounced off the metal skinning vats and slammed into the meat carcasses with loud *twacking* noises, and the air filled with divots of bloody meat and gore.

There was such a tornado of noise and devastation that it took Rourke a moment to realize that the hammer on the tommy gun was falling on an empty chamber. He felt rather than heard a movement behind him.

He whirled just as a giant of a man in a bloody leather apron rose up from behind the second skinning vat. Rourke saw the maw of an old Colt Peacemaker point at his face and it seemed that at any moment he would see the hammer falling and the bullet coming at him from out of the bore.

Rourke threw the tommy gun at the butcher's face and the man ducked sideways, just as one of the gaping, bloodied carcasses came along the conveyor belt and swung from its meat hook, slamming into the butcher's back. The man's Colt fired, the bullet passing so close to Rourke's head he felt it lift his hair—and the butcher tipped forward, into the scalding vat.

The man shot back up out of the boiling water like a geyser, screaming, thrashing, and Fio shot him in the face.

The slaughterhouse fell into an eerie silence then, but for the tinkle of falling glass and the hiss of steam from the water leaking out of one of the vats onto the bloodied floor, the creak of the conveyor belt that still swung around overhead.

"Give it up, boys," Fio called out to whoever of the rodmen might still be left alive in the office.

He was met with silence, a piece of wood settling, and then the crackle of more falling glass as something came flying through the shattered window, to hit the floor and roll slowly toward them.

A Chicago pineapple.

Rourke had already pushed up onto his feet and was running toward it, his feet slipping and skidding in the puddles of blood, and bullets dancing and pinging around him like hail. He heard Fio scream "Shit!" and then the firing of Fio's .38, giving him cover. No sooner did Rourke's hand close around the grenade than he was throwing it back through the office window and hitting the floor, covering his ears with his hands. The small bomb exploded as it hit the desk, ripping through the metal with a sound like a tearing scream.

A scream that fell into a deafening silence as the world was filled with the smell of cordite and smoke and bloody, butchered meat. Cow and man.

Time hung suspended for a moment, and then they heard the slap of running feet from outside and the *whoop-whoop* of sirens. Rourke met Fio's eyes across the killing floor. Fio's face was filmed with cow's blood, and his sandy hair was sticking straight up in stiff tufts. His eyes were so distended they were white all around the edges.

"Are you happy now?" Fio said, his voice croaking.

Rourke didn't answer, for he was scooting now at a crouch over the bloody, littered floor. He knelt beside Casey Maguire and tried to close the holes in the man's chest with his hands.

Case's eyes fluttered open and focused on his. "I swear it on the blue star," he said, the words thick bloody bubbles on his lips. "I didn't kill Charles St. Claire. The bitch set us up, Day. She set me up to take the fall."

Rourke pressed his hands into the wounds. The blood ran through his fingers, but then after a while it stopped.

He stood and walked across the slaughterhouse killing floor toward the open door, which showed black, heavy clouds settling into a hot night. It still wasn't going to rain.

Chapter Thirty-Two

Lucille was out on the deck of the houseboat, taking down the wash that was hanging from a line strung between the outriggers. She was smiling as she watched him walk up the gangplank, until she got a look at his face, at the blood that was all over him.

He stood before her, his hands hanging useless, thick at his sides. He could feel his face hardening in preparation for being able to bear himself what he was about to do to her, and he wanted to stop it, but he couldn't. He stood before her and destroyed her life with words, and there was no way of doing it without pain.

She listened, staring at his face, and her own face was empty, barren. "You did this," she said.

He looked back at her, and once again there were no words left for him. He couldn't say how he had done it, but he knew he had.

She stood with her hands fisted at her sides, and then she threw her head back as if she were screaming, although she made no sound.

He went to her and touched her, and her face shattered. He tried to gather her up against his chest as she fought him, beating at him with her fists, and she made a noise like a rag tearing, a sound that broke into words he couldn't understand, and then he did.

"You killed him, Day. LeRoy loved you, and you killed him."

Somehow he got his arms around her and he held her tight, as if they both might die there on a hot summer's evening on the Bayou St. John.

Rourke lay on the bed in the dark, with his shoes off and his shirt unbuttoned, a whiskey glass resting on his naked belly. It was his own bed, and he was alone in it.

The heat still beat relentlessly through the night. He'd gone from the houseboat out to the swamp, to break the news to LeRoy's grandmama and his brother, LeBeau, and then to the station house before he had been able to come home, and all the while he was smelling the death and blood on himself. He could see it too, without even having to close his eyes. Slices of it in frozen, three-dimensional images, like photographs in a stereoscope.

Red blossoms bursting open on Casey Maguire's chest. A fly crawling around LeRoy's open and bloody mouth. LeRoy, lying dead in a field of sugarcane, who didn't look like he'd ever been alive.

Remy with tears and tenderness both in her eyes, looking into his eyes, and lying, lying, lying.

We had lit the candles in the sconces by the fireplace and he held up his glass and looked at the light through the champagne, like you do, to see the bubbles, and he laughed and said something about Cain having a lot to answer for.

Lying, and setting up Casey Maguire to take the fall.

It hadn't struck Rourke as important at the time, although it should have—LeRoy saying that he hadn't told his lawyer anything, that he hadn't even seen the man in over a month. Remy Lelourie had known all along that Maguire had killed his brother, and so she'd come up with a way to send Rourke out to Angola and maybe discover that knowledge for himself, figuring he would take it one step farther and decide that the bootlegger must have killed Charles St. Claire as well.

Setting him up to take the fall.

Daman Rourke lay in the dark with the glass of whiskey resting warm and heavy on his belly, and he thought how even now he couldn't bring himself to believe she had really done it—killed her husband and done all those other things besides. She had always been able to twist him inside out, until he didn't care anymore what was truth and what were lies, knowing only that if he listened to her long enough, hard enough . . . Remy Lelourie.

He had nearly drifted off to sleep at last when the screams woke him.

He was out of bed instantly, with his gun in his hand. He pounded down the stairs of the *garçonnière* and across the courtyard, into the house. He found Katie standing in the middle of the hall, screaming in her sleep.

He gathered her up in his left arm, lifting her onto his hip, and the movement woke her up enough to stop her cries. She looked up into his face out of heavy, groggy eyes, and he touched her forehead with his lips, feeling for a temperature. She hadn't been well since the shooting—restless, frightened, a little feverish.

"The gowman was coming to get me, Daddy."

"Shhh, honey. I'm here and nothing's going to hurt you."

"But I saw him, Daddy."

He jerked the chain on a small crystal lamp that sat on a narrow pier table against the wall, and a gentle yellow light pooled around them. "There now, see. No gowman. Just you and me."

The door to his mother's bedroom opened, and she stepped into the hall. She stood there for a moment, disoriented and barely awake herself, and then her eyes widened as she took in the sight of Katie in his left arm and the gun he still held against his thigh dangling from his bandaged right hand.

"She just had a bad dream is all," he said to his mother. He kissed the top of his daughter's head; it felt hot under his cheek.

Maeve gripped the collar of her robe closer to her neck as if she was cold, although there was a film of perspiration on her face. Barefoot and with her hair hanging down in a thick braid over her shoulder, she looked young and frightened, as if she'd just been awakened from a scary dream herself. "I'll make her some hot milk," she said.

Katie's lips fluttered a little snore against his neck as she settled deeper into him, spreading her legs around his hips, her arms tightening around his neck. "No, that's all right, Mama," he said, keeping his voice low and crooning. "I don't think she ever quite woke up all the way. You go on back to bed and I'll stay with her for a while."

His mother stood there for a moment in a peculiar stillness, as if even her breath had stopped, and then she nodded and said, "It was only a bad dream."

He carried his daughter back into her room and laid her down on her bed. He kissed her cheek and then both her eyelids. He set the gun on the nightstand and adjusted the fan so that it wouldn't blow directly on her. He heard his mother's bedroom door close, and then, as if in response, the beat cop dropped his wooden club on the banquette outside. It was one of the city's oldest customs— a signal that all is well and that someone is on guard.

Rourke's heart was pumping wildly again, though, as he lay down beside his sleeping daughter. His ribs ached from the battering they'd taken rolling around on the slaughterhouse killing floor. The cut on his hand burned like fire. The rush still coursed through his blood, though—the high that came from danger and destruction.

He turned his head and stared at his gun where it sat on the nightstand, the metal of the barrel glinting in the light that spilled through the door from the hallway.

Katie sighed in her sleep, and the sound of it was swallowed up by a sudden splash of water on the windowpanes. It was raining.

Daman Rourke leaned against the brick column at the entrance to the Criminal Courts Building the next morning and watched as people thronged the streets around the Parish Prison. A chant started up, with the heat and beat of drums: Re-my, Re-my, Re-my Lelourie.

The chant broke into cheers and whistles as the crowd undulated and parted, and she emerged. A white rose flew through the air to land at her feet, and then another and another, until the sky rained roses.

Fiorello Prankowski thumbed his hat back farther on his head for a better look at the show. "Fuckin' reporters," he said. "They got no shame. All we've been hearing for a week is how we've been dragging our asses in arresting her, and now they're all over our case 'cause it turns out some other guy did it."

Rourke pushed his hands deeper into his pockets and leaned harder against the column, as if he were now what was holding the building up. He watched her start to get into a duck-green Pierce-Arrow he had never seen before, but then she paused for a moment to lift her radiant face up to the sky and she was smiling.

"I guess Vinny McGinty must've thought that if he went to a lawyer and spilled his guts about what went down, Maguire would figure there was no sense anymore in killing him," Fio said, still working the case over in his mind. "Jesus . . . Like he couldn't add up that one squealing goon plus one grandstanding lawyer is only gonna get you two dead bodies."

"Except that wasn't how it happened," Rourke said. "He told me with his dying breath that he didn't kill Charles St. Claire."

"And you believe him?"

"He swore it on the blue cross."

Fio tilted his head back to stare at Rourke, trying to figure it out. Trying to figure Rourke out. Rourke kept his face averted, not helping him any.

"These are not happy thoughts, partner," Fio finally said. " 'Cause if Casey Maguire didn't kill ol' Charlie, then somebody else did."

Rourke said nothing. The crowd had surged around the car, unwilling to let her go. A little girl in a starched white pinafore held a magnolia blossom up to the window. Remy Lelourie leaned out, laughing, to take it with both hands, and it was as if she were embracing them all. She was theirs once again. Innocence redeemed.

Fio sighed and tugged his hat brim back down over his eyes. "If she did it after all, then she's home free."

Rourke's gaze followed the Pierce-Arrow as it pulled out into the traffic and disappeared around the corner. *Home free.* They had tried, convicted, and executed Casey Maguire yesterday in that shootout on the slaughterhouse killing floor. He and Fio were hero cops, the press had their hot story, the Department could close out the St. Claire murder case, and the Cinderella Girl was home free.

The crowd was moving away now, leaving white roses scattered and trampled on the sidewalk and floating in the rainwater in the gutter. Rourke wondered what she would do now that it was over. She would leave, he thought, go back to the good life of champagne baths and tango dances and petting parties in the purple dawn. He wondered if this time she would tell him good-bye.

"Well, partner, this is sure an exciting conversation the two of us are having about how we probably fucked up the case," Fio said, "but I'm done detecting for today. Plumb wore out. I'm going to go home, is what I'm going to do now. Maybe pluck out a song or two on my parlor organ."

"Play one for me," Rourke said, and he smiled, but his heart wasn't in it.

Rourke watched Fio leave and then pushed himself off the column and began the hot walk down Saratoga Street toward City Hall. He had himself announced into his father-in-law's office, only to go without a word of greeting to the window.

The palms and statues were still there in Lafayette Square, but this morning a spasm band was entertaining the loafers on the park benches, their bottle-capped shoes striking sparks off the paving stones as they danced. He couldn't tell for sure, but he thought the boy strumming the washboard was LeRoy's baby brother, LeBeau.

"Hambone, hambone, have you heard? Mama's gonna buy me a mockingbird."

"Well, hello there to you, too, Day," Weldon Carrigan said to his back.

Rourke turned around and braced his shoulder against the window's wide wooden casement, crossing his legs at the ankles.

"Officially, I got to reprimand you for the way you handled this Maguire mess," the superintendent was saying as he opened the bottom drawer of his mahogany desk and pulled out a bottle of bourbon and a pair of cut-crystal tumblers. "The newspapers are calling it the Slaughterhouse Bloodbath. Going in there with guns blazing, a half a dozen citizens dead—although none of them innocent, praise the Lord."

He poured a couple of fingers of the bourbon into each glass and pushed one toward the edge of the desk in Rourke's direction. "Unofficially, now . . . you've saved our collective asses, Day. For one thing, there isn't going to be any Trial of the Century."

He smiled and raised his glass in a toast, then took a sip, seeming to savor the taste of the bourbon with pleasure, although his pleasure faded some when Rourke made no move to pick up his own glass. "Since when do you got something against drinking before noon?"

Rourke slanted his father-in-law a hard look from beneath the lowered brim of his hat, but inside he was feeling unclean just being in this room, as if he were sticking his hand in a spittoon. "What do you got to celebrate, Weldon? I would think you'd be missing Casey Maguire and the pad he had y'all on here at City Hall. Or has the next one like him already come along?"

The other man's face went tight with anger for a moment, then eased into a smile as charming as any Rourke could produce. "I think you should go on home now, Day. Maybe take a few days off the job. It's been a long and tiring week."

"LeRoy Washington is dead. Shot to death by the gun bulls while trying to escape."

Carrigan studied his glass as he twirled the booze around a couple of times before taking another slow sip. "I'm afraid I don't—oh, yes. The unfortunate Negro boy who went to prison for killing Bobby Joe Maguire."

"He wasn't a boy."

Carrigan raised his head, his gaze meeting Rourke's. His face still held its customary look of affability gloving an iron fist, but a small tick had begun to pulse below his right eye. "What exactly is this about?"

"It's about LeRoy Washington and the boss cop he said came to him while he was chained to a toilet and looking at a murder rap that had 'sure thing' written all over it. A boss cop with the juice to cut the kind of deal that gets a colored man prison for killing a white man instead of the electric chair."

A flush seeped slowly over Weldon Carrigan's cheekbone, and the tick beneath his eye picked up its beat.

"And it's about a bent cop by the name of Roibin Doherty," Rourke went on, "whom I saw leaving your house the evenin' of your birthday party, and a few hours later he turns up dead. He was shot with a .38. A cop's gun. Except for that one time he lost his temper and strangled his brother, Maguire preferred to do his killing secondhand. He used Doherty to get rid of Sean and Vinny for him, and that just naturally makes me wonder just who he used to cap Doherty."

Carrigan carefully set his glass of bourbon on the desk, lining it up between the onyx postage-stamp box and the cedar humidor. "I think you'd better shut up now, boy, while you still got a job."

Rourke managed a laugh, although it came out scratched. "Cut the shuck, Weldon. We both know you'll never get me fired. You're too scared of what you think I can prove."

He straightened slowly and came to stand next to the desk, leaning over it so that Carrigan started to lean back in his chair, away from him, before he stopped himself. "I will have my quarter back, though," Rourke said.

Weldon Carrigan glared up at him, his face now showing the iron fist ungloved, but if there was one thing he understood it was leverage, and at the moment Rourke had it all.

"What are you talking about?" the superintendent said. "What quarter?"

Rourke smiled. It was not one of his nicer ones. "The two bits I gave you for your honor . . . I overpaid."

His ribs were still too sore for him to play his sax, so Rourke went flying instead.

He took the Spad up until the earth was a smear of brown and blue and green beneath him, an impressionist palette done by the hand of an indifferent God. The wind was one long screaming note in his ears, and the dying day had turned the sky the color of blood dried by the sun. Up here you could feel the vastness of the universe and understand how slender, how fragile, was the thread that held you to it.

Fly hard enough, far enough, fast enough, and the string would break.

The stars were popping like hot sparks in the black sky when he went out to Sans Souci later that night.

He parked the Indian at the top of the oyster-shell drive and walked around to the back of the house. The air was taut, waiting, as he crossed the yard. It was so still that each leaf on the pecan and oak trees looked etched in metal.

He climbed onto the porch of the old slave shack and looked out toward the bayou. The water was like a sheet of black glass, mirroring the moon.

Nine nights ago, Charles St. Claire had been dying here, drowning in his own blood. Before that moment came, maybe he had stood like this out on the porch and seen that bad ol' moon come rising up to float in the bayou. Maybe he had seen his killer coming for him from out of the hot, wet darkness, the midnight heat.

Rourke blinked, and the moon in the water shattered into pieces.

He went inside.

He stood in the dark for a moment, and it seemed he could hear the panting breaths, could feel the screams come bubbling up, bursting in his own throat, feel the cut of the knife and taste death in the hot blood that filled his mouth.

Could hear the rattle of the banana leaves and the locusts' scratching song falling into a breath-held silence. Hear rotting wood groaning beneath a footstep—

He whirled.

Her face was white in the moonlight, and beautiful, but her eyes burned wild. Crazy.

She came toward him across the porch and through the door. He only breathed again when he saw that her hands were empty.

She came all the way to him, and his heart was still racing, running even faster now. She wore the same white satin robe she'd had on the night he'd taken her on the floor of Sans Souci, the robe and nothing else.

When she put her hands around his throat, he didn't try to stop her. She pulled his head down to her mouth and she was tasting him with her mouth, kissing him, moving her tongue with his. Her hands pulled him closer, so that their bellies and hips ground together. Her skin was hot.

He reached up and wrapped his hands around her wrists and thrust her hard away from him.

She was trembling all over, and she looked at him as if she would devour him. "You don't know what it's like," she said, "to have to wait and wait and wait for you for years, and then to have to wait some more."

He wiped his mouth with the back of his hand, then wiped it again, but he couldn't get rid of the taste of her. "You *bourréed* me good, baby," he said. "You really had me believing you didn't do it." He wiped his mouth again. His hand was shaking. "I guess my first clue that you were lying all along should've been when you told me there was no other man."

She stared at him, saying nothing, and the sight of her was like the sound of a saxophone, and that could cut you in half when you were alone.

Her eyes closed for a moment, and her mouth tightened with

something, pain, regret—it didn't matter because by then it seemed that what he was seeing was so far away it wasn't even in this world.

"I had to lie to you about that, Day. You would never have believed anything else if I told you I'd been sleeping with Casey Maguire."

"Oh, lady, you got that right." His laugh was sharp, cutting himself more than her.

She brought her hand up to her throat, was rubbing her throat as if the secret were buried there, right above her collarbone. "You don't understand," she said. "He was the closest I could come to you. He had your blue star."

Sweet Jesus.

"And I lied to you about Charles going up to Angola to see that colored boy because I had to get out of jail. I saw a way of getting you to see how Casey Maguire could have done it all, but I didn't do any killing myself. Not this time." She smiled, but it cracked midway and turned into something else. "I lied to you, Day, over and over, and yet still I'm saying you must believe me. You must believe *in* me."

This time the laugh that came out of him was ragged, desperate. "Baby, wanting to believe you has never been my trouble."

She reached up and touched him, a light brush of her fingers across his cheek. "Then do. Believe in me, love me. Love me, Daman Rourke, if you dare."

She left him, then, walking out the door without looking back, left him feeling strangely bereft and empty, like a promise unfulfilled.

Chapter Thirty-Three

From the editorial page of the New Orleans *Times-Picayune*, Friday, July 21, 1927:

KEEP IT IN CHICAGO, BOYS

New Orleans has once again sent a message to all organized criminal outfits to get out of town and stay out. Mr. Casey Maguire and his gang of Mafia-financed bootleggers were involved in a shootout with police Wednesday evening that has left six of their number dead, including Mr. Maguire. When the heroic law enforcement officers—who had reason to suspect the bootlegger was responsible for the brutal slaying last week of prominent New Orleans attorney Mr. Charles St. Claire—arrived at Mr. Maguire's slaughterhouse to question him, one of his men panicked and opened fire, and a veritable bloodbath ensued. This time, however, it was the ones responsible who paid the ultimate price for their lawlessness. Yes indeed, a message has been sent to Mr. Al Capone and his ilk, those criminals who might think to conduct their dirty business here in New Orleans: Abandon all hope ye who enter here. Keep it in Chicago, boys.

A couple of days ago we issued a cautionary note in these editorial pages to those who were calling for a hasty arrest in the St. Claire murder case. Instead we urged that the perusal of all the evidence to hand be conducted with care, thoroughness, and fairness. Mrs. Remy Lelourie St. Claire was arrested for the crime of murdering her husband late Monday evening. Two days later, Mr. Maguire, in resisting his own arrest for the same crime, proclaimed his guilt to the world. Yesterday, Mrs. St. Claire was released from the Parish Prison with all due dispatch. As we have already said on these very pages: The truth will out and justice will prevail.

Charles St. Claire's cut throat gaped rawly open and his eyes stared unseeing into Rourke's. He lay there sprawled in all his naked and exposed indignity, his blood black, his body pale and mutilated.

Who killed you, Charlie St. Claire, and why?

Rourke closed the case file folder and put it into the Open basket on his desk, with the other murdered ones who remained unspoken for.

Outside, the late Saturday evening sky was full of a buttery sun that seemed to be melting and dripping from an oyster-blue sky. He drove himself home to the Conti Street house and got out the ice-cream maker and all the fixings, and he and Katie and his mama sat in the courtyard beneath the mimosa tree. Maeve ladled the peach custard into the freezer can, giving the big blue bowl to Katie for licking, and then Rourke took over. He put the dasher in the can and fastened the cover, then put the can in the wooden pail and packed crushed ice all around it. He teased Katie about making her do the cranking, and she teased him back, saying it was a daddy's job, and so he smiled and started cranking, slow and easy as it should be done, while they all took the edge off their appetites with *panné* sandwiches and soufflé potatoes, and inside he still felt restless, fragmented, the case file in the Open basket haunting him.

He told himself that on Monday he would simply begin all over again. He would begin with the given, the obvious; he would have a talk with the Ghoul and go over the forensics, shifting the puzzle pieces into yet new patterns, trying to see them in a way he hadn't seen them before.

The water in the fountain made sweet music, and a breeze was coming in through the carriageway that smelled of summer, hot dust and tar. Katie sat down on the bench next to him and he saw that there was a dime with a hole in it tied around her ankle.

"Why are you wearing that good-luck *gris-gris*, honey?"

She went a little quiet and then shrugged. "That's so the gowman won't get me."

He tried to think of what to say to her. He couldn't go on insisting there was no such thing if she was going to be so persistent in her belief of it. He went on cranking the ice cream instead, figuring that for this one evening at least he would just let it go, let it go.

Just then a banjo and a harmonica started up out in the street, one of the impromptu parades that could spill out of the speakeasy next door whenever the customers got to feeling a little frisky. Katie ran out into the carriageway to have a look.

"It's wearin' her down, this fear she's got," Maeve said to him once she was out of earshot. His mother was sitting on the edge of the fountain with her arms wrapped around her drawn-up legs. She had on a big straw hat and she looked young in it, pretty.

"I don't know what more to do about it, Mama," Rourke said. "How do you go about proving a negative?"

"Maybe one of us ought to take her out to where the gowman is supposed to be living, show her that he isn't there."

"One of *us*?" he said, teasing her a little. "Lord, you are such a city gal, you'd get yourselves lost and wind up food for the gators."

She let go of her legs and drew herself up, pretending to take offense. "I'll have you know I wasn't always a city gal. We can ask LeBeau Washington to take us out with him in his pirogue some day next week. We can make a picnic out of it, the four of us."

The crank was getting hard to turn now, he had to put his

whole back into it. It felt good, the pull of his muscles as he worked. The world smelled of peaches.

The banjo player had spotted Katie and was giving her a serenade. "She's old enough," he said, "to have figured out that just because you can't see a thing, that doesn't mean it isn't there."

"Maybe. But she has this need inside her to face things square on, does Katie. She's like you in that."

One of the working girls was showing Katie how to jig the Charleston. Katie's braids were flying and her knees were knocking. As he watched her this time he saw not Jo in her, nor anything of himself, but the woman she would be.

She stopped dancing suddenly, as if she were a puppet whose strings had just been cut, and Rourke felt a shiver of fear that had no basis except that he would always be frightened now of bullets flying at his Katie from out of a smoky rain.

He watched her come through the carriageway into the courtyard, and her face was white, her mouth trembling. He was already up and running to her, when he saw LeBeau emerge from the brick-red shadows behind her. The boy had his straw hat clutched tightly in two shaking fists, and his face was swollen from crying.

"Miss Lucille, she sent me to tell y'all," he said. "Miss Augusta, she be dead."

The sun had had been baking the bayou mud all day, and so the air was filled with the smell of it, of ripeness and decay. The houseboat floated silent on the green, still water. It looked deserted.

Maeve walked up the gangplank as though she had been here before, but Katie stopped on the edge of it and would go no farther. She was scaring Rourke with the way her chest kept making these small jerking hitches but her eyes stayed wide open and dry. All he knew to do was to squat down next to her and grip the sides of her head with his two hands and kiss her face.

"I can stay out here with her, Mr. Day," LeBeau said. "We go lookin' for frogs, uh-huh. They's frogs out here big as baseballs, Miss Katie." He held out his hand, and she seemed to turn away from her father with relief. She put her hand in the boy's and she even managed a little smile. "You let me show you some of the biggest frogs you ever hope to see," LeBeau said. "Big as baseballs."

Rourke walked up the gangplank alone. He stopped in the doorway to the cabin, and his gaze went first to the bed. The sheet had been pulled all the way up underneath Augusta Durand's chin, but her arms lay outside, folded together over her chest. The proud bones of her face stood out in relief against the pillowcase that had been scrubbed clean by her daughter's hands and bleached white by the Louisiana sun.

Augusta had spent last evening with her daughter, trying to see Lucille through the grief of losing her man. It was LeRoy's brother, LeBeau, who had told them how Lucille was taking it so hard, sitting out on the deck in the rain and sobbing a noise that sounded like crunching bottle glass under your feet. They'd all been worried Lucille would do herself a harm, LeBeau had said, which was why Augusta had decided to stay over, but it was Augusta who had died of a stroke during the night.

Rourke saw that Lucille and his mama were at the foot of the bed, facing each other, and with a ragged silence between them, and then Lucille said, "What you think you can do for me now, after all this time and misery done passed?"

Maeve's face flinched as if she'd been slapped. "Your mother . . . Augusta was my friend."

"Well, she gone now, gone out like a candle in the rain. If you come to tell her something, then you too late."

Lucille must have sensed his presence in the doorway then, for she turned. She stared at him a moment, and her eyes were those of a woman who had gone through to the other side of hell, where the scorching, merciless sun can burn you down to nothing but ash.

"I don' want nothin' from you either, Mr. Day," she said. "But if you want to show me respect, you can get out of my house. That what you can do."

Rourke went back up on deck and stood at the aft rail. He watched Katie and LeBeau as they walked through the canebrakes, stirring up clouds of insects, their images blurring in the waves of wet heat that were coming off the water.

He looked back through the open door and he saw that his mother had taken the chair beside the bed. She sat in stillness, with her hands folded in her lap and her head bowed, as if she prayed, although if she had spoken with God in his presence before it had never been with clasped hands and bent head.

Her shoulders made a sharp, jerking movement, and then she leaned over and took Augusta's face in her two hands. It was not a gentle touch; it was hard, desperate. Maeve held the other woman's face in her hands as he had done with Katie's face, as if she could make Augusta feel her touch even in death. As if by feeling her hands on her face, Augusta would have been able to understand what she was trying to say to her.

Chapter Thirty-Four

The first time she'd had to get his baby cut out of her, she'd gone herself to a woman on Pailet Lane. The woman had done it in her kitchen. Lucille had lain there on the old rickety pine table and looked up at a ceiling that was stained with rust, up at a dim, bare lightbulb that must have been burning out, because it kept flickering, or maybe there had just been something wrong with her eyes. She had gotten an infection from that time that had left her sick and weak and bleeding.

So when Mr. Charlie found out she was pregnant again, he said he'd arrange to have a doctor come along to the flat on Rampart Street and they'd take care of it there.

Mr. Charlie. She only ever called him Mr. Charlie. She guessed he didn't know that it was Negro slang for "white man," and that it wasn't a compliment.

She hated him with all her heart, hated him for what he had made her into, and for what he had taken from LeRoy. Hated him for being white, and for him being able to look at her in that way of his, with that *Love me, love me* look he would get in his eyes, and not understand that the whole of her life was defined by the color of her skin. If you were born a Negro like me, she would think when he looked at her in that way of his, then you might as well have been born in sin, because they can do whatever they want to you, and short of dying you can't stop them.

Sometimes the hate inside her was so strong she could have beaten herself to death with her bare fists. It had grown up inside of her, the hate, the way the swamp grows, with the water slowly flooding the land and the next thing you know you're looking at the black skeletons of dead cypress trees and you've gators snapping at your heels. Sneaks right up on you unawares does a swamp, does the worst kind of hate.

Sometimes he would cling to her, holding her in a way that had nothing to do with what passed between them through their bodies. In that dark room, on that bed of soft Irish linen sheets, he would cling to her, and she would look through the gauzy veil of mosquito netting at the moon floating across the window, or sometimes there would be rain slanting through the arc of light cast by the street lamp, and she would reach, grasping, for the certainty of who and what she was. "Hold me," he would whisper to her in the night. "Just hold me."

She had wanted to keep it a thing that happened between them only on the bed with its veil of mosquito netting, like a prostitute would do, but he hadn't let her. Or maybe it was her own pride that hadn't let her, because she would find herself doing things for him, as though she cared for him and he for her. Like cooking up some red beans and rice and fried *sac-à-lait*, so that when he came through the door he would say, "My, that does smell good," and kiss her on the back of the neck and cup her bottom with his hands. Or she would help him with his bath, washing his back for him, rubbing her hands over his wet, slick skin, breathing in the steam and the smell of him, touching him, touching him.

She began to listen to the thing he most wanted to talk about, his work, and she realized he was doing real good for her people—a white lawyer taking their part before a white judge, using the white man's laws against them when he could. She didn't know why he was doing it, what need in him was driving him to do it, but it got done nonetheless. She didn't understand how he could do such wrong to her and have this one place of righteousness, of decency, inside him, and so she made herself despise him for it.

One evening, while she waited for him to be done with the writing of a letter, she went to stand out on the balcony, leaning her elbows on the wrought-iron railing, enjoying the promise of coolness that came with the falling darkness and the smell of jasmine rising from the courtyard below. Across the way someone began to play the saxophone, "Sweet Georgia Brown," and the soulfulness of the music drew the words right out of her. When she was done singing, the night had come and was lying gentle now on her heart.

She turned around and he was standing in the doorway, one shoulder braced against the jamb, with his hands in his pockets. The white linen of his shirt glowed blue in the dark, and there was no mistaking the feelings on his face.

"Do you know how the wheels on a gear work?" he said.

She shook her head, not because she didn't understand about gears, but because she didn't want him talking about those feelings that were showing on his face.

"How the teeth of one wheel intermeshes with the other, so that the one wheel drives the other? It's what I feel when I'm with you. That not only is my wheel meshing with yours, but that you are the driving force of my life. Or could be." He pushed himself upright, laughing a little, shrugging. "Lord. I don't know if I could have possibly put it more unromantically. I don't . . ." He waved his hand now as if his words were clouding the air between them. "I tell myself that this shouldn't be possible, that it can never be, but there it is. I love you, Lucille."

She made her eyes go hard and her mouth go mean, but she had to lean back against the balcony's lacy, wrought-iron railing, her legs were shaking so. "You don't need to be tellin' me no lies like that, Mr. Charlie. You know what you want you goin' to be gettin', without you havin' to be tellin' me lies."

She thought he'd turn angry with her, wanted him to, but instead his face clenched with pain, and his eyes were begging her, *Love me, love me, say you love me.* She told herself that it was a weakness in him, this need to be loved, a hunger that drove him to cruelties, and had long since cost him all his honor.

He closed the distance between them, and she tightened up all over in preparation for his touch. Even so, when his fingers oh so lightly brushed the curve of her cheekbone, she shuddered.

"If you were white," he said, "I would marry you."

She twisted away from him, unable to bear it. "Oh, Mr. Charlie, you don' know what you sayin'. You don't know. You don't know."

But he had said it, and it changed things between them.

She caught herself thinking of him at odd moments, and her heart would give a hard, painful twist she didn't understand. While wringing out a pillowcase to hang on the line, while picking over cantaloupes in the market. While walking down a brick banquette that was slick with rain, a jasmine-scented wind lifting her hair. Sometimes she would dream at night of a man's lips and hands touching her, and they wouldn't always be LeRoy's. Sometimes they would be his.

If you were white.

The memory of those words was like a whiplash on her heart. It was bad enough to be betraying LeRoy with her body, over and over, but now her betrayal was one of the spirit. She was wanting to be something she was not.

He tried, but he was not always able to stop himself from coming inside her, and although she got potions and charms from Mamma Rae, that hoodoo wasn't always known for working.

Still, it had come as a surprise that morning when she got out of bed only to fall back into it with her belly roiling and her head reeling. She lay there with her knuckles pressed hard to her mouth, unsure whether she was stopping a scream or a sob. A baby. She was pregnant with da massa's baby. Again.

She hadn't told him about it that first time, just took care of it herself. Only he found out later, when she had got so sick, and he made her promise not to keep such a thing from him again.

So she kept her promise when the inevitable *again* came rolling back around, even though she was uneasy about it, the words sticking in her throat like tough pieces of jerked meat, sticking and choking her when she saw the hardness come over his face and eyes, showing up the mean place in him that had driven him to take her in the first place.

"We're going to have to get rid of it, of course," he said.

She stood before him unable to breathe, swaying dizzily. What did he think she was? As big a love-fool as she must look, uh-huh. What did he think? That she was wanting to have this baby, a white man's baby, and with her LeRoy up in Angola for another forty-eight years? A white man's baby, a little girl, who would grow up looking at her skin and the way it was coming up light and always be wondering who her daddy was. Knowing that no matter how light her skin was coming up, her *skin* was the reason why her daddy wanted nothing to do with her, wanted none of her.

But it was the way he'd talked and that look on his face, in his eyes, *get rid of it*, like it was just so much garbage that had to be washed down the gutter. Like some monster that had to be cut out of her.

In that one moment the hate she felt for him was so deep and so black, it was as alive as the child she was growing in her belly.

The doctor had a neck that was thick with rolls of fat, like pink sausages, and dark, heavy-lidded eyes. He had that way about him of some white men, where he was always having to make sure she knew her place. He made her feel dirty in the way he touched her body, and in the way he looked at her. Da massa's woman. He ended up hurting her as badly as had the woman from Pailet Lane.

Afterward she lay in the azure gloom of dusk on sheets that were soft and cool and smooth to the touch. Out the window she could see lights glimmering behind the slatted blinds of the house next door. Someone was frying up a chicken for supper. She could hear the doctor and Mr. Charlie in the next room, hear the clink of a glass and the rap of something on wood.

"Well, that's taken care of," the doctor said. "And not before time. Christ, Charles, aren't there enough pickaninnies littering the world without you makin' more of them?" And Mr. Charlie laughed.

He laughed.

She could forgive him for making her into a whore and she could forgive him for killing their babies, but not for that laugh. She was never going to forgive him for the way he laughed.

Chapter Thirty-Five

Early Monday morning and almost two weeks now since the murder of Charles St. Claire, Rourke found the Ghoul sitting on a stool in front of the chipped enamel drain board, slicing a scalpel into something that looked like a human heart.

"Lieutenant Rourke. Just the man I wished to see," the coroner said. He lurched and lumbered to his feet, trailing smoke. "I realize that the St. Claire case is officially closed, however—"

"It's open."

The Ghoul's eyebrows came up a little, but all he said was, "Indeed."

Rourke went to the wall where the photographs of the murder were still thumbtacked to the corkboard. He studied the sprawled and mutilated body with its gaping throat wound, the black splatters of blood on the walls, the dark smears of it on the oiled wooden floor. "Footprints," he said aloud. "Did anything ever come out of the footprints?"

"Which footprints?" the Ghoul said. "The ones made during the murder or the ones left by the patrolmen who answered the call and trampled all over the scene with their big flat feet? I managed to recover three partials belonging to the victim and one nearly perfect match to Mrs. St. Claire's left hallux, where it had been planted right next to the body."

"Then there's nothing to tell us whether a third person was in that shack the night of the killing, before the cops arrived."

"Besides the domestic who discovered the body? No, there is no way of proving it conclusively one way or the other."

Rourke stared at the photographs, thinking, then he shrugged and shook his head. "What do you want with me?"

The Ghoul blinked behind the veil of his cigarette smoke. "What?"

"You said you wanted to see me."

"Oh. Yes, indeed." He went to the counter that held his microscopes and began to rummage through a stack of specimen slides. "I met Mrs. St. Claire briefly that night of the murder, when I arrived at the shack. That other detective, the big Polish one, was interviewing her, and I passed by her close enough to detect her perfume. Very distinctive, it was. Sandalwood and lily of the valley, with a hint of musk. The smell of that perfume was pervasive in the hair of the victim, and then there was that bruise on her cheek—Ah, here we are . . . " he said, fishing a couple of slides from out of the pile with a flourish.

"It was the bruise, you see—it kept nagging at my subconscious, and then at the last possible moment before the mortuary hearse was about to cart away the body for embalming, it suddenly occurred to me what I should have thought to look for in the first place. I only had time to make a quick examination and to preserve some samples, but over this weekend I was finally able to study what I had found. I must say it was a great satisfaction to me to discover that I had been right to play my hunches, as you say. Do you play your hunches, Lieutenant Rourke?"

"All the time."

The coroner took a deep drag on his perpetual cigarette as he put one of the slides beneath a reflected-light microscope and turned it on. "Forensics is telling us, Detective, that Mr. St. Claire engaged in sexual congress with a female between the time he last bathed and his death."

Rourke gave the microscope a dubious look. "Sweet Jesus. You didn't cut open his cock, did you?"

The Ghoul tried laughing, but hacked instead. "No, no. That wasn't necessary. What I did find, though, was evidence of dried semen and vaginal fluid on the organ. And two hairs from a female pubes entangled among his own. The sex act was violent, or at the least extraordinarily vigorous, as the hairs had been pulled out by their roots."

"Are you finally getting around to telling me that Charles St. Claire raped somebody right before he died?"

"Raped or engaged in extremely rough lovemaking, yes. It was that bruise, you see, that kept nagging at me, and the smell of her perfume in his hair."

Rourke thought of Remy lying on those stained linen sheets, torn, bruised, her voice broken from screaming. He remembered her as he'd first seen her that night, drenched in blood.

"If he hit her, raped her . . . " Rourke said, and heard a sudden, murderous, roughness in his own voice.

"You are thinking that it could have been self-defense. But a prosecutor could say she was his wife, and that gave him conjugal rights over her. A prosecutor could say she had no legal right to deny him, certainly not to murder him. I am speaking, of course, hypothetically, as if the case were still open, as if we haven't all decided that it was a bootlegger and not his wife who murdered Charles St. Claire."

Rourke bent over and put his eye to the microscope. Magnified, the hair was a curled sheath filled with dark, fibrous matter. He could see the white bulb of the root. He knew he had to ask, although he didn't really want to. Maybe Case had been right, after all. Maybe he should just be letting it go.

"Could this have come from a Negro?"

"An interesting question, but I do not know that you can always tell." The Ghoul scratched his cheek, lost in thought a moment. "The pure African Negro's pubes would perhaps be distinctive. But the American Negro, where there has been such a hybridization with the white race . . . " He shrugged. "All I can say is that the hairs are of a human, not an animal, and most likely a female; and the degree of pigmentation indicates she wasn't much over thirty years of age."

Which described them all, Rourke thought. Remy, Lucille, Belle. Belle . . . Sweet mercy. Had Remy walked in on him raping her sister?

A skimming of clouds enshrouded the first stars in gauze when Daman Rourke went back out to Sans Souci later that evening. He parked out on the bayou road and walked toward the house through the oaks and pecan trees, his shoes crunching on the rotting seed husks. The breeze was light and gentle, like the breath of a sleeping baby.

Light blazed onto the gallery from the open French doors. He saw their shadows first and then the women—Remy, Belle, and Heloise—walking slowly along the gray-painted cedar boards. In the deep purple dusk, they might have been ghosts from another time. From where he watched among the trees, their voices came to Rourke in whispers, like the rustle of hooped skirts and the click and flutter of fans.

He wondered if they spoke of the coming baby. Belle would be showing soon, and so she would have to go away. If Remy intended to raise the child as her own, then she would be going away as well. It would not be the first time such a thing was done in a house like Sans Souci. Belle's baby would become one of the secrets of *la famille*. One of those secrets not confessed and never spoken of, but remembered somehow.

It was an ugly thing, the seduction of one sister by the husband of another. Yet such was the way things worked in the South with *la famille*—you could be at each other's throats, but when trouble came your way you always knew your family would stand by you.

Heloise, Remy, Belle. *La famille*. Family is what you are born into, not what you marry. A girl is known by her maiden name until the day she dies, and after, long, long after.

A mother and her two daughters making birthday pralines for the daddy who had deserted them.

He died screaming.

Rourke thought of the Mardi Gras mask thrown into the cistern and the white enamel paint and purple spangle driven under Charles St. Claire's fingernail. The killing had been planned. Perhaps they all three had killed him together. Or perhaps, like Vinny, Remy Lelourie was supposed to be the bone, the one who was supposed to look guilty so that the other two could get away with it.

Whatever the Lelourie women were speaking of this night, though, they were done with it now. Rourke watched Belle and her mother come down the gallery stairs and walk along the oyster-shell drive toward Esplanade Avenue and home. If they looked his way, they didn't see him.

He did not go up to the big house, but rather he stayed among the trees and watched the gallery, which was empty now, the way he liked to watch the graveside after a funeral, and which was why he was still there when Lucille Durand came up over the bayou levee and walked right up onto the sagging porch of the old slave shack.

She went inside, but a few moments later she came back out again. She stood on the porch and looked up at the big house. Rourke followed her gaze and saw that Remy Lelourie had come back out onto the gallery. The two women looked at each other across the green lawn and over the fronds of the banana trees. They all made a haunting triangle, Rourke thought—the white woman on the gallery of the big house, the colored woman on the porch of the slave shack, and the man watching the both of them from among ancient southern oaks that dripped moss like strings of tears.

The Greater Liberty Baptist Church on Desire was baking in the summer heat. Even with the door and windows wide open and all the fans going, it was stifling inside. The air was thick with the smell of bay rum and sugary perfumes, of melting starch and the chicken gumbo served at the wake.

The ladies of Pailet Lane flapped their cardboard fans and

touched at their wet cheeks with the backs of their wrists. Lucille, sitting in the front pine pew, wasn't weeping. She stared at her mama's coffin with eyes that had turned to stone.

Watching her from where he sat in the back of the church, with his own mama and daughter, Daman Rourke thought that for Lucille it must be as though she had put all the good left in her life into that coffin for burying.

The Reverend Jackson Powell was a man who towered above his pulpit and whose deep voice resonated off the rafters and white-washed walls like a bass saxophone. "Augusta Durand was a good soul," he proclaimed with uplifted hands, as if he would gather to him all the answering amens and hallelujahs. "A good soul and a good woman, who spoke her mind and shared the bounty of her heart, and loved her Savior, the Lord Jesus Christ in heaven. Amen."

Rourke thought it the finest and truest compliment he'd ever heard paid to anyone. She was a good soul.

They took the casket to the cemetery in a hearse pulled by horses wearing black plumes. Everyone walked alongside, and the funeral band played "Nearer My God to Thee." The drummers had put handkerchiefs under the snares of their drums, making a *tunk-a, tunk-a* beat in time with the horses' hooves striking the road.

The Durand family didn't have one of the whitewashed brick crypts. At a corner of the cemetery, the procession stopped in front of an open vault that was shaped like an oven and set high up in the brick wall. The pallbearers slid the coffin into the vault, wood scraping against brick. Reverend Powell spoke, his melodious voice making of the words a song of glory.

"Yea, though I walk through the valley of the shadow of death, I will fear no evil: for thou art with me, thy rod and thy staff they comfort me."

The drummers pulled the handkerchiefs out from under the snares and rolled their sticks on the drum heads, and the band broke into "When the Saints." The mourners opened up their umbrellas beneath the cloudless sky and left the cemetery dancing.

Rourke stayed behind with Katie and his mother, who had

brought flowers—tea roses and jasmine—as a gift for her own dead. He filled a verdigris vase for her with fresh water from a faucet on a pipe.

She took the flowers to the Lelourie family tomb, with its dancing marble child-angel and the wall with those names of her scandalous past engraved on the stone: REYNARD LELOURIE, her lover; MAUREEN, the daughter she had borne him. His baby sister, born of his mother and her lover many years ago. He wondered what she would be like now, this fruit of Maeve and Reynard's sin, if she had lived to be a woman grown. This sister who had shared half of his blood, and half of Remy's blood as well, he realized.

Maeve bent over to fit the vase of flowers into the tomb's *immortelle*, everlasting metal memorial wreath, made to go on existing long after all the bones had turned to dust and even the memories had died. He could tell nothing of what she was thinking, feeling. She kept her silence as she always had.

They sat in the hot shade on a stone bench beneath a fig tree, while Katie played hopscotch on the flagstone path. "When you were a boy," his mother said, "it seemed the only time I saw you was in a cemetery."

She had said something like that to him once before, but he couldn't remember when. As a boy, he'd had no memory of her as his mother before she had left. He had seen her only that once, when his father had dragged him to see her naked in the bed of her lover. They hadn't spoken words until the day after his father's funeral, but by then he was fifteen and believed he no longer had any need of her.

In the Irish Channel, when a body is laid out at a wake, a saucer is placed on the dead person's chest for friends and family to put in nickels and dimes, money for the undertakers. Mike Rourke's sons, though, had had no need for charity. Their father had died a hero's death in the line of duty, trying to break up a knife fight between two shrimpers on the wharf. His funeral had been attended by every policeman and fireman and politician in the city.

Rourke had gone back to the cemetery the next evening by

himself. It had been hot that day, as well, and the murmur of the insects in the weeds outside the crumbling, chalk-white walls had made it seem as if the heat itself had a voice.

They had surprised each other at the ovens, where the many mourners had left mountains of flower bouquets and a gold and red banner had been draped over the wall reading CRESCENT CITY POLICE. He hadn't wanted to be there with her, but he wasn't going to let her chase him away. So he stood in the hot sun before his father's vault, saying nothing, with the heat of the flagstone path rising through the soles of his shoes and sweat running off his face.

Then she had spoken to him, the first words he could remember hearing from her, asking him if he wanted to come and live with her now, now that he'd been left on his own, what with Paulie gone into the seminary and his daddy gone to Jesus in heaven.

He had laughed in her face.

Then years later, before another tomb, with a silent and faintly fragrant rain falling and the stones beneath his feet feeling wet and cold, and his heart feeling wet and cold and missing his wife . . . Yes, that was when she'd said it, he remembered now. We shouldn't only be meeting at cemeteries.

"Your father was a good and decent man at heart."

He'd been watching Katie while he'd been lost in his thoughts, but now he slowly turned his head and looked at his mother. From the way she sat, though, so composed, her face etched with grief and yet in a strange way also empty, he wondered if he'd only imagined her speaking, for he thought he could hear the fig leaves rustling above their heads although he felt no wind.

In the years since he'd brought his infant daughter and come to live with her in her lover's house, they had never spoken of his father, and he had wanted it that way, because all the words left unspoken and all the thoughts left unacknowledged spared him from having to admit that the life he lived now felt like an act of betrayal.

"He was a good man," she said again, and this time he watched her mouth form the words and so he knew they were real.

He waited for her to say something more, but what? To say she was sorry, sad, indifferent? She'd had a choice between her sons and her lover, and she had chosen her lover. His father had had a choice between them and the bottle, and he had chosen the bottle.

She had kept her face averted from his gaze, but now she turned her head and met it square on.

"I loved Reynard Lelourie," she said, and he saw in her eyes an emotion that was both an anguish and an ecstasy. "Oh, how I did love him. With all that I am, I did love him. I won't even say I couldn't help myself, because that wouldn't be true. I wanted to love him, I allowed it to happen. I *chose* it. And I won't say I regret it, for I don't, not a moment of it. Not a moment of it." She stopped, closing her eyes, and after a moment a tear gathered on her eyelash and fell onto her cheek.

He didn't put his arm around her or touch her in any way. "It's done now," he said. "And they are both gone."

Her eyelids clenched tighter, and then she let out a slow breath and nodded. "Yes. They're gone."

They sat together for a while longer, fallen once again into their familiar and safer silence. He was about to ask her if she was ready to go home when she stood up and went back to the tomb with its dancing marble angel.

She opened the gate and went inside so that she could trace with her fingers the name MAUREEN carved into the stone. "I had her with me for a time after she was born. I rubbed my nose against her cheek and it was soft. Her hair was so soft beneath my hand."

A footstep scraped on the brick path behind them, and they turned together. Lucille came up to them and stopped before the gate to the tomb and then she went inside, as though she, too, wanted to read and trace the names. Her face held a hard and flushed intensity.

Maeve started to raise her arm, as if she would wrap it around the girl and draw her close, but then she let it fall.

"I want to go up t' Angola, see my LeRoy's grave," Lucille said.

"Could I ask you to drive me up there, Mr. Day? Could you do that one thing for me?"

He would have liked to touch her in some way too, but he could see that she wouldn't let him. "Tomorrow, if you like," he said. "We'll go tomorrow."

"That would be fine," she said, and walked back down the brick path without having once looked at either one of them.

Fog was coming in thick off the river when they drove through the gate of the Louisiana State Penitentiary. The old stone buildings looked black in the damp. The air was so still and heavy that sounds bounced and echoed—the clang of the metal gate, the bullying shout of some gun bull, and, incongruously, a baby's crying, coming from one of the small clapboard cottages where the hacks and their families lived. The "free people" the prisoners called them.

"I've never seen fog like this in summer," Rourke said, trying to pull Lucille's gaze off the bleakness of the camps. She sat with her arms wrapped tight around her waist, her face closed to him. "I hope LeBeau has the sense not to take the pirogue out into the swampland in this soup, otherwise it won't be much of a picnic that he and Mama and Katie will be having."

"LeBeau didn't say nothin' about takin' out no pirogue," Lucille said, although she still didn't look at him. "Last I seen him, he had his pole and bait bucket and was headin' for the Black Bridge."

The cemetery was mostly wooden markers with a few rusting tin cans of withered flowers. He'd made sure to ask at the guard-house which one was LeRoy's. They got out of the car and found it easily. It was the freshest mound. Lucille stood looking down on the oblong of soft dirt, and her face had gone back to being stone.

"This is an ugly place," she finally said.

"I'll have him moved down to New Orleans for you. You can put him next to your mama, if you want."

She nodded slowly and carefully, as if her head might fall off. "I want you to know I don' blame you no more for what happened. I

397

know you didn't put the thought in his head to go runnin' so's the bulls could shoot him in the back."

He reached out and slid his hand beneath the hair on her neck, a simple touch of comfort. "I liked it better, though, when you were blaming me rather than yourself. It wasn't any one thing any of us did, including LeRoy."

She wrapped her arms tightly around her waist again. "Oh, I did plenty. Plenty. An' I've killed. If anyone should be put on trial for killin', sent to Angola for killin', it should be me."

She began to move back and forth, back and forth, rocking her upper body. Silent tears poured over her face.

"Luce. Did Mr. Charlie give you a baby?"

A great moan tore out of her throat, and she rocked harder, her hair beginning to whip from side to side. "Oh, Lord God, Mr. Day. How? How did you find out?"

"It was only a guess. You've been feeling poorly, and three or four times a week for two years is a long time to be lucky," he said, thinking of Belle, who had only needed the one afternoon.

She let out a harsh laugh. "You've never been able to leave things alone. You keep proddin' at 'em and pokin' at 'em 'til you get at the truth, and never mind how the truth can be ugly."

She stopped her rocking and stared forward, into the nothingness of the fog. "He gave me a baby, all right. Twice. And both times I got it cut out of me. But that last time, that last time had me feelin' so sick. So sick. I left Mr. Charlie's place, but then I couldn't even make it down the block, I was bleedin' that bad again, and all's I could think of was makin' it as far as the house on Conti Street. Only you and my mama weren't home, there was only Miss Maeve, and I don' know what happened 'cept I think I must've fainted, 'cause the next thing I was wakin' up, lyin' in my old bed, from when I was a little girl in that house.

"I could hear Mama and Miss Maeve out in the hall, talkin', and Miss Maeve, she was cryin', too. They thought I was too sick to hear what they sayin', but I found out that day where I come by my light skin."

She lifted her arm up in the air, turning it over, and she laughed. Hard, sour. "Not that me knowin' changed what *is*, though. Don't change what I am. Uh-uh. Lucille, the white man's whore."

"No, you're not."

"Don't you be tellin' me what I'm not." Her hand curled into a tight fist, and she drew it back down against her chest. "I couldn't stay out of that white man's bed. Even bein' sick I couldn't stay out of that bed. I went back to bein' with him through the night too soon, and the next mornin' I was bleedin' again and Mr. Charlie, he got scared and called up that white doctor to come over. An' that doctor he does what he has to do, an' then he go back out into the front room and he and Mr. Charlie start at it again, talkin' 'bout how they no need to be bringin' no more pickaninnies into the world, how the world's got enough niggers. Out the same mouth that was all the time talkin' 'bout how much he loved me, Mr. Charlie was callin' his own babies those awful names.

"So after that doctor left, I made myself get outta that bed and go on in to Mr. Charlie. I thought he should know who-all who he callin' nigger, whose babies he been killin'. So I tol' him how my daddy was Mr. Reynard Lelourie, but he only laugh like I knew he would. Sayin' how they lots of niggers walking 'round N'Awlins today with Lelourie and St. Claire blood in 'em. Sayin' how it didn't mean nothin'. Sayin' how a St. Claire was never goin' to be namin' no nigger as his kin.

"I waited 'til he done laughin' and crowin' and then it was my turn to laugh."

Her head fell back and Rourke watched her tears come again, watched her throat convulse, and all he could do was stand there as if he'd been kicked.

" 'Cause then I tol' him who my mama is. My mama is Miss Maeve, I said, and so what does that make your wife, huh, Mr. Charlie, Mr. High an' Mighty White Man? If Miss Maeve is my mama, and that Reynard Lelourie was my daddy, then what color does that make your wife?"

• • •

He didn't knock on her front door this time either. He walked in and down the back hall to her bedroom. She was sitting at her dressing table, fastening a string of pearls around her throat. He stared at the nape of her neck, at the feathering of dark hair there.

Slowly, she lifted her head, and their gazes met in the mirror. She did not turn around.

"My partner, Fio, he once had this theory that you had an ugly secret you couldn't bear for the rest of the world to know, and somehow your man found out about it and so you killed him."

She said nothing, and it seemed he could see the shadows darken under her cheekbones, but the rest of her was so pale, so pale.

"I took Lucille up to Angola this mornin'."

She flinched at Lucille's name, and her eyes slowly closed, although the rest of her remained still as stone, and then she said, "What did she tell you?"

"What you killed them for—Julius and Charles. What you didn't want found out, Remy darlin'. What nobody wanted found out—that you and Lucille Durand are sisters."

Chapter Thirty-Six

A strange green light haloed the tops of the oaks and cypress trees that summer's day in 1916, as if the spirits of the bayou were gathering there. It had grown suddenly quiet, expectant. Even the locusts had paused in their screeching.

Remy Lelourie stopped on her way to the slave shack and looked back at the big house. Sans Souci. The house seemed to shimmer in the ghostly green light, a thing built not of wood and stone but of wantings, longings. Her love for those graceful colonnettes and sweeping galleries had come to her with her mother's milk, become a part of her flesh and bones. For so long Sans Souci had been the only thing she felt she belonged to, and yet it would never be hers.

The door to the shack stood open, but she could see no one inside. "Julius?" she said softly, strangely reluctant to disturb the hot stillness.

The beads clattered open with the sudden sweep of an arm, startling her.

"Well, well," said Julius St. Claire. "If it isn't Remy Lelourie. So you've decided to keep our little rendezvous, after all."

The ends of his hair were dripping sweat, his face pale, sickly. He trembled as if he had a fever. He took a step toward her, and she saw the old French revolver in his hand.

She looked to see if the hammer had been cocked. It had.

She looked from the gun back up to his face. The black centers of his eyes had almost swallowed up all the blue. He was scaring her. The Julius she knew was a sweet, kindhearted boy, who just yesterday had asked her to be his wife and kissed her on the mouth, gently, so gently, as if she were a breakable thing. She had first seduced him when they'd been sixteen, yet he kept on treating her as if she were some delicate, swooning blossom of southern womanhood, even when he ought to have known better.

"Are you going to shoot me if my answer is no?" she said, feeling a little afraid now, but liking it.

The sound that came out of his throat was meant to be a laugh. He swayed a little on his feet. "I regret saying this, darlin', but my offer of marriage must be withdrawn. It doesn't count, you see, when the young lady in question isn't all she appears to be."

That made her laugh. "Oh, Julius. I've never *tried* to be what I appear to be. But since I can see I'm no longer wanted, I'll just—"

"No!" The gun jerked up, pointing at her face. "I said I was no longer interested in marrying you, but that doesn't mean I still might not want to have you one more time for old times' sake. Go on into the bedroom now, darlin'. Get!" he shouted, waving the gun wildly when she didn't move.

She passed by him close enough for her arm to brush his belly as she went through the beads and into the bedroom. The other, matching, revolver, she saw, was lying on the bed. A light-headedness came over her, from the fear that was surging through her whole body like an electrical current, and the excitement.

She could play this game; she had invented it.

"Take off your clothes," he said.

She took off her skirt, shirtwaist, chemise and drawers, leaving them to fall where they may. She stood before him naked, her hands at her sides.

He stared at her forever. The noise of the locusts sawing in the bamboo outside the window filled the room. The heat of the evening was like hundreds of hot, panting breaths.

Suddenly his face pulled, twisting, and he moaned. "Oh, God,

God. You are so white, your skin is so white. If I hadn't seen the truth with my own eyes." He made a harsh, choking sound, as if he were gagging. "I loved you. I *loved* you."

The gun jerked in his hand again, his finger nearly pulling the trigger. She flinched, but only deep inside herself where he couldn't see it.

"If you're going to rape me, Julius. Then do it."

"Rape you? I intend to die with you, darlin' Remy, to take you in death. They will find us arm in arm on this bed, two lovers who couldn't be together in this life and yet couldn't bear to part, but not rape, not rape. I want you still, still . . . but I really shouldn't. I shouldn't so defile myself anymore as to lie with a Nigra."

"What? You aren't making . . . What?" she said again, shaking her head, her mouth kinking up in a funny way, and she felt something go wrong with her heart, felt it pause and then take up its beating again in slow, unsteady lurches.

"Last night," he was saying, and he was weeping now, the tears mixing with the sweat on his face. "Last night, I told Daddy how we were going to be married, and this morning he brought me into the library and he showed me everything. Told me all about you Lelouries."

He took a step, closing the distance between them. He put the barrel of the gun underneath her chin and forced her head up. She couldn't stop her throat from swallowing.

"So white, your face is so white and yet he showed me . . . showed me . . ." He dug the muzzle deeper into the soft flesh under her chin. "He kept her slave papers, the bill of sale, the birth certificate—he kept it all, my great-granddaddy did. The duel, Remy. You know the story of the duel. My great-granddaddy Pierre killing your great-granddaddy Henri under the dueling oaks with this gun. Well, Pierre's sister, who was Henri's wife, she was near mad with grief over losing first her man and then her baby. But the slave had a get that was coming up light, white as white can be, and so they brought it into the plantation house and passed it off as Henri Lelourie's child. Your great-granddaddy's child, Remy-girl. We keep the secret for y'all, my daddy says, for *la famille* and a promise that was made, but we keep the truth, too. So no St. Claire will ever destroy his name by joining with the Lelouries' tainted blood."

She closed her eyes, as if by not seeing him she could close out his words. She didn't want to understand what he was saying, but she did, she did. Those stories of her Mama's, going year after year to the places where it all had happened, the dueling oaks, the house on Conti Street. It was like one of those Valentine hearts that are torn in two and the lovers must match the pieces up together again. Her mama had given her half a heart, and now Julius had given her the other. The pieces fit, but the rip was still there.

She felt the gun barrel slide up along her jaw to her mouth, press against her mouth. She tasted the oil and metal, and smelled the sharp, familiar tang of fear. She opened her eyes in time to see his head lowering toward hers as if he would kiss her, kiss her or kill her.

"I loved you," he said through tears, but the gun in his hand was steady, the muzzle still pressed hard against her mouth, bruising her lips and knocking against her teeth. "I was going to marry you, but now I can die with you. Get up on the bed, Remy."

Slowly, she backed up a step, and then another, her gaze flickering between his face and his finger on the trigger. When the backs of her thighs hit the bed, she scrambled up on it and snatched up the other gun.

He came at her.

She cocked the hammer. "Don't."

He kept coming, up onto the bed with her. "We'll die together now, Remy. You must want to, you know you do. This will be our marriage bed, my love, the only one we'll ever have."

Her breathing was coming too fast, and her arms were trembling. But she wasn't going to die. Not for him.

"Don't make me do it for you, Remy, please. Don't make me, don't make me do it."

He held the gun in his hand down at his side now, but she knew what was coming, she knew the barrel would be coming up, that soon she would see the round gaping maw of the muzzle. She already saw her death in his eyes.

She pointed the pistol at his face and shot him.

"I almost told it all to you our last evenin' in the willow cave. But I thought that if you looked at me, then, the way Julius had, I might as well have let him kill me. There was that part of you I could never touch, you see, no matter how I tried. And I was so afraid that was the part of you that would fall out of love with me if you ever learned the truth."

She was sitting, still, at her dressing table, but now he knelt before her, with his face pressed into her belly, holding her tight, as if he were a bandage that could stop the bleeding.

I will always love you, he thought, although he didn't say it, for it seemed as though he had forfeited the right.

Her hand was stroking his hair, over and over, stroking him. He raised his head. She was looking down at him with eyes that were wide and dark, and the pulse was beating in her throat, hard and fast.

"I would have run with you," he said, the words coming out funny, as if their edges had got broken. "Or stayed and lied for you, if that was what you wanted."

She bent over and took his face in her hands, her thumb lightly brushing across his lips. Then she leaned closer and put her mouth where her thumb had been, almost with reverence. He reached up and wrapped his arms around her neck, holding her, and he laid his head on her shoulder, and she rested her chin on his head. The fog was thick outside the window, warm and enveloping like a womb.

He didn't know how long they stayed that way, holding each other. Slowly, she pulled away, her hands lingering a moment, touching him, and then they let him go. He looked at her and he thought he had never felt pain like this, it was so pure.

"Remy—"

"No, Day. It was wrong, what I did." She lifted her arm and looked at her skin, and it made him think of Lucille holding her

405

own arm up to the sky and talking about coming up light. "Your partner, that policeman, he was right about me—I couldn't bear to be found out. I tell myself that the gun was coming up, was firing at me, that Julius was going to kill me with that old French revolver unless I shot him first, but I can no longer remember the way it really was. I only remember that I didn't want to be found out."

She let her hand fall back into her lap and her face went oddly dreamy, as if she were remembering someone else in a place long ago and far away. "It was such a strange and frightening thing—to suddenly not be the person you thought you were. To be something you'd been taught all your life was ugly and tainted. Something *less*, in the eyes of the world you'd always known. I was a coward, I know, but I ran away from it. I only knew that if I stayed and tried to hold on to what I'd always thought I was, while trying to understand what I really was—then I would be pulled apart until all that was left of me would be shattered. As surely as that revolver shattered poor Julius's face."

Rourke wanted to be holding her again. He felt flayed down to his soul, yet oddly cleansed. He wanted to tell her this, but there were no words that would measure up against all that she would be feeling. He thought of their world and the way it was, of what their world had done to Lucille and LeRoy, of Lucille telling him how he could never know, because he wasn't colored.

"It didn't work, though," she was saying. "Running away. I'd see a sign on a theater door—whites only—and I'd want to laugh to think that if they only knew, I wouldn't be allowed through that door to watch my white self up on the movie screen. I'd hear some man on the radio talking about how Negroes 'must know their place,' and I'd wonder, Where is my place? With that white man on the radio or with them, with Negroes, and I'd feel ashamed and dirty, and then I'd despise myself for feeling that way. I'd wonder: Where is my dignity? Where is my pride? But I couldn't find the courage to be true to myself, and I'd feel so alone."

"You're the bravest person I know and you aren't alone anymore," he said.

She shook her head. "No, no, Belle and Mama, they must never know," she said, misunderstanding him. "You musn't ever tell them, Day, for you know how they are, how they've been raised to think and be and feel, and you know how they would never be able to bear it. Only four of us know the secret now—all the rest are dead. Me and you and Lucille, and Lucille's mama, of course. Your mama."

Rourke thought again of Lucille, holding her arm up to the light. The Lelourie girls, because of how they had come out, were allowed to keep the secret, but Lucille had to bear it before the world.

Remy's eyes had grown unfocused now, warming with a curious light. "I ran away after I killed Julius, but something just wouldn't let me stay gone. I kept thinking how I wanted to come home so bad, if only for a little while, and that night at the premiere party, I could tell Charles's daddy had died without passing on to him the Lelouries' ugly secret. He was being so sweet to me that night, courting me, and so I thought—"

She stopped, shaking her head as she reached down to stroke his cheek, once, lightly, with her fingertips. "No, I'm lying a little bit about that part. I wanted to fool them, fool a St. Claire and New Orleans, like I was fooling the whole world, making them pay for all their signs and their laws and their blindness. Making them love *me*. And I wanted to take up the dare, too, Day. A double dare, to see if I could get away with it. But then Charles found out. My sister told him. My sister, Lucille."

She had lost herself in thought, but her hand was stroking his face again, over and over, and he didn't want to go beyond, to the next place, where she would tell him how Charles, like Julius, had to die. "Don't," he said, but she failed to hear, or perhaps to understand.

"Julius," she said, and her voice broke over the name. "He had been broken by knowing what I was. But Charles was still Charles. I used to think there was nothing akin to softness anywhere in Charles, no part of him that was vulnerable, but he was. Once he told me that I seemed to him like a sad book he'd read and loved a long time ago. It was Lucille he was thinking of when he looked at me, when he lay with me, although he never knew it until the very end. He loved Lucille, I think as much as he could love anyone. The night he learned the truth, he came to me drunk and high and furious, but also strangely excited, exhilarated. He said he was going to tell everyone, everywhere, that the most beautiful woman in the world, this woman they'd all been worshiping for years, was a Negro and then, oh, how he would enjoy watching them all jump and squirm. He was laughing about it, and then he hit me. He raped me, and then he started crying like a child does, beating his fists on the floor. And then he left and went out to the shack."

A strange smile was pulling at her mouth now, a smile born of hurt and tenderness. "And here you are, Day, still thinking that I followed him out there, that I followed him out there and killed him."

"It doesn't matter," he said.

She reached up and pressed her fingers against the hollow of his throat, as though to feel if he still lived. "Yes, it does. To you it would always matter. I understood how much it mattered to you that night you came to arrest me, when I turned from the window and saw your face, saw what was in your eyes as you looked at me. You looked at me as though you were seeing the gowman come to take away your soul."

"The gowman," he repeated, and that was when it all suddenly came together in his mind, the pieces meshing like fine gears, while he knelt there on the floor of her bedroom with the fog pressing against the windows and the blood draining cold from his heart.

The Mardi Gras mask, and the chips of white enamel and the purple spangle under the nail of Charles St. Claire's severed finger.

LeBeau seeing a creature in white with snakes for hair come flying out of the slave shack on the night of the murder.

Katie walking in her sleep that night, seeing the gowman, Katie telling him over and over how she had seen the gowman in their house on Conti Street.

"Oh God. Katie."

Chapter Thirty-Seven

Even big sins begin with little deeds, so Maeve Rourke's mother used to say. Her mother, who had chosen to end her life with the slash of a razor. So had she thought, in that moment before she made that first cut, of all the other moments and little deeds and choices that had gone before?

There were moments with Reynard, in those early years, when Maeve truly believed she had everything she'd ever wanted. When she found out she was with a child by him, she had even more. There is a moment when a child comes out of your womb, that very instant of birth, when you feel a surge of pain that is like a death, a moment when that child is separate from you, and yet still a part of your body, and that moment stays with you forever. Your child is born, lives, maybe even dies before you, but that moment is always a part of your heart.

She was so pretty, was little Maureen, the prettiest thing you'd ever hope to see and hold and snuggle up to. With all her fingers and toes and wide, bright eyes. You couldn't see it at first, what was different about her, but then the days passed and you couldn't not see it—her skin, her hair and mouth and nose. On the day when the truth was first spoken aloud between her and Reynard, when the truth was faced, he had stared down at his baby daughter, his *Negro* baby daughter, lying in her bassinet, and he'd had such a look on his face, as if he were seeing all their sins come to life.

Maeve had pushed past him and snatched the baby up, her fingers digging into the blankets so hard that little Maureen started screaming with fright and pain, wrapped the blankets up tight around the plump flailing legs, and went and sat with her in a chair by the window, holding her close, so close. "Go away," she said to Reynard. "Go away."

She sat in the chair, rocking back and forth, back and forth, her eyes looking through the window. The shutters of the house across the way shone with a new coat of paint. A man with a banjo sat beneath the tin canopy of the saloon on the corner, playing a lively jig for pennies. Sunshine made rainbows in the puddles left from that morning's shower, but for her there was no light in all the world, and she was cold.

It was that time of day when you can sense the night is coming even though the sun still clings to the rooftops across the way when she heard Reynard's step coming up behind her. She wanted to tell him to go away again, but she didn't. He knelt before her, putting himself between her and the window, so that she would have to look at him.

"You can't keep her, Maeve," he said. "You'll destroy me if you keep her."

She knew that. She knew how it was in New Orleans, how it would be for Reynard if the world were suddenly to learn that underneath his white skin, colored blood was pumping through his veins.

"I've spoken with the laundress," Reynard was saying. "Augusta Durand. She has agreed to take the child and raise her as her own."

She is mine, Maeve wanted to say, to insist. But she did not.

On the day they buried the empty casket in the St. Louis Cemetery, in the Lelourie family tomb with the name MAUREEN

carved on the stone, it occurred to her that either she would have
to forgive him or she would have to stop loving him.

She'd wondered why he hadn't accused her of sleeping with
another man, a colored man, but then he told her about a story
handed down through the years in the Lelourie family. About how
his granddaddy had fallen in love with a slave girl and brought her
here to this Conti Street house, lived with her here, until he had
been killed in a duel. "I must come down from her, from this
house," Reynard said, his face twisted with shock and horror and
a strange kind of wonderment. "I've a Negro's blood. A slave's
blood."

It became after that as though a cancer had invaded him. She
would come upon him looking at himself in the mirror and she
knew he was searching for traces of the disease. How have I
changed? he would say to her, to that face he saw in the mirror. I
have the same heart and mind and soul. What has changed?

She would come awake in the middle of the night and he would
be standing naked at the window, and he would say, as if to
himself, I wonder what became of her? And Maeve knew he was
thinking of the slave girl. They took her baby, she wanted to say
back to him, and it broke her heart—that is what became of her.

There was an outbuilding in back of the cottage where the old
kitchen had been, with rooms above where the servants and slaves
had slept. He would spend hours in those rooms, and after a time
she began to feel a fury with him that was like a knotted fist in her
belly. What was so weak about him that he couldn't find a way to
live with it? For him she had given up all her babies, Paulie and
Day and their little baby girl, who had a new name now, Lucille.
Every one of her babies she had given up for him, and she had
found a way.

One evening, after he had been to the outbuilding, he came
into the parlor where she was reading, and he had a cane knife in
his hand. The blade was rusted and pitted black, and dull from
being buried in the root cellar beneath the old kitchen. "The way

my family always tells the story," he said, "is that when my grand-daddy first saw her, she was cutting cane in a field."

Later, Meave saw that he had cleaned up the knife and sharpened it.

It was when she and Augusta were washing the abortion blood off of their daughter's legs that they first thought of killing Charles St. Claire. That man had almost been the death of her, of their Lucille. He was destroying the life of their Lucille and killing her babies. It would only be justice that they kill him.

Justice and atonement.

They played a game with cards, high card winning, to let God decide who would be the one to do the actual deed, and Maeve was chosen.

Maeve did not intend to die herself, though, or to go to prison, and so she and Augusta prepared, they thought it through. How it would be done, for the method of execution ought to be a fitting one. How they would keep from being found out.

Of the two of them, Augusta was the better at planning. She thought of the cane knife, and the white cape and Mardi Gras mask—that distinctive Medusa with snakes for hair—should anyone happen to see them that night.

That night the air was alive with sounds. The locusts screeching and the frogs croaking down in the bayou, the wind rattling the leaves of the banana trees, leftover rain dripping from the eaves.

Augusta had come up with a plan to lure him out of the house, but in the end he had come out on his own, crossing the yard to the slave shack.

Maeve followed him.

She waited for a time under the shadows of the oaks that were like pools of dark glass on the lawn, and then she went around to the side of the shack where the bedroom was.

She took off her white cape and hid it in the bamboo thicket, where it would not get bloodied, the white cape Augusta had made from a sheet stolen off the laundry line of the bordello next door to the house on Conti Street.

She took off her white cape and underneath she was naked.

She climbed through the window and went to the bed. She sat on the bed, behind the drape of the mosquito netting. Her breath steamed beneath the mask she wore, making her face hot, but the rest of her was cold, so cold. She waited until she felt the moment come upon her.

She listened to him moving around in the other room. Once she heard him laugh. When the moment came, she gripped the cane knife tight in her hand and rose up from the bed, and she went to him.

She swung the knife at him, over and over, cutting him, killing him, killing him, killing him, killing him.

The cypress trees were wet and black in the yellow light. Fog clung to their flooded roots and hung from their bare branches like strips of wet cotton. Daman Rourke pushed the pirogue through the grass and cane, his ears straining, hearing nothing. Miles of water and marsh and drowned cypress trees, and they could be anywhere.

He told himself that Maeve loved her granddaughter too much, too much, to ever do her any harm. But the heart is never rational when it comes to your child, and so he felt as though he were moving deep underwater and he had no breath left, and that he was never going to live through this.

He felt a touch on his thigh, saw Remy's face floating before him in the mist. "We'll find them," Remy said. "She's only doing what she said—taking Katie out here to convince her there is no such thing as a gowman. No matter how frightened she is of being found out, she would never be able to hurt Katie."

He breathed, nodded, but he was seeing Charles St. Claire on the floor of the slave shack with all those bloody gashes in his dead, white flesh. She had done that.

He heard a rustle and a splash, and snapped his head around so hard his eyes blurred. He saw a white crane rise out of the marsh, with wings gilded gold from the unearthly light.

Katie, always walking in her sleep. She must have been out in the hallway that night, come awake for half a moment and seen her grandmama leaving her bedroom wearing the Mardi Gras mask and something white, and she thought she had seen the gowman, and he hadn't believed her. She had told him, but he hadn't believed.

A great wailing cry floated to him on wisps of fog, followed by a splash, like a body hitting the water, and in that moment Daman Rourke finally found his limit, found his stopping place, found that sharp, black edge where the fear was more than heart and soul and blood and guts could bear, and hell ceased being a figment of your imagination, and became the place where you burned.

He pushed the pirogue toward the scream, praying, begging God, making oaths and promises and vows, awash, drowning, dying by fear.

He saw the bow of a pirogue appear out of the white, sun-spangled mist. He thought it was empty and then he saw her, huddled in the bottom with her knees drawn up under her chin.

He nearly fell into the water himself going for her. He wrapped her up in his arms, hugging her so tight he felt the breath push out of her chest.

He heard someone sobbing and he realized it was him.

"Grandmama fell into the water," Katie said.

He pulled back just enough so that he could grip the sides of her head and look into her eyes. They were full of tears and fear, and he crushed her up against him again, crushed her against him until her chest was pressed to his throat and he could feel her breath hitching, hard and fast, as if she had the hiccups, but alive, alive.

She put the flat of her hands on his shoulders and pushed away from him. "Daddy, you need to go look for Grandmama."

"I will, honey," he said. "I will."

They searched for her through the thick green water and the clinging, sucking stalks of marsh grass. They never found her.

We are all haunted, thought Daman Rourke, by the demons of choices made badly many years ago, both by ourselves and by those who came before us. You can never really know another's heart. It's all there in each of us—all the good and all the evil in the world. We only differ in the choices we make, and in the end we must make those choices alone.

He would never know for sure all the whys for what his mother had done. He thought that the same love-born fury that had driven her to take the life of a man by slashing him to death with a cane knife had in the end been what had driven her to spare him and Katie and destroy herself.

La famille.

He knew that he would never stop wondering about her, and about what parts of her he carried inside himself.

One evening the four-o'clocks opened up in the shade of the levee, and the breeze had just a touch of coolness to it, a promise of the end of the hot days of summer. On that evening he and Katie and Remy bought some cartons of shrimp and dirty rice and took them, along with his saxophone, to the houseboat on the Bayou St. John. They ate and drank from a jug of sour mash, and when the sky grew dark enough for the first star to start its shining, he picked up his sax and sent a deep sweet note floating out over the water, and Lucille put all the pain into a song.

He looked at Remy's face, pale in the light of the dying day, the dying summer. Growing up here, he thought, it's so much a part of life you don't even see it. The signs on the drinking fountains, the screens in the streetcar, all those places they aren't even allowed through the door. They live among you, cooking your food, cleaning your houses, rocking your babies to sleep, and you don't see them. Until that day the "they" becomes you, or the ones you love.

LeRoy had been right. You live in the world and either you just don't see it, or you tell yourself there's nothing you can do and you let it go. But LeRoy had also been wrong. You can change what is. Somehow you have to figure out a way to change what is.

Later that night, in bed with her lying in his arms, he said, "Be my wife, Remy," and she cried and then she said, "It's against the law for a white man to marry a Negro."

And he said, "Laws in this city get broken all the time."

He pulled his arm out from underneath her so that he could rise up and look at her face and kiss her mouth, and he thought that he would never leave her, no matter what.

One morning in October, when the sky was a hard, crisp blue and the smell of woodsmoke was in the air, a postcard arrived in the mail, bearing a Brazilian stamp. On the front was a photograph of a woman sitting on a rock, looking out to sea, with her back to the camera's lens. On the other side was printed the address to the house on Conti Street and nothing else, but then nothing else was needed.

A son would always know his mother.